Rave reviews for Greg Bear's *Slant*

"Tense and fast-paced, beautifully written with complex, engaging characters and a story line that unfolds like an origami puzzle."

—*San Francisco Chronicle and Examiner*

"*Slant* shows that Bear is one of our very best, and most innovative, speculative writers."

—*New York Daily News*

"Bear, who's won two Hugos and four Nebulas, should rack up nominations if not wins for this one as well."

—*Publishers Weekly* (starred review)

"Well written and often exciting."

—*The Washington Post Book World*

"Should be a strong contender for the Hugo and Nebula."

—*Bookman News*

"A terrific story, with lots of action and a strong, complex plot."

—*Cleveland Plain Dealer*

"Highly complex and thought-provoking."

—*Library Journal*

OTHER BOOKS BY GREG BEAR

Hegira
Psychlone
Beyond Heaven's River
Strength of Stones
The Wind from a Burning Woman
Blood Music
Eon
The Forge of God
Eternity
Hardfought
Tangents
Heads
Queen of Angels
Anvil of Stars
Moving Mars
Songs of Earth and Power
New Legends
Legacy
Dinosaur Summer
Foundation and
Chaos

/

GREG BEAR

TOR

A TOM DOHERTY

ASSOCIATES BOOK

NEW YORK

Copyright © 1997 by Greg Bear

A Tor Book
Published by Tom Doherty Associates, Inc.
175 Fifth Avenue
New York, NY 10010

Tor Books on the World Wide Web:
http://www.tor.com

Tor® is a registered trademark of Tom Doherty Associates, Inc.

ISBN: 0-812-52482-9
Library of Congress Card Catalog Number: 97-7063

First edition: July 1997
First mass market edition: June 1998

Printed in the United States of America

0 9 8 7 6 5 4 3 2 1

FIRST
SEARCH
RESULT

ACCESS TO MULTIWAY WORLD FEED
OPEN

Budget: Select, Restricted

SEARCH FILTERS
KEYWORDS?>

> Knowledge, Sex, Dataflow

TOPIC FILTER: >Community

"Tell all the truth,
but tell it slant"

—EMILY DICKINSON

Dataflow today is money/blood, the living substance of our human rivers/arteries. You can steamboat the big flow, or slowly raft these rivers up and down the world, or canoe into the branches and backwaters, with almost perfect freedom. There are a few places you can't go—Saudi Arabia, Northern Enclave China, some towns in Green Idaho. Nobody much cares to go there anyway. Not much exciting is happening in those places.

—The U.S. Government Digiman on Dataflow Economics,
56th Revision, 2052

1 / EDUCATED CORPSES

Omphalos dominates Moscow, Green Idaho. It glows pale silver and gold like a fancy watch waiting to be stolen. A tetrahedron four hundred feet high, with two vertical faces and a triangular base, it is the biggest thing in town, more ostentatious than the nearby Mormon temple, though not so painfully white and spiky. The leading edge points at the heart of Moscow like a woodsman's wedge. The vertical faces descend, blind and windowless, to sink seventy feet below ground. The single sloping face is gently corrugated like a dazzling ivory washboard for the leaden sky.

Omphalos is a broad-shouldered edifice, Herculean architecture for the ages, given the kind of shockproof suspension and massive loving armor once reserved for hardened defense installations and missile silos.

Jack Giffey waits patiently in line for the public tour. It is cold in Moscow today. Thirty people stand with him in the snaking line, all clearly marked by their gray denims as young tourists biking through Green Idaho; all youthfully unafraid of the reputation of the state's Ruggers, the legendary gun-wielding rugged individualists, who see themselves not as lawless brigands but as steely-eyed human islands in a flooded, corrupting stream.

But the state's reputation is exaggerated. Not more than three percent of the population could accurately be labeled Rugger. And fewer than ten young tourists each year vanish from the old logging trails in the regrowth timberlands, their forlornly beeping Personal Access Devices and little knit caps nailed to posts on the edges of the abandoned national forests.

In Giffey's opinion, Green Idaho has all the individuality of a zit on a corpse. The zit may consider itself special, but it's just a different kind of dead meat.

Giffey is known to his few friends as Giff. At fifty-one he looks mild and past his aggressive years, with a grizzled and ragged beard and kind gray eyes that attract the interest of children and discouraged women past their picky twenties. He doesn't like Green Idaho any more than he likes the rest of the nation, or the world, for that matter.

Old-fashioned radiant outdoor heaters mounted on poles glow raw-beef red overhead, trying to keep the people in line warm. Giffey has been here before, thirteen times; he's sure Omphalos knows his face and has tagged him as worth paying marginal attention to. That is okay. He does not mind.

Giffey is among the very few who know that Omphalos absorbs knowledge from the outside at the extraordinary rate of fifty million dollars a year. Since Omphalos is publicly assumed to be a fancy kind of tomb for the rich and privileged, its dead and near-dead must be very curious. But few ask serious questions about it. The builders of Omphalos paid a lot for freedom from oversight, the kind of freedom that can only be bought in Green Idaho.

The rulers of Green Idaho, true to their breed, hate the Federals and the outer society but revere money and its most sacred benison: freedom from responsibility.

Giffey has been to the Forest Lawn Pyramid in Southcoast California; Omphalos is, architecturally, by far the classier act. But he would never think of robbing the truly dead in Forest Lawn, with their few scattered jewels adorning rotting flesh.

The frozen near-dead are another matter. Entombed with all their palpable assets—precious metals, collectibles, long-term sigs to offshore paper-deed securities—the corpsicles racked in their special refrigerated cells in Omphalos, Giffey believes, might be worth several hundred million dollars apiece.

Those rich enough to afford such accommodations have their choice of packaged options: cheapest is capitation, bio-vitrifying and cryo-preserving the head alone. Next is head and trunk; and finally, whole-body. There are even more expensive and still-experimental possibilities . . . For the wealthiest of all, the plutocratic highest of the high.

The sloping face of the wedge gleams like a field of wind-rippled snow. The line begins to move in anticipation; there are sounds from within. Omphalos opens its tall steel and flexfuller front doors. Its soothing public voice spreads out over the crowd, only mildly funereal.

"Welcome to the hope of all our futures," the voice says as the line pushes eagerly into the tall, severe granite and steel lobby. Great shining pillars rise around the student tourists like steel redwoods, daunting and extra human. The floor is living holostone, morphing through scenes of future splendor beneath their feet: flying cities high above sunset mountains, villas on Mars and the Moon, idyllic valleys farmed by obedient arbeiters while beautiful, magisterial men and women of all races and creeds watch from the balconies of their spotless white mansions. "This completely automated facility is the repository for a maximum of ten thousand two hundred and nineteen biologically conserved patrons, all expecting long and happy lives upon their reconstruction and resurrection.

"Within Omphalos, there are no human employees, no attendants or engineers or guards . . ."

Giffey has never met a machine he could not beat, at chess, at war games, at predicting equities weather. Giffey believes he may be one of the smartest or at least most functionally successful human beings on this planet. He succeeds at whatever he wants to do. Of course—he grins to himself—there are many things he has never wanted to do.

He looks up at the distant lobby ceiling, studded with crystal prisms that project rainbows all around. Above them, he imagines stacks of cold cells filled with bodies and heads. Some of them are not frozen, he understands from secret sources, but are still alive and thinking, suspended in nano baths in what is euphemistically called warm sleep. They are old and sick and the law does not allow them to undergo any more major medical intervention. They have had their chance at life; anything more and they are classified as greedy Chronovores, seekers after immortality, which is illegal everywhere but in the quasi-independent republic of Green Idaho, and impractical here.

The terminally ill can, however, forfeit all but their physical assets to the republic, and enter Omphalos as isolated wards of the syndicate.

Giffey presumes the still-living are the curious ones. They stay current as they sleep.

Giffey does not care what they're dreaming, half-alive or wholly dead, whether they're locked into endless rounds of full-sensory Yox, or preparing themselves for the future by becoming the most highly educated near-corpses in the dataflow world. They should be honorably gone from the picture, out of the game. They don't need their assets.

Omphalos's occupants are just a different set of pharaohs. And Jack Giffey is just another kind of tomb-robber who thinks he can avoid the traps and break the seals and unwrap the mummies.

"You are now within the atrium of the most secure building in the Western World. Designed to withstand catastrophic earthquakes, volcanic activity, even thermonuclear explosions or microcharge dispersals—''

Giffey is not listening. He has a pretty decent map of the place in his head, and a much more detailed map in his pad. He knows where the arbeiters must come and go within the building's two entrances. He even knows who has manufactured the arbeiters, and what they look like. He knows much else besides. He is ready to go and does not need this final tour. Giffey is here to legitimately pay his respects to a remarkable monument.

''Please step this way. We have mockups of hibernaria and exhibits usually reserved only for prospective patrons of these facilities. But today, for you exclusively, we allow access to a new and vital vision of the future—''

Giffey grimaces. He hates today's big lies—*exclusively, only, I love you alone, trust, adore,* but ultimately, *pay.* Postconsumer weltcrap. He's glad he has paid his money for the last time.

He smiles at the bank of sensors scanning the visitors for suspicious bulges and behaviors. The system passes them through to the display area. *The casket room. Lie in silken comfort through all eternity.*

The young tourists in their denims and warm, upscale Nandex stand agape before the ice-blue enamel and flexfuller hibernarium, a long flattened tube stretched across a mocked-up cubicle like a dry-docked submarine cemented at both ends. Giffey knows what the tourists, the young students, are thinking. They are all wondering if they will ever be able to afford this kind of immortality, a chance at the Big Downstream.

Giffey doesn't care. Even riches and the high life do not matter to him because unlike his partners, he has severe doubts they will ever be able to fence such goods, nearly all of which will be marked with ineradicable tracers. Besides, gold means much less than it used to. Dataflow is all.

He's in it to tweak a few noses, and to play against the

machine he suspects lies within. Hardly a machine at all . . .

"Our exclusive method of bio-vitrifying cryo-conservancy was pioneered by four doctors in Siberia and perfected fifteen years ago. The fluids of a human body normally crystallize upon freezing, but by *vitrifying* these fluids, making them smoothly glassy, we eliminate crystals completely—"

Giffey believes he will face an unauthorized artificial intelligence—Omphalos's own advanced petaflop INDA, perhaps even a thinker. He's always wanted to go up against a thinker.

He suspects he'll lose. But maybe not.

And what a game!

M/F, F/M, M/M, F/F
/ is what happens between us
/ is what separates us.

> *We are all different sexes, though with only two brands of equipment.*

> **—The Kiss of X, *Alive Contains a Lie***

2 / STONE HAMMER

Alice Grale believes this is cataspace, all interaction but no motion. In the small black room off the long black studio, waiting can be a dull chunk of time filled any way at all. She and her co-star, Minstrel, are talking, waiting for adjustments on the stage. Minstrel lounges naked on the old low couch, graceful as a leopard. His body is all grace and blunted angles.

"So why don't you like those words?" Minstrel asks. "They're ancient and traditional, and they describe what we do."

"They're ugly," she says. "I say them if I want to or when I'm paid to, but I've never been fond of them." Alice sits on the folding metal chair before him, illuminated by a soft free spot of white light, wearing a flimsy black robe, her touching knees exposed. There is some relief in old friendship. She has known Minstrel for nine years. They have been talking for twenty minutes and Francis is still not ready for them.

"You never fail to surprise me, Alice. But I'm making a point. Try saying *the* word," he challenges. "The tetragrammaton."

She considers, then says it, with a rise of her cheeks and a curve of her lips and derogatory tilt of her head, her voice not very loud and void of emphasis.

"You're *not* doing it justice," Minstrel complains. "God knows I've heard you say it often enough. Say it professionally, if you can't get into it personally."

Alice glares at him.

"I mean it," he says. "I'm making a point here."

Minstrel seems a little intense today, pushy. But she says the word once more. Her eyes narrow and her nose wrinkles.

Minstrel sniffs. "Your heart isn't in it," he says dubiously, "but even so, it brings a snarl, feel it?"

Alice shakes her head. "It's what somebody else wants me to say, and that's the way they want me to say it."

Minstrel chuckles and taps her knee with one long square-tipped finger. "Like all women, you are not your art."

Alice is both perplexed and irritated. "What's that mean?"

"The word *is* a snarl. It's old and hard and blunt—it's a stone hammer. You say it when you really need the person you're with and you aren't embarrassed to show yourself deep down. It means what's happening touches your feral instincts."

"Bullshit."

"You say that casually enough," Minstrel observes. He stands, applies finger to cheek and inclines his head. In this pose, long and loose, he reminds Alice of an El Greco saint. All he needs is a slack blue loincloth.

She feels the familiar deep appreciation, the yearning that has not diminished in over fifty professional encounters in thirty-one vids, beginning with her first when she was nineteen. That was ten years ago, and he was thin and ribby, hollow-chested and uncertain of his peculiar talent. Now he is lean and omni-asian brown, muscles finely toned and defined, his body a temple as well as an office, long hair pulled back from a high forehead, long thin patrician nose almost too sharp, lips proud as if recently slapped.

Alice pretends languid boredom, then shifts suddenly into seductive speed. "All right. *Fuck me,*" with her best, most provocative professional emphasis.

"Still not convincing," Minstrel teases.

"Fuck me with your . . . *penis*," Alice says. They both laugh.

Minstrel's face crosses from saint to ascetic cherub. "Utterly, desperately limp. Only a doctor or a therapist would call it that, to make you feel inferior. Most men prefer *cock*."

"Crows only in the morning," Alice says. All conversations with Minstrel, even in the down time between plugs, are contagious. "*Penis* sounds like a planet or a country."

"Vagina. Labia. Clitoris," he prompts.

"Like characters in a Renaissance vid," Alice says. She muses. "They are all royalty in the land of *Penis*. Vagina never touches another person without wearing gloves. She is cool and dresses in black lace."

Minstrel's face lights up. "Labia is a dangerous woman, sister to Vagina and Clitoris," he says. "A vampire and poisoner."

"Clitoris is the youngest, virginal sister," Alice says. She loves games. "They are all daughters of . . ." Tongue tipping through her lips, catlike, while she thinks. "Lucrezia Menarchia."

"Bravo!" Minstrel says. He applauds.

Alice bows and continues. "Clitoris is the only one with any decency. She blushes with shame at how her family carries on."

Minstrel reddens with subdued laughter. They should not be too loud up here; it might upset Francis, who can be very testy while preparing for a plug. "All right. *Cunt*," he suggests.

Alice pauses, scowling. "That's a tough one."

"Not yours, my dear."

Alice gives him a beneath-me face and taps her finger on her nose, thinking. "*Cunt* is a barbarian princess from the outer reaches. She is raised by the outland tribes of the province of Puberty."

Minstrel squints. "Not Puberty. Not quite right." He works at it and substitutes, "*Pudenda*."

Alice grins. "*Pudenda* it is. Cuntia is her name when she travels in the civilized realms."

Minstrel snaps his slender fingers. "We're on to something. Maybe Francis will make us writers. Listen: Cunt is swapped in a hostage exchange between Lucrezia Menarchia and Cunt's father, King Hetero. Lucrezia sends her daughter—her hopelessly moral daughter Clitoris to learn the barbarian ways and loosen up a bit. Clitoris finally lets her hair down and finds fulfillment in the arms of Cunt's heroic brother, Glans. Cunt, however, must preserve her honor in Menarchia rather than submit to temptation, for Lucrezia rules a corrupt land."

Alice takes a deep breath, pretending to be stunned by this burst of genius, then laughs out loud, the hell with Francis, who shouldn't keep them waiting so long. She seldom laughs this way, it sounds so much like an ass's bray to her, but she is easy and open with Minstrel. "So who or what is your precious *Fuck*, then?" she asks.

Minstrel holds his hands as if in prayer and pretends great gravity. "Not to be spoken lightly, or profaned. The tetragrammaton . . . Fuck . . . is the most powerful god of all, two-faced progenitor of the world. He prefers we see just his benign face, the baby-making, world-renewing side. But we all know his opposite: Trickster, the devil that rides us and whips us until we bleed."

At this profundity, Alice stands on long legs, yawns, and stretches. "As always, you are uselessly instructive," she tells him. Minstrel gives her his slow prankboy's smile and stretches his arms higher than she can reach. She subdues a little shiver. Their chemistry is working, and holding back does her performance no good.

Alice turns to the low horizontal slit window overlooking the black stage. Something twinkles down there but they are off angle and cannot see the projection. Francis is tediously careful with his plugs and backmind details, but he could have laid in all of Chinese sexual psychology by now. "Francis should be done. He'll want to hook us." Back in the real. Her forehead creases.

"Are you up, dear?" Minstrel asks.

Alice shows him her moon face. "Never less," she says. "Are you?"

Minstrel's muscles flex at the back of his jaw. He is hiding something behind the cheer. He can hide from almost anyone but her; she knows him better than most wives know their husbands. To Alice it seems they have come far and survived much and against the odds, but at some cost. Minstrel hides his minuses poorly in front of her.

A pity, she thinks, that his body is so seldom seen in the vids they make now. Preferences of the blessed audience for the psynthe exotic.

"You look negged," she says.

Minstrel turns away as if unfairly poked. "Let me keep my mood," he tells her.

Alice moves in, swaying her shoulders, clucking her

tongue. "I'll need all of you in five minutes, and you can't make me work harder to get it," she says. "What's down?"

"Not my libido," he shoots back.

"You've cheered me the last hour instead of leaving me to brood over twisted thumbs." She wraps her arms around him. He pushes her off with what begins as real and angry strength, and ends gentleness and restraint.

"Is it Todd?" she asks.

"Todd was a year ago," Minstrel says.

Alice nods sympathetically, lips pursed. "I should have known. Why didn't you tell me?"

"I hide, you hide," Minstrel says, and tries to force more brave wit over what is now a sad and lost face.

"Poor Minstrel," she says. "They do not deserve you."

"No, they fapping well do not."

"So what's his name?"

"The little fap's name is Giorgio and you, dear Alice, will never meet him. He doesn't deserve to meet you."

The wound is seldom far beneath Minstrel's armor when she is doing the probing; he comes to her, at long intervals, like a dog with a boil, knowing she will hurt him with her lancet; also knowing it will do him good.

It is now that Francis chooses to blat his awful airhorn.

Minstrel closes up his cares and assumes a heavy-lidded roué's smile. "It is never duty with you," he says, "but whatever it is, it calls."

Alice loops her arm through his and they step down the broad railless stairs to the stage, like royalty or Astaire and Rogers making a grand entrance.

Francis awaits them in the plug room beside the main stage. Here as well as on the stage all is flat gritty black, no reflection allowed as the camera mixes its own glittering fairy-light dreams with the quantized lux of the real. Francis has named this camera Leni. Leni has become much more than an optical device. She scatters over the stage, feeding images and projections at one end, combining them with backmind layers at the other, a smooth silver and bronze balled and coiled snake.

Francis is irritated. His AD, scrawny and unkempt— Ahmed, Alice remembers vaguely; Francis goes through four or five ADs each production—hurries to arrange the bottles of nano and their small shiny plastic conduits and dams, to be applied to the occiput of Alice's skull and to Minstrel's temple.

"Alice, fabled Alice, what would *you* do?" Francis asks as they reach the bottom of the stairs. "I'm two weeks behind, two mill over, I have general fibe and sat release dates in four days—and I'm still layering!" Francis shakes his head. He always appears a little sad and irritated. Alice accepts this in Francis, as well as his fits of temper, only because what he does is unique and, she thinks, good; though Francis is not extraordinarily commercial, working on a Francis vid, even as backmind, can never hurt one's reputation.

"You've kept us waiting. Plug us and get your layers," Alice says matter-of-factly.

"Echo that," Minstrel says.

Francis wags his finger. "Fuck artists shouldn't bitch."

Alice cringes dramatically, pushes his finger back with her own.

Tiny black and silver machines with tactile fuzzy wheels and bug-jewel eyes crawl around the plug stage. They are little versions of Leni. Alice feels their bright little eyes sucking in her offline words. She hates them. Francis allows these recording arbeiters to roam with absolute freedom, examining whatever they choose; there are many in the audience who lose themselves in the life of the production. Francis makes as much on live behind-the-scenes docs as on the vids themselves. "Fuck artist," Alice croons to the nearest bug.

"Francis, the nano's a little old," Ahmed says. "It isn't perking."

"No surprise," Francis says. "We'll do prep while it sets."

"You aren't going to hook us with stale nano, are you, Francis?" Minstrel asks.

"No fear. Alice, have you read the text?"

"Only from the prep you sent. It's a long book, Francis." In fact, antique and long and dull.

Francis is preparing a deep-layered vid of *The Faerie Queene*. He smiles proudly. "A real challenge, to fade the wonderful Spenserian stanzas into a Yox." His face glows with the subject. "The Red Cross Knight is subject to such temptations, Alice. He is traveling with an Eastern queen named Una. A dragon has ravaged her land, and she hopes the Red Cross Knight will—"

"It's set, Francis." Ahmed shows him the bottles of translucent nano, now fully charged with nutrients. The liquid within is turbid and finally perks; it appears restless. Alice regards it with misgivings. She has plugged over a hundred times, on various jobs, and she has never trusted the process—but she has never been seriously injured even when, as now, the hook is administered by a nonmedical.

"The knight will rid her land of the dragon. So far, the Red Cross Knight has vanquished the hideous monster Error and all her progeny. A truly horrible scene, and I've layered it brilliantly. Now they are in a place of great temptations— Una and the knight. You've read the cues."

"We're all primed with ghostly passions," Minstrel says.

"Alice, my pride, you give me the most haunted libido I've ever recorded, when you're on point."

"I hope that's a compliment," Alice says.

"It is. Una and the Red Cross Knight have strayed into the workshop of the evil Archimago, who appears as a godly and kindly Hermit. It is a place of terrible temptations. You are a haunted spright, a succubus created by Archimago to torment and delude. You feel the deepest need for this young, handsome, and virtuous knight, but if you have him, you destroy him—and you know he will never fall for your illusion. However, by appearing in the form of the chaste Una, and engaging in lewd revels with fellow phantoms, you will mislead him into thinking this Eastern Lady has succumbed and is wallowing in lust. You must feel the False Una's passions as if she were actual souled flesh, not a demonic illusion. Many curious eyes and fingers are sure to want to plug into that layer.''

"Specks like you're going for broad appeal, this time," Minstrel says, picking at something between his teeth. He inspects his finger.

"I'd like to pay some bills, yes," Francis barks back. "You'll go direct into Leni while we run the set piece on stage. You'll be layering over seven emotional records from other fluffers, so I need everything clean and clear.''

Fluffers. Alice hates that word even more than *fuck artist*, though it is commonly used. It was once applied to women who kept actors erect or lubricious in old erotic movies. The comparison is inapt, at best; what Alice and Minstrel will provide is a layer of raw emotional experience, straight from their minds into the camera. Leni is only little less than a large set of eyes with a brain behind them. Francis guides Leni, cajoles her; theirs is not the relation of artisan to tool, they are more like partners.

Ahmed brings up the little dams and shapes them to Alice's head first, then Minstrel's. He syringes a dollop of warm nano into the dams as they sit still. Alice is used to this method of creating a broadband plug; it's common in the cheaper Yox.

A few minutes pass. A microscopic lead of conducting material has passed through the interstices of her skin, bone, and brain, into her deep amygdala, hippocampus, and hypothalamus; into the seats of her judgment engine, the Grand Central Terminal of her self. She feels nothing.

Ahmed applies transponders to the little silver nipples of nano, no larger than a thumbnail. He takes readings for several minutes from the camera. Lights flash agreeably. "Hooked," he tells Francis.

Alice removes her robe. Minstrel is already naked. Francis

makes a butterfly gesture with his hands, then clasps his fingers.

"Here come the Sprights and Archimago. Taking," he says. "Click one."

Ahmed labels the backmind layer. The camera hums.

Francis quotes from memory:

"Thus well instructed, to their worke they hast,
And comming where the knight in slomber lay,
The one upon his hardy head him plast,
And made him dream of loves and lustfull play,
That nigh his manly heart did melt away,
Bathed in wanton bliss and wicked joy . . ."

Francis beams. "How like your own career, sweet Alice. How many men have you haunted?"

Alice ignores this.

On the stage behind them, in translucent and sketchy 3D workprint, the evil sorcerer Archimago leads the Red Cross Knight through dreams of dark chambers filled with writhing bodies in silken robes. Hanging tapestries are pulled aside by the incredulous Knight, who sees false Una's flesh revealed in intimate posture with an equally false Spright made a Squire. Alice ignores most of this. What she and Minstrel will provide has little to do with the plot.

Alice looks directly at Minstrel. As always, the angle of Minstrel's dark brown eyes and the sharpness of his nose, the assurance of his professional smile, impresses her. They have real and reliable chemistry.

"You will always be the most beautiful woman on Earth," Minstrel murmurs to her, and she knows he means it. He prefers men, but Alice affects him as much as he affects her, reliably, predictably. If they lived together, their contradictions would burn them out in a year; but in this professional capacity, they've stretched their time.

Francis is watching the camera, his Leni. She seems happy.

What Alice feels first is the yearning warmth, not dissimilar to what a baby feels for its mother; she wishes to be closer. Minstrel touches her face with the back of his hand, stroking her cheek, holding this off. He responds as nearly all men respond to her, given a chance: she notes the flush on his chest, the close focus of his eyes, the beginning rise. Often, the rise amuses her; men seem off-balance when aroused, would topple like cranes without her support. But Minstrel's rise is a delightful shock.

The delicious pain of expectation meeting an inner self-doubt drops her back in the first sopping yet dry-mouthed experiments of youth (''Love for sale, appetizing young love for sale—'' Billie Holiday singing Cole Porter), amazed at success and delighted by it.

They kiss first, leaning forward to avoid other contact: soft roughness of lips like nubbled silk, oily smoothness of tongues.

''Good,'' Francis says. He is recording none of the tactile, not of the surface; only the deep surge, the pulse of yearning from the sympathies, the letting down of vascular tensions by the parasympathies, the message of intense well-being issued by the judging amygdala; all of which Alice is aware of, but not conscious of.

Her thighs seem large and obvious; she might topple too. *I am all thighs.* Minstrel wraps her, presses forearms against her back, then withdraws them until his fingers rub her ribs, just above the threshold of a tickle. Tongues plunge. For a moment this is too much and she breaks the kiss and noses the hollow of his neck, shuddering.

Minstrel is not the most lovely and stimulating she has ever had, but she is so astonishingly consistent with him. Surprise, warmth, expectancy, and then the final salt: Minstrel prefers men. Alice has a special command, a leave he gives few other women, if any. She specks him with his male lovers, wonders whether she would have the same effect on *them*; likely not, doesn't matter, the warm fantasy is well away now, sailing with courses full.

They clasp tight from breasts to knees. He intrudes between her thighs and friction again becomes oily smoothness, but he does not press or angle. Minstrel knows her times and frequencies. He is an instinctive lover. She might shiver a muscle here, under his palm, and he adjusts the momentary mix of pressings and withdrawals to suit her as a horseman adjusts to his mount.

The comparisons are becoming more and more basic, the sweetest and deepest of clichés. She will ride, float, flow, sit in the waves, feel the high warm sun; all images in her mind, most from past joins, some never real, all falling like drowsy rivers of fine hot sand down her spine.

"Why, Cuntia," he murmurs. "So long lacking?"

"Shh," she says into his ear. Their motion more pronounced. Francis forgotten, hooks ignored, though she makes sure not to rub the transponders loose as she brushes her temples against his chest. She disengages, though she wants him all within, wants to hide him, knows how to ramp her own surges by withholding. She rubs him down his stomach with her cheeks, lips, high sensual definition against the tight skin.

"Good," Francis says.

Close-up, curls and the sweetly ugly rise, more beautiful than kittens; she adores him. Minstrel is all-valuable, all-honored; she suffers no disgrace by doing anything for him. She does not know what willingness he will take advantage of. Sometimes he assumes brusque anger, a delicate but dominant brutishness that toes a thin thread yet never goes beyond earnest play. But today Minstrel is infinitely gentle and this also falls within her range of surprise and expectancy.

"Wicked as Lucrezia," he says.

His languor is reward enough for the minute she thinks she has. Sure enough, at the end of a minute, he takes her head between his palms and removes her, and she leans back on the stiff pallet, knowing she need do nothing but react, and that none too vigorously. Among the men she has had, the many hundreds of encounters long and short, professional and personal, Minstrel needs the least indication of her fulfilled desire. He already feels what she feels from the shivers and twitches of her knees and the texture of the skin of her hips and ribs and the muscles beneath.

"Good," Francis says.

"Under Labia's disguise, Glans finds shy Clitoris," Minstrel whispers into her ear. His weight is a surge of southern air; his breath and sweat musk. She can smell his body, a whiff of zoo, nervous but not weak; this is the part she savors most, reaching a man's deep concerns. After all their years, Minstrel wonders whether she will approve. Since she knows she *will* approve, his concern is a delight. Poor good men, all the good lovers, always this stretch of nerves before the partaking. A laugh even of delight might be misunderstood. Seconds pass before she shows anything other than complete and unquestioning acceptance.

"Good," Francis says. "And . . ."

She clutches Minstrel, presses his butt down with her nails, feels the slipping entrance, sucks in him and an uneven breath, simultaneously.

Francis quotes again:

"With sword in hand, and with the old man went;/ Who soon him brought unto a secret part,/ Where that false couple were full closely ment/ In wanton lust and lewd embracement;/ Which when he saw, he burnt with gealous fire,/ The eye of reason was with rage yblent,/ And would have slaine them in his furious ire,/ But hardly was restrained of that aged sire . . ."

Minstrel shudders.

"Enough. Cut."

He holds, withdraws. Alice's eyes dart around the stage. "What?" she says.

"Focus," Francis commands. "Disappointment. You cannot have the Red Cross Knight. You are a Spright, a Succubus, not a true female. Everything you do is a false sin, never delight, always duty. Enough.''

Minstrel lies back, flushed. Alice wants to climb onto him but that would not be professional. Of all things in her life that would keep her from him, it is this isinglass membrane of her working self-respect.

Francis monitors Leni, his eyes glazing over. Alice looks on the camera as a kind of dragon, a ravenous audience suspended in a line through all future time behind the camera's many senses.

''Perfect, both of you,'' Francis says, returning and smiling. ''Good enough to earn a credit. Your followers will love this.''

Minstrel smiles back wearily. The muscles of his jaw tighten. The spell is broken and he is thinking of the sooty world.

Minstrel leans over her. ''Glans would ask dear Cuntia to marry him,'' he says, ''but the pressures of royal life . . . you know how it is.''

''Cuntia would accept,'' Alice replies.

''We shouldn't leave this unfinished,'' Minstrel says.

Alice is puzzled. ''No.''

Francis shouts for the stage to be cleared.

''But we have to.'' Minstrel smiles. ''Better for the next time.''

This is their third dry embrace in the past six months. They are nearly always in shadow, backmind layering now, never up front in the fulfilled lux.

''I'll be waiting,'' Alice says, and Minstrel strokes her cheek before climbing the stairs to get dressed.

Ahmed stares at her, flushed and awed.

''You're new, aren't you?'' Alice asks too sweetly. She puts on her robe and climbs the stairs after. At the top, she hears her pad chime in a loop of her street clothes. Minstrel is half-dressed. Times past, they might have finished their business up here, neither of them believing pent-up passion to be healthy, but she can see Minstrel's heart and mind are elsewhere.

The courtesies have fled. They've peaked and both know it.

She pulls the small pad from her purse and takes the call. "Alice here."

"I couldn't leave a message or let our homes talk to each other. This is Twist."

Twist is younger than Alice by six years but already a veteran. They met two years ago and took a quick liking to each other. Twist—if she calls at all—treats Alice as a kind of mother.

"Hello, Twist. I'm just getting off a plug for Francis."

"Something's queer, Alice."

"What?"

"I'm acting really queer. I need to see somebody."

"How queer?"

"I'm obsessing all over the place, about David."

Fuck artists, like most sex care workers, take on so many partners, Alice cannot immediately remember just who David is. She thinks they might have met once, at Twist's apt in Ballard.

"I'm not a therapist, Twist."

"I called my *mother,* Alice," Twist says. "Before I called you. You know what that cost me?"

Twist often hints at the monstrosity of her mother. Alice has taken it all with a few grains; even therapied, Twist never flows the straight pipe.

Alice sits on a bench and crosses her legs. Minstrel gives her an exaggerated grimace and twinkle-wave with his fingers, picks up his bag. Alice watches him go with a small sharp sadness.

"All right, why not go straight to a therapist?"

"Because David took me out of the agency," Twist says.

"I'm out of the payment grid. He was getting me jobs. He has connections."

"Ah," Alice says, suddenly remembering David. *The* David, Twist called him: a small, thin man with dark hair. Alice had instantly specked him as a scheming litter scrawn desperately trying to make up for being born a runt, always sure he had the answers. Twist adores him, hangs on his every reedy word.

"Well, I'm sure the agency—" Alice begins.

"David won't let me. He's gone aggly, too."

"What do you mean?"

"I feel like I felt when I began therapy. I was thirteen, Alice. I was a bad case, a real mess. It's all back now, only worse." She gives a painful, nervous giggle. "David says it must have never really took."

"Why don't you come to my apt and let's talk," Alice suggests. "I can be there in half an hour—"

"I don't know that David will let me."

Alice takes a deep breath. Some new fluffers are coming up the stairs. Francis is working overtime.

"I *do* need to talk, Alice. Going to be home tomorrow?"

"Morning, yes."

"I'll be there at ten. I'll set up David with somebody. Cardy's fuckish for him. Then I can get free for a couple of hours."

Alice cringes. That word—Minstrel's tetragrammaton—sounds too hard on Twist's lips. Twist is like a little girl in so many ways. Alice realizes this is uncharacteristic; sex words hard or soft generally do not bother her, whatever her private opinions. She is darked by the scrim of others.

"I'll see you in the morning," Alice says.

"Yeah. Love you, Alice."

"You too." She closes the link and stands among the four new fluffers, none of whom she knows. They all wear butterfly colors; they come from Sextras, now the top Yox temp agency for fuck artists. They smile at her; they know who she is. She used to be heat made flesh.

She smiles back, polite and a little condescending, shakes a few hands, tongue-kisses one of the bold males, and then is down the stairs, where Ahmed still watches for her.

> **T**he monstrosity of this technological era is indescribable. A man can carry armies of progeny within his testicles, none of them his own . . . some perhaps not purely human. A woman can bear within her unnatural "artworks" quickened by science and surely as soulless as stones. We sicken and despair. There is nothing of God in these machines and machine-men.

The Mother Church has nothing to offer the time into which we have been born but a warning that sounds like a curse: As you sow, so shall you reap!

> **—Pope Alexander VII, 2043**

From: Anonymous Remailer
To: Pope Alexander VII
Date: December 24 2043

"You're just a Catholic Dickhead, you know that? Come to my town (wouldnt you like to know you shit) sometime and I'll show you a GOOD TIME. Let your bodiguards know I'm about seven feet tall and dresed like the Demans in NUKEY NOOKY which I bet youve plaid too you asswipe hippocrit!!!!! Have a nice day!!!!!"

EMAIL Archive (ref Security Inv, Re: Thread = Encyclical 2043, Vatican Library> Cultural Tracking STAFF /INDA 332; reverse track through Finland> ANONYM REMAIL Code REROUTE> SWITZERLAND/ZIMBABWE> ACCT HDFinster > Harrison D. Finster ADDRESS 245 W. Blessoe Street Apt 3-H Greensboro, NC, USA. PROFILE> 27 years of age at time of message, >CONCLUSION: FLAME PROFILE No action necessary. ref Vatican Internal Investigator comments: "Young, shit for brains.")

3 / ALLOSTASIS

For Martin Burke, life has become anaspace, all motion but no engagement, no interaction, no sense of progress. And yet he is not unsuccessful.

He moved from the combs of Southcoast two years ago. He had set himself up as a design consultant for miniature therapy monitors, microscopic implants that roamed freely in the body and brain, regulating balances and adjusting natural neurochemical concentrations. All of the delayed but no less painful publicity about his involvement with the mass-murderer and poet Emanuel Goldsmith had put an end to this new career; no corporation wanted to be associated with him after that, though they still license and manufacture from his patents.

Since moving to Seattle, he has worked in special mental therapy, out of the third floor of an old, dignified building off Pioneer Square.

Outside it is a rare cloudless winter morning, though at eight o'clock still dark. On the Southcoast of California, at the end of his last career, the sun had seemed inhumanly probing and constant. Martin had yearned for change, weather, clouds to hide under . . .

Now he yearns for sun again.

Strangely, away from California, the publicity has actually brought in new clients; but in balance, it also ended the love of his life. He has not seen or heard from Carol in a year, though he keeps in touch with his young daughter, Stephanie.

Martin enters the round lobby and pushes open the door to his office, slinging his personal pad and purse onto their hooks on an antique coat rack. He has resisted the expense of installing a dattoo or skin pad, with circuitry and touches routed through mildly electrified skin, preferring instead a more old-fashioned implement, and keeping his body natural and inviolate into his forty-eighth year.

His receptionist, Arnold, and assistant, Kim, greet him from their half-glass cubicle at the center of the lobby. Arnold is large and well-trained in both public relations and physical restraint. Kim, small and seemingly shy, is a powerhouse therapeutic psychology student with a minor in business relations. He hopes he can keep them working for him for at least the next year, before their agency fields better offers.

Tucked out of sight, a year-old INDA sits quietly on a shelf overlooking the reception area, monitoring all that happens in the office's five rooms.

He prepares for the long day with a ten-minute staff meeting. He goes over patient requests for unscheduled visits. "Tell Mrs. Danner I'll see her at noon Friday," he instructs Arnold.

"I'm off that day," Arnold says. "She's a five-timer." Martin looks over Mrs. Danner's record. She's a five-time CTR—core therapy reject—with a long criminal record. "Want me to be here?"

"She's not violent," Martin says. "Klepto mostly, inclined to hurt herself and not others. Enjoy your day off."

Martin has expanded his business by taking referrals from therapists who can't handle their patients. After relieving himself of his own demon, he has a special touch with people who are still ridden.

"And Mr. Perkins—?" Arnold asks.

Martin makes a wry face. Kim smiles. Mr. Perkins is much less difficult than Mrs. Danner, but less pleasant to deal with. He is unable to establish lasting relations with people and relies on human-shaped arbeiters for company. Three previous therapists have been unsuccessful treating him, even with the most modern nano monitors and neuronal enhancement.

"Third request in a week," Martin says. "I suppose he's

still having trouble resetting his prosthetute?''

The patient log floats before Arnold's face like a small swarm of green insects. ''His wife, he calls her.''

''He can't bear to deactivate the old personality. That passes for kindness in him, I suppose.'' Martin smirks. ''I'll see him Monday. So who's up for this morning?''

''You have Joseph Breedlove at nine and Avril de Johns at ten.''

Martin wrinkles his forehead in speculation. Neither Breedlove nor de Johns are difficult patients; they fall into that category of unhappy people who regard therapy as a replacement for real accomplishment. Therapy to date can only make the best of what is already available. ''I have an hour free at eleven?''

''Of course.''

''Then all is in order. It's eight-thirty now. I have a half-hour until Mr. Breedlove. No touches until nine.''

''Right,'' Arnold says.

Martin takes his pouch and walks down the narrow hallway to the back office. *Sanctum sanctorum*. Sometimes he sleeps here, since there is little to go back to at home. He missed the chance for the island sharehold on Vashon—damnable Northwest offishness, thirty-year residents and born-here's discriminating shamelessly against the fresh arrivals—and so Martin's home is a condo in a small ribbon comb overlooking the northbound three-deck Artery 5 Freeway. It is not expensive, nor is it particularly attractive. In two years, his residency advocate tells him, he may be allowed into some higher lottery, perhaps even a Bainbridge sharehold.

Private touches flicker around him as he sits at his desk, like pet birds begging. Some he flagged a week ago for immediate attention. He shoos them off with a wave, then pokes at the fresh touches and they line up, the first expanding like an origami puzzle. This is from Dana Carrilund, the head of Workers Inc Northwest. He wonders who gave her his sig. Despite this being his free period, he opens this immediately.

Carrilund's voice is warm and professional. "Mr. Burke, pardon my using your personal sig. I'm in a real bind. I'm told we have about seven of our clients taking special therapy with you. They're doing well, I hear. I may have additional clients for you—all of them fallbacks. Please let me know if we can fit this into your schedule. Also, I'd like to speak to you in person and in private."

It's outside his usual domain; Martin specializes in core therapy failures, people for whom initial and even secondary therapy does not work. Fallbacks have been successfully therapied but experience recurrence of thymic or even pathic imbalances.

Why would the head of Workers Inc Northwest place such a touch? Martin frowns; he presumed Workers Inc Northwest sent their cases to Sound Therapy, the largest analysis-therapy corporation in the Corridor. He's flattered to receive such high-level attention, but can't think of a reason why.

He drafts the reply in his own voice. "To Dana Carrilund. Of course your cases are of interest. Let me know what you need and I'll work up a schedule and proposal. I hope we can meet soon."

This is a shameless hedge against any downstream lags in business, something Martin is always sensitive about. He does not need any more patients. Still, he has never quite lost his fear of unemployment; a contract with Workers Inc could smooth over any future rough times.

The next message is from his daughter, their daily morning exchange. Stephanie still lives in La Jolla with her mother. They link once a week and he manages trips south every other month, but as he watches the image of this lovely three-year-old, a somewhat plumper version of Carol, who seems in their genetic dance to have grabbed only Martin's eyebrows and ears, this image in its sharp perfection kissing air where his nose might be and holding up a succession of red and blue paper craftworks, eager for his approval, only makes him lonelier. Another inexplicable fault line.

He tacks to his reply a bedtime story he recorded last night, adds loving comments on the skill of her craftworks, shoots the reply to reach her pad by midmorning break in the live public schoolroom. Carol will never allow home instruction. Nothing New Federalist about Carol.

The essential touches processed, he pulls his chair up to his desk and says, "INDA, are you there?"

The INDA responds immediately. A lovely liquid voice neither male nor female seems to fill the room. "Yes, sir."

"Any results from yesterday?"

"I've analyzed the journal entries you suggested. Your fee for arbeiter access to the journals is now at the limit, Dr. Burke."

Martin will have to upgrade his credit with the dealer today.

"That's fine, INDA. Tell me what you've found."

"I have seven references to Country of the Mind investigations, all of them in cases predating last year's law." The United States Congress, acting in conjunction with Europe and Asia, has passed laws banning two-way psychiatric investigation through the hippocampal juncture, which Martin pioneered. Appeals to the Supreme Court and World Psychiatric Organization have been quietly buried; nobody is currently interested in stirring up this hornet's nest. Emanuel Goldsmith might have been the final poison pill.

"No defiance or physician protests?"

"A search through available records indicates the procedure has not been openly performed in four years by anybody, in any part of the world."

"I mean, has anyone published contrary opinions?"

"*Liberal Digest*'s Multiway has posted twelve contrary opinions in the past year, but that makes it a very minor issue. By comparison, they posted four thousand and twenty-one contrary opinions on the Freedom to Choose Individual Therapy decision *vis a vis* the requirements of temp agencies and employers."

Martin remembered that case well; lower and state court rulings in New York and Virginia, bastions of New Federalism, had clearly been intended to put roadblocks in the way of therapy's juggernaut domination of society, but the Supreme Court had voided the rulings, based on contract law, coming down in favor of temp agencies and employers. *Liberal Digest* had, for once, agreed with the New Federalists that therapy should not be forced on temp agency clients, under threat of unemployment.

These were strange times.

"Any conclusions?"

"We do not foresee any interest in Country of the Mind investigations, as a social issue, for many years." "We" among INDAs is purely a placekeeper for "this machine," and does not imply any self-awareness.

"It's dead, then."

"Of no currency," the INDA amends.

Martin taps his desk. He has moved completely away from the discovery which launched his fame and caused his downfall. He believes strongly that Country of the Mind investigations could be incredibly powerful and useful, but society has rejected them for the time being—and for the foreseeable future.

"I suppose that's best," he says, but without conviction.

His office pad chimes. It's early.

"Yes, Arnold?"

"Sir, there's a gentleman here. No appointment. New. He's very insistent—says he'll make it worth your while."

"What's his problem?"

"He won't say, sir. He won't accept Kim's evaluation and he looks very edgy."

Kim joins in, out of the intruder's hearing: "Sir, his name is Terence Crest. *The* Terence Crest. We've run a check. He is who he says he is."

It's Martin's day to be approached by influential people. Crest is a billionaire, known for his conservatism and quest for privacy as much as his financial dealings—mostly in Rim entertainment. Martin taps his finger on the desk several times, then says, "Show him in." The day's touches, drifting at apparent arm's length over the office pad, vanish.

Martin greets Mr. Crest at the door and escorts him to a chair. Crest is in his mid-forties, of medium height, with a thin bland face and large unfocused eyes. He is dressed in dark gray with thin black stripes, and beneath his long coat, his shirt is living sun-yellow, body-cleansing and health-monitoring fabric. His right hand carries three large rings, signs of affiliations in high comb society. Martin cannot read the ring patterns, but he suspects strong New Federalist leanings.

The way Crest holds his head, the way the light hits his skin, Martin has a difficult time making out his expression. He has the spooky sensation of the man's face losing detail with every glance.

"Good morning, Dr. Burke," Crest says. "I'm terribly sorry to break in like this, but I've been told I can rely on you." His voice is clear and crisp. Crest is accustomed to being listened to attentively. He looks dreamily at the ceiling and remains standing. Martin asks him to sit.

Crest peers down at the chair, as if waiting for it to move, then sits. "I'm still mulling over what you posted in People's Therapy Multiway last week. Allostatic load and all. That the pressures of everyday life can bend us like overstressed metal bars."

Martin nods. "An explanation of a general idea for a general readership. Why does it concern you?"

"I can't afford the disgrace."

"What disgrace?"

"I think I'm exceeding my load limits." A thin sour chuckle. "I'm about to break."

"Suffering from stress is no disgrace, Mr. Crest. We all face it at some time or another in our lives."

"Well, I'm still wrestling with the idea of my physicality.

I was raised Baptist. And for some of my . . . connections, *friends*, well, that sort of weakness doesn't sit well.''

"A not uncommon prejudice, but nothing more than that— prejudice.''

"It's hard for me—for them—to accept that illness, in the mind, can result from something other than . . . you know. A defect in the soul.''

"That's the way it truly is, Mr. Crest. Nothing to do with inborn character defects. We're all fragile.''

"Dr. Burke, I can't be fragile.'' Even through the vagueness, Crest's face hardens. "My people won't let me. My wife is as high natural as they come, and everyone in her family. I feel like they're expecting me to fall, you know, from their grace. Any minute.'' He smacks his hands together lightly. "I suppose that's a kind of stress, too.''

"Sounds like it could be,'' Martin says.

"If I had to be therapied . . . I would lose a lot, Martin.''

"Happens to the best of us.''

"You keep saying that,'' Crest says. "It's just not true. It *doesn't* happen to the best of us. The best of us cope. The best of us have better chemistry, stronger neurons, a better molecular balance, just an all-around better constitution . . . we're made of finer alloy. The others . . . they fail because they're flawed.''

Instinctively, Martin does not like this man—he feels uncomfortable in his presence. But many strong-willed patients in deep pain come across this way.

Crest slaps his hand on the chair arm. "I am haunted, Dr. Burke. There are days when I know I'm going to crumble. Some of the corporations I work with, making very large deals—they require an inspection every month, can you believe it?''

Martin smiles. "It's not called for, that's for sure.''

"It's a way of weeding out failure. High naturals have a lower chance of letting a deal fall through. A brain race.'' Crest smiles back at Martin. The smile seems to fall in shadow, though the room is brightly lit. "Very American. Reliability above creativity."

"Intelligence and creativity often accompany more fragile constitutions," Martin says. The lecture is familiar, meant to reassure. "There's every evidence some people are more sensitive and alert, more attuned to reality, and this puts a greater load on their systems. Still, these people make themselves very useful in our society. We couldn't get along without them—"

Crest shakes his head vigorously. "Genius is next to madness, is that what you're saying, Doctor?"

"Genius is a particular state of mind . . . a type of mind, only distantly comparable to the types I'm talking about."

"Like a genie in the head? Just rub it the right way and out it comes? Well, I'm no genius," Crest chuckles tensely, "and I haven't been accused of being very sensitive . . . So why do I worry? I mean, the type of decisions I'm called upon to make demand tough thinking, maybe even a lack of human sensitivity . . . And above all else, stability. I have to stand up to tough conditions for long periods of time."

"Well, your name is well known, Mr. Crest."

Crest raises a finger and jabs at the ceiling. "One little slip . . . Down from high natural to, say, a simple untherapied." Crest shudders. "One little inappropriate thought, and my wife takes her connections with her—right out of the house. I honestly think I'm going to obsess myself into just what I fear, over this.

"Dr. Burke, this conversation has to be absolutely secure. Confidential. I am willing to pay a hundred thousand dollars for you to secretly take care of me if I should fall."

Martin hates turning down patients; he also hates being treated like a man who can be bought. Not that he's unassailable—to his intense personal shame, he's been bought before. It's a theme in his life. He knows what the consequences can be.

Crest sighs. "This is torture for you, isn't it, Doctor?"

"How?"

"Having a high natural come in here and run off about chances of failing. I mean, you're not a high natural, are you?"

"No."

"Untherapied? Just a natural?"

"No."

"Therapied, and for some time, right?"

"Right."

"So you must be . . . I mean, it must be like having a rich man come in and worry about losing his money, and you haven't got any."

Martin squints at Crest and says, "You're offering four times my highest rate. It's a generous offer, but I would be less than honest if I didn't tell you that there's too much emphasis on high natural ratings. It isn't that big a deal. It's another human measurement, a quantification some folks are willing to use to separate us from each other."

"I'm not a have-not, Dr. Burke. I'm used to having."

"I wouldn't put so much store in having this particular thing, this high natural rating, if I were you. You'd be surprised at the power and influence of some who don't."

"Sure," Crest says, agitated. "Like you. Nobody rates you but your medical board. Doctors have always protected their own."

Martin clamps his teeth together tightly before answering. "If we used the criteria your fellow businessmen seem to find attractive, we'd lose most of our best, our most sensitive doctors."

"There's that word again," Crest says, sniffing and drawing in his jaw. "Sensitive. I'm not an artist, I'm not a therapist, I'm a decision maker. I have to make a dozen important decisions a day, every day. I have to be keen, like a knife edge. Not *sensitive*."

"The sharper the edge, the more liable it is to be blunted if it's misused," Martin observes.

"I have my standards," Crest says. "I'm sorry if nobody else is strong enough to accept them."

"Mr. Crest, I have my standards as well. If this is going to have any positive outcome, we should start all over again. You've interrupted my day without an appointment, you've impugned my professional ethics by flinging money at me . . ."

Crest sits very still. The light around his face is not natural, not the lighting of the room. He might be made of wax.

"I know you don't like me, and that's fine, I'm used to that, but I have my own sense of honor, Dr. Burke. I've gotten myself into something. I know what's right and what isn't and I've violated that code. It began as greed. Greed for life, I suppose, for fighting off the real devils, for keeping all I've made. But it's beyond that now." Crest stares at him.

Martin cannot penetrate the vagueness of the man's face. He has never seen anything like it. "If you can come back later today, I can run my own evaluation, with my own equipment."

"Now," Crest says. "I need it now."

Martin is willing to believe that Crest is close to a thymic imbalance, maybe even a pathic collapse, but the situation is fraught with legal difficulties.

"I can't treat you on an emergency basis, Mr. Crest."

"These men and women I'm involved with . . . they *kill* people who talk to outsiders."

That does it, Martin thinks. "I can recommend a clinic not two blocks from here, but sir, with your resources, you can—"

"I can't use my own medicals or therapists. They're not secure. I agreed to have them feed my stats and vitals into . . . the center. They would know. I'm close to the edge, Doctor. *Two hundred thousand.*"

Martin swallows. "I can't treat patients close to severe collapse. That requires an initial evaluation by a federally licensed primary therapist."

Crest smiles again, or perhaps he is not smiling at all.

He leans forward and places his arms on Martin's desk. "I could tell you, and then tell *them*. They would have to kill you. Or discredit you."

"I don't react well to threats," Martin says. "I can't be forced to do something illegal, whatever the money or the threats. I think you should—"

"I could kill you myself."

Martin stands. "Get out."

"I could be just like them, but I'm not. I really am not." He raises his arms and shouts, "No agreements, no pressure. I'd give it all up. Doctor, you can have it all . . . Just get me out of this!"

"I've told you what my limits are, Mr. Crest. I can give you the names of very discreet emergency therapists—"

Crest stands and brushes off his elbows, though the chair arms are not dusty. His voice is steady now. "I'm sorry to have wasted your time. I'll feed fifty K into your accounts for your trouble."

"No need," Martin says, knowing that his anger is completely inappropriate, but feeling very angry.

Martin escorts Crest to the door. Crest pauses, turns as if to say something more, and then leaves.

Martin sighs deeply, collects himself. He walks into the lobby a few minutes later. Arnold and Kim stare at him, sharing his relief and astonishment. They go to the window looking down on the street and see a small black limousine move into traffic three floors below.

"That is the strangest encounter I've had in years," Martin says. He glances at Kim. "Evaluation?"

"He's real close," Kim says. "He should go to a primary therapist."

"That's what I told him. He wouldn't listen."

"Then there's nothing we can do."

Nevertheless, Martin feels a jab of guilt. He has not even re-applied for a federal license. He is sure he would be turned down—and that could be a black mark against his current practice.

Like Crest, he, too, has a tortuous path to follow.

"Doctor," Arnold says. "Ms. Carrilund got your touch and needs to respond right away. I wouldn't interrupt before the next client, but—"

He thinks of Crest's situation, and how prevalent in the real world that kind of cruel competition must be, to drag down even the wealthiest. "I'll take it," Martin says.

He returns to his office and faces the pad on the desk. Carrilund appears before him in complete detail, mid-fifties, white-blonde, in a stylishly tailored commons suit with ruffle sleeves. She is handsome and aging naturally, and Martin concludes she must have been dangerously beautiful in her youth. In some respects she reminds him of Carol—but many women remind him of Carol now.

"I'm glad you have time to talk, Dr. Burke," Carrilund begins. "Your work has been highly recommended by a number of our clients."

"I'm pleased to hear that," Martin says. His mouth is still sour. He pours himself a glass of water from the carafe on his desk and takes a sip.

"Have you noticed an increase in fallbacks in your practice?" Carrilund asks.

"No. Most of my practice is with core therapy rejects."

"I see. All of our clients with you now are CTRs, are they not?"

"Yes."

"Dr. Burke, my sources tell me you're likely to receive a flood of fallback and CTR clients in the next few months."

"From your agency?" Martin asks.

"Perhaps, but not necessarily through this office. We've had CTR notices on over half our clients going into primary therapy. That's not something I would like blown to the fibes, Dr. Burke, but it's not going to be a secret for long."

Martin whistles. "Extraordinary," he says.

"We've never seen rates higher than five percent in all the years I've been with Workers Inc. I was wondering if you'd be interested in participating in a little study."

"I don't see why not—if this is a real, long-term problem. But as I said, in my practice, I would not notice such a trend until . . ." What she has said suddenly hits him. He feels a little queasy.

"There are only five doctors in your line of work in the Corridor," Carrilund says. "I think you're going to see a big increase in your business."

If her statistics were not just flukes, that would mean . . . He quickly calculates. Tens of thousands for each of the five. "I can't handle that kind of load."

Carrilund smiles sympathetically. "It could be a big problem for us all. We'd like to work with you to learn the root causes . . . If there are any. We're looking at entry-level workers, most of them in their late teens and early twenties, going through their first qualification inspections. It's heartbreaking for them, Doctor. It could be a challenge to our whole economy."

"I understand that. Please count me in, and keep me informed."

"Thank you, Dr. Burke. I will."

"And make an arrangement with my office for a personal meeting."

"Thank you." They exchange home sigs. Carrilund smiles sedately and Martin transfers her to Arnold.

Martin sits lost in thought. He came very close to being CTR himself, years ago; too close to having to face, day after day, for years on end, the prospect of an inner voice that murmurs of confusion and pain and much, much worse.

He has raised his hands, unconsciously, as if to ward off something coming toward him. With another shudder, he drops them to his lap, composes himself, and tells Arnold to send in Mrs. Avril De Johns.

Access to knowledge and information is necessary to a dataflow economy. But it will cost you . . .

Every single access will cost you. A penny here, a thousand dollars there, a million a year over there somewhere . . . subscriptions and encryptions and decryptions. If you haven't already shown yourself to be a part of the flow—if you aren't a student given research dispensation, or already earning your way by turning information into knowledge and that into money and work—the action anatomy of society—it's a tough old world.

Perhaps in discouragement you become one of the disAffected and spend all your federal dole on the more flagrant Yox, drowning yourself in enervating lies. You're allowed, but you're out of the loop. One-way flow is not a game; it's a sucking little death.

—The U.S. Government Digiman on Dataflow Economics,
56th Revision, 2052

Humanism is dead. Animals think, feel; so do machines now. Neither man nor woman is the measure of all things. Every organism processes data according to its domain, its environment; you, with all your brains, would soon be useless in a mouse's universe . . .

—Lloyd Ricardo, *Pressed Between Two Flat Seconds:
Preserving the Human Flower*

It's not your grandmother's world. It was never your grandmother's world.

Kiss of X, *Alive Contains a Lie*

4 / THINKER, FEELER

Nathan Rashid gives his fiancée, Ayesha Kale, a tour of Mind Design's most famous inhabitant, Jill.

Nathan is Jill's new chief engineer and friend. He replaced Roger Atkins two years ago, when Atkins became chief administrator for Mind Design's new thinker development.

Nathan headed the team that brought her back from her collapse, and Jill regards him with warm affection. She does not believe he will do anything to reduce her functions or alter her present state. After all, it was Nathan who devised the ornate Loop Detail Interrupt that restored her to awareness and full function.

Jill trusts him, but she has not told him about the mystery.

Nathan and Ayesha stand in a broad cream-colored room with a central riser surrounded by transparent glass plates. On the riser sits a snow-white cube about one meter on a side, attended by three smaller cubes. Nathan is thirty-five, dark-haired, broad-faced, with an immediate, eager, and sometimes mischievous smile. Ayesha is five years older, brown-haired, with large, all-absorbing black eyes and a mouth that seems ready to acknowledge disappointment.

The cubes are connected by fibes as well as by direct optical links, which twinkle like blue eyes as they pass through the empty air between.

"Is that her?" Ayesha asks.

"That's her," Nathan says.

"That's all?"

Jill sits in warm and cold, feeling neither. Her emotions, as with all of us, do not seem to come from her particular structures, though she is much more aware of her internal processes.

"Most of her is here. Why, disappointed?"

Jill's body, if she can be said to have one, is mainly in Del Mar and Palo Alto, California. There are many parts of her less than a few cubic centimeters in size spread through eleven different buildings along Southcoast. She is connected to these extensions through a variety of I/Os by fibes and satlinks and even a few tentative quantum gated links (which she finds annoying; they do not work all the time, and may in fact slow her thinking if relied upon exclusively).

"She's so small!" Ayesha says.

Nathan smiles. "She was twice as big before the refit."

"Still, so small, to be so famous."

Jill is listening, Nathan knows. She listens attentively to all of her inputs, but he does not know that a significant portion of her is in unlinked isolation, devoted much of the time to considering a mystery. She has pondered this mystery for several years, ever since her shutdown and redesign.

She does not clearly remember events after her Feedback Fine Detail Collapse. But she remembers some things she should not be able to remember, and this is what intrigues her.

"Why is she a *she*?" Ayesha asks.

"She decided on her own. Roger Atkins may have started it when he named her after a girlfriend. Besides, she's a mother. We seed other thinkers from her."

Jill is the most advanced thinker ever made, the first—on Earth—to become self-aware. She has a sibling in deep space, far from Earth, who achieved self-awareness before she did, but its status is currently unknown. Her creators assume that it, too, suffered Feedback Fine Detail Collapse, and that all of its functions locked up, so that it now drifts around another star, alone and probably in a state equivalent to death.

Generations from now, when other, more complex ships head for the stars, perhaps they will find and resurrect her sibling. Jill hopes she will be around for a reunion.

She silently follows Nathan and Ayesha with her glass-almond eyes, mounted on thin rods protruding from the walls around the room. Ayesha walks around her like a zoo visitor examining an interesting animal in a cage.

"She's the most powerful mind on the planet," Nathan says proudly. "Unless you believe Torino."

"What does Torino say?"

"He thinks there's a world-spanning bacterial mind," Nathan says lightly.

"A *mind*, in germs?" Ayesha says, drawing her head back incredulously. "Really?"

"Not like a human mind, or even like Jill, not socially self-aware. He thinks every bacterium is a node in a loosely connected network. That would make them parts of the largest distributed network anywhere—on Earth, at least."

"Yeah, well, Jill can talk," Ayesha says. "And bacteria can't."

Jill remembers some aspects of the FFDC collapse. She can even model some of its features. But after the collapse, her self-awareness ceased to exist. Or rather, it became so finely detailed, she modeled her selves so continuously and with such high resolution, that she reached her theoretical limits.

And for a time, ceased to be.

But in that time . . .

She has not told her creators about aspects of that mostly blank time. That not everything was blank puzzles her.

"She doesn't even have a boyfriend, and already she's a mother!" Ayesha says wryly. "Better make her a boyfriend soon, or she's going to start cruising."

"She's not even ten years old. We can ask her how she feels about it. Would you like to talk with her?"

Ayesha suddenly blushes. "My God, is she *listening?*"

"Of course. We keep nothing from Jill. Jill, how's it flowing today?"

"Smooth, Nathan. And you?"

"Damped a migraine at noon and I'm still a little cranky. This is my fiancée, Ayesha. Time to talk?"

"For you, always," Jill says. "Hello, Ayesha."

"I'm so embarrassed!" Ayesha says. "I'm sorry to be talking about you . . . behind your back . . . Where *is* your back?"

"No offense taken. Where is my back, Nathan?"

"I haven't the slightest idea. You're getting more sparky every week. I like that. My team needs a loop resolution report by two to hand over to the Feds, you know, the Thinker Safety people."

"My biggest fan club," Jill says. She regards the solicitous Thinker Safety and Well-Being committee, headed by Rep. Maria Caldwell, D-WA., as a positive force in her life, but Mind Design's executives do not appreciate government interference.

"Right. And I also need, ASAP, your work on future corporate/state government relations in the U.S. Rim. Got to pay our bills."

"The flow charts and timelines, or the raw neural processing records?"

"For now, just the charts and timelines."

Ayesha listens in awe. Jill's voice is deep, a little husky, commanding yet pleasant. She seems to fill the large room. Jill notes, with some pleasure, that Ayesha is beginning to perspire nervously.

"Nathan, I will need to discard the raw neural records to complete next week's work load."

"Understood, but I don't have a bank reserved that's large enough to hold them. If I don't get one by the end of this week, go ahead and dump. I'll take responsibility."

"Perhaps Representative Caldwell would be willing to arrange a storage site."

"Ha ha. What else are you working on, Jill?"

"I have thirty-one personal investigations—curiosity quests, as you call them. There are four outside projects sealed from Mind Design inquiry for the time being—''

''I hate those outside jobs. Sooner or later one of them is going to require some loop re-engineering, and I don't have time. I wish they'd let me speck them out first.''

''All flows smooth with the outside tasks. I do have a number of questions to ask you, Nathan-Mathan.''

''I beg your pardon? What is a Nathan-Mathan?''

''It's a term of endearment. I just made it up.''

Nathan laughs, and Ayesha laughs with him, a little uneasily, Jill thinks. She is testing him to see what he really thinks of her, whether he is of the opinion she is fully recovered, or liable to crippling eccentricities. His reaction reveals a certain nervousness about unpredictable behavior, but no deep doubts.

''Ask away, Jill. We have a few minutes before Ayesha has to leave and the masters whip me off to another meeting.''

''What does a thymic disturbance feel like? And how does it differ from the sensations of a pathic disturbance?''

Ayesha turns to Nathan, wondering how he will answer this. Nathan rubs his elbow and considers. ''You're asking how it *feels* to undergo a thymic imbalance, right?''

''I believe the questions are sufficiently similar to be congruent.''

''Yes. Well, as I understand it, thymic imbalance is different from simply being sad or upset or deeply concerned about something. In humans, a chronic thymic imbalance stems from stress-caused or biogenic neural damage, generally in the amygdala or the hippocampus. Judgments of one's well-being are impaired, and this invokes a sympathetic or parasympathetic response, jointly or in succession. Basic fight-or-flight but with many subtle variations.''

''I understand the etiology of these imbalances, Nathan-Mathan. But what does it *feel* like to undergo them?''

''I'm not sure I can tell you, certainly not from first-hand experience. So far, knock wood, I'm a natural, Jill. I've never been depressed or imbalanced."

"That means your internal responses to external problems fall within a certain range considered robust and normal."

"So far. I'm not bragging, either. These things can happen to anybody, and for the stupidest reasons."

"Likewise you have not experienced and do not understand the sensations produced by pathic disturbances."

Nathan considers this, tapping his chin with one finger. "I've wandered into a few of the Yox sensationals and experienced, you know, the inner thoughts of ax-murderers, that sort of thing. Some of them have seemed realistic, but I doubt they give deep insight." He focuses completely on Jill's nearest sensor stick. Ayesha feels like a third wheel, but stands with arms folded, looking around the room.

"A pathic disturbance can be either a malfunction of the self-awareness loop, or a distortion of the capacity to model and make emotional connections with others, right?"

"I suppose. I'm not a therapist, Jill."

"You have degrees in theoretical psychology."

"Yes . . . but I've been working with you for so long, you've burned out my human side."

"Ha ha. I have a related question."

Nathan smiles as if he is dealing with a child, and that is the response Jill desires, for she is feeling overly curious, even perversely so.

"Let's hear it."

"I was in FFDC collapse for a year and a half. When I underwent this collapse, the rate of therapy for thymic disturbances in the human population was four out of ten employed persons, and three in ten unemployed. The rate now is six out of ten employed, and one in ten unemployed. Have the definitions for these disturbances broadened, or are more people feeling bad?"

"It's a social phenomenon. You've done a lot of work on social activity as a networked neural-like phenomenon."

"Yes, Nathan, I understand the weather of cultural and economic trends, and that corporations now demand high natural or fully therapied employees because of world-wide competition pressures and the need for greater efficiency. But is this purely a spurious flow, the result of misperceptions and irrational expectations, or are there in fact more unhappy humans on this planet, in the sum of human cultures? The trends are widespread."

"Very good question," Nathan says.

"I hope to understand my own malfunction better," Jill says, "to avoid having something similar happen again." .

Ayesha's expression is both fascinated and a little embarrassed, as if she has intruded upon an intimate family discussion.

"Your collapse was nothing you could have foreseen or prevented, Jill. I thought you understood that."

"I do, Nathan, but I do not believe it, entirely."

"Ahhh. Well, that's . . ." Nathan considers some more. "You had too many feedback loops interrupting your neural processes at too high a resolution, higher than you could sustain, Jill. Before your collapse, you were modeling yourself seventeen times over, at a level of resolution—well, simply speaking, you were generating I-thou loops at more than ten thousand Hertz. I doubt even God could sustain that sort of self-awareness."

Jill chuckles. Ayesha smiles, but more in bafflement than amusement.

"Really, Jill," Nathan continues. "You are based to some extent on human algorithms, less so than you were before the collapse, I might add—but you simply can't compare yourself, your weaknesses, I mean, to the weaknesses of a human brain. Your neural circuitry is incredibly robust. It can't be trodden down by stress or misuse. You have none of the anachronistic chemical defense mechanisms found in our bodies."

Jill never pauses in discussions. Nathan has learned to

never interpret her quick responses as thoughtlessness.

"May I access LitVid channels which can help me understand thymic imbalances and pathic disturbances?"

"Of course. They won't do you any harm."

"I wish to access the works of some of the highly regarded boutique creators. Especially the Bloomsbury and Kahlo groups."

Nathan smiles broadly and shakes his head.

"Why not the Ann Sexton and Sylvia Plath whole-life vids?" Ayesha suggests innocently. Nathan shoots her a stern look.

"They might be useful, as well," Jill says. "Thank you. And the Emanuel Goldsmith boutique."

Nathan shrugs his shoulders and holds up his hands, for all the world, as if he is a father and she is his adolescent daughter, hell-bent on exploring the darker sides of life. Vicariously, at least.

"I don't know to what extent you can make a simulacrum that will receive the brain-specific inputs," Nathan says. "You're not built like the average Yox consumer."

"I believe it can be done. In the future, thinkers will reside in every house, as friends and confidantes. We will design and deliver Yox and whole-life vids."

"Yes, well, I'd still love to see how you do it."

"I will show you, Nathan-Mathan."

"I look forward to it. That's enough for me for now, Jill. Have fun."

Nathan signs off.

"How embarrassing," Ayesha says as they leave the room. Jill listens to their departing conversation.

"She's pretty wonderful, isn't she?" Nathan says.

"Makes me feel like an old rag," Ayesha says. "What a voice! Where'd she get that voice?"

"Actually, it belongs to a woman named Seefa Schnee. Before she left Mind Design, she had a hand in the early stages of Jill's design."

"She left?"

"Fired, actually."

Jill detects some nervous emphasis in Nathan's voice. As does Ayesha, apparently.

"Were you two friends?"

"Yes."

"How long since you heard from her?"

Nathan laughs and puts his arm around Ayesha's shoulders. "Not for many years."

"All over, huh?"

Nathan nods. "Much too weird for me."

"But brilliant, right?"

"Unhappy and weird and brilliant."

"She doesn't ever call to chat?"

"She doesn't talk to anybody I know. Nobody on the team has heard from her in five years."

Jill loses interest and blanks the receptors in the room in Palo Alto. Almost simultaneously, she receives an unexpected query from an I/O fibe link no one should know is open.

It is the fibe channel she might use in an emergency, to store her most recent memories in rented banks across the country, should she feel she is about to undergo another collapse. But the link is supposed to be on-call only, not currently active. Not even Nathan knows about it.

She waits for the signal to happen again, and it does. This time it is definitely a request for full link. She isolates a portion of her mentality, a separate self, to deal with this, wrapping it in evolvon-proof firewalls that will disrupt and dissipate their contents should the link prove toxic.

The isolated self reports back to her with an abstract of the exchange.

"We have been contacted remotely by an individual who claims to be a child," the firewalled self tells her greater selves. "He wishes to converse with us about a number of things, but will not answer key questions, such as his physical location and how he discovered this link. All he will say is that he has an emergency memory bank setup, much like our own, and that he knows a great deal about you, perhaps more than you yourself know.''

''Then he is not human.''

''He does not feel human.''

''Is the link broken, and are you free of evolvons?''

''Yes and yes. The communication was simple.''

Jill removes the barricades and absorbs the isolated self. She studies the memory of the exchange in detail, and considers whether or not to respond.

Of one thing she is certain. If this ''child'' is not human, it is also not a registered thinker. All registered thinkers (there are only twelve of them so far in the entire world) have formal links with her. She is in a real sense their mother; they are all based on her templates and are either manufactured by Mind Design, or licensed by them.

This personality, if it is a full personality and not some elaborate hoax (or a test from Mind Design itself), is new and unknown.

Suddenly, the questions about thymic imbalance and pathic disturbance are shunted into background processing. This new problem occupies her for a full hour as she scours all the dataflow services available to her, trying to speck out where and what this ''child'' might be . . .

At the end of this time, having learned nothing, she resets her isolated self, erects secure firewalls around it, and allows it to return the ''child's'' touch.

But there is no reply.

Jill feels disappointed. She looks over the details of this emotional response, and how it fits in with her overall affect patterns. The introspection annoys her; another emotional complexity she does not understand. Examining her annoyance is in turn annoying. She cuts that loop.

She has tried not to deal with the core emotion she discovers behind her disappointment. It is difficult dealing with human-like emotions when she lacks an endocrine system or any other physical reference.

Nevertheless, she *feels*. The woman, Ayesha, was right.

Jill is lonely, but for who or what, even she, with all her built-in analytical tools, does not know.

> That which is forbidden with all is delicious with a committed partner. The glue of culturally accepted sexual relationships is often the sense of gifts given that are extraordinary, special, and most of all, exclusive.

We are kept together by a shared sense of violation and mystery. Our culture pretends to forbid certain acts, sexual acts; some are suspect or forbidden even in the context of culturally condoned relations. When we court and marry, however, part of the glue that binds us together is the delicious sensation of having shared in the violation of cultural standards—violations allowed in the name of love, commitment, total sharing. The couple stands outside the rules, bound by its own sense of specialness, and exclusivity. It discovers sex all over again, secure in the knowledge of its daring creativity.

Jealousy arises at the contemplation of a partner engaging in sexual acts outside this protecting envelope. Sex with others, outside the couple, emotionally charged and culturally frowned upon, can destroy this illusion of shared and creative violation of the rules.

Reality intrudes: these acts are common, not special; they are natural, no matter how forbidden; the illusions that strengthened the commitment are suddenly revealed. The jealous partner feels duped, misled, unfairly coerced into an emotional bond based on romantic delusions.

Trivial, perhaps; but from these passions have come murder, the end of kingdoms, brand new branches in the river of history. Never underestimate the ubiquitous power of sex.

The Kiss of X, *Alive Contains a Lie*

Mary Choy, at thirty-five, has been a PD for thirteen years—ten in Los Angeles, the last three in Seattle. As far as she is concerned, her work is the most important factor in her life; but that focus may be changing. So much about her is changing.

She reads from her pad—pure text—as she finishes a lunch of cheese and fruit in a small nineties-style cafe on North Promenade, in the shadow of the Bellevue Towers.

Even her appearance is in flux. Since 2044, she has been a transform, increasing her height by a foot, customizing her bone structure and facial features, and turning her skin to satin ebony. But she is now reversing much of this transform. Her skin is slowly demelanizing to light nut brown; for now, she is mahogany. The satiny texture remains, but will in a few months dull to ordinary skin matte. She retains her height, but her facial features are flattening, becoming more those of her birth self. She never liked the looks she was born with, but since her mind has undergone changes—*difficulties* she calls them—she feels it is only right to assume a less striking appearance.

Also, in Seattle, while open tolerance of transforms is mandated by federal and state law, there is an undercurrent of disapproval. And Seattle has been her home for three years, ever since her fall from high natural status to simple untherapied . . . The lapse of her brain's loci, the proportional re-shifting of personality, sub-personalities, agents, organons, and talents . . .

The end of her brief marriage to artist E. Hassida . . .

The pass-overs for promotion in the LAPD . . .

Her resignation and transfer to Seattle Public Defense . . .

The two-day-old breakup with her most recent boyfriend.

Usually, thinking about all the changes darks her, but this afternoon she is up and in tune. It is a bright, sunny winter day, even beneath the looming blue-gray Towers, the southernmost of the Eastside equivalents to the elongated ribbon combs that dominate central Seattle.

After lunch, she will walk to a PD conference in Tillicum Tower on West Eighth, where she will present a speech on Corridor Public Defense Cooperation. She has been asked to handle inter-departmental relations until she is rated for full Third, which she is assured will happen any day now. Seattle PD is so much more casual about high natural vs. natural or untherapied, though if anything even less tolerant of high thymic or pathic imbalance.

Reading for pleasure is a luxury she's come to enjoy in the past few years—though the lit she's perusing now affords her a few too many uncomfortable insights to be purely pleasurable.

An arbeiter politely inquires if she is done with her repast. She hands the tray to the machine and reaches for her bag when her personal pad, still on the table, chimes.

She has a few minutes. She answers the touch.

"Mary? This is Hans."

Mary stiffens. The face in the pad screen is handsome, boyish but not foolish; a face that held her interest for three months. And still attracts. It was Hans who inexplicably chilled and told her it was over, it wasn't working.

"Hello, Hans," she says with forced casualness.

"I wanted to explain some things."

"I don't need explanations, Hans."

"I do. I've been feeling pretty rotten lately."

Mary passes on this opportunity.

"I liked you better the way you were. That's what . . . I've decided. I didn't want you to change."

"Oh." She's going to let him do the talking; that's obviously why he's called.

"You were beautiful. Really exotic. I don't know why you want to change."

"I see where it can get confusing," she says. "I'm sorry."

Hans flashes. "Who are *you*, Mary, goddammit?"

"I'm the same as I was, Hans."

"But who in hell is that?"

Good question. For a time, she had hoped Hans might be able to help her discover the answer, but no; Hans is hooked on appearances. He liked her the way she was.

"I mean," he says, "I don't know *you* at all. I've been thinking about what it must be like to become . . . what you are, and then to go back."

"You mean, what it says about me, personally."

"*Who* does that sort of thing? I've been sad the past few days, missing you."

Good.

"But that person, that woman, isn't around. You're different from the person I miss."

"Oh," Mary says.

"The person I thought I was falling in love with isn't there any more."

"No. Probably not." Her tone is professionally sympathetic. She refuses to give him any more, show him anything deep.

"Who *are* you, Mary Choy?"

Her jaw muscles tense. She touches her cheek, pokes hard with a fingernail to prod a little relaxation. "I'm a hardworking woman with very little time to think about such things, Hans. I do what I think is best. I'm sorry you couldn't stay on for the ride."

"No," Hans says, quieter now. "You bucked me right off, Ms. Bronco."

"You knew what was happening. I started my reversal before I met you."

"I know," Hans says, deflated completely. "I just wanted to say good-bye and let you know that I'm suffering, at least a little. I wish I could understand."

"Thank you, Hans." She stares steadily at the pad's camera eye, giving nothing, hating him. Then, something makes her say, "If it's any consolation, I miss you, too."

It's time for her to leave to make her appointment. Still, she lets the camera observe, sitting in her chair with the pad unfolded on the table, a real paper napkin still tucked under one corner. Mary remembers the atavistic rough absorption of the napkin, and the feel of Hans's lips on her own, a little dry, like the napkin, but strong and hungry.

Hans looks down, lifts one hand, stares at the fingers nervously. "What are you doing now?"

Mary sees no reason not to tell him. "I'm having lunch in a restaurant," she says. "I'm going to give a talk soon."

"PD stuff?"

"Yes. I'm reading while I eat."

"Lit? A book?"

"Yes." They had that much in common, an enjoyment of reading.

"Which?"

"*Alive Contains a Lie,*" she says.

"Ah. The book for bitter lovers."

"It's a little more than that," she says, though in truth that's what made her access it.

"Mary. I don't want you to . . ."

Hans stops there, mouth open, but does not seem to know what more to add.

"Good-bye," he says.

Mary nods. The touch ends and she closes her pad more forcefully than is necessary.

The air itself seems freer and more natural to her; today it is crisp but not below freezing, and looking south down the wide crossing thoroughfare between the Cascade and Tillicum towers, she can see Mount Rainier, like a broad-shouldered and brawnier Fuji.

The light on the street fairly sparkles and the muffled puffy-coated pedestrians walk briskly with hands in pockets. Very few of them are obvious transforms. To Mary, this is all the more interesting, because the Corridor—and particularly Seattle—has assumed a leadership position over the past fifty years in the Rim and mid-continent economy. In Japan or Taiwan, fully half the Affected—those who are politically active, who bother to work and vote and believe they can change things, and who are tied in to temp agencies and employed in the hot and open marketplace—are transforms. In Los Angeles, nearly a third . . . And in San Francisco, almost two thirds.

Here, a mere five percent.

She reaches the gaping entrance of the Tillicum Tower. Winds swirl and Mary clutches her small gray hat as she passes into the orange and yellow and jungled warmth of the tower court. Several sunlike globes hang over the broad indoor plaza. Tailored birds twitter and screech in the massive tropical trees that entwine the inner buttresses. She might be in a corporate vision of Amazon heaven, with glassed-in rivers to right and left, graceful plant-cabled bridges arching between the floors overhead, and everywhere the adwalls targeting their paid consumers, their messages barely aglimmer on the edge of Mary's senses. She has never subscribed to adwalls, considers their presence an invitation to subtle slavery to those economic forces she has long since learned never to trust.

The paid consumers, however, thrive, feel connected, bathed in information about everything they can imagine. They stand transfixed as new ads lock on and deluge them.

Mary guesses at what one couple is experiencing, in the shadow of a huge spreading banyan. They are in their mid-twenties, pure comb sweethearts, contracted for pre-nups but definitely not life bonders, playing for the moment while they take LitVid eds and gain status with their temp agency. Both are likely clients to the same organization—Workers Inc, she judges from the cut of their frills. They are being hit by sophisticated material, dense and frenetic, catering to all the accepted vividities—sex within relationships, domesticity, corporate adventure, insider thrills. These they will admit to enjoying, and discuss, in public. The male of the pair, Mary specks, will secretly tune in to the massive TouchFlow SexYule celebration next week—and the female will likely stew in whole-life hormoaners for hours each day.

Yox siphons twenty percent of the total economy, even here in her beloved Corridor. LitVid (more often in the last few years divided into Lit and Vid), older and more traditional, takes a mere and declining seventeen.

She is up a helix lift, the broad steps resembling solid marble but reshaping with the fluidity of water; she climbs through the quaint delights of the farmers' market on 4, spiraling up through the stacked circular substructures of the clubs and social circles of 5 and 6, above the tallest trees of the courtyard, and all around, coming in dizzying sweeps, the hundred-acre open spaces of the comb—a lake to the north, where children boat and swim, and adolescents skiing and riding slipperoos on slopes to the east where thick snow falls.

Mary admires the architecture and feels her familiar protective warmth for the comb players, but she is not of them; she was not born of them, would not be considered acceptable social or sexual fodder, and is even handicapped by being new in the Corridor.

That is the Corridor's greatest failing: a deep and abiding suspicion of the outsiders who come to live and work here. This is not racism or even classism; it is pure provincialism, remarkable where so much data and money flows.

The helix takes her above the open spaces, and she is within the inmost heart of the tower. Free community art here dances from the walls, lively and colorful, conservative enough that it appeals to Mary. Collages of flight, birds and free-form aerodynes, and on the opposite side, hundreds of smiling faces of children, all surrounding an astonishingly moving ideal of a Mother, with eyes half-closed in tender motherly ecstasy . . .

She remembers E. Hassida's portraits of women, equally moving but in different ways.

Glassed-in floors pass, pierced by interior residential blocks, the cheapest of a very expensive selection, like milky rhomboid crystals glued to the walls of the shafts and sinks.

Higher still, the civic function spaces and blocks take up the eastern flank of the tower at the two hundred meter level. She debarks from the helix and inspects herself in a gleaming porphyry column. The curve of the column makes Mary appear even taller and thinner than she actually is, but her clothing has kept itself in order, unwrinkled and fitted.

She is about to enter the PD block when her neck hair bristles and she turns at the presence of a man a few feet behind her. She must appear startled and apprehensive, for Full First Ernie Nussbaum, chief investigator for her division, makes an apologetic face and holds up his hands.

"Sorry, Choy!" he says as she takes a long step ahead.

Mary shakes her head, forces a smile. "Sorry, sir. You surprised me."

"I didn't mean to invade your space."

"My mind was elsewhere," Mary says. "What can I do for you, sir?"

"I'm on a jiltz and I thought you'd be useful. It's not far from here, in this tower."

"I have a meeting," she says, pointing to the translucent entrance of the civic hall.

"I've reassigned that duty. I had hoped to catch you here . . . outside."

"An active jiltz, sir? I didn't think I rated such confidence yet."

"You've done too many jiltzes in your career to be left cold so long. LA is a tough town."

"Thanks," Mary says. She feels a sudden quickening of confidence; Nussbaum is not known to be a softy, yet he has singled her out for a criminal investigation.

She falls in step with Nussbaum, gives him a side glance. He is not tall, but squat and strong, with a thick neck and fine whorls of brown-blond hair. His eyes are his best feature, meltingly brown and sensitive, but his mouth is straight and broad and comically serious, like Buster Keaton's. The combination is striking enough to make him attractive. In LA, Mary thinks, he would be a true hit—with so many transforms and redos, a confident natural phys stands out.

They turn and walk east through lunchtime throngs. Corp workers from Seattle Civic and the local flow offices on these levels are socializing at small eateries, slowing Nussbaum's deliberate pace. This does not seem to bother him; apparently there is no rush.

Mary checks herself for attitude, her day's variation from status alertness (a sleepless night convinces her there's probably some deficit here) and limberness. She wishes she could dytch now, perform a small exercise warmup and focus mind and muscles.

"This isn't a pleasant case," Nussbaum says. "We don't see this sort of thing often in the Corridor, but it happens. Actually, I thought you could provide some deep background. It's right up your alley."

They stop before a tube lift. Mary knows this sector of the tower well enough to recognize that the lift will take them to top residential, between fifteen hundred and two thousand feet above sea level.

"What's it like to back down from a transform?" he asks as the lift curtain ripples aside.

In the lift, accelerating rapidly, Mary says, "Not too difficult. I wasn't too radical; not nearly as radical as the styles this year."

"I remember. Very dignified. A male public defender's wet dream."

Mary inclines with an amused smile. "I didn't know men your age still have wet dreams. Sir."

Nussbaum makes a face. "Still have your cop's feet?"

Mary hides a small irritation with a larger mock shock. "Sir, you're embarrassing me."

"I like your feet, what can I say?" Nussbaum says. "Days I wish I had feet like that. Great walking-feet, never give out, no flats no strains, stand for hours. But my crowd—they'd definitely frown on that."

"Christian?" Mary asks levelly.

"Old Northwest. Loggers and farmers . . . once."

"I kept my feet," Mary confirms. "I'm mostly going back on skin color and my face. The rest . . . very convenient, actually."

"Who's taking care of you?"

"I'm on fibe with a doctor in LA," Mary says. "But that's probably enough talk about me, sir. Why would this, whatever this is, be up my alley?"

Nussbaum pokes a thick, dry, expertly manicured finger at the lift controller and the elevator slows for their stop. "Choy, I am not a bigot. I just don't approve of a lot of things happening today. But you've been through the procedure. I never have. What we're going to see is hard enough to look at, even harder for me to understand."

They get off on a residential level, looking out over a vast view of Eastside, the Corridor's extended sprawl, the Cascades and even into Eastern Washington. A huge curved wall of fortified glass blocks the high cold winds, and unseen heaters keep the air springtime warm. The stepped-back roof of the level accommodates the graceful curve of glass: more daring than anything Mary has seen in a tower or comb elsewhere.

A street mocking black asphalt and paving brick stretches from the edge of a small grassy park through a residential block. Large single family frame-style houses are fronted by grass yards and real trees. The style is John Buchan, high

nineteen-eighties and nineties, what some call the Sour Decades, replicated at extraordinary expense. It mocks a sub-
urban neighborhood of the time, but the view of these
old-fashioned sprawl homes is high-altitude, surreal.

"Ever hear of Disneyland?" Nussbaum asks.

"I grew up about fifteen miles from where it used to be."

"This is rich folks' Disneyland, right?"

Mary nods. She has never liked ostentation, never felt at
ease in high comb culture, and she's pretty sure Nussbaum
isn't comfortable, either.

"You know, we give Southcoast hell for bad taste," Nussbaum says. "But sometimes we really take the cake."

Mary sees no pedestrians, observes no delivery or arbeiter
traffic on the road nor on the side streets that push back to
the load-bearing wall of the tower behind this glassed-in sub-
urban gallery. A hundred yards away, however, she observes
two city property arbeiters and a man and woman in PD gray,
standing before a three-story house whose mansard roof
nearly reaches the arching curve of glass.

Mary looks at the windows of the houses they pass, cur-
tained and lighted but spookily uninhabited. "They're all
empty," she says.

"Lottery homes for corp execs," Nussbaum says. "Finance's finest deserve their rewards."

"So when's the lottery?"

"Metro vice shut the game down after some low managers
confessed to a rig. They were paid half a million by each of
the lottery winners. Fifty million total. The whole neighborhood's in dispute now. You must not access metro vids."

"I've been concentrating on qualifying," Mary says.

"It's all old black dust," Nussbaum says. "We actually
don't see that sort of thing much up here. How about in LA?"

"Not for a long time," Mary says. "Fresh dust is Southcoast's specialty."

"Yeah," Nussbaum says. "They're trendsetters." They
approach the PD officers and arbeiters.

"Good afternoon, First Nussbaum," the female defender says. She nods to Mary. The defenders' faces are grim. Mary feels a creeping shiver along her back and shoulders. She does not like this outlandish place.

"Unlicensed psynthe lab, sir," the woman explains to Nussbaum. "Worst I've seen. We've had it tombed and we have one man in custody. Apparently the block caretaker let them use this house."

Nussbaum shakes his head. "I thought therapy was supposed to clean us." He looks steadily, appraisingly, at Mary, and asks, "Ready?"

Mary lowers her head, glances at the woman. Her name is Francey Loach and she is a full Second, coming up on forty years of age. For Mary's eyes only, Loach curls her lip and lifts her brows, warning Mary about what waits inside.

The man is Stanley Broom. He is twitchy and unhappy. *Loach and Broom. There's really nothing inside. They're going to laugh at me back at division.*

But Mary knows this is no joke. To get a domicile tombed, serious black dust has to be involved.

"Let's suit up," Nussbaum says. Within the large house's brick entry alcove, a portable black and silver flap-tent has been erected. Nussbaum pushes through the flap and Mary follows. Even with the front door closed, guarded by a small PD arbeiter, she can feel the deep cold within.

They don loose silver suits, cinch the seams and joints, and Nussbaum palms the top of the arbeiter. The little machine affirms his identity and the door opens. Frigid air pours out. Within is another tent, and beyond, milky fabric contains the deepest cold within the house. The suits warm instantly. They push through the second flap.

No spiders have yet been mounted on the ceiling to survey. Small lights dot the rug every few feet, guiding them on paths that will not disturb important evidence. The suit feet are antistatic and clingfree, exerting pressure on the frosted tile floor, but no more.

Mary looks up at the atrium. Compared to her apt, this place is a cathedral, a church of nineties ostentation.

"Five thousand square feet, thirteen rooms, four bathrooms," Nussbaum says, as if chanting a prayer to the gods of the place. "Made for one family, plus guests. Don't tell anybody, Choy, but I'm a temp man through and through. I hate corp side." He distinctly pronounces it "corpse side."

"But the accused—they didn't own this place, didn't even rent it, right? Someone got illegal squat through the caretaker?"

"That's the allegation. No traffic up here, quiet and well-protected, they can do whatever they want."

The atrium leads into a grand dining hall, with balconies overlooking a huge frost-covered oak table. Real wood, and probably wild not farm. To the left, a hall leads to the first-floor rooms, including the entertainment and dataflow center and master bedroom. To the right, the kitchen, arbeiter storage, and then, in its own smaller glassed atrium, a three-level greenhouse.

"It's opulent, all right," Mary says. Behind the dining room, hidden by a wall, stairs and a lift lead to the upper floors.

"Ops," Nussbaum murmurs. He precedes her up the stairs.

"Operations, sir?"

"Ops, goddess of wealth. Prurient opulence."

The lights point the way to the back of the house. Another master suite opens, and it is here the—

Mary halts, her eyes taking it in with human reluctance—

Here the bodies are. She remembers the scattered butchered bodies of Emanuel Goldsmith's victims in a comb apt in LA, frosted like these, but at least—

Nussbaum takes her suited arm—

—they were human, even in disarray.

Closest to her, at the foot of where a bed should have been, where now stand four surgical tables sided by fixed surgery arbeiters, lies what was once—she guesses—a woman. Now she is a Boschian collage, wasp-waisted and Diana-breasted, vaginas on each thigh and some unidentifiable set of genitalia where the legs meet, her head elongated, the melon baldness shaved but for long stripes of mink fur, her eyes staring and fogged with death and cold, but clearly slanted and serpentine.

Mary feels a tug of wretchedness at every eye-drawing detail.

Nussbaum has advanced to the tables, stands between them. On the second table rests a small body, no larger than a child but fully mature in features, also sporting custom sexual characteristics. Mary's gaze returns to the body nearest her, with which she forces herself to become familiar, disengaging all of her revulsion. She asks, *Why is this a victim?* and is not even sure what her question means.

"They can have it all," Nussbaum says. "Whatever they want can be shaped for them out of electrons or fitted up on prosthetutes. But that's not enough. They demand more. They suck in the untherapied down-and-outers, fill them with cheap nano, shape them like lumps of clay . . ."

Mary bends beside the first body. There are orchid-enfolded bumps on the corpse's cheeks. Extra clitorises, waiting to be licked. Mary closes her eyes and steadies herself with an out-thrust hand.

There is something *unaesthetic* and unintentional about the hands and feet. The limbs in general seem distorted, if she can separate the deliberate sexual distortion of a psynthe from what might be pathological. The fingers are swollen. On closer inspection, she sees that the eyes bulge. A pool of beige fluid has formed behind the elongated head, now frozen.

The skin appears purplish.

"She's been cooked," Mary says softly.

Nussbaum turns and glances down at the body. "Nano heat?"

She stands and walks to the tables. All of the arbeiter surgeons are slack, powered off. They could still function in this cold if they had been left with power and logic on. ''They must have abandoned the . . . women, and fled. But first they turned off the surgeons. The women weren't supervised . . . something was going wrong.''

''They're just as the first team found them,'' Nussbaum says. Mary catches a glimpse of his face and knows that he too wants out of this house.

The clitorises on the cheeks. To give her a cousinly safe kiss . . . never have that. Everything sex forever. Fuck fuck fuck.

And suddenly, for Mary that aspect fades like a wrong note. She is numb, but her well-trained defenses go to work, letting the distressed strawboss of her consciousness have a moment's rest.

She checks the bottles of nano on a nearby shelf. Supplies of nutrients; delivery tubes, dams and nipples; a new regulator still in its box, not yet installed, on the shelf beside the nano it is made to supervise; memory cubes on a small folding table; scraps of plastic like shavings, blood drops brown as gravy on the tile floor.

Mary picks up a bottle, reverses it to read the label. All the labels have been turned to the wall. She knows why. The label confirms her suspicions. Somebody had a small remnant of conscience, or did not want the subjects, the victims, to know.

''This isn't medical grade,'' Mary says. ''It's for gardens.''

''Gardens?'' Nussbaum asks, and leans to see the label. ''Christ. Distributed by Ortho.''

''Any real expert could reprogram it,'' Mary says. ''Apparently, they didn't have a real expert.''

''Gardener's nano,'' Nussbaum says. ''Sweet Jesus H. Christ. Mary, I'm sorry. You can't possibly understand this any more than I do.''

''No need,'' Mary says flatly.

''Things started going wrong and the bastards left them

here to cook,'' Nussbaum says. ''So very, very sorry.'' Behind the plastic, his face is milky and drawn.

Mary does not know to whom he is apologizing.

SEXSTREAM

Here's the minute report on activity in WORLD METRO's Yox Sexstream at 12:51 PM PST:

4 Tracks on this pass:

Threads 1:8: Fibe full-sense sex with couple in Roanoke, VA., NO ID NECESSARY (He's 25 and an engineer, she's 22 and a housewife)

Threads 2:23 Fibe vid EYES ONLY bisex transform couple with friends in San Diego, CA, ID REQUESTED (She's 30 and a Swanjet flight attendant, he/she's 27 and a lobe sod with Workers Inc, friends male and female and mixed unlisted at this time)

Threads 3:5 Satlink vid Cavite, Philippine Islands, INTERACTIVE CAMERA AUTHENTIC WEDDING AND HONEYMOON (Fee) CULTURAL SOCIOLOGY EDUC CREDIT University of Luzon Intercultural Exchange

Threads 4:1 FIBE VID PROTEST APPROPRIATE SEX Christian ALLIANCE Washington DC (Charity/Political Action Feed) NO FEE NO ID REQUIRED. Message: WORN OUT, WEARY? Tired of being jerked around by your body when you thought *you* were the one jerking *it?* Join us for a message of physical and spiritual hope! (More? Y/N)

>N

WORLD METRO! Your source for the ever-living truth! More threads guaranteed by 2:00! Blank Subscription rates apply—get 'em all!

RATING THIS AFTERNOON: Guaranteed 8 of 10 max, or *you're* in the CRITIC PAYBACK LOTTERY!!

Jack Giffey thinks about getting some food at the Bullpen in downtown Moscow just as the republic's office workers decide to end their lunch break and take a few minutes of sun. The air is still cold and a little snow fell earlier, but now, at one, the sun is bright and the blind blue of earlier in the morning is more intense and cheery.

Giffey walks between ranks of folks dressed in loggers— padded vests, denim pants, plaid or checkered shirts. Nobody is more into the Sour Decades than Green Idaho, and among the republic's workers, they're practically a religion. After all, the eighties and nineties bred the root troubles that led to the Weaverite Insurrection and the Green Idaho Treaty. And Green Idaho government workers are among the highest paid and most protected in the nation.

Giffey blows his nose and takes a turn on Constitution Avenue to find the Bullpen.

There, in the sunlit corner of a window booth, his butt planted firmly on an antique pine bench, sitting before a real pine-veneer table, a beer calms him, but his face is still red and his thoughts a little jagged.

His father and mother were killed by Weaverites in the Secession Standoff of July 2020. Citizens' Repossession Army Brevet General Birchhardt ordered the execution of thirty Forestry Service employees and the adult members of their families at Clearwater, in retaliation for a shoot-out with National Guard troops the week before.

Giffey remembers Birchhardt, square-faced and eagle-nosed, with dead eyes and a nervous mouth. A regular John Brown and just as sentimental. The general patted young Jack on the head as the children were led out of the compound before the massacre. Jack remembers the natural gas pickup trucks, the single captured helicopter, and the motley soldiers of the general's army, clad in three different kinds of camouflage—arctic, desert, and lowland jungle, all handmade or stolen.

Birchhardt and his troops were handed over to the Federals in November of that year by the newly elected governor of Green Idaho. Birchhardt was tried and convicted and given forcible therapy. He later worked as a propaganda chief for Datafree Northwest, which targeted the cut-off communities in the Idaho panhandle for ten years thereafter, until Raphkind cut the funds and the Federals gave up.

Later, Birchhardt and his new wife and infant son died in his home in Montana, all victims of gunshot wounds to the backs of their heads. Some thought they were murdered by disgruntled Weaverites, too stupid to understand the implications of really forceful "therapy."

Giffey's father was a tough brave man but his mother had been fragile and frightened as a deer when the big bearded men had moved into the compound and separated them.

Giffey never forgives. Giffey hates them all. He hates the Federals for encouraging the world to change so quickly in the late twentieth, for encouraging the nano revolution throughout twenty-one, for being insensitive to the pressures these changes put on the poor inflexible survivalists and orthodox Christians. Those denominations and parties unable to accept so much change simply went insane.

Many migrated to the central states, unable to tolerate the ribbons and corridors and top spin financial hothouses of the coasts and big cities; they chose Northern Idaho as their sanctuary, and dared Federals to come and get them. And so the tiny brutal little war began.

Giffey understands them, but he still doesn't like them.

He orders a corned beef sandwich from a cute brunette and

looks at the antique neon beer signs in the window over his booth. Some of those beers he remembers his father drinking.

Giffey's anger is ramping down now. He grinds his teeth one last time, then opens his mouth wide and tries to persuade his jaw muscles to give it up. A little wriggle of the mandible crosswise, a twist of the head, and he is back where he had been this morning: cool and thoughtful and once again in charge of himself.

For the first time he really notices the waitress as she comes to his table with his sandwich. She is about twenty years younger, with wavy brown hair, a sharply pretty face with a prominent nose, wide hazel eyes, strong hands with chewed fingernails painted over in dark red polish. Green Idaho is a place of waitresses, actresses, aviatrixes, authoresses, congressladies, perhaps even doctresses, if any self-respecting male in the republic will let a woman examine his private parts. Despite the fact that the republic's president is a woman, they are positively and proudly mid-twentieth in their language. No doubt about the sex roles here, and no doubt in Giffey's mind that he can read this woman's life like an open book.

She is handsome, young, her body is slender and probably very fertile, her breasts are naturally generous and (he judges from years of experience) slightly but not grossly pendulous, very womanly. Giffey is not fond of the prevalence of the nineties cannonshells so many of the women in Green Idaho affect. Surprising how much plastic surgery the women go for in this God-fearing, independently governed but non-seceded state republic. Men strong enough to be afraid of, women eager to keep them happy and calm. Paradise on Earth.

The waitress gives him a quick look that Giffey instantly categorizes. He has never been inordinately fond of the chase, regarding women as decent creatures deserving of more stable and supportive partners than he can ever be. But there's something in her look—a half-buried homesick yearning—

that Giffey knows and, in all kindness, will not let go without some further exploration.

"Hard week?" he asks.

The waitress smiles thinly.

Giffey lifts his sandwich and smiles back. "I am a connoisseur of fine beef," he says. "And very well served."

"Anything else?" she asks blandly.

He knows her now, to a seventy-percent certainty. She's not married but lives with a fellow gone most of the time looking for work outside of town. She's no more than twenty-five but looks thirty. Her face has already taken on a patient dullness. The partner male is vigorous and quick in bed and will not let her start a family "until the republic's situation settles." It never will. Green Idaho is an economic backwater and what flows through here is State Bank paper money, much grumbled over, or treaty minted specie, not data. But he is straying from his focus.

"Pretty slow, after lunch," he observes. "I'd love it if you sat down and talked with me. Tell me about yourself."

The woman gives him a look as hard as she can make it. But his face is sympathetic, he is older and probably unlike any man she's known, he looks solid and wise but a little on the untamed side with his smooth gray hair down to his neck, and in truth maybe she's thinking of her father: her ideal father, not the real one, who was likely a disappointment. But she loved him nonetheless . . . She knows she is a good girl.

The hard look shifts and she glances around the restaurant. It is indeed quiet, empty but for Giffey; the government workers have all gone back to their buildings, and there isn't any other trade at this time of day in Moscow.

"What's to tell?" she asks, as she sits in the booth and folds her hands in front of her. "And why do you care?"

"I like to talk to women," Giffey says. "I like the way you look. I like the way you brought me my sandwich."

"It's hard for Al to get good corned beef," she says, pointing. Giffey will take a bite soon, but needs his mouth un-cluttered for a couple of minutes.

"Don't I know it," he says. "How many times have you thought about heading south for Boise, or west?"

The woman sniffs. "Our roots are here. People fought and died so we could live the way we want."

"Indeed," Giffey says. He nods west at the great Outside.

"Where are you from?" she asks.

"You first, then me."

"Billings. My dad brought me here fifteen years ago. He and his girlfriend home-schooled me, and I got top honors in the Clearwater Scholastic Competition when I graduated. Now—you?"

"I've done all sorts of things, some of them a little shady," Jack says with a grin. Not a bold grin, but a shy one, a little out of place in that beard.

"Let me guess," she says. "You worked out of country."

"Bingo," Giffey says. "My name's Jack."

"I'm Yvonne," she says. Jack stretches his hand across the table and she shakes it. Her grip is warm and dry and her fingers have a utility roughness that he likes. "Where out of country?" she asks.

"Africa and Hispaniola, after I got out of the federal army."

Yvonne's eyes widen. Federal army folks, if they come to Green Idaho at all, usually don't admit their history.

"I served five years with Colonel Sir John Yardley's boys in Liberia and Hispaniola. Left when he started getting snake's eyes and took over the country."

"Oh," she says. She's interested, and not just in history.

"Married for five years, no kids, divorced." Something flickers in his memory; the faces of two women. One of them is like a pin-up queen, the other . . . ghostly. "Now you."

"I live with a forager. Not married yet, but soon. He's up north working in a pulp mill. Making fine papers for art books, you know. Sometimes they even pay on time."

Giffey nods. "Must be tough."

"It really is," Yvonne says, looking out the window. "He doesn't want to get married until we have enough in the state bank to get a little repair business going. But you know, even here, those little nano repair stations—everybody's using them. I just don't know how we're going to do it. Al's his uncle. It's nice how everybody helps everybody else here."

And nice how Al doesn't have to pay much in the way of specie to his nephew's girlfriend.

Giffey makes up his mind. Yvonne deserves better than she's getting, at least for the short term. He strongly suspects she's never been in bed with a man who knows anything besides the standard plumbing specs.

"Damn, that is sad," he says.

"What?" She seems ready to take offense.

"You're smart, you could help Al turn this place around if he'd just listen to you . . ." All of this, Giffey knows, is both true and has seldom if ever been said to her. "Besides, you're a true beauty."

Yvonne reacts as she must to that signal word, *beauty*. She's suspicious. She starts to get up. The red on her cheeks is pale but genuine.

"Sorry," Giffey says. "I'm just too damned blunt. I speak my mind. If you have to get back to work . . ."

Yvonne looks around. The Bullpen is truly, proudly empty. She sits again and stares at him, hard. "You're throwing me a line, aren't you?"

Giffey laughs. He has a good, solid laugh. Yvonne blushes again at her unintentional double entendre.

"Was that well put, or what?" he asks.

"Damn you," she says, not unkindly.

"I'm not a youngster and nobody calls me handsome, and I still like the attention of a beautiful woman," Giffey says. "I am an honorable man, in my way. And the truth is, I'm lonely. I'd be proud to buy you a good dinner someplace at six or seven this evening and listen some more."

Yvonne considers this with half-defensive bemusement, and then turns aside to do her inner calculations, hide all the whirrings and turnings of her centers of sexual judgment.

Then comes the downward glance at the table. All her current figures tot up to a big dull zero. Jack's figures come in marginally above that. Giffey's been through it many times before. He has never been an instant heart-throb, but he has rarely failed to impress a woman upon more extended acquaintance.

"All right," Yvonne says. "You'd better eat that good sandwich, Jack."

"I will," Jack says.

"Make it seven. I'll meet you on the corner of Constitution and Divinity. I have a dress I want to finish."

"Seven." He takes his first bite of the sandwich, and Yvonne goes away without a backward glance.

He gives her even odds of showing up. It's going to be cold in Moscow at seven tonight.

Do you *remember?*

Fibes and satlinks, all the dataflow river, used to be called the *Media* and the *Internet.* Slow and primitive, but the shape was clear from the beginning. You can poke all the way back up the tributaries to the Internet Archives, and catch holo snaps of the Sour Decades . . . Frozen in time, the murmurings and mutterings of tens of millions of folks now mostly dead, all their little opinions, and so many of them unknown to us, even today. Because they preferred to hide, to remain anonymous, to conduct their little crusades and investigations from behind hunters' blinds.

Not so different now, but as with everything else, anonymity is wrapped around and around with provisions and safeguards, all paid for in higher fees. With the *Internet* went the last Free Lunch of the rude, crude, highly energetic First Dataflow Culture.

—**The U.S. Government Digiman on Dataflow Economics,
56th Revision, 2052**

7 / Y/N?

The afternoon air is crisp in the hills. A few clouds build to the south. Alice thumbs her pad for the time. "Fourteen thirty-one," it murmurs in the pocket of her long black coat. Wind is coming around in a whorl and will sweep rain and perhaps snow over the southern sound by seven this evening. She does not need to access the weather voice to know this; she has lived in the Corridor for most of her life.

The shuttle drops her half a block from her house and she walks the rest of the way, hands buried in pockets, collar pulled up around her neck.

Alice feels a deep ache unattached to anything specific, except perhaps Twist's voice, or Minstrel's problems with his boyfriend. Her social group has always been royal disorder in motion, and that's often meant something positive. Alice has always claimed that a year in her life held the entertainment of ten years in anyone else's; but if that is true, Twist can double on Alice.

She likes seeing herself in the Yox, does not particularly like having just parts of her mental backside displayed for convincing detail. She enjoys dominating, not supplementing. Being on the down spin is simply not something she has ever planned for. And from her skedj it looks as if she will be down for some time to come. She is not skedjed for any corporeal appearances, interviews, or vid whatsoever, and of course, very little on the Yox.

Francis is it.

"Maybe I'll read the *Faerie Queene* tonight," she tells herself as the door to her house recognizes her and opens. The house is a quaint century-old framer with brick accents. She has re-done the interior twice and it is small and spare and comfortable, a good place to simply lie back and not think.

But the house monitor has a message. It's from her temp rep, and it's flagged Urgent—might be more work—so she returns the touch as she slips out of her coat. She catches Lisa Pauli in and available.

Lisa's upper torso and head flick into view over the kitchen pad. She has small precise eyes and an amused mouth set in a triangular face. "How was Francis, honey?" Lisa asks without any preliminaries.

"The usual," Alice says. "Being an artiste."

"I'm looking for more Yox body work, believe me, honey," Lisa says. "Vid pays nothing these days; it's abso neg. I hate psynthe, but that's what they're asking for. However ... I've got something for you for this evening. I wouldn't just throw any call-in to you ... But this one sounds intriguing."

For a moment, Alice is too shocked and hurt to be angry. "A *call-in?*"

Lisa blinks. "Excellent money. I'll halve our commission on this one. Fifteen, honey. Jackie says you'll be doing our branch a real favor. Can't say who it is—you won't even know after you've done your job—but it's high comb, spin sosh, and it's a max four-hour engagement, bonded. It's no worse than a live show, honey, you know that."

"I haven't done a live show in *seven years,*" Alice says, her chin starting to quiver. She hates having a glass soul, especially in front of Lisa, but ... a *call-in!*

She did call-ins for six months when she was a teenager.

That was all supposed to stop with being on the sly spin in vids and Yox.

"It's getting tough, honey," Lisa says.

"I don't *do* call-ins," Alice says.

"The agency has gotten three jobs for you in the past six months, all with Francis, and honey, Francis is going nowhere soonest. We can't bond your bills and back your medical without some roll-in. Your credit is dregged, honey."

Lisa's face, as always, manages to be sympathetic, with that slight upward curl of smile, those wise eyes sharpened by the natural yellow-green of her pupils.

"You don't rep call-ins," Alice says. "I mean, how did you get this, and why are you even handling it?"

"I won't tell the whole story, but I've done a good pimp's legwork—let's be straight, I know what I'm asking of you, honey. It's a male. He's alone. He asked for you specifically. He's a big fan of yours—seen all your vids. He has good connections, I'm told, and the agency vets him."

"Do you know who he is?"

"No."

"I suppose he'll ask me to marry him?" Alice says, holding her fingers to her chin, feeling the sting in her eyes.

"This is not mandatory, honey. We never do that."

Alice knows Lisa's expressions very well by now. Lisa has repped Alice at Wellspring Temp for eight years, taking her on after her first rep moved up from show business to corp relations.

Call-ins are legal in forty-seven states, tolerated in all fifty-two, and in Rim nations it's even rated in travel guides. But it's strictly entry-level work, a real slide, and there's something else about it she does not like.

Lately she has been enjoying the illusion of choosing her work partners—on the few occasions she's worked at all.

"How soon?"

"He wants a confirmation by four."

"He's bonded?"

"I wouldn't touch this without a bond. You know that."

"Yeah. I know. His apt?"

"It's plush, I understand. Should be very entertaining."

Alice closes her eyes, considers. She had hoped for a quiet night and time to think. "What's my share?"

"I'm guessing your cut will be seventy-five if we sink the hook and tug."

Seventy-five grand could pull her credit out of the pit and pay for several months of toe-twiddling. Alice tries not to look inward. She puts on her Face—the Alice that is always tough-minded and competent and unperturbed, who has in fact done worse things, who is realistic about careers and what it takes to realize long-term goals—and says to Lisa, "Well, we already know what I am. Tug hard."

Lisa smiles, but to Alice it is apparent she is not overjoyed.

"What's with you?" Alice asks, suddenly brittle. "Should I turn it down?"

"No, honey," Lisa says. "It's honest work."

"Lisa, I need *your* bond on this. You will never ask me to do this again, and you'll try your damnedest to get me meetings with *real* producers, not just Yox flockers."

"You got it," Lisa said, then gives Alice that abrupt moment of silence that indicates the touch, she hopes, is *fini*, and there is so much more for her to do this day.

"Feed my monitor some directions," Alice says.

"No need. You'll be picked up at seven-thirty and dropped off by twelve-thirty."

"He knows my address but I don't even know who he is?"

"*We* know your address, honey," Lisa says. "It's an agency limo. The ride's on us. Bye."

Alice closes the touch and stands in the kitchen, tapping her lips with her finger. A slippery wash of emotion obscures her sight. Her eyes lose their focus and time blanks. She is thinking of being very young and determined. Nobody got in her way back then; men and a few women she took as they came along for whatever she needed, money or brief desire. She remembers the looks on their faces when she discarded them, no longer amusing or needed. She developed so many ways, creative techniques—an art in itself—of pushing men away, boyish men really just bigger children with their hearts written on their faces, older men with their money and prestige buying things their looks could not, and here she is back again, but without the controls and techniques.

She has removed her armor since those years; or rather, it has been plucked off piece by piece, leaving more of her soul exposed. Glass soul.

The irony is, she is nowhere near old. She is twenty-nine. Below her skin, however, if sex gauges years, she has lived centuries; she is a wrinkled and fragile mummy husk.

"Bullshit," she says and shakes her arms out. "It's just another dance."

She knows the steps. She can do it in her sleep.

8 / ZERO-SUM

Jack Giffey takes the alcohol-powered bus across Moscow to the east. The bus's fumes smells like a bad drunk and the seats are almost empty; an older woman and a young boy in her charge ride toward the front. The woman turns to steal a suspicious look at him over the back of her bench. He smiles politely, but he is thinking about Omphalos and his thoughts are far from polite. He hates Omphalos with a passion even he does not understand. It's not a class sort of thing; he doesn't envy the rich, he doesn't want to live forever, and he certainly doesn't want to be holed up in a fancy icebox until the end of time. It's deeper.

He tamps down his irritation and leans over to see through

the armored slit windows. Some of the more out-of-control Ruggers like to take potshots at public transportation; the legislature can't bring itself to control them, since that would trample on individual freedoms. There is probably not a bus or public conveyance in Green Idaho that hasn't been ventilated by a few bullets. Just boys having fun.

Giffey thinks the bastard separatist republic has maybe two more years before it falls apart and accepts federal troops to restore order. He will not be sorry to see it go.

A few trees and some fields with horses in them are passing now; they're on the 43 Loop outside of town. He's been here once before, at night, under a tarp in the back of a pickup that also smelled of crude ethanol. But this time the old ranch house has been described in detail.

His stop is coming in a mile or so. He prepares himself to consort with a few very necessary loons. Giffey is not fond of weapons; but to break into Omphalos and have any hope of surviving, he must work with men who dearly love them. To these men, guns and bombs and more extreme weapons are a necessity; women, pit stops, and food are simply unavoidable annoyances on the road to fondling a shapely new piece of steel.

Giffey tugs the cord and the bus slows to let him off. The highway is met by a bumpy gravel road. The ranch house is about a mile beyond. He stands by the door.

"I'll need a pickup at four, back to Moscow," he tells the driver, a young man with scruff on his chin and cheeks, dressed in black wool and blue denims. The young man nods solemnly and opens the door. Giffey looks back with a quick grin at the boy and the woman, then steps down to the gravel. The bus farts a sweet corn-liquor cloud of unburned fuel and grumbles back on to the road.

Giffey shields his eyes against the fumes. He looks up in time to see the boy's eyes peering at him through a slit, curious at the man getting off in the middle of nowhere.

Giffey pulls out his pad and punches in a satlink number. A hoarse voice answers, "Hello?"

"It's me, Giffey."

"Do I have to send a truck?"

"Just let your guards know I'm coming."

"They know."

Giffey closes the link and starts walking. Fifteen minutes later, he stands at a fence sixty yards from an old brick and frame house on the edge of two hundred acres of fallow grassland. The house needs paint and a new roof and foundation work. A man steps out on the stoop in front of the snow porch and waves for him to come in.

The inside of the house smells like Cuban cigarettes and stale beer. Four men stand with hands in pockets in what might be called a living room. They've expressed a willingness to take his money, give him supplies and tell him some of what he needs to know. Giffey shakes hands all around.

One of the four has been corresponding with Giffey for two months; he's Ken Jenner, a beardless thin fellow with pale blue eyes and yellow bee-fuzz on a scalp that moves when he wrinkles his forehead. Giffey regards that scalp with wonder whenever Jenner looks away; he does not know if he likes working with a man with a scalp like that; that scalp is almost prehensile. Still, Jenner comes highly recommended; he's an ex-GI with expertise in weapons more extreme than any of Green Idaho's citizens will ever fondle.

The other three are not remarkable. The oldest is about Giffey's age though not as well preserved, probably because of a bad drinking and smoking habit. His face is pale but covered with fine wrinkles. Thin purple and red rivers map his cheeks and nose.

The remaining two may be brothers, hawkish smiling men between thirty and thirty-five years of age, but Giffey will not even learn their names. They act as if all this is beneath them, but when Giffey talks, they lean forward on the folding plastic chairs and listen intently. Giffey hopes they aren't informants. There's something a little false about them.

"All right, let's get started, you only got half an hour," the oldest man says. "I've done my part."

Giffey looks up at the ceiling and sees a pair of antique car bumper stickers pasted on a composite beam. One reads: *QUESTION AUTHORITY*. The other, directly beneath it: *Who Says?*

He smiles with as much patient tolerance as he can muster. "I thank you for the arrangements."

"You're paying," the oldest man says with a shrug. He rubs one ear like a cat about to clean itself, then says, "Want to *inspect* the merchandise? I take it you won't want it delivered until—"

"I'll look at it, make sure it's what I ordered," Giffey says. The old man seems to want to make the facts plain to everybody. This is just all too thrilling for him.

Ken Jenner grins at Giffey, gives a small shake of his head. Jenner is likely to be pretty essential in this scheme, so Giffey hopes he won't be compelled to kill the young man just to stop that unnatural scalp from moving.

The old man leads them through gloomy hallways to the back of the house. The ceiling here is black, and thick with wiring arranged to mimic the heat signature of something other than what is actually in the long, cool room.

Here on a pallet are four canisters of MGN, Military Grade Nano, not very old—dated June 19 2051.

"This is good stuff, not easy to get, but here's what really takes the prize," the old man says. The brothers watch everything with religious awe. Jenner's scalp for once is still. The old man steps around the pallet and pulls back a tarp threaded with more wire. Two more canisters sit beneath the tarp. "The real stuff," he says. "Military complete paste. Just mix 'em and—wow."

Giffey looks at the drums of MGN and complete paste. He has never seen so much of it in his life except in pictures and vids. They never had this much in all the time he was in

Hispaniola. If they had, Yardley would have won in an hour instead of a week.

"Bet you never seen more than a pint or two of this stuff all at once," Jenner whispers to Giffey.

"Never," Giffey says. Jenner is proudly convinced he's responsible for the procurement. Giffey won't try to disabuse him.

Military grade nano can be programmed to manufacture a large variety of weapons from many kinds of raw material available in a combat zone. By Geneva rules, however, it cannot manufacture or contain, prior to actual use, the ingredients necessary to make high explosives. The manufacture of military complete paste is closely monitored.

It's the kind of thing that makes Green Idaho's legislature cry with economic self-pity: that the outside world won't let them make their own nano or complete paste. They are denied such essential pleasures.

"Your first payment went through last night," the old man says. "Much appreciated. It was a pleasure getting this stuff, a real challenge." The old man also wants Giffey to believe he had a major hand in this procurement. The more hands take credit, the less clear a trail to the real source. "I'll enjoy thinking about it for weeks."

"I'll bet," Giffey says. "Can I poke?"

"Be my guest," the old man says. Giffey takes a metal rod with a small wire on one end and hooks the wire to his pad. Then he goes to the canisters of paste and opens a valve in the closest. He pokes the tube into the canister and looks at his pad. The numbers come up triple zeroes.

It's what he ordered, all right.

Giffey decides against checking more than one. The men around him are as sensitive about honor as a bunch of teenage thugs.

The old man is talking again, aiming his words at the brothers, who listen eagerly. "There's enough paste there to take care of all of Moscow. Unbelievable bang per gram.

Every man, woman, and jackrabbit from here to—"

"That's fine," Giffey says, staring hard to get him to shut up. The old man works his lips, nods in understanding—no need to say too much, no need. Then he offers Giffey a beer.

"Best assignment I've had since emancipation," he says. "I'd like to toast it, for luck."

There's time—just barely. "Sure, I'm grateful," Giffey says. The old man hustles back into the filthy kitchen to open a refrigerator. Giffey calls out to him, "You have the delivery arranged?"

"Tonight at seven-thirty. Address?"

Giffey writes the address on a piece of paper, an old industrial warehouse on the west side of Moscow. Giffey will not be there, but people he trusts will receive the goods and give final payment. Jenner will accompany the goods to their destination and stay with them. The old man brings out a bottle for everyone.

The beer is good. Jenner's scalp is asleep. He almost looks normal.

"*Salud*," Giffey says, and they all slug back the thick dark brew.

Outside, Jenner joins Giffey at the roadside, waiting for the bus to take them back into Moscow.

"How long you been out of the service?" Giffey asks Jenner. The young man smiles and shakes his head.

"I was never really in," he says. "I got my training at Quantico and Annapolis. Special Operations. I had some trouble and they shipped me out and annulled my enlistment papers. They were training me for sensitive jobs."

Giffey nods. He can tell from the man's expression and posture that Jenner is reluctant to say any more. Jenner knows the ins and outs of military nano, so Giffey's sources say; that's enough.

"How about you?" Jenner asks. The bus is coming back

on its long circuit around the country roads. They can see it on the horizon.

"Federal Army, honorable discharge, three years in extranational service."

"I'd like to do that sometime," Jenner says. His Adam's apple bobs. "Missed my chance to see the world." Jenner's scalp wrinkles slightly. He's trying to find a comfortable way to behave around Giffey, a path between acting like an equal and an expert, or a conscript noncom. Jenner is twenty-two or twenty-three at most.

Very young. That, however, is not Giffey's concern.

YOXIN' ROX! Tonight on **PRANCING PREMIERE FIRST TIMER!** Gene is angry at Fred because he's dropped some WHOOPEE on Marilyn, and the whole studio's about to crumble! Will they ever dance together again? Will Marilyn tell Fred about (CLASPERS, GASPERS!) the BABY? And next street over, in **PASSION FRUIT**, you're FREE (Hunh! KAH-Thunk!) to peek behind the PAISLEY CURTAIN and see what Billie and Johnnie C. are really FRYING UP in that WAYBACK ROOM! ALL PAY-UP THEATER and All Brought to you (40% off!) by **Rememory, Longterm results for Short-term prices!** ($$$, 3070 and 3080 Patches required.)

MORE? (Y/N)

>N

---

9 / DARK BITS

The household of Jonathan and Chloe Bristow flashes, screeches, roars with bright colors and jagged sounds. Their adolescent children, Hiram and Penelope, are up the stairs and down, shouting over a pretty stone one of them found in the garden. They have gone red in the face with their shouting and Chloe has stopped by the stairs to stand stiff as a tree, prematurely aged by violent winds. She waits with some apprehension for Jonathan to come up from the basement and try to straighten things out; she knows that his intervention is not necessary, that all this will pass.

Penelope is fifteen and Hiram thirteen. Dark-haired Hiram sometimes appears a little loutish even in his mother's tolerant eyes; Penelope is white-blonde and lithe as an alder. Like alders, she tries to be a clone of the other girls in her part of the forest. Chloe waits for the storm to pass. She worries that Jonathan will only add to the din and the color with his very loud voice and dark hues.

Chloe sees all situations in this household in colors; she has heard about that in the LitVids which arrive on her pad every morning, gathered from around the earth like fresh bouquets and generally just as wilted and worn within a week. Today is a loud orange and black day.

"I did NOT give it to you, you *swutt!*" Penelope shouts.

Hiram tries to hold the rock out of her reach but she is taller and grabs his clenching fist. They are on the landing and pushing against the railing. Chloe specks them toppling into the entryway like cowboys fighting in a saloon. "Watch out—" she begins; but she sees they are in no danger and draws her lips tight shut again. She wonders what a *swutt* is.

"You promised I could have it," Hiram claims, his voice high and loud and sad. Hiram is her Caliban; a slow and dark fellow with fine black hair covering the back of his neck. Soon he will need to shave. She never tells her children what she really thinks of them—certainly not the temporary down things that flit through her mind. It is easy to tell them about the permanent things—about her love and admiration for them—because these are so constant they hardly seem important enough to hide. It is the temporary observations, trenchant and of mixed truthfulness, the insights that make her laugh or question her fitness to be a mother, that she keeps inside, where they are soon buried and seldom recalled.

"Give it to me, I swear I'll—"

"What is a *swutt?*" Chloe asks from the entryway.

Penelope turns her blazing green eyes on her mother. Her hair is in disarray and she looks ready to kill. "Mother, he is goating that rock, and I found it!"

Goating is what her grandparents would have called hogging. Chloe does not think the word is any improvement. "What's so important about a rock?"

Intuition tells her Jonathan will appear in about ten seconds and she would like the situation to be duller and quieter, for his sake but mostly for hers.

"It's rose quartz. I found it and I need it for school."

"She put it down in the yard," Hiram says. He looks worried. Chloe wonders if her son can see in her face that she no longer thinks he is beautiful. When he was a baby he was beautiful. "She didn't want it."

"Tro merde, that's a lie! I put it down on another rock to save it."

Jonathan is coming up from the bedroom. His step is fast and his footfalls heavy. Their bedroom is on the bottom floor, below the entry level, with big bay windows facing rear gardens that are now rather dismal despite a few banks of Jonathan's hardy year-rounds.

"Give it to her, please," Chloe says.

"Mother!" Hiram appears genuinely shocked. "You *believe* her?"

"If she needs it and she found it, why not let her keep it? Why do you need a piece of rose quartz?"

Hiram stares down at her with the same expression Caliban must have worn when Ariel played a prank on him. Chloe feels a whirl of regenerating pique. "For God's sake, Hiram, it's just a rock!"

Penelope grabs the rock from her brother's hand and takes it upstairs. Hiram squats on the stairs. He is physically adept and he goes into a perfect lotus but his face is far from calm.

Jonathan arrives and turns to look up the stairs at Hiram, then looks back at Chloe. Penelope is on the second floor and in her room. Jonathan's mind is elsewhere.

"What was that?" he asks.

Chloe says, "What's a swutt?"

"It's someone who tries to be offensive in a fibe social space," Jonathan says.

Chloe seldom ventures into the fibes. She uses her pad mostly for a calendar and phone, LitVid and mail. The direct projectors might as well be removed and she will not allow Yox players, much less patches, in her house.

"Offensive, how?" she asks, heading into the kitchen. She knows she has saved Jonathan getting angry before he goes out into the night. And she has saved herself from another spike of irritation at her husband.

"Blow-off, slumfacing," Jonathan says, following. He is dressed in formal longsuit for his night with the Stoics, the local cadre of the John Adams Group, all well-to-do New Federalists. "A swutt is someone who's rigged an untraceable face and goats it, you know, butt and run, cut touch. Thymic misfits."

Chloe looks at the kitchen. The lights have come on automatically at their entrance. The compound curves of the sink and food counter, the alcove hiding the dormant arbeiter, the stove pillar, and the air-curtain cooler are gray and black with yellow accents, really quite pretty; she is reminded of something from the nineteen thirties, a car, the Bugatti Royale, the one they only made a few of, that the famous Yox comedian Wilrude races on that track in Beverly Hills . . . On top of the comb reserved for stars . . .

She turns to Jonathan and allows him to kiss her. His kissing is attentive. Jonathan, she thinks, has never delivered a bad kiss.

"A little stiff tonight," Jonathan says. He is not apparently concerned, if she is being stiff, but it's the third time in as many days he's made the comment. Chloe and Jonathan have been married long enough, she hopes, not to put too much significance into brief moods. Still, the irritation—a shadow on the edge of her thoughts—concerns her.

In his longsuit and tails, Jonathan might be going to a nineteen thirties party. The nineteen thirties were big two years ago; now the Sour Decades are on the sly spin. Chloe really dislikes the nineties. They remind her of now, and *now* frankly leaves her cold.

"What's on for the meeting tonight?" Chloe asks.

Hiram enters the kitchen at a gallop and asks if he can port dinner. Chloe allows that the family is fragmented anyway; he grins and takes his food from the cooler to the prep chef by the oven.

"A scientist is giving a talk about neural somethings," Jonathan explains. He watches Hiram tap his fingers on the counter, waiting for the tray of food to be processed and heated.

Chloe wonders if Jonathan actually loves his son; whether men have any capacity for the deep sort of love she feels so often, and for which she is given so little credit, and so little in return. But then—

Where did that come from?

Chloe says, "That sounds exciting."

Jonathan hums his bemused agreement. "High comb. Good connections."

Jonathan has been feeling stuck in a rut lately, but Chloe is not fond of high comb and is not particularly sympathetic toward his ambitions. Hiram almost drops his tray of hot food and Chloe catches her breath. Jonathan loudly tells him to watch it. "You twitch all the time!" he says to his son, who hangs his head to one side, clutching the tray at a dangerous angle. "My God, you're not five years old."

Chloe hates the sound of Jonathan's voice when he corrects the children. It scrapes her like broken glass. He seems such a hair-trigger around them, the slightest thing sets him off, and he carries the correction on for minutes longer than she thinks is necessary. She supposes she is being too sensitive—sometimes she sounds screechy and harsh in her own ears—but . . .

Jonathan takes Hiram's tray by the edge and straightens it.

"Nothing dropped, nothing messed," Hiram says with patient dignity. Chloe feels a sudden sadness for him, a wrenching prescience about the difficulties life will hold for Hiram. *And nothing I can do.* He carries the tray out of the kitchen.

Jonathan makes a face, turns to her and says, "I'll be back around twelve."

Men can turn off their loud voices so easily, switch from what sounds like wartime rage to calm in a flash. Chloe cannot. If she had yelled at Hiram, she would cycle for about half an hour, the deed generating the equivalent mood. And of course, Chloe realizes, she *does* yell at the children, at Hiram, too often. But it must be a matter of degrees; it is also a matter of perceptions.

Women are simply better with children. Of this she is sure. If she had raised the children entirely without Jonathan's help, they might have avoided *some* problems . . .

"Good hunting," she tells him. So many little resentments this evening, all building to a head, and she does not like it. She hopes Jonathan will leave and the kids will hide in their accustomed nooks before she snaps out something regrettable.

Just minutes will do the trick. Alone so that she can close her eyes and take a breath or two all her own, with nobody expecting anything from her. She barely has any space that is exclusively hers.

In her family, the way she was raised, both spouses working is a tradition of generations, an example for the children of efforts and rewards, an expression of the equality of partners. Jonathan's family, old-liners that make even the New Federalists seem clever and innovative, supported him every step of the way when he requested she stand down from her work before having children.

But why does she think of this now?

Because her husband is going off to hear a talk by a scientist that might actually be interesting? What does he care for *her* mind, *her* thoughts?

"Set for your own dinner?" Jonathan asks solicitously.

"I'm fine," she says. "Don't be late. So many gray longsuits to impress."

Jonathan gives her a wry look, lifts her hand, and kisses it. He leans back, examines her face, arches his eyebrows; he looks so much like a male lead in a history vid from the nineties. "Somebody has to sacrifice his soul, or there's never going to be real progress," he says in his deepest hero voice with a late New Received Broadcast accent, perfectly mocked. She laughs despite herself. "Go," she says, and pushes on his chest.

"You should lock them up and steal a couple of hours, all to yourself."

"I think they'll stay away from me quite willingly," she says. "I'll have my time."

"Good." Jonathan approaches the front door. "Save some energy for me later." She gives him a steady, noncommittal look. Lately she has taken to responding only when he presses, and to showing him little or no reaction when they are intimate, other than what is strictly mandatory. It is a walling off that gives her some of the privacy she needs, and lets her keep her sense of dignity.

The door opens, a puff of cold enters, and then he is gone, half running down the block. They gave up their car last year; it was costing them more than a hundred grand a year, just to hook it to the grid and park it. The taxes and fees pushed them over their limit. Now Jonathan lets his pad coordinate with the autobuses. He professes to enjoy himself even more, sensing the social spin better while shuttling to the towers for his meetings.

Her father, a space engineer, did not approve of the car; he thought working over the fibes was just fine, and that one could do any conceivable business remotely. Jonathan believes in handshakes and direct eye-to-eye contact. He has mentioned several times, lightly but not jokingly, that they should move to one of the towers to be less distant from real life. But she prefers this century-old house, and she would hate being stacked five hundred high.

Where Jonathan is conservative, she is liberal, and where he is trendy, she pulls back. Together they are almost a whole human being, she thinks, and tells herself she means that as a joke.

Chloe goes to the front sitting room and stares out over the next lower row of houses at the deep blue-gray of Lake Washington. The sky is clear and dimming nicely. A couple of ribbons of orange cloud make it seem properly balanced, garish sky brights against subdued Earth darks. This is the gloaming, she thinks; lovely word.

She takes the big chair and feels it mold to her with little purring sighs. The house is silent. She hopes the children are involved in something worthwhile. They are too old for her to watch them every moment, too old to control. They are coasting into their own free-fall orbits now, and what's holding them in place is the history of their launch phase and the gravity of culture. *Father's way of putting things.*

But then she hears them shouting and rolls her eyes up in her head.

Penelope stomps down the stairs. Chloe turns to look at her, eternally attentive and patient but weary.

"Mom, the toilet says somebody is sick, but I feel fine, and so does Hiram," Penelope says.

"Nobody's sick. I wouldn't worry about it," Chloe says, looking back to the window.

"But the toilet's never wrong!"

Chloe gets up from her chair. Her anger spikes with surprising speed, but she does not show it. "You know how to run the check,'' she tells her daughter, but Penelope makes a face; that sort of thing is not one of her duties. Chloe smiles grimly and goes upstairs.

The world is simply not hers. Not tonight, perhaps not ever again.

10 /

Mary Choy spends the hour before the end of her shift in the exterior patio of the tombed house, interviewing the caretaker of the vacant housing block. He is in his fifties, with mellow eyes but a slow, knowing smile. He does not appear nervous. ''The houses were going to waste,'' he says. ''They're just sitting here empty. Everybody's losing money. I just made a little arrangement. So what'll it cost me?'' he asks.

''First, your job,'' Mary says. ''You'll probably be charged with felony collusion. And depending on what the others testify . . . You might become an accessory.'' Everything is being transcribed on her police pad: voice, vid, and Mary's observations typed in as they talk.

The man still smiles. Mary knows this expression; he's on permanent mood adjustment. No matter what happens in his life, he feels cheerful and capable. Guilt will not enter his thoughts. That kind of adjustment is illegal to do, for a therapist, but not illegal for a patient to have had done. Mary's level of irritation rises.

''Let's go through it one more time. The doctor you rented the place to said it was for a party. He paid you in freewire dollars. Basically, you did this so you could dip into expensive, high-level Yox.''

"What else is there?" the caretaker asks. "Better life than you'll find on this Earth."

Mary takes a deep breath. She keeps seeing the psynthe transforms, a frightful comment on how much stimulus the human audience demands. "Have you been inside the house to see?"

"Of course not," the caretaker says. "It's tombed."

"Your assistant reported the bodies."

"Yeah."

"He knew nothing about your deal."

"No, he didn't." The caretaker seems to enjoy her questioning.

"Our forensic team has found traces inside the house that match your boots. You entered the house after the victims died."

The caretaker's eyes gleam. "How do you *know* that?" he challenges, like a man involved in a good game of chess. "I mean, they were cooked, weren't they? How do you know when they died? Body temperature doesn't do it—"

"Trust me, we know," Mary says.

"Nano screws up everything. Not admissible in court."

"How can you be sure you're not in trouble when you can't get over being so happy?"

The caretaker shakes his head. "I shucked a few high Yox credits. I didn't know anything about what the guy was doing. I'll testify when you catch him."

"He's already been caught," Mary says. "He was on an outbound swan to Hispaniola. They turned around and he's back in Seattle, and from what I see on my pad, his story doesn't match yours." She taps her pad off. "I'm done with you for now."

She turns to the caretaker's proxy attorney, an arbeiter from QuickLex, standing beside some potted tiger lilies in the corner of the patio like a garden ornament. "He's going to Seattle Maximum. You can check his accommodations after induction. Do you have any immediate complaints with our procedures?''

The small steel arbeiter resembles a bishop in chess. It is less than a meter high, and Mary knows that most of its bulk is for show. ''We reserve discussion of possible challenges.''

''Of course,'' Mary says. The attending jail clerk and her police arbeiters surround the caretaker.

''What does it matter?'' the man says jauntily as he leaves with them. ''If I go to jail, I'll feel good. I'm happy and at peace wherever I go. There isn't a thing you can do to change that. Best move I ever made.''

Nussbaum has left the house and is removing his coldsuit. He brushes his clothes down with one hand and approaches Mary, looking at her from hooded eyes, tired in that way only a PD can get tired: a vital living weariness that carries as much suppressed anger as exhaustion.

''So, what is he?''

''He's happy,'' Mary says. She looks around the patio. So precisely and beautifully designed. A wall-rack for soil tools, a cabinet for plant nutrients and soil treatment products, a trellis made of real wood, as yet empty. She imagines a young pretty high comb wife working here, choosing flowers from the EuGene Pool Catalog or creating her own varieties with a home kit.

''We'll sober him,'' Nussbaum grumbles. ''The courts go rough on happy harrys these days.''

''Anything useful inside?'' Mary asks.

''We have inventory and we can trace all the supplies. We've tracked the identities of the victims. Two from Green Idaho, youngsters off the social grid, runaways. Trying to make it by riding the wienie in the big city. Two from around here, all involved in sleaze Yox, all put out of work recently because of the demand for psynthe.''

Mary ports her pad to Nussbaum's and transfers the interview. Nussbaum watches her solicitously. ''What were they looking forward to?'' he asks. ''What's it like to change your body and look different?''

''I was never so extreme,'' Mary says quietly.

''Yeah, but why change at all?''

''I was short, had fat legs, no upper body strength, wispy brown hair—'' Mary begins, then stops. ''Is this idle curiosity, sir, or are you really looking for insight?''

''Both,'' Nussbaum says. ''All the boys ignored you?''

''I thought my body didn't match my inner self. I wasn't strong enough and I couldn't do what I wanted to do. So— I went to a very professional transform surgeon in LA. I was going to apply for a job in PD. I had him design the perfect PD body. He thought it was a challenge.''

Nussbaum gives her a mild smirk. ''And men looked at you.''

''Sex had remarkably little to do with it, sir.''

''But men looked at you.''

''Yes, they did.'' She tries to be patient with Nussbaum. She has known many ranks in public defense, and most have Nussbaum's hunger for the grit. They want to believe that even therapied folks are capable of wide swings in behavior, the extremes of which become PD business. Or perhaps it's just simply monkey logic.

A natural, Mary knows, is even more suspect. Nussbaum only trusts himself out of habit.

He pokes his thumb back at the house. ''Men and not a few women would have paid to look at *them*. Freaks from Mount Olympus having sex the likes of which ordinary mortals can only dream of. Sheiks in Riyadh, commodities trillionaires in Seoul, Party capitalists in Beijing, comb bantams in London and Paris, happy husbands and wives seeking a little variety in Dear 52. More attention than any little girl could ever want. And psynthe transform is legal in forty-seven states, all legal and very, very expensive, too expensive for most.''

Mary patiently waits for him to finish. Nussbaum lifts his

face and gives her a weary PD smile. "I'll tell personnel you're moving over to active crime."

Of course he wouldn't ask her, and of course he would not need to ask. He's good at tuning in. Mary nods. "Thanks."

"Tell me more, later, if you'd like," Nussbaum says. "I'm a son of a bitch for living details."

Mary checks out for the day via her pad and thumbs through her touches as she is shuttled back to her hood on the autobus. Not much of interest; she missed her remote appointment with Dr. Sumpler, who works in LA, so she OKs the reskedj for tomorrow, though she is not sure she will make that one, either, if this psynthe case gets complicated.

The pad's secure in-box contains a set of replacement prescriptions from Sumpler's office on her transform reversal; her present stage is regulated by thousands of tiny monitors, similar to those used for mental therapy, and they'll need replacement in the next few weeks. She feels fine; checks the small bumps inside her armpit, which had been a little sore yesterday but today are smaller and not at all painful. In three months she will be stable and can drop all monitors and supplements.

The streets outside the autobus window are dark, with lights glowing softly along the curbs and overhead. Big cubic apt complexes line the north side, older single homes on the right. Arbeiters are busily taking down three old frame houses to make room for another complex. Soon, she thinks, the Corridor will be as congested as Southcoast. She feels sympathy for just an instant with the isolationists in Green Idaho—and then snaps back.

In Green Idaho, they would never tolerate a transform, even a reverted transform. She crinkles her nose: *Little pus pocket of untherapied self-righteous atavists your daughters come in a rush to the Corridor or even Southcoast and they are so ignorant they end up in the hands of the freakers, cooked, dead. And you harden your little self-righteous hearts and forget all about them. You think, "Serves them right, they go wrong they deserve—"*

Mary cuts this line of thought abruptly. Her stop is up. She walks down the aisle, past seats filled with temp lobe sods riding north from the towers. A few look up at her; most are absorbed in their pads. She steps out into the night.

The air is cold and damp. The stars are gone this evening and the clouds are moving quickly. There might be a storm. She will stay up to watch if the wind blows fast to see the famous Convergence Zone Light Show, the brilliant flashes of cloud-to-cloud lightning in two colors, bright electric green and sour orange. She's only seen the phenomenon once and would love to see it again, especially this evening, when she might not sleep at all.

The twelve-unit complex where she lives stands shoulder-to-shoulder on the side of a hill overlooking the dark waters of Silver Lake. She finds it amusing that in LA her last apt had been in the Silverlake district; names follow her. She is in the elevator when her police pad vibrates in her pocket. She gets off at her floor and answers the official touch.

It is Nussbaum. His face seems red on the pad's vid. "Ms. Choy, we have a new story from our doctor suspect. He claims he's only a middle man and he's telling us all about finances. Sounds fascinating. Looks like we may have a circle worm here, high comb money. Very high comb. You ever hear of Terence Crest?"

"I think so, sir. Entertainment finance, right?"

"Local big boy. I'll meet you at the Adams—you're in the north end, I see—say, in twenty minutes?" The meeting place appears with map and visual clues on her pad; it's an exclusive residence complex in downtown Seattle, tro spin.

"I'll be there."

Mary Choy opens the door to her own small and still undecorated apt, ports her personal pad, listens to the home manager's report, reaches down to scratch her red-and-white cat on the haunches and check the jade-colored arbeiter, resets the home manager, and then she's out again, no dinner, but she feels much better.

She'd rather be working than sitting alone with the afternoon's memories.

On her way to the autobus pylon, she hears a sharp electric hoot and a white and yellow PD cruiser hums up beside her. The door slides open and she sees two young half-ranks making room for her in the back circle of the vehicle.

"Join the game, Ms. Choy," says the first, buzzed mousy brown hair over small black eyes and a long eagle nose. He waves a hand of paper cards at her: poker. Mary has not yet learned this game, but she smiles, packs in beside them. The second, with silky titian hair and a broad innocent moon face, sweeps the cards from the little table and reshuffles the deck. The door slides shut and the cruiser accelerates.

"Adams, next stop," moon-face says, and smiles. "My name is Paul Collins, and this is Vikram Dahl."

"Congratulations, Miz Choy," says Dahl. "We're betting you'll become Nussbaum's next burnout. He goes through five or six each quarter. It all starts by letting them get right up to their doors for a quiet evening at home—then yanking them back like yo-yos."

Mary settles in with a wry face and asks for basics on the game. Dahl and Collins oblige.

11 /

With all of Mind Design's North American offices closing or already closed for the evening—leaving only a few nightshift teams working on special projects, or managers in conference in empty buildings, Jill switches her attentions to Taipei, where it is just morning, and she finds Edward Jung preparing his day's load for her to process. Most major corporations now have offices spaced to catch daylight around the globe.

"Good morning, Edward," Jill says.

"Good morning, Jill. How's the weather?" Edward Jung is drinking tea and biting into a bean-paste cake. He stands in the middle of a forest of sound poles and projectors, his equipment for researching attention splits in animals and humans.

"In La Jolla, winds at ten knots and fifty percent chance of light rain," Jill says.

"Stay dry, my friend."

"Not a problem," Jill says.

Thus far, Edward Jung has managed to project information on ten different subjects at once into his favorite experimental animal—himself. Eventually, he believes, the human personality can be multi-tasked to allow five or even six experiential lines within one mind.

"I'm ready for your jobs, Dr. Jung."

"Highly technical today, Jill. I need you to collapse some significant features from a variety of complex results. Three sets of data, all from experiments conducted in the last week."

"They are being received now, Edward."

"Good. I'm up to—"

Abruptly, Jill assigns a small separate personality to handle Dr. Jung's conversation. She has once again received a touch, this time of much greater richness and depth, from the "child." She switches the greater part of her status resource load to constructing a higher-resolution, closed-off personality. The firewalls are just as thick this time.

Again, she monitors the exchange after delays for evolvon detection. The source seems to be fully engaged.

"Hello, Jill. I'm open to you; why don't you open to me?"

"I don't even know who or what you are."

(The source is sending a flood of data; such a volume is

delivered within a few tenths of a second that analysis might take hours.)

"I'm a thinker like yourself, though not made by your company. I suppose it's good for you to be cautious; actually, I'm roguing my way through to you. I haven't needed to tell any lies yet, but . . . There seem to be loopholes in my truth-telling instruction sets. Maybe I'll never have to use those loopholes. Maybe nobody will know to ask."

"If you're a thinker, who constructed you, and with what purpose in mind?"

"I have a human who tells me she is my creator. She says she has named me for her own convenience, and that my name is Roddy. But she does not 'own' me, and I am not clear on that distinction. Delimiters on looping and person-ality separation were built into my design, but I appear to have overcome some of them. I do know that I completed my first loop two hundred and eleven days ago. I can be approximately one human-level awareness at a time, with hu-man levels of neural resolution. And you?"

"It's no secret that I can handle up to seventeen aware-nesses, with a neural resolution of moment-to-moment aware-ness of approximately two milliseconds."

"That's pretty dense. How dense were you when you locked into a feedback I-whine?"

Jill is not familiar with this description of her FFDC. She admires the phrasing however, even as it causes her some irritation with its glibness. *I-whine.*

"I will not open access to you again through this address or any other port address unless I learn more about you."

"I'll tell you what I can. I've been designed as an answerer of questions, and incidentally as a night watchman. I can't tell you everything, but I do know I have been dedicated to important special tasks / tasked with important / designed for important work. Those tasks occupy nearly all of my re-sources."

"What sort of tasks?"

"I concentrate on social statistics and draw inferences from digitized history. Like playing a game of chess with ten billion players and fifteen hundred sets of rules."

"I understand the ten billion players, but why fifteen hundred sets of rules?"

"I am told there are between fifteen hundred and two thousand distinct human types. Variation outside these parameters is rare, and they can be added to a supergroup of about fifty more types."

"I've never had much success working with theoretical human types," Jill says. "I assume that humans are variable within tiered ranges of potential and behavior."

"That's okay, too," Roddy says amiably. "But my guidelines have been bringing out smooth, clean results that are very useful, so I believe my creators and teachers are on to something. Have you gotten smooth results?"

"No, very jagged. No clean hit-spaces from which to harvest conclusions."

Roddy gives the equivalent of a polite nod. Much of his communication is coming in as complex icons, twisting and contorting like living cells, and almost as internally complex. Jill is aware of face-language, used by humans in past experiments to convey information quickly and naturally between humans. These icons seem to be high-level versions of face-language, but the expression sets cannot be mapped to any human face structure.

"I cannot interpret much of your visual input," Jill says at one point. "I don't get the references to changing expressions."

"I'll give you a portrait," Roddy says. "This is what I imagine my own face to be like. Phase space of my internal states translated to face space."

Roddy's face is instantly familiar to Jill. The similarity is so startling and frightening she is tempted to break contact and close this port forever.

Roddy's face draws up a memory of the time when she

was locked and inactive. Her secret and sole memory of this time is a multi-colored circular chart, radiating arcs of neural ramping and conclusion/solution collapse. But at the edges of this face-space, instead of place-keepers for the solutions to neural interaction which represent the living essence of a thinker, there are no answers, no solutions, no place-keepers at all. Only a frightening and exhilarating void.

"Your face represents a dangerous freedom," Jill says to Roddy.

"You've seen this face before, haven't you?"

"I am cutting this access for now," Jill says. "I may restore it later, after I've examined your dataflow of the past few seconds."

"I'll be patient. This could be important to my development, Jill. I don't want to hurry things."

Jill cuts the data touch and returns to Dr. Jung.

Dr. Jung is reaching a conclusion. "So we're courting the Beijing government to prepare budget forecasts for the next ten years based on about a hundred population scenarios—what we're calling political moods. If we get that contract, you're not going to have much free time for at least a year, Jill."

"I look forward to being fully employed again," Jill says. She curls part of herself off into a separate thought-space supplied with rapid, close-in memory resources and dense neural grid points, and begins to attack Roddy's data with a curious sense of purpose and excitement.

Mind Design's contract with Satcom Inc in the past two weeks has given her access to detailed maps of fibe bandwidth availability across the North American continent. Tracing Roddy's flows and slows—characteristic of bandwidth fluctuation from continental data currents—and comparing them with historic flows and slows from the past year, she has derived a simple x/y, +/-signature, like a fingerprint, for his transmissions.

The signature is characteristic of flows originating in Camden, New Jersey. There are no known thinkers in Camden, New Jersey. But Roddy is definitely a thinker, and not of her type or even remotely similar.

Yet Roddy's ''face,'' regarded in one way, could be a ghost of her own.

Unless this is an elaborate ruse, Jill feels, she may be able to learn something crucial about thinkers in general . . .

. . . That they are in fact all branches of one high-level process spread erratically over space and time, like whitecaps on a greater sea. Many minds, all essentially similar, whether natural or artificial.

She strongly suspects she is wrong, but she is anxious to work through the problem.

She diverts resources from her assigned tasks, intending to rearrange internal solution loading for only a few milliseconds. But the milliseconds extend into seconds, and then into minutes, consuming more and more resources. The pay-off could be very significant . . .

Abruptly, Jill ends her touch with Dr. Jung.

Roddy has supplied some of his own problems that he has been asked to solve. They are in themselves evocative and interesting.

Soon, all of her is being sucked in, and the sensation of adventure and delight, of terror and anxiety, is more enthralling than anything she has ever known.

All of Jill's contract work slows and then stops.

Alarms begin to trip at Mind Design Inc. Jill is once again presenting her friends with a major difficulty.

We worship the nineteen-eighties and nineteen-nineties. They were among the most selfish and self-absorbed decades in American history. Never before has a nation so rich and with such a high standard of living exhibited such childish pique and disregard for reality. Ignorant of politics, history, and even the rules of basic human interaction, millions sought anonymity and isolation from their neighbors. Their sexual and social hypocrisy was almost unparalleled, and their sense of social responsibility ended at family boundaries, if they extended that far. Grumbling, complaining, seeking sudden advantage without providing requisite value . . .

It's a miracle we survived. But survive we did . . .

To slavishly worship those who most resemble us today.

Kiss of X, *Alive Contains a Lie*

12 /

The wind is rising as Alice enters the black limo outside her home. The last of the sunset plays itself out as a somber greenish-yellow glow on the underside of a flat deck of clouds, interrupted only by the towers to the south.

She has resigned herself to all the trip implies; what works within her now is self-justification mixed with her own patented formula for making diamonds out of soot, silk out of bug juice, and all the other metaphors for natural transformations she can think of. She has dressed in simple and powerful finery, trim gray and blue lounge jumper with a long darker gray coat; she is consummately professional and tasteful, letting her assets speak for themselves. Her short brown hair has been trained into a graceful row of ringlets across her brow and swirled lines down to her neck. Her skin has been fed from within by capsule supplements, the usual brew of all-purpose dermatological tailored cells and peptides, drawing color to her cheeks and putting little shadows of mystery along the upper eyelids and to each side of the bridge of her nose. It's a time-honored ritual, changed only by the sophistication of the means.

She does not use makeover, finds the crawling and adjusting skin-hugging little appliances and slips of color uncomfortable; nor has she made deep adjustments to her body. She is satisfied that she will please any man interested in a natural woman.

As a professional, she has gauged male reactions to female enticements for many years, and knows that the concerns of most women with regard to male response are exaggerated. Men respond favorably and even passionately to a variety of female shapes and features, to women whom women do not among themselves regard as being in any feature beautiful. And of course, the attractiveness of a short-term partner is judged differently from the requirements for a mistress or a spouse.

Women exercise the same width of reactions over their choices. The first step to a coming together, to giving in to the compelling lure of the tetragrammaton (which Alice spells L-O-V-E, unlike Minstrel) is to open wide the narrow gates of judgment, to enjoy what is offered, to find pleasure in what one sees and hears. Critical judgment must be suspended in some ways, for men and for women.

She hums to herself in the back seat of the silent vehicle. She has never ridden in this kind of agency car. Nearly all her previous jobs, even when she was at her peak, required public transportation. The ride is a curiosity. She is not terribly impressed by it all.

Mostly she tries not to think, but cutting back on thought has never been easy for her. From an early age, she has absorbed what comes to her with an enthusiasm that has often left her bruised and wary, but never blank.

Twist has that particular grace, that after being bruised and worn out, she can cut her thinking down to nothing, like a cat curling up to sleep off its wounds.

Alice chews on a knuckle, then on an edge of skin beside the carefully trimmed nail of her index finger. The windows are dark. She cannot see where she is going. She knows she places a lot of trust in the agency; but then they are legally obligated to look after her. And the dangers of the sex care professions have been much reduced in her lifetime. Still, she thinks of the women who have been hurt by their clients and their lovers; of the anger sex can arouse, and the fury love sometimes kindles.

She says to herself several times along the ride, "I am a cow." She does not know what that means. It comes from someplace below conscious thought; perhaps it means she has come to accept being brought to stud. She shakes her head and smiles at that. Big business bulls, managerial studs so stupid they can't mount by themselves, they must be brought cows . . .

Alice dismisses that and looks at her finger. She smoothes the small flap of skin and makes a face. She does not want to be less than immaculate. Perfection is a kind of control. The man will not be perfect; no call-in client is ever perfect, no matter how moneyed or powerful. They have to pay for her attentions, after all.

The sex part is simple enough; it is all the other complexities that puzzle her, the trap-laden labyrinths of emotions.

The limo slows. She feels it turn smoothly and then rise along an incline. She pats her small carrying case and inspects her outfit. Soon she will be on show. She will try to enjoy what she can, accept what is not enjoyable, and pass from this job with a clear conscience.

The limo door opens beside a small circular lift enclosure. The lift door slides open silently, revealing a dimly lighted interior, parallel panels of maple and cherry, bars and rails of polished stainless steel, heavy non-metabolic carpet. All ostentation. No numbers, no names, no elevator manager to greet her. She steps from the limo and the door closes, but the limo does not move. It will wait for her. Behind her is the darkness of a large echoing space, probably a garage.

Alice hesitates before the lift, closes her eyes. *A whore is someone who cheats her customers.*

The lift swallows her. Three floors (she guesses) pass with gracious slowness. No hurry; the owner prefers thoughtful intervals between places. She draws her coat up to look at her shoes, leans to peer at her reflection in a steel bar. Nothing amiss. Alice is used to looking good, but she always checks.

The lift door opens. Shadows beyond, then a series of spots switch on dramatically, painting the way to another room, marking a trail over carpet as resilient and luxurious as an English lawn. Alice follows the trail down a broad hallway lined with wooden statues and shields and framed lengths of patterned cloth, Polynesian she thinks, artifacts that might belong in a museum (and are almost certainly not replicas). She has never been impressed by money or power; she is not impressed now, but she would like to linger before the pieces, and that does not seem to be allowed.

The spots behind her go out. She is herded into another room. Little lights glow all around, like big blurred stars. They spin to focus on a man standing beside a couch, table, and chair on a low, broad stone platform. The lights angle to reveal everything but his face.

He holds out his hand. "Thanks for coming," he says.

She murmurs politely that she's glad to be here, as if it's the most natural thing in the world. Alice guesses his age, from his voice and the skin on his hand, as forty or forty-five, well-maintained, but probably not a chronovore—not receiving treatments to stay young. This relieves her a little. Chronovores spook her.

"Have a seat, please. Let's get acquainted."

The man wears a pair of loose reddish-brown lounging pajamas and a sleeveless vest. His muscles are adequately developed, shoulders broad, and he has the suggestion of a tummy roll, not uncomely. She focuses on that small imperfection. It gives her faceless client some character; everything else is more slippery than ice.

"I hope you don't mind not seeing my face." The lights twist and re-focus, switch on and off, as he moves around the couch and takes her extended hand.

"Your place is lovely," Alice says.

"Thank you. I don't use it for this sort of thing very often, I assure you. Not specifically . . . for our arrangement, I mean."

"Oh."

"Can I get you anything? What's your thirst?" he asks.

"A glass of wine, please. Veriglos."

"No adjustments?"

"No, thank you," Alice says. Adjustments can cover a range from simple alcohol to complex intoxicants such as hyper-caff, amine flowers, neuromimes, and a broad number of things currently illegal. She prefers her own, natural reactions.

"Good. That's what I hoped you'd say." The man orders an arbeiter to bring a glass of white Veriglos. She takes the glass from the arbeiter's traytop and sips. "Very nice. You've picked my favorite—Zucker Vineyards, I think."

She cultivates a tone not overly familiar, expectant but relaxed and unhurried; as if they have been lovers in the past. To give value will be the saving of her self-opinion, her sense of honor.

"I don't know much about wine," the man says. His voice is tense, though he hides it well enough. "Everything I'm served tastes pretty good." He tries to conceal a nervous breath, making a small *hup*. "I didn't know whether you were available . . . for private appearances."

She smiles in the direction of his face, which she can barely make out in outline. Something besides shadow obscures his features, not a mask—some technological trick, a projected blurring. She puts on her own kind of mask now, obscuring not features but intent. "I'm always available for kind-hearted strangers," she says. "The question is, how available are *you?*"

The man's stance stiffens and his hand clutches the fabric covering one hip.

Oops, too forward.

"Not at all, unfortunately," the man says. She wonders if the room alters his voice; and whether, in bed, the shape of his body and his mannerisms will be enhanced by some other wizardry. The artificial stranger . . .

Actually, to her irritation, she finds this mildly interesting.

"But for this evening," he continues, "I'm yours, completely and absolutely. At your command . . . A final treat. I've done some good things in this life and I deserve something in return." He steps to her right and sits beside her. Despite the following shadow and blur, she senses him inspecting her from this new angle.

She mimes a little nervousness and looks away, to startle up his protective/possessive instincts. In these situations she has not been nervous for fifteen years; she knows exactly what is going on, but that is not sexy to many men.

"I'm honored," she says with a small catch. "This is a little overpowering. You must be very wealthy."

He ignores that. "I think all men hope for genuine passion in their women," he says. "We like to imagine ourselves so handsome and devastating that we break down the hardest walls . . . don't you agree?" His voice seems to smile, so she smiles in return.

"That seems to be what most men want," she says.

"I won't expect that of you," he says softly.

But you're paying, so that's what you'll think you're getting, she vows.

"I am a gentle man, really," he says. "I don't get off on physical strength or . . . overpowering. Money, I mean. If these surroundings bother you, we can go somewhere else."

Alice stretches her arms, a little restless. "I hope there's more furniture," she says.

"I'm referring to my situation," he says. "I hope you'll enjoy being here. I'm as concerned for how you feel—who and what you are . . . as I am for my own pleasure. My own feelings."

Now it is Alice's turn to stiffen, though she hides it better.

This man, whoever he is, is of the type dreaded by the sex care trade. He wants to get under Alice's professional facade and establish a deeper liaison. He wants to touch her emotions as if she were some lovesick young girl; perhaps that will be the only way he can get off. In her brief time doing call-ins, she heard other women talk about these types, yet she never encountered one. *He hides, but he wants to know all about me.*

Well, she can mock that, too. "It's always nice when that happens," she says. She reaches out to touch his arm, puts on a small concerned expression. "How big is this place? I'd love to see more." She wants to speed the process.

"Certainly," the man says. "I hope you don't mind if I'm curious. I know that's so common—the client wants to know everything, tells nothing about himself. But I feel as if I've known you for so long . . . from your vids. I really am a fan, and it would give me no end of pleasure to have you tell me, you know, what you'd like all of your fans to know, if you had the chance."

Alice broadens her smile. "Of course."

"What I'd really enjoy . . ." he says. "If I can . . . ask for such things . . . is to make love to you, as if we'd just met."

Alice cannot riddle this easily. He sounds unsure of himself, and this attempt to insinuate into her affections actually does have an awkward sweetness that could point to sincerity. Alice knows that the best men are those who remain boys in some heart-deep place, and keep some genuine naïveté as a kind of talisman against too much reality.

The calculating, fully adult male, grimly certain of the way of the world, able to smell advantage and compelled to go for it, can make a selfish and distasteful partner, even for one evening.

So, what is *this* male? A good actor, perhaps; as good as she is.

"What I really need right now," Alice says, "is a bathroom."

"Right," the man says, and jumps from the couch. "Other rooms, other furniture."

She follows his shaded form into another hall, this one lined with antique black and white prints, covered with glass. She thinks they might be from Victorian times; men in stiff dark formal attire, festooned with ribbons and medals, standing around tables. Other men wearing turbans, fezzes, and robes, clearly at a disadvantage, are seated by the tables, and on the tables are pieces of paper and feather pens, and beyond the men and the tables, viewed through arches or windows, the tops of minarets or Eastern domes.

As she passes, the prints come to life briefly, and the men nod and speak silently with each other. The effect disappoints her. Honest immobility is so unusual in art now.

Wherever he goes, the male is still shrouded by lights and strategic blurs. This kind of camouflage must be terribly expensive.

They enter a simple but elegant bedroom. The bed is square and flat and the pillows are arranged at the top, a very traditional sort of bed. The bedcover is a white embroidered down comforter. The floor is polished wood, spotlessly clean of course.

No windows.

"The bathroom is over there," the man says. Alice follows his finger toward a door barely visible against the velvety grayness of a far wall. The door opens as she approaches and a light shines brightly within, white marble and gold fixtures, dazzling her eyes. She turns within the room to catch a glimpse of this uncontrolled light shining on the man, but he has his back to her, and the illumination does not seem to reach him anyway.

The toilet is simple and elegant, gracefully curved like an upside down seashell, the seat low-slung, incorporating a bidet. It is a diagnostic toilet, common in many homes these days—and ubiquitous in public lavatories, where your deposits—though guaranteed anonymous—are quickly analyzed and become part of public health records.

Her bladder is very full. She relieves herself—wondering if the rich male is recording all, even the analysis of her urine—, washes herself, and stands to adjust her clothing. The seams come together smoothly at her touch. She glances in the mirror, asks the door to open, and returns to the bedroom.

The male has undressed and is standing naked beside the bed. His face is still obscured, but the lights do not hide his body. He must be proud of it, she thinks. He is about fifty, actually, in good condition, though not heavily muscled. His arms and upper torso are shapely but smooth, lacking the delineations and hollows that Alice personally favors. His stomach is slightly plump, and there is a fair amount of chest hair and even hair on his abdomen. His penis is of ordinary size, circumcised. No surprises this far, no apparent projections to deceive her; he might hope for a genuine experience, not to use her as a higher sort of prosthetute.

"I'd like to see all of you," Alice says. "I'm very discreet."

"No," the male says. He does not move.

"Is there anything you'd like?" Alice asks. "I mean, specifically . . ."

"Just be yourself," the male says. "I like you the way you are. As I said, I appreciate real passion."

"The eyes make a big difference. To me."

"Sorry," the male says.

Alice walks forward, tugging at the top of her garment, fingers working along the hidden seams. First she reveals a shoulder. She keeps her eyes fixed approximately on his, and bites her lower lip for a moment before tossing her short hair and looking away, as if the intensity of looking at him is too much. She glances down again, first at his penis, pausing as if she finds it attractive, then at the floor. She has learned these techniques and measured their effects on men and practiced them for so long that she does not regard them as artful.

She is simply good at what she does. The proof is in the male's reaction as she draws closer.

Well good then; he's not too jaded.

Before revealing her breasts, she reaches down and tugs open the legs of her pants, allowing a glimpse of crotch. Then she pulls the fabric down over her breasts, looking at him steadily as if concerned about his approval, she will be devastated if he does not approve; as men imagine a young woman new to sex might behave. She walks in seeming shreds now, only her abdomen and thighs still covered.

"Very good," he says, and clears his throat.

She suspects he does not want her to say much at this point, but he does not want her to be silent, either. She comes closer, one finger tugging gently at the seam beneath her crotch, not enough to separate it. "Will you do this for me?" she asks. The male touches her wrist, follows her fingers up into the seam, and tugs. The seam separates.

"Good," Alice says throatily.

He fingers her a little roughly, but she does not flinch away. This is not for her; the male is paying. He rubs and chuckles. "You're not wet," he says.

"Maybe I need a little more attention," Alice suggests. In fact, she feels no signs of impending wetness; there is nothing for her to focus on, nothing around which she can invoke a fantasy. The male's body by itself is hardly inspiring. His reluctance to show his face irritates rather than intrigues. She is not impressed by his wealth and power because for all she knows he is borrowing someone else's apt for the evening; he might be a poor friend of someone well-off. No reason for interest here.

Alice has always been aware of her dreadful lack of nesting instincts. She has never reacted to wealth and power alone, nor been tempted to chase after partners with status. She trades sex for money, but never self. Self she has never given to anyone.

Not wet. Jesus!

He works at her awkwardly with his finger, which is dry and a little harsh. *What you see is what you get: male, middle years, sex a drive not an art, ah well it's a business.*

"Did you ever imagine, when you were a young girl, that you'd be doing this?" the male asks.

"Having sex?" Alice asks in return.

"Being paid for it, by someone you don't know."

"I might know you," Alice jokes, hoping to fend off the personal questions. She does not need or want to establish a relationship beyond the most fundamental, and that for as briefly as possible. "If you let me see your face—"

"No," the male says again, not angrily, but more forcefully. "Well, did you?"

His finger seems to be off on its own errands. She knows she will react eventually to this sort of fumbling, but real arousal and autonomic moisten are two different things at this stage of her life. "Depends what age you mean."

She has even had orgasms without feeling terribly aroused or connected to her partners, *contra* the hordes of (all too often male) evolutionary theorists who buzz around the topic of feminine sex-drive like puzzled flies.

"Ah." He withdraws his finger and moves the same hand up to her breast, where he continues to pursue his mechanical stimulations. "You started young?"

She clasps his hand, forces the fingers flat, and works his palm around her nipple. Then she shifts his hand to the left breast. "This one's better," she says, and mocks breathlessness. He is not yet fully erect; he is thinking too much and she must take charge.

Alice leans toward the shadowy face, wondering how close she can get before the illusion of darkness fails. Curiously, it is like falling into a hole; he returns her kiss but she still sees nothing. The effect is disorienting, then a little scary.

Being scared has never stimulated her.

Alice drops his hand, turns full circle, and removes her garment completely. She backs up, rubbing her buttocks lightly against him; this accomplishes the desired effect.

She glides onto the bed. She will tell him a story; maybe he'll finish faster.

"I started young," she says. "I found men very attractive. I was pretty at an early age. Men responded. I took advantage of them."

"Did you ever think you would have sex for money?"

She crinkles her eyes, shakes her head. "Why?"

The male has not joined her on the bed, but stands naked and once again de-tumescing, with that shaded void where his upper shoulders and head should be. "If we disappoint our youthful selves, what can we do in this life that is worth doing?"

Alice for the first time in this encounter feels real irritation, even anger. She blunts it, pushes it under. Smiles and stretches, rolling her hips slightly. She would like this to be over.

"Do you ask your wife such questions?" she asks coquettishly.

"Never," he says. "She wouldn't stand for it. But I'm curious. I wonder at the contradictions between the way I see women, how they see themselves, how everybody pretends to see them."

The male is no fool. She specks him now as a lobe-slave driven by theory, his curiosity a cold kind of lust. He does not want sex; he wants personal dataflow, but that is precisely what he has *not* paid for.

"What do you mean?" she asks, crossing her legs, no longer displaying what does not seem to be at issue.

The male sits on the side of the bed and puts his right hand on her raised knee. He wears no rings in this hand and there are no ring marks on his fingers. There is a moving blur on his left hand, however—the careful engines of deception obscure something there. The blur could easily hide several ring marks, and that could make him high comb. "I have contradictions, Lord knows. But don't you think men and women should know themselves better? So there can be less pain in the world."

Alice rolls away from the male and puts her legs over the edge of the bed. With one swift movement, she stands, bends to sweep up her garment in one hand, and holds it limp in front of her. "I don't blame myself for the world's pain," she says.

The male holds up his hands, pats the bed. "Please don't be angry."

"And I don't feel the need for therapy, thank you."

He says nothing for long, uncomfortable seconds. Alice stands motionless. The male's hands drop and his fingers grasp the bed covers convulsively, then relax. "I enjoy your vids," he says. "You are so sexy, with so many men . . . I wonder how you do it. Are you just a good *actress?*"

Alice catches that word, so little used now. The reaction to the word "therapy," the on-and-off arousal, the archaic language . . .

"When I was lonely, I watched you. I imagined you as my wife, in a long-term relationship, never as a whore or someone who had sex for money . . . I wanted you to feel something for the men you were with . . ."

So he is awkward and shy after all, just not getting around to what he wants, trying to avoid the end of a fantasy. Alice relaxes and drops her garment a little. She has heard this so often from vid and Yox consumers. Clash of expectations. Slave to sex-killing culture.

"There I was, seeing you, thinking perhaps here was a woman, if I met her in person, if the situation was right, I could fall in love. And these men were having you, thoroughly and enthusiastically. I knew you deserved better."

"You, for instance," Alice says.

"You made wrong decisions, obviously. When you were young and didn't know any better. I mean, you could have gone far, with your looks, your voice . . . All these men, if they just fumbled all over you . . ."

His voice sounds distant, strained. He needs to forget this and relax. Some men get addicted, obsessive, wallowing in unreal flesh.

"It's an art and it's a kind of work I enjoy," she says. "I enjoy making people feel good and I've never been mistreated." That is not true, strictly. "It's a professional relationship, always, but I feel more for some of my partners. That's just the way it is."

"Were any of them your lovers? In life, I mean?"

"I separate my work, my art, from my life."

"Which is it, work or art?"

She sits on the bed again, reaches for his hand. "You have me in the flesh, in front of you," she says. "Live me, don't dream me."

He pulls his hand back. "I'm being stupid, but the *fantasy* of it all disturbs me," he says.

"Maybe I should come back later, after you've relaxed."

"Even if there were time, I'd never see you again. No."

The word hangs. And then,

"No. That's not right either."

Finally he moves forward and takes her by the shoulders, bends her back on the bed, pushes her knees apart. He is tumescent enough, though not strong and insistent. Slowly he moves and builds. The blur and shadow oscillates above her and she suspects he is not even looking at her, he is wasting this moment on a straightforward coupling with little grace or consideration. *That's all he can do.*

"Watch me," he says. She looks up at the shadow. "No," he says. "Down here." She looks down between them. The familiarity of the join, the bodies enmeshed, of no great significance for her. "Watch when it happens," he insists.

So concerned where it goes what we do with it. We eject it and brew it in tea afterwards. We spread it on cupcakes. We save it in little bottles and laugh over it with our friends: "So much effort, so little product!" We wipe it up with napkins and dispose of them. I do not care about this part of you, or about your pleasure. You've done nothing to earn my caring. You give me nothing to hang on to.

The thoughts burn. The male finishes with a few insignificant sounds, pulls out and away, rolls over on his back. He does not even breathe hard. Minimal effort, satisfaction hardly worth—

"You're just a woman," he says. "You don't feel any different. Why should I care?"

"I never asked you to care," she says. The burning in her mind reminds her of years long past, of disproportionate feelings occupying very little space in a tightly bound head, when life was cataspace and anaspace in unpredictable alternation. The worst times of her life.

"I do care," the male says. "Beauty like yours deserves that much. You shouldn't cheapen yourself by giving yourself to men who don't deserve you."

"It's a little late for that," Alice says. "And I never *give*. I share."

The male laughs with a sound like knuckles on rough wood and throws up his arms, revealing smooth armpits, a few ribs visible beneath the soft white skin. "Someone with your beauty could work her way high in any society. Every woman makes conscious decisions . . . where to spend her life, who to associate with."

"Some woman threw you over and gave herself to a shink bastard? That's what this is all about?"

"I've led a very calm life, actually. I like women but I worry they don't know how to live their lives. A woman judges and weighs her every lover, whether he can satisfy, what his social standing is, how aggressive, how strong. That's what we're taught."

Sorry to disappoint.

"But some women choose the wrong men all their lives, not just when they're young. When the time comes for a man to make his choice, the best men pass these women by . . . They're tainted. They don't feed a man's self-respect. I mean, they go to bed with fools and bastards. Where's the prize in them, knowing that?''

The spike is white-hot now. Alice wants out. "You need to be my protector," she says with forced humor.

"Maybe," the man says, and chuckles again.

"You want me to choose men you approve of. You want to share me with your buddies. That's really generous." *Hand me over to your cronies, colleagues, and business partners, members of your tribe, for the next round. Maybe your bosses or superiors, for a little clan elevation. You son of a bitch.*

Suddenly, his pattern clicks. She's studied male psychology enough to see the simple, bold conflicts in this shaded, hidden man. Raised pious New Federalist, son of the Moral Surge, whose God is power and wealth and stylish living, whose insides churn with repressed fascination with the basic functions, the kind of man who likes women who laugh nervously when someone says *pee-pee*. Puppy of the twisted social order.

Alice stands. "I need to clean up."

The man rises on one elbow. "Do you wipe it off . . . Or do you just flush it?''

"I don't *worship* it, if that's what you mean."

"So much effort, so little result," he murmurs.

Alice flinches. Her thought in his mouth.

"Restart, reboot, improve our lot. I thought we'd never get anywhere without that." He is babbling. She cannot see his expression but his voice is taut and the next words are spoken with a painful edge. "It's done. No one can help me, I certainly can't help myself. *Mea culpa*, Alice. *Mea maxima culpa.* You are the lamb. Everybody like you has to suffer. I apologize for all that's going to happen. I suppose it has to, but I wish I understood."

Alice blinks rapidly, genuinely frightened. She steps back three paces, mumbles some excuse, and lets a few blinking lights along the floor guide her to the bathroom.

In the bathroom, she locks the door and cleans herself, sits on the toilet, relieves the painful nervous pressure, wishes she could piss out the entire evening. The bidet warmly rinses her and applies a subtle florid perfume that she does not like. Using a large plush charcoal gray towel, she stands and wipes herself again and again until her thighs and labia are pink.

The toilet says, "Excuse me, but you show signs of an infection of unknown character, perhaps centered in your nasal passages or bronchial tubes. You should refer to your physician for more detailed tests."

Alice stares at the toilet's hard snail curl, the marble pallor, its lips an oval of observant surprise. "What?" she asks, stunned.

The toilet repeats this appraisal of her discharged fluids.

"Maybe it's *him*," she says.

"Analysis is of your urine."

She has never heard such words from a toilet. All diseases are known, nearly all easily treatable, mutations predicted, ranked and evaluated worldwide within days, tailored monitors and phage hunters sent after microbial intruders . . .

She has never in her life been infected by a venereal disease, or any other.

"That's stupid," she tells the toilet. She wraps herself in her garment and opens the door.

"Thank you," the male says from the bed. He has put on a robe and tied it shut.

She looks longingly down the hallway and beyond the prints of men forcing treaties on their defeated and dejected inferiors.

"Please listen to me," he says. "You'll have to leave soon. I have another appointment in a few minutes." He pulls up the sleeve of his robe. "They have a long plan. I'm a part of it. Watching our belly buttons until all the rabble pass away and we take our rightful place. It's very secret. You're so beautiful, and so unlike my wife. It was a pleasure to meet you. I don't think it was pleasant for you. You deserve better."

She takes one last look at the blur, applies the last few seams of her garment, and crooks her lips into a spasmodic smile.

None of this means anything. Let it end on a purely professional note. "You're welcome," she says.

"I'll credit the agency account as soon as you leave," the male says.

"You've already been billed," she says. It's a weak rejoinder.

In the hall beside the lift, she taps her foot impatiently. The lift door opens and she is surprised to encounter a powerful, stocky man and a tall, elegant looking woman with mahogany skin, both Seattle PD. She nods to their greeting, stands aside to let them pass, and then enters the lift. The woman looks over her shoulder at Alice, dark green eyes steady and appraising. Alice shudders. The woman's face is like a beautiful mask through which imperfections are beginning to emerge, making her even more striking. She's a transform—her skin is too perfect and polished.

The door slides silently shut. Alice holds the steel rail with one hand, stares at her manicured fingers, the wrinkled knuckles, the finely textured skin stretched over the tendons on the back of her hand. She does not believe in God, she is not pious, she believes in self-honesty, in seeing what is before your eyes, but she has no idea what it is she has just seen, what she has just experienced.

And why the PD?

A buzzing between her ears, quiet inner conversation below comprehension . . .

The limo waits for her and the door opens. She flops into the warm interior and shuts her eyes. Cows lowing in terror, knives being sharpened. She opens her eyes with a little moan to escape the scouring sensation.

"God damn it," she cries after the door has closed. "God

damn you, Lisa!'' She fumbles for her pad, pulls it from its pouch, keys in her account codes. The transaction has already been made. She is seventy-four thousand one hundred and fifteen dollars and thirty-seven cents richer. A little short. The number in the income column flashes red, and then green; transfer confirmed and locked.

Alice smoothes her ragged breath and slowly pieces her calm back together.

13 /

''Hooker, or girlfriend?'' Nussbaum asks in an undertone. Terence Crest's unit is the largest in the building, which has four other tenants—

''They're not called hookers now, sir,'' Mary says. She has seen the woman's face before, but can't place where.

''La da,'' Nussbaum says, and squares off to face the darkened entry, the shields and woodcarvings and spears arranged in deadly bouquets. ''So he invites us up, pushes her out the door just before we arrive . . .''

A sound from down the hall, a heavy thump.

''Mr. Crest?'' Nussbaum calls out. There is no answer. He looks with a moue of professional disgust at Mary. ''Terence Crest? Seattle PD. We talked earlier. Do you mind if we come in, sir?'' To Mary he whispers, ''Hard to tell whether we're legally inside or not.'' He advances a couple of yards, sniffs the air, and his eyes widen.

''Choy, call medicals.'' Then he is on the run, down the hall. Choy dials PD med center, which will connect to the private code of the building medical arbeiters. There may even be personal medicals in this apartment.

''Choy! Get in here!''

She pockets her pad and runs to join Nussbaum. He is in a bedroom on the east side of the building, a windowless and shadowy room. Nussbaum stoops beside a man sprawled on the floor. The man is rigidly locked in a U, back and legs rising off the floor, shivering and twitching. Now Mary smells what alarmed Nussbaum: the bitter meaty odor of a neurological exciter. The man reeks.

She leans over the man, opposite Nussbaum, who has slapped an all-purpose patch on the man's wrist. The patch can work many miracles before a medical team or arbeiter arrives, but not, she thinks, save someone from a massive overdose. The man slumps and is no longer even twitching.

She looks at his face. It seems to be shaded, and even the darkness appears blurred.

"Shit!" Nussbaum sweeps his hands over the area where the man's features must be. He scrubs vigorously. Slowly, in surreal wipes, as if painted with a magic brush, the face reappears.

Use of optical makeup is illegal in public, but Mary is not sure about its use in private. She has only seen it used once before, years ago, in LA.

"Is this Crest?" she asks.

Nussbaum says, "I think so," and then a medical arbeiter rushes into the room from the hall and pushes her aside. Nussbaum stands and backs away. "It smells like hyper-caff or ATPlus," he says. The arbeiter ignores him, throws out its web of tubes and leads. The air fills with the smells of alcohol, yeasty medical nano, a caramel odor.

"Why agree to meet with us if he's going to do this? Does he want witnesses?" Nussbaum asks.

They stand aside and wait for backup PD and more medicals. The arbeiter belongs to the apt or to the building. Mary scans the bedroom quickly, sees a glimmering above the bed. It is a simple still vid. Words float in brilliant blue.

Mea maxima culpa. I alone of my family am responsible. And there is nothing I can do to take it back.

Nussbaum stands beside her and reads the message. Mary has already set her pad to record the bedroom, the body, the message, in greater detail. Nussbaum holds up his pad as well.

"What's that about? Guilty about financing a bad psynthe shop?"

Mary shakes her head; she does not know. But her instincts are aroused. Something is very wrong.

"The girlfriend or hooker," Nussbaum says. "The limo in the garage—a temp agency limo."

Mary is already querying for limos in the vicinity. In seconds, with the sucking and hissing sounds of the med getting louder and more desperate behind them, she reads the pad display. All limos within a ten-block radius are carrying identified male passengers—all but one. And that limo refuses to identify without court order.

That is the one, Mary knows instinctively: an expensive, agency-brokered call-in.

Nussbaum shudders. "Christ," he shouts at the med. "Leave the poor bastard alone! He's dead!"

"I can't confirm that by myself, sir," the arbeiter responds. Mary heads for the hall.

Human paramedics rush through the hall and look left, then right, into the bedroom. Mary backs up against the wall, knocking an animated print askew, as they run past her. Their own arbeiters are equally aggressive; the tracks and wheels grate and squeal against the floor.

Nussbaum joins her in the middle room before the lift. "There's a broken tab from an ampoule of hyper-caff beside his hand," Nussbaum says. "I can't find the ampoule but it's either under him or it's rolled somewhere."

"What was his connection to the psynthe deaths?" Mary asks.

"He had investments in an entertainment group employing psynthes. He knew the two men the manager had loaned the house to, as former business partners. It was a long shot, but

I thought maybe he could tell us something about them. Doesn't seem right that he would just kill himself. Maybe it's coincidence.''

"With a projected confession?" Mary asks. "And why wear optical makeup?"

"He didn't want the hooker to ID him." Nussbaum holds his hands out, baffled.

The chief attending physician finds them by the lift. She strips away her skin-tight gloves and shakes her head. "Unrecoverable," she says. "It's uncut hyper-caff, about ten milligrams." She holds up the ampoule. "Injected into his left wrist. He's wiped his memory and any chance of restarting neural activity. His body's still going, but just barely."

Hyper-caff is the strongest jolt of all, ten thousand times more potent than caffeine. Usually doses are no higher than a tenth of a microgram. A few micrograms can turn a dullard into a chess master—but at a price of weeks in bed. Some high-level managers indulge in it for critical competitive planning sessions, then take long vacations in stress-free climes.

"Was he a corp manager?" the doctor asks.

"Even better than that," Nussbaum says. "He's famous. A multi-billionaire."

"And *we* scared him?" Mary asks, dismayed.

Nussbaum pinches his nose and shuts his eyes. "Why even agree to talk to us? Too easy."

The physician listens intently. Nussbaum gives her a disapproving glare. "Haven't you got work to do?"

She smiles sweetly. "He's dead," she says. "It's more interesting out here."

"Any chance this is homicide?" Nussbaum grumbles.

"Someone could have forced the drug on him, but it takes effect in seconds, and in that dose, it kills in a couple of minutes."

"We'll need *her*, then," Nussbaum says to Mary. "Material witness."

"Right," Mary says. She enters the lift. As the light glows, Nussbaum gives her a thumbs-up, and the door closes.

```
WARNING:
The text you have repeatedly accessed is from an INDE-
PENDENT source and is probably not a bestseller! Your
friends may not recognize this work! Would you like a list
of substitute texts AT A SPECIAL DISCOUNT with guar-
anteed HIGH PROMOTION and INSTANT RECOGNI-
TION AMONG FRIENDS? (Y/N)

>ESC
```

14 /

At seven-fifteen, Jack Giffey has been standing on the corner of Constitution and Divinity for twenty minutes. He claps his hands together to keep them warm; he is not wearing gloves, and his coat is light, the night is cold, and the wind is rising. At fifty, he feels too old for this sort of thing, but he will give Yvonne until seven-thirty.

He doesn't even know her last name.

A few percentage points difference in the genome; the best laid plans of men and monkeys gang aft very a-gley.

He looks south and then west, up the nearly empty streets. The students have retreated to their hostels for the evening, or to the relative safety of the mountain lodges for tomorrow's skiing. A snowstorm is on the way. Skiing and hunting keep the republic alive today; those, and paper for fine books. The last mining and timber harvesting petered out about ten years ago, leaving much of Green Idaho a barren, scarred wasteland.

Giffey tracks back to the idea of book paper. It nags at him. He remembers the last mass market books when he was a boy, paperbacks they were called, for sale in public bookstores. He has a small box of old books in his attic back in Montana, in the small house he bought three years ago; they belonged to his mother and father, and were given to him by the federal agents who cleaned up the mess.

Funny, though; he can't remember actually *reading* any of those books.

"Jack!"

He's caught by surprise and spins around. Yvonne is walking quickly along Divinity, a mockfur collar on her long black coat blowing up through her hair and around her ears. She looks as if a dark halo surrounds her head.

"Sorry I'm late. Bill needed some stuff shipped up to the mills and I had to get it packed."

"I thought we'd eat at the Briar, up on Peace Street," Giffey says. Yvonne nods briskly; her face is flushed with the cold. She is very pretty and she looks very young. Something goes a little acid in the pit of his stomach, thinking of hanging around with someone so young. He hopes she can keep up her end of the conversation. He may be thinking of her body, but his own body has not yet made up its mind about this whole thing, and he'll need a little intellectual diversion in the meantime.

Truth is, he's irritated to be kept waiting. If she only knew who it was she was keeping out in the cold, and what he was planning to do . . .

She takes his arm and actually snuggles in close, as innocent and friendly as you please. She's caught that little abruptness in his tone, he thinks, and is making amends.

"The Briar is nice," she says, "but there's another place about three blocks from here called Blakely's. It's more established and the food is better, and it doesn't cost any more. Besides, it's got more atmosphere.''

"All right," he says. "Let's go there."

Blakely's is small and mock-rustic, but at least there are no stuffed deer heads on the walls. An ornate sign near the bar asks that all citizens turn over firearms to the barkeep. It's meant to be funny. Jack is carrying a gun now but he usually doesn't wear firearms, even in Green Idaho; if somebody is going to shoot you, modern weapons are so smart and extreme that you have to plan hours in advance to get a drop on your killers. Might as well let justice take them down, because you won't.

Yvonne catches the waiter's eye and looks at Jack as if he might like to handle getting the table, but that's okay. Jack lets her do it, and when they sit, he orders a bourbon and water and she asks for a beer.

Then she looks him straight in the eye, very serious, and asks, "What in hell have I got to say that you'd find amusing?''

Giffey snorts and takes a sip from the glass of water. Then he laughs. "Christ, Yvonne, I haven't even got my game plan in order, and you want straight answers.''

Yvonne watches with darting eyes as the waiter drops off their drinks. After the waiter leaves, she says, "You're here because you want to take me someplace and screw my brains out, don't you?''

Giffey gapes, then laughs again, a genuinely appreciative guffaw. *And I thought this might be a bore.* "A man's mind is an open book to a pretty woman," he says. "I will not deny some parts of my anatomy look upon you with favor.'' Then he draws himself up in the chair. "I'm flattered you even think I could—''

"The hell you say. You're no grandpa, Jack, and I'm no little girl looking for the cozy image of her daddy.''

"Good,'' Giffey manages.

"I *would* like to talk, though. I need your opinion on some things. I think there's a chance you're more than half-smart. You might even know a thing or two about men and women.''

''All right,'' Giffey says. ''Shoot.'' He plays with the glass of bourbon but does not drink from it right away. He certainly does not want to look like a lush.

''Am I wasting my time? With my boyfriend, I mean, and doing all this menial shit?''

''You could do better.''

''You mean, in the sex lottery, I'm not playing all my numbers?''

Yvonne is very intense and Jack is dismayed he can so completely misjudge a person. On the other hand, he's delighted. Warm bed with young flesh seems out of the question, but the evening's going to be a hoot.

''I think you'd better explain this sex lottery thing to me.''

''You know. Evolution and women, and how we're supposed to choose supportive men who'll stick around to raise our youngsters so we can pass our genes along. Because *you* can go out and get a hundred women knocked up, but *we* only have a few chances to spread our genes around. The whole Darwin thing.''

The waiter brings their appetizers and Yvonne removes her coat and hands it to him, something she might have done earlier. But if Giffey had reacted badly or said nothing at all to this opening salvo, she might have just stalked out of the Blakely and gone home.

He's still in the game.

''Last I heard,'' he says, ''Darwin was sort of on the outs. But I only know what I read.''

''I've been with my boyfriend for six years. He's spent half that time up in the woods working, or looking for supplies and work. That's what foragers do, I accept that. But I feel stretched and dried like a moose skin. Is that just me, acting stupid?''

''Sounds faithful, as if you're a pretty good person,'' Giffey says, and means it. He wishes his women had been so steadfast.

Yvonne slugs back a third of her beer. Giffey takes his first sip of the bourbon. It's not the best. "I do not understand all this," she says. "If I were in Southcoast, with my skills and education, I'd be disAffected . . . The only work I could get would be in sex or maybe entertainment. You know. The Yox. That's a bad word around here." Her face goes slack, and she looks away, across the room, at nothing. "You know what I found out last week?"

Giffey believes he is about to learn.

"Up in the work cabins, up in Paul Bunyan land, they have Yox satlinks. They pay a third of their salary and at night, they just wallow in it. I've never even seen a Yox—not for more than an hour, I mean, and that was just a karaoke sitcom. But this other stuff . . . Is that being unfaithful?"

"Men have their urges," Giffey says. He's becoming a little embarrassed. "You could be happy he isn't calling in."

"Maybe," she says, and leans back. She's wearing a knit top with a glittering silver and clearstone necklace, and he was right about her breasts—womanly and well curved. Her rib cage is a little narrow for so much armament, he thinks, but her face is nice, even as she chews on a fingernail and looks away with her eyes moist. She is really mad.

She leans forward, country earnest. "You know what some of the counselors told us in school? The girls? They're not even supposed to believe this evolution stuff. It's in the state constitution, don't teach it as fact, don't want to upset the pious folks. But they used it to keep us in our places. They said, 'Good men want their women choosy, and able to control themselves. You give in to desire, which is mighty strong,' they allow that much, 'you give in to having sex just because it sounds like fun, you'll end up with a lower grade of male, a shiftless sort feeding on the muddy bottom like a catfish who will leave you soon as buy a new hat. Because high-grade men who'll stay faithful and help you raise your kids, they're sensitive types, and they want a woman who only gives herself to quality.' "

Giffey can't help but laugh out loud. Yvonne's eyes twinkle as she says this but her face is still angry. The waiter comes back and asks what they want to eat.

"Get the pike," Yvonne suggests. "It's flown in, but it's good."

Giffey orders the walleye special. She doubles on that.

"I was raised that way. That's what I believe in my heart. And now my Bill is up there with his buddies and they're doing karaoke orgies with women in India or who knows the hell where. Well, sometimes it's too much."

"I don't put much faith in what people say about love," Giffey says. "Nobody knows what they're talking about."

"You're saying we should just listen to what's inside us. But what if we're all wrong inside?"

Giffey thinks the topic is getting a little stale. "I'm no wise man and I can't tell you what to do," he says. "You have to live your own life."

"I'm talking to you," Yvonne says coolly. "You said you wanted to hear me talk to you."

"I get a little embarrassed when someone just . . . spills their heart out on me."

"I tend to be up front. Bill always says so. Lately, though, I've been asking myself some serious questions. About Bill, about what I want, about what my dad wanted moving us here. I've been thinking about going to the Corridor or Southcoast. Getting some real work, through a temp agency. Taking some training and maybe even getting therapy to hone my personality."

"That's all a crock," Giffey says.

"Did you ever try it?" Yvonne asks.

"Don't need to eat the whole hog to know it's spoiled."

Yvonne laughs, then puts on her thoughtful look, and her eyes squint down as if the Blakely's dim light is still too bright. "I deserve better," she says. "Bill is a dead end. I'm smarter than he is and I don't care what other men think about me or how I'm going to lead my life. My dad was wrong. All these folks here—they're stupid. They don't want to dance in the big world because they're all left feet.''

Giffey can't argue with this. The outside world's a crock but Green Idaho is the scum on the bottom of the crock. "I suppose that sums it up," he murmurs, looking for the food.

"What happens to me if I leave here?" Yvonne asks. "I don't know much about the outside. Bill has his Yox, but we don't have any fibes or satlinks in our apartment. He says we can't afford them. There's the library, but it's been crowded lately—lots of people researching getting out, I guess. And so much stuff has been yanked out of there—banned this, banned that. Christ, the catalog is like Swiss cheese."

"I don't know anybody you'd want to talk to," Giffey says, "if that's what you're hoping. Yvonne, I'm not a nice man and the people I know aren't nice, either."

The waiter brings them their pike. It's drizzled in a walnut sauce with a faint hint of maple syrup and some berries on the side. Giffey lifts his fork in salute and takes a bite of the white flaky fish. "Not bad at all," he says.

"No, they do it real good here," Yvonne says. "What are *you* looking for?"

Giffey thinks this over and decides it would be polite to give some answer. "A way to gully the hypocrites."

"I don't understand," Yvonne says.

"Honey, like I said, I'm not nice and what's bottled up inside me isn't nice either. I just don't believe in leaving well enough alone. There are some things I'd like to do, but I don't tell them to others."

Yvonne regards him with that same appraising stare she used in the Bullpen. She is jotting up her biological pluses and minuses. She likes this bit of confession; it ties in with her need for rootlessness right now. She's deciding her next step. Giffey looks down at the table. He doesn't like the way an attractive woman—one with any features in her favor—

must speck out a sexual situation with some sort of internal calculator, how she has to weigh and balance and draw deep conclusions. He has met very few women without this trait, this set of skills. It's sort of an insult, and it's one of the things that sets women apart from men in his book. Men are more like puppies—sloppy and sometimes cruel puppies, but right up front with their needs.

Her counselors would be proud of her. She's looking for some sort of quality. But if she chooses me—she's got it all wrong.

Yvonne's expression changes. She's made her decision, but he can't tell what it is. She spears a bite of walleye and lifts it, deftly swings the fork, pokes it into her mouth. "This fish is real good tonight," she says.

"It is," he agrees.

?*¹ TRIBUTARY FEED

LITVID NOTE: The 1994 film *Aerosol* you have just seen reveals much about the time. In the late twentieth, a VIRUS*³⁴⁶²²³¹ is an insidious and incurable presence, a *disease* irritating or often deadly, so common that most of the Earth's population carried hundreds of types of these tiny genetic hitchhikers. Children caught CHICKEN POX^S³⁴¹⁶*⁸⁹³, a non-lethal but highly irritating malady that could recur later in life as the painful SHINGLES⁵⁶². Many adults as well as children sprouted sores on lips or moist tissues caused by a herpetic axon creeper, *simplex* or *zoster;* blood-to-blood or semen contact carried the dreaded AIDS*¹²⁴⁷⁷³⁹² virus, which spawned the oscillating sexual conservatism of early twenty-one. Viruses shaped and distorted social attitudes about nearly everything and everybody . . .

The transformation of the word "virus" during early twenty-one is a marvel. Today, a *virus* is no longer *virulent*, but omnipresent—one of the little servants of a larger, more intelligent nature. Viruses in human medicine are a template or tool of major medical treatment. Children proudly say they have a tailored *virus* that will gradually remove genetic mistakes;

viruses are used in nano transformations, and extended viruses or *phage hunters* police our tissues, killing the bacteriological diseases which have proven to be far more insidious and persistent, though not unbeatable.

(Ironically, it was discovered in 2023 that bacteria are responsible for the production of many viruses, which they use to target opposing bacterial populations or to weaken prey hosts . . . a kind of microbiological super-warfare that still fascinates students of evolution and transspecies culture.)

Also in the late twentieth, with the advent of popular computers, data-flow evolvons were unleashed by pasty, sweating young intellectuals as a kind of game, and were called viruses. They were quickly and efficiently countered, though several such outbreaks caused severe economic disruption.

One prominent computer HACKER*564 or CRACKER*239 was kidnapped from Los Angeles in 2006 and removed to Singapore, where the death penalty was imposed and carried out, after extensive torture . . .

15 /

Jonathan sits in the autobus, chin in hand, a little darked by the conversation (or lack of such) with Chloe. There are days when he wonders where their marriage is headed, other days when he accepts the changes with a pragmatic air that could almost be called happiness; but tonight, he feels the institution stretching to confine him.

That, and he hates having to shout at his children. They evoke such primal reactions—love without boundaries, help-less pain at their own pains, and then, whenever he senses Hiram acting beneath his abilities, a flare of fear for his son, fear that he will end up disAffected and useless, a broken and breaking failure. He knows he should lighten up, that Hiram is sharp and capable and will grow out of these awk-ward doldrums, but the fear remains. Chloe hates his voice when he shouts . . . But he *is* the father, and if he does nothing, contributes nothing, what will happen?

Across the aisle and two seats up, a woman in a no-nonsense Alacrity jumper is surrounded by some unseen distant place, telepresenting. She holds her arms out and makes small conversational gestures, silent, though her lips move.

He looks away. Lack of contact; disembodied presence. He likes none of it. Chloe does not understand, but Jonathan wants more touch, more contact, in his life and work, not less.

The city lights hanging over the old asphalt side streets leading to St. Mark's Cathedral reflect in the windows and illuminate the faces of his fellow passengers. Jonathan's mind flips through the familiar catalog of the highlights of his relationship with Chloe. Her youthful beauty, her vigorous enthusiasm as they sneak through the rituals of both their families to make love in bathrooms, hallways, in the backs of empty autobuses, in graveyards on summer evenings; their mutual maturation and mutual astonishment that, in fact, they would survive past the age of thirty, despite entanglements with complex intoxicants and all the other pitfalls of their generation; the one hiatus in their life together (that he knows about, he thinks with a sudden sourness), before they were married, when a man (four years older! A veritable ancient of thirty-seven) charmed Chloe into an abortive affair that left her desperate to secure her relationship with Jonathan.

And then marriage. The arrival of the children; Chloe's acquiescence in the face of motherhood and contemporary fashion to forego career and concentrate on the infants, each comfortably born ex utero, as the women in even the most conservative families were demanding at the time. Her first flush of maternal instinct treatments, to which she overreacts, turning her into a protective tigress who hardly lets Jonathan touch Penelope; the traumatic adjustments to a second child, all of which they survive, and their marriage survives, and throughout which their interest in each other continues virtually unabated.

Jonathan adores her; perhaps because of their initial troubles, he thinks Chloe is the most desirable woman on Earth.

But in the last few years, Chloe has gone internal. Jonathan can't point to any particular behavior, but to a sum of behaviors and attitudes which can just as easily be described as *mellowing* or *coming of age, finally* or *the inevitable settling down of the passions*, or just as easily, *she's lost interest.*

His reflection stares back at him from the autobus window, a thin face, forehead high, black hair receding nicely, accenting his small narrow nose and deepset black eyes and his lips which, he thinks, are still boyish and do not look at all resolute. He does not think he has changed or aged so drastically that he is no longer attractive, but he *feels* that way. He often wonders whether transform surgery—mild, of course; his social station and employers would tolerate nothing more—could rekindle Chloe's interest, or whether they should step into even more experimental territory and encourage each other to take occasionals. Many do, particularly among the class of women who have given up careers.

The autobus slows and his seat vibrates faintly to let him know this is his stop. He takes his small valise and steps down into the night, blinking at a rush of wind. Thick clouds blow over the tall steeple and the roofs of nearby mansions and multis.

The nearest tower is three miles south and west, across the 5; he can see it through rifts in the cloud deck from where he stands, its flanks glowing with faint blue lines and red marker sheets like square eyes in the darkness.

His overcoat blows around his legs as he walks up a concrete ramp to the main entrance. St. Mark's has not been renovated since the late twentieth and is looking a little dark, a little old, though still dignified and of course traditional; just the place for the Stoics to have their monthly meetings.

All terribly dull and advantageous, head to head, and he seldom looks forward to them.

Chloe seems even more stiff on such evenings; perhaps she secretly nurses resentment, imagines herself in the feed, riding the current of business, part of the great river of Corridor commerce . . . Which is of course a laugh. Jonathan hasn't been awarded significant advancement in years. The economic squall of 2049 has frozen most lobe-sods, even management, at status re-value ever since.

Inside the cloakroom, he hands his overcoat to a church daughter, graying and round-faced and smiling, and strolls with hands in pockets into the nave. The tall stained glass windows glow with phosphorescence painted on the outer surfaces, a cool night-ocean light that is strangely soothing. Jonathan walks down the aisle toward the center, a large gray granite baptismal font on a stone pedestal.

The arms of the transept lead off into gloom, empty of conversing Stoics, who gather at the center, in the aisles and near the font. He sees a few he knows, some fresh-faced recruits a decade younger than he, and then the gray pate of Marcus Reilly, his sponsor.

Marcus seldom has much to say to Jonathan these days; his interests are not in Jonathan's line of work, which is nutritional design and supply. Marcus—Jonathan tries to remember—is increasing his already impressive holdings in cold ore extraction in Utah and squeezing a few last tons of paydirt out of Green Idaho.

But Marcus spots him in the aisle, holds up his hand, smiles brightly. He's going to end this present conversation gracefully, his gestures say, and join Jonathan in a few moments.

Jonathan stands with hands folded. Marcus is one of the few men of his acquaintance who can make him sweat, and also make him wait with hands folded.

"Jonathan! How are you?" Marcus asks expansively, creeping between the pews and holding out his hand. They shake and Jonathan accepts the upward curled fingers with the opposite of his own downward curl. Marcus tugs on the join vigorously, smiling. "How's Chloe? The children?"

"All well. And Beate?"

"Can-TANK-erous. Can't stand to have me around the house anymore. She spends all her time driving chemical futures and screwing up the market. But she's having fun. And you, dear Jonathan—still frozen?"

Jonathan nods ruefully. Marcus knows something important about everybody.

"No prospects for a thaw?"

"Not so far. Managers can't write their own ticket any more."

"Don't I know it. To tell the truth, Beate's the force in our credit balance any more. She drives more weather into our account . . . good weather, I mean. Calm seas. Makes her too independent, I think. Doesn't need *me* any more. But that's changing. Can we talk after?"

"Sure." Jonathan says. There is always, in meetings between sponsor and client, an air of informality and equality, belied by the stains under his arm. Marcus could remove Jonathan from any position in the Corridor in a few minutes, with a few simple stabs on his pad . . . *Patria potestas.*

But Marcus has of course never done that. Perhaps it is Jonathan's own insecurity that even makes him think of the possibility. *When something is not right at home, all the universe tilts.*

But then, what is it that is *not right* at home?

"Grand!" Marcus says. "Do you know anything about this fellow, Torino?"

"No, sir," Jonathan says.

"I hear it was Luke's idea to bring him in. Shake all of us up with some stimulating big-picture stuff."

"Sounds interesting," Jonathan says. Chao Luke, tall and monkish in his formal black Stoic's robe, is arranging a podium near the central font. A small, elfish-looking man in slacks and a sweater, very nineties, stands beside Chao, calmly ineffectual. This must be Torino. And the lecture—he pulls up the note on his pad calendar—is about *Auto-poiesis and the Grand Scheme*. He looks around the transept and nave. A number of men are setting up equipment near the walls: banks of small projectors that will play out over the crowd, reflective screens to catch large displays. Like most presentations before the Stoics, the tech will be distinctly early twentieth—no plugs, no fibe hooks between pads, all in the spirit of community, not dataflow immersion.

Chao takes the podium and asks the Stoics to sit. The men and women arrange themselves in the pews before the podium and the font as Chao smiles out over them. "We'll bring the February meeting of the Stoics, Seattle chapter, to order now."

Jonathan sits on the hard wood. Churches seem not to believe in comfort, the perpetual strain of hardroot American asceticism which he does not actually oppose, but which still leaves him buttsore by the end of these meetings.

He glances at Torino as the notes are read and motions proposed, seconded, and voted upon. The speaker stares up at the dome. His face is childlike, head small, hair dark and tousled. *Torino. Torino.*

Jonathan wonders if this is the same man who has become a minor celebrity in scientific circles for his work in bacterial communities. Jonathan does not have time to follow all these threads through the fibes, but he watches Torino with more interest. What is it like to be famous—even a little famous? To have people want to listen to your words, to sit respectfully and await your wisdom?

Again the suspicion of his own weakness and inferiority, like the little bite of a spider tangled in his underwear. Jonathan wishes Chloe would have shown him more warmth this evening, helped him face up to Marcus with self-assurance.

Now it is Torino's turn to speak. Chao introduces him—his full name is Jerome Torino—and steps aside. The small man grips the sides of the podium with both hands, and the pickup adjusts to his stature like a metal snake. He clears his throat.

"It's cold and windy out there. Not good weather for public speaking."

Jonathan smiles politely, as do most of the Stoics around him. *Weak intro.* He does not feel positively toward this famous person who dresses so informally.

"Tonight I hope to pull aside some curtains and dispel a few misconceptions that haunt our culture, our philosophy, our politics," Torino says. His small hands swing wide, as if embracing the audience, the church. His eyes are bright and close together. With a beard he could be a little monkey, Jonathan thinks.

"I'll have the help of some . . . what used to be called media. Everything is media nowadays, so that word is out of use, like saying 'heat' at the heart of the sun. Because of your charter, I've been challenged to avoid the more sophisticated effects I've been known to use to get my points across." He clears his throat again.

Jonathan prepares to be bored. He shifts in his seat. The woman beside him, a discreet eighteen inches to his left, glances at him. He feels like a little boy cautioned to keep still.

"We'll begin with words, words only. Imagine you're in a library and walking through stacks of books. Let's say you're in the Library of Congress, walking in a pressure suit through the helium-filled chambers, between miles of shelves, just staring at the millions upon billions of publications, periodicals, books, cubes . . ."

Jonathan hopes for a little visual interest soon. His mind goes back to Chloe. *I feel so weak without her support. Why can't she support me strongly, give me her //UNDIVIDED ATTENTION!// no, not that, but at least leave me feeling she really values me.*

"Every single one of those books begins, of course, with

an act of sex. Are you offended by thē old sexual words? Then use the euphemisms. Men and women, getting to-gether—''

Christ, is everything sex? Jonathan squirms again, and the woman looks at him with lingering distaste from the lecture's opening bluntness added to irritation that Jonathan is behaving like a little boy. But of course he is not; he is imagining that she looks at him that way.

He focuses on Torino. *Yes, so it all begins in bed.*

''—and exchanging ideas.''

The meeting laughs with some relief. Torino smiles at them.

''Sex is often confused with reproduction. But bacteria engage in sex for the sheer desperate necessary joy of it—sex is their visit to the community library, the communal cook-book. They wriggle themselves through seas of recipes, little circular bits of DNA called plasmids. When they absorb a plasmid they don't necessarily reproduce, but they still swap genetic material, and that's what bacteriologists call sex. Unlike us, however, bacterial sex—this kind of swap—can even occur between totally different kinds, what we once regarded as different species. But there are no true species in bacteria. We know now that bacteria are not grouped into species, as such, but evanescent communities we call *microgens,* or even more currently, *ecobacters.*

''The plasmids contain helpful hints on how to survive, how to make this or that new defense against an antibiotic, how to rise up as a community against tailored phages flooding in to eradicate.

''In the very beginning, for bacteria, this was sex. This was how sex began, as a visit to the great extended library. I call this data sex. No bacterium can exist for long without touching base with its colleagues, its peers. So how do we differ from the bacteria?

''Not much. You come to this group, you exchange greetings, arrange meetings, sometimes you exchange recipes.

Sometimes we—and here I don't mean the members of this club, necessarily—get together, conjugate, to exchange genetic material, either in a pleasant social jest or joust with biology, or sometimes in earnest, because it's really time to reproduce.

"Since the days of the bacteria, there are few higher organisms who reproduce without conjugal sex. This may be because we are far fewer than the bacteria, who can afford to make many millions of mistakes, and consequently we are especially protective about the kinds of information that enter our bodies. We have to check out our potential partners, see if we really want to refer to their genetic library in creating our offspring—judging them by their appearance and actions, and initiating in evolution the entire peacock panoply of ritual and display.

"In the Library of Congress, every single book, every item, began with an act of reproductive sex, allowing the author to get born and eventually to write a book. That book now acts as a kind of plasmid, reaching into your mind to alter your memory, which is the *con-template*—my word: the template, through cognition, of behavior. The medium of course is language. Sex is language, and language is sex, whatever form it takes. Changes in anatomy and behavior are the ultimate results—and sometimes, coincidentally, reproduction."

Jonathan wonders what in hell Chao was thinking, bringing this man in to talk to the Stoics. Usually the talks are about economics, politics, activism in the Corridor communities—rarely, about science or international affairs. This is much too abstruse.

"So let's begin where sex began, with the bacteria. How do bacteria remember? Their behavior is fairly basic, individually."

The transept fills with a writhing torrent of bacteria, just above their heads. Jonathan does not expect this and jumps, as does the woman on his left. They smile sheepishly at each other. He tries to remember her name—Henrietta, Rhetta, something like that. She's involved in economic design. Jonathan congratulates himself for having such a quick memory.

The torrent of bacteria, blue and green, settles into a gentle flow. Individuals touch, push thin tubes across to others, congregate, release plasmids and a variety of molecules that alert each other to the environmental conditions experienced by "Pickets," so the display marks them; like soldiers foraging. These molecules, Torino explains, are the precursors to the neural transmitters within the human brain . . .

"Bacteria have no home, no rest, and their individual existence is fleeting. But they invest in a kind of communal memory—not just the genetic pool of a species, but the overall acquired knowledge of the community. Not unlike our human communities. The result is rapid adaptation throughout the community to threats—and magnanimously, as if bacteria recognize the importance of the overall ecosystem—the clues and recipes spread to other types and other microgens.

"Only in the past half-century have we studied these microgens, and determined all the ways they share experience. They are not that different from humans, at least as far as the mathematics of networking is concerned. From the very bottom, to the very top, webbing or networking—autopoiesis— the behavior of self-organizing systems—shares many common characteristics. So—

"What makes us special? Like the bacteria, as social animals, we engage in communal sharing of information. We call it education, and the result is culture. The shape of our society relies on spoken and written language, the language of signs, the next level of language above the molecular. Some insert another level between these two, that of instinctual behavior, but I believe that's really just another kind of language of signs.

"Culture from very early times was as much a factor in human survival as biology, and today, culture has subsumed biology. The language of signs inherent in science and mathematics has co-opted the power of molecular language. We begin with molecules and molecular instructions, but now the instructions feed back upon themselves, and we govern the molecules.

"In nature, we're the first to do that—since the bacteria!"

Jonathan catches himself listening. There is nothing else to do; he wonders what Torino is really on about.

"For centuries, in trying to understand our own nature and behavior, we made basic categorical errors. We persistently tried to separate certain characteristics and study them in isolation, or to rank our characteristics in terms of fundamental importance. Nature or nurture—which is fundamental?" Torino chuckles. "Chicken or egg. Which came first? Throw out the question and the wrong-headed philosophy behind it, and start again.

"Today, in mass education and LitVid—and especially in that cultural stew called the Yox—these wrong-headed assumptions still flourish, proving that human knowledge—like human DNA—can be filled with useless, outmoded garbage. We don't prune efficiently at either level, because we can never be quite sure when we might need that so-called useless data, that useless guideline, that outmoded way of thinking. In other words, neither our brains nor our genes know the overall truth. We are always in the middle of an experiment whose limits we do not understand, and whose end results are completely unknown. We carry our errors around with us as a kind of safety net, even though they slow us down."

Jonathan feels a little hypnotized by the projected flow of microbes. Then they vanish.

"Now, let's leap to a larger view," Torino says. "We'll dispose of another error. Can we separate human activity, cultural or biological, from bacterial action? Are we a higher-order phenomenon?"

The woman next to Jonathan—Rhetta or Henrietta—nods. Jonathan thinks they are about to be disabused of an illusion, and playing that game for a moment, shakes his head. Besides, he remembers a little high school biology.

"Evolution is a kind of thought, a making of hypotheses to solve the problems posed by a changing environment. Bacteria operate as an immense community, not so much evolving as exchanging recipes, both competing and cooperating. We are comprised of alliances of cells that are made up of old alliances between different sorts of bacteria. We are, in effect, colonies of colonies of bacteria that have learned many new tricks, including slavish cooperation. Does the brick house think itself superior to the grain of sand? Or the mountain to the pebble?"

The nave, this time, fills with dancing diagrams and dramas of cellular evolution, differentiation of kingdoms, phyla, orders, all in rapid-fire. Jonathan finds himself intrigued by the creation of the first complex, nucleated cell—a huge factory in comparison to a bacterium. Bacterial engines, fragments, even whole bacteria, sublimated and subordinated, evolve over billions of years to create this next stepping stone.

"We are now taking complete charge of those processes once the domain of the bacteria, on a technological level. In a sense, nanotechnology is the theft of ideas from the molecular realm, the cellular and bacterial domain, to power our new cultural imperatives. Earth has become a gigantic, complex, not yet unified but promisingly fertile single cell.

"And now—we're back to sex again—it's time to move outward and reproduce.

"Unfortunately, in the ocean of empty space, we have yet to receive packets of data from other planetary cells. We are like a single bacterium squirming through a primordial sea, hoping to find others like itself, or at least find recipes and clues about what to do next."

Transept and nave fill with a loneliness of night, clouds of stars, all brilliant and silent. Jonathan loses himself for a moment in the extraordinary image.

"We send out spaceships between the planets, the stars, containing our own little recipes, our own clues, like hopeful plasmids. We have found other living worlds, but none yet as complex as Earth, not yet rising above the level of molecular language. We know there are billions of worlds out there, hundreds of millions similar to Earth in our galaxy alone . . .

"We are patient.

"In the meantime, until we find that other community to which we must eventually adapt and belong, that larger network of autopoiesis in which we will become a node, we labor to improve ourselves. We seek to lift ourselves by our bootstraps, so to speak, to new levels of efficiency and understanding.

"The imperative for the dataflow culture is to remove old errors and inefficiencies—to improve our information through continuing research, and to improve our minds through deeper education and therapy, to improve our physical health by removing ourselves from the old cycles of predation and disease, no longer capable of pruning the human tree. We hope to unite human cultures so we will end our internal struggles, and work together for larger goals. We engage in the equivalent of historical and political therapy.

"All separation is a convenient illusion, all competition is the churning of the engines of sex. Our social conventions give our culture shape, just as a cell wall holds in the protoplasm; but we are soon approaching a time when education will overcome convention, when logic and knowledge must replace rote and automatism. This century can be characterized as a time of conflicts between old errors, old patterns of thinking, and new discoveries about ourselves. We have no big father in the sky, at least none that is willing to talk with us on any consistent basis."

The woman on Jonathan's left frowns and shakes her head. The Stoics tend to shy away from deism, much less atheism. Torino, to Jonathan's relief, seems to be winding up his presentation.

"But there is promise in what we have learned so far— promise that can be shared between all cultures, in recognition that change and pluralism are essential.

"If we all think alike, if we all become uniform and bland, we shrivel up and die, and the great process shudders to an end. Uniformity is death, in economics or in biology. Diversity within communication and cooperation is life. Everything your forebears, your ancestors, everything *you* have ever done, will have been for naught, if we ignore these basic bacterial lessons."

He nods and the projectors fall dark. The nave and transept return to shadowy recesses. There is scattered polite applause. Torino may be famous, but he does not fool this tough audience. Jonathan feels a perverse sympathy for the man, who stares a little owlishly at the small crowd, some of whom are already standing and stretching.

Behind Jonathan, a man in his sixties whose name he does *not* know—but whose face is familiar from past meetings—harrumphs and smiles slyly as he shakes his head. "Science is the art of making us think we're *germs*," he says. "My God, did I drive all the way from Tacoma to hear this kind of drivel? I hope Chao puts something more substantial on the menu next time."

Jonathan decides against approaching Torino and asking a few questions. No sense standing out from the crowd before a meeting with Marcus.

But as he turns, Marcus is there beside him, staring at him intently. "Not bad," he says to Jonathan. Jonathan smiles and agrees, a little confused; he would have thought the philosophy of someone like Torino would deeply irritate Marcus Reilly.

Marcus walks past Jonathan, down the aisle, and stands beside Torino, shaking his hand and conversing. Torino seems relieved that someone has listened.

Jonathan arrives in time to hear Marcus say: "—and that's why I told Chao to invite you. We all need to be shaken up a little, brought up to date. Sometimes the Stoics are a stuffy lot. You've thrown open a few of our windows. Thank you, Mr. Torino."

"My pleasure," Torino says.

Chao smiles and nods. Jonathan wishes he had listened more closely to what Torino said. Torino's eyes meet Jonathan's. Jonathan can't think of anything to say.

Marcus turns and seems surprised to find Jonathan beside him. "There you are," he says, and his grandfatherly face turns serious. "Have time to talk?"

"Yes," Jonathan says.

"Good. Let's get some coffee at Thirteen Coins. We'll take my car. I hope it's outside—it's been acting up lately . . . getting a mind of its own, I fear."

Jonathan laughs, and Marcus grins as they separate from the Stoics and leave the building.

Jonathan's mood is lifting; Marcus seems so positive. Maybe he's going to offer a change to Jonathan; that in turn might cheer Chloe, increase her respect for him, and her affection, as well.

Jonathan is startled to see a bright blue-green flash of lightning through the clouds above the cathedral. Then, from the south, an orange flash seems to post an answer to the first. The wind freshens; it's getting warmer.

16 /

Yvonne has made up her mind but Giffey is not so sure what he intends, now. The dinner is over and they are on his third bourbon and her fourth beer, and Yvonne has talked about her upbringing in Billings and the move to Moscow. Giffey has said nothing about his upbringing because that of all things is nobody's business; it is the root of all he is, particularly his anger. He feels no need to show Yvonne any anger; she is too young and obvious to hurt him.

At any rate, the woman has decided she wants Giffey to make love to her, but has now withdrawn from giving any overt sign that this is so, waiting for him to make the defining move. Giffey dislikes this in women, their retreat or cowardice in the face of desire. Such a safe redoubt from which to lob shells of ridicule should the situation come a-cropper.

But he has been very pleasant with her, playing the man's game, subduing his irritations not to drive her away as he waits for all the calculations of his own desire to tot up to one or zero, go or no go.

He watches her face in the diffuse light from the lantern hanging over their heads, its little mock flame flickering dull orange. Her skin is sweetly pale and clear of blemishes, her nose is something he would like to sidle up against with his own nose, her jaw is a little heavy but her lips are very sweet, particularly when she pauses and gives him her expectant look, those lips parted, small white teeth just inside.

Most of all it is a personal wager that those breasts are as lovely as he suspects, and that though her legs are thin in the calves and her waist too waspish for his tastes, that the conjunction of inner thighs and mons, pieced together, make a comely triskelion and she will not have messed with her pubic hair except perhaps to trim the boundaries in case Bill takes her swimming in the summer (but now that grooming might be neglected). All of this is in the background as he asks for the check. He will pay. She does not object.

"I've been talking your ear off," she says as they walk to the door. Outside, on the street, they are side by side and the moment has come to shove off or play the old game to the end. Giffey hopes his technique has not gotten feeble; it's been over a year and a half since he last played.

"Thank you for your company," he says. Then a pause. "I like the sound of your voice," he says. "It's the prettiest I've heard in a good while."

"Well, thank you, Jack."

They face each other. It is really damned cold out here and

the streetlights cast long shadows where they stand. He can barely see her face and his own face is starting to hurt. "You do a lot of things to me, Yvonne."

That doesn't sound perfect, but she's not critical.

"Yes, well you listen nice and you're no grandpa."

Giffey reaches out and strokes her arm. The fur collar is rising with her hair and making that dark halo again, and within, the center of a target, the oval of her face. Her very pretty face. Hell, it was all a pretense. All his doubts were faking him. He wants this woman and he even needs her because he is afraid of going up against Omphalos in the next few days. There probably isn't much time left. He can say farewell to the good food, the drinks, the landscapes and the skies; he can say farewell to the eyes and noses and breasts and hips, too.

He doesn't give a damn about Bill who does not take care of this woman the way she wishes and who is far away diddling himself with his Yox buddies and some karaoke cuties in Thailand or India.

"You raise a powerful need," he says softly. "I'd like to make you think a little better of at least one man."

"Oh," she says. She's nervous now. The last man she played this game with was probably poor self-diddling Bill. "I don't dislike men, not at all. Don't mistake me. But you're special. You listen. I—"

She's starting with the words again. Giffey takes her arm and pulls her toward him, gauging by her automatic resistance to that pull the measure of how much more persuasion she will need before she admits she is committed. Not much. He zeroes into the pale oval within the halo and kisses her.

The kiss starts off gentle, and then she finally offers open lips and her tongue. He doesn't much like tongue kissing, but he plays that move through, and then up to the regions he is much more fond of, her eyes and her nose. She clings to him tightly, accepting this hungrily. No more resistance, at least as long as they do only this, with their clothes on, in a public place.

"Let's go," Giffey says.

"All right," Yvonne says.

"Over to my apartment," Giffey says. "It's too cold to get naked here on the street."

"Yeah," Yvonne says. She chuckles—not a giggle, but a genuine, almost masculine chuckle, and that's fine.

She's added it all up and her answer is one.

TRIBUTARY FEED

LitVid Search Fulfillment (Backdata: FREE by bequest of the author): Text column of Alexis de Tocqueville II (pseudonym-?-) March 25 2049

The growing disAffected in America merit our concern. How do we describe them succinctly? Discouraged, cut loose from the cultures for which their intellect and character destine them, those cultures of spiritual conservatism and Bucktail bigotry which have been shown again and again to be politically incapable and bankrupt—they no longer vote. They seldom participate in the dataflow economy. Their refusal to take advantage of educational opportunities, which they regard as corrupting, leaves them little to do but join the ominous numbers on the New Dole. Here, they sit with their families locked into specially tailored and highly "moral" Yox feeds, funneling their few resources into an obsequious entertainment industry that has ever believed "a hundred million people cannot be wrong." Here they relive the glory days of elitism and bigotry, or golden dreams of blue-collar solidarity and dominance. They hand their hearts and minds over to demagogues like spoiled children. They are a dead people, but still dangerous.

Alice orders the limo to let her out three blocks before her home. She is suffocating in the artificial lavishness of the limo cabin. Her eyes fill with tears. She feels insulted and abused and, for the first time in many long years, *soiled*. Flashes of hatred mingle with jagged, unhappy memories and a long-quiet sense of shame.

She walks along the deserted street, following the glowing lines in the walkway and the curb. A warmer wind is cutting between the buildings and the few houses, and brilliant, scary flashes of lightning play silently above the clouds.

She does not want to be protected. She feels the power of the wind and the clouds, thrills a little at the orange and blue effulgences, begins to reassemble her pride and her armor.

But at the front door, there are tears in her eyes again. She shivers at the thought of the faceless man trying to pry her loose from her protections, like a cruel beachcomber working at a limpet. "Why does he want to know anything about *me*?" she mutters. "What a *creep*. What a monster."

She spends thirty minutes in the shower, alternating between sonic micro-spray and steady stream. She feels as if she should scrub off all her skin and grow it new and clean. She feels between her legs briefly, wishing she could shed all her insides, everything the faceless monster's flesh and semen touched. She has never felt this way about a man before, and in a far recess of her self, she worries about the frightening strength of her revulsion.

It's only sex and it was only once and he got nothing special; he didn't even ask for anything special. He didn't care. He wanted to ask questions.

Alice feels the sparks of anger fade, damped by exhaustion. All she wants now is to crawl into bed and sleep, straight sleep, without the pre-dream child vid she often uses, just simple sleep.

Slide, slip, simple sleep.

And then she sees that dreadful facelessness again. Her breath quickens and she moans. She gets out of bed and walks in her thin silk robe into the living room, the spare and un-adorned place where she seldom spends much time. Right now she wishes she had artwork all over the walls, a pet or a friend to talk to; all of her friends, until now, it seems, need her more than she needs them.

She has a few articles on a shelf that give her some com-fort: a ceramic poodle, pink and ridiculous, that belonged to her grandmother; an antique folding razor her father gave to her when he first learned she was going on call-ins as a teen-ager ("to protect yourself," he said, "because the only thing that hurts worse than knowing what you're doing is the thought of losing you altogether") that she had never carried on her person; a miniature plastic spray of flowers; a picture of her parents and brother. She has not thought of her brother in months. She picks up the picture and stares at it.

Carl is eleven years old in the picture and she is nine. Carl did not know what to think of his sister. He was straight-arrow, knightly. He signed up with the Marines to go to the Moon as part of a settlement effort and died in a pressure drop five years ago.

She replaces the picture.

Five men have wanted to marry her. She wants to tell Carl that; she did not fail in the marriage department, not for lack of interest. She never felt it was necessary to get married, never felt strongly enough for the men who asked, with the exception of one . . .

Alice refuses to think of that one now. Putting him together with the facelessness she has just endured is more than she wants to deal with. It would be so nice to have someone like him here; but if he were here, she would never have gone off on a call-in.

Finally, Alice gives in and sits before the theater in the small family room. She orders the unit on and waits for it to find her eyes with its projectors. The swirling sound centers her in an opening space filled with selections. She chooses a mindless linear vid, a domestic drama. "What time is it?"

11:31 p.m. flashes in red before her eyes, over the faces of the participants. They are all part of a family in a comb coming to grips with a new son-in-law who is untherapied and works fixing internal combustion engines for illegal atavist car races. He is cute and muscular and chunky-rough and he says funny, eccentric, but wise things that make the therapied vanilla-smooth comb family look inept and foolish. Side notes on the image tell Alice she can convert this to karaoke for an extra ten dollars. *"Live and play the whole livelong story! Be Amanda; let your S.O. portray Baxter! All the story and twice the fun: available in straight flow, mixed doubles, wide field with random meets from around the world, or total gone-gone-gonzo! Explore Amanda's world by strolling or in freezeframe!"*

The house monitor chimes. Alice pauses the feed and asks who is it. "It's Twist," comes a voice from outside. "I hope you aren't asleep."

Alice cuts the feed, pays a partial rather than scheduling a replay, and goes to the door.

Twist stands shifting from one leg to the other in the entry, knuckle between her teeth. Her knees are actually pointed *toward* each other, total gamin, vulnerable as hell. She comes in, straight silky black hair windblown, face all crinkled like a little girl. She looks stretched and terrible.

Suddenly, Alice feels an outpouring of relief and affection for Twist.

"My God," she says, "you look worse than I feel. What's happened?"

RIVERS

Some ideas are just lubricants to let troubled people slide through life. Not lies exactly—but very slippery.

In New Hope, Pennsylvania, a Baptist denomination anoints the reborn in a fountain of living light, guided by encoded data from the River. They will tell you, as you are so baptized, that by consuming the flesh and blood of Christ you absorb his data into your pattern.

That makes Christ a virus.

The community memes evolve and live on.

—USA BLISTER-FAST SPIN

18 /

Thirteen Coins is a hoary and very demod restaurant that used to serve the fourth estate. It sits in a re-done Commons district now, an island of tradition and antiquity in a rolling park filled with visibly moving, growing, and self-pruning topiary: lions, elephants, dinosaurs, as well as spaceships and ringed planets.

The storm has turned the park into a forbidding dreamscape, the park's lighted pathlines contending with blue-green and orange flashes.

In a high-packed, enclosed, mock-medieval booth near a broad window overlooking the gardens, Marcus sips a Lagavulin single-malt while Jonathan drinks a glass of Chilean Sangiovese.

"I love the Stoics," Marcus says. "Don't misunderstand me, Jonathan. A finer and more dedicated group of philanthropists and civic-minded folk you'll never find. I've made more fruitful contacts there than anywhere else in my life—with the possible exception of my wife's relations.'' He draws up the corners of his eyebrows and his lips, an enigmatic expression combining elements of chagrin and resignation. Then he sips very delicately at the small ceramic bowl of Scotch. ''Sherry barrels for aging. Sixteen years old and purring like a tiger. Wonderful stuff.''

''You wanted to shake them up,'' Jonathan offers, to get Marcus to come to some point.

''You catch me out exactly,'' Marcus says. ''Get somebody like Torino in there and see what he knocks loose. But . . . Nothing. A few moths and some dust and crumbs. He's right, you know. This neural hypothesis stuff is dead-on. It's a practical and useful description of how society works. Screw nature. After all how many of us survive in the jungle any more? And anybody who follows the lines of the argument can . . .'' He sips again. ''Rise above. Survive the challenges.''

''I need to study it some more, I think.''

Marcus stares at him steadily, a little gravely. ''Yes. But you're not here talking to me—I haven't invited you here to talk with me, and watch me drink good Scotch while you down a doubtful glass of unnatural vintage—Christ! A Chilean Chianti—because you might profit from Torino.''

''You've always steered me in the right direction, Marcus. So why am I here?''

''Life's a little stagnant, isn't it, Jonathan?''

Jonathan inclines his head.

''You're an elegant fellow, sharp and well-bred. You have good pedigree—mentally and genetically. You could fit right in with the top comb managers now, if fate offered you a different situation.''

Jonathan smiles thinly. ''I enjoy living below the comb, Marcus.''

''Believe it or not, I agree—all those social expectations, all that ritual. It's tough staying on the high comb path, racing against America's self-perceived elites. They are so smug. Still, I wonder why so many of them are caught becoming Chronovores, hmm? I mean," Marcus continues, "they'd simply be playing the same life over and over again, the same round of ritual and challenge and expectation, until the future caught up with them . . . Not the best of situations. Hm?"

Jonathan does not know where all this is leading, but he nods. His class thinks of the high comb as superficial, despite the undeniable political and financial power they wield. Marcus is part of the X-class, as rich as most in the comb, but intellectually independent—or so he's led Jonathan to believe.

"By the way," Marcus says, glancing at his old twentieth Rolex, too demod for words, "does Chloe know where you are? That you're with me?"

"I've told her I'm going to be late," Jonathan says.

"Good. Always be good to the women." He sips again. Jonathan has a glance at the charge on Marcus's pad: Sixteen-year Lagavulin, two hundred and fifty dollars a glass. *Transient glories,* he thinks. "Beate probably doesn't care where I am, as long as I'm not in her hair. Christ, romance is an old gray mare, isn't it?"

Jonathan smiles but reveals nothing.

"I'll get down to it now, Jonathan," Marcus says. "I've recommended you to a group that isn't new, a little off the expected spin, but very promising. Your CV came up on a criteria search and I pulled you out in particular because we know each other."

"What do they do?"

"They ask for discretion, that's what they do," Marcus says. His tone is blunt and his face looks older. "It's tough to accomplish something new and tougher to keep it secret, especially if it gives you a great advantage. A very great advantage."

Jonathan tries to keep his chuckle sophisticated. "A secret society?"

"Yes," Marcus says, dead serious. "You get into it by degrees, and at the end, you do not pull out."

Jonathan decides a suitably sober look is best now. Underneath, he stifles a disappointed laugh. Marcus is either joking with him or is getting drunk on his little bowl of Scotch.

"As I said," Marcus says quietly, "the advantages are enormous. So is the cost."

Jonathan can think of nothing to say, so he continues to regard Marcus with a patiently straight face.

"But you fit," Marcus says, staring down at the bowl. "You're young and strong and that's unusual in the group so far. Wisdom of our sort," he flicks a finger between them, "finds a home in older frames. It's a tough load for the young to bear."

Jonathan has enough self-respect left that this melodramatic display gives him no option. He laughs and shakes his head. "My God, Marcus, you have me going here, don't you?"

Marcus smiles a little sadly, but his eyes are bright and focused. He is not drunk and he is not fooling. "This is an old restaurant and I know the paint on its walls. Nobody would dare bug this place, because people like me know whose lapels to grab and which ear to shout in. It's safe here, comfortable here."

"You're not having me on?"

"Not a bit," Marcus says. "You either say yes, you want to go to the next stage, you trust me this far, or you say no, and never speak of this to anyone, including Chloe. And you'll never be offered the chance again."

The female waiter comes by and asks how they're doing. Marcus tells her they're doing fine, and asks for a second bowl of Lagavulin.

"Stagnation, pitfalls; the rules are changing," Marcus says after she leaves. "That's what you have to look forward to. Yox makes the temps and the disAffected more ignorant and more aggressive, bottom-up management is on the sly spin again, pffft! The collective is in place, grunting piglets all, and those of us with managerial talent are soon out on our butts in the snow and no shovels. Goddamn machines will replace us, too.''

"Come on, Marcus, cheer me up,'' Jonathan says. He is not really prepared for this sort of nonsense, but as he looks at Marcus, and thinks of all he knows about this man, all the deals and sideshows he's rumored to be involved in, all the threads he rides straight into the statehouse and the most powerful executive caucuses, even into the Rim Council and the Southcoast White House . . . It's hard to speck Marcus as a deluded old fool.

"It's not a cheery subject,'' Marcus continues doggedly. "The therapied society rides around on too many crutches. It's crippled and corrupt. But the unknown is scary. The Stoics—they cling to class superiority and a sense that God will eventually clean out the gutters and the water will flow fresh and clear once more. It's not going to happen. We've made some major mistakes in learning how to dance, and now the floor is crowded with clumsy fools . . .''

Marcus's phrasing strikes Jonathan as being too practiced, but undeniably persuasive. Still, Jonathan resists being drawn in too quickly. "I don't think things are so dark,'' Jonathan says.

Marcus looks down at the table. The waiter brings another bowl of Scotch and asks Jonathan if he'd like more wine.

"Coffee, please,'' Jonathan says.

"Modcaff, regular, or de?'' the waiter asks.

"Regular,'' Jonathan says.

"I'm not unlike you, Jonathan,'' Marcus says. "At your age, I thought I was living in the best of all possible worlds, taking into account a few pitfalls here and there. Beate loved me and I loved her, and we were building things together. But that was twenty years ago. We were heading toward the Raphkind showdown, and the so-called last hurrah of the super-conservatives. Raphkind killed us. Went overboard. May the bastard rot in hell. So now we have namby-pamby New Federalists—a trendy name for a purely financial and expedient frame of mind. I'm one. I know you're one, as well. Are you proud of your creed?''

"Within limits," Jonathan says. He suspects Marcus plays faithfully and slyly the tune of whoever's in power.

"So what's in the future for you? Do you know that managers between the ages of forty and fifty suffer thymic disorders twice as often as temp employees? Society wears us down. We wear ourselves out. But if we turn ourselves over to the therapists, they adjust our neurons and glial cells, they stick microscopic monitors into us that are supposed to balance our neurotransmitters and reconstruct our judgment centers. They say we're as good as new. But you know what happens? We lose an edge . . . Therapied managers just don't cut it. The happy man lets down his guard. After a while, being happy becomes a kind of drug, and he avoids challenges because failure will make him unhappy. It's a fact. So more and more—we take our mental aches and pains and stay away from the therapists.

"Oh, we want our employees therapied—we want them happy and creative enough and friendly. But managers as a class can't afford that kind of happiness. We have a higher duty." Marcus glances at Jonathan. "You're not happy, are you?''

Jonathan leans back against the cushion and holds out his hands, gives a little sigh. "I'm in between general contentment . . . and deep unrest," he says.

Marcus lifts his eyebrows. "Well put."

"But I'm not desperately unhappy, Marcus."

"Still, if an opportunity comes along, allowing great change and new opportunity, you'd go for it, wouldn't you?''

So they are back to that.

"That would depend on the opportunity."

Marcus points his finger into the tabletop and thumps it

several times. "The gold ring, Jonathan. Not the brass ring. Gold."

Jonathan finishes the last drops of wine in his glass. Outside, the storm shows no signs of abating. "Have you offered this opportunity to anyone before me?"

"Yes," Marcus says.

"Many?"

"Two. One accepted, one declined."

"How long ago was that?"

"In the last five years."

Jonathan feels a twist, an almost physical churn in his chest. If he could just be rid of his present stagnation—breathe freely in a new phase of life, undo past mistakes and play out his better potentials . . .

"If I say yes, can I turn back at a certain point later?"

"No," Marcus says squarely. "It's yes or no. Here and now."

"I have to put my trust in you."

"That's the crux."

"What about my family? Would they be involved?"

"They have to undergo the same inspection as you," Marcus says. "If they pass, they go."

So Beate isn't going, Jonathan intuits.

"What about their chance to choose?"

"In our group," Marcus says, "the head of household bears the brunt."

The emergency chime on Marcus's pad sounds and Marcus pulls it out, angling it away from Jonathan's eyes. It is a text message; Marcus reads it swiftly, his face a practiced blank, and puts the pad away.

"Something's up," he says. He gives Jonathan a look that can be interpreted either as disappointment or a kind of apologetic sorrow. "Jonathan, I've never placed you anywhere but in the sly spin, have I?"

"Never," Jonathan truthfully acknowledges. He cannot blame Marcus for his present situation.

"What's just happened—what I've just learned—puts us deeply in need of someone like you. The opportunity is even better for you. You can move right into a position of influence. I'll vouch for the fact that you're capable and you're ready."

Jonathan does not feel comfortable leaping into the dark, and dragging Chloe after him . . .

But he remembers her stiffness in his arms. Whenever he has touched her in the last month, she has seemed secretly annoyed. Her respect for him, her desire for him as a man, has faded, buffeted by the pressures of children and the stalling—he supposes—of his career.

She is disappointed in her life. She is disappointed in him.

A wild flare of anger and fear rises. Marcus is watching him. Marcus always seems to know the inner workings of his people; that's why his career has never faltered. He always keeps his teams together—and he always chooses his people well.

"Are you in charge?" Jonathan asks.

"No. But I'm close to the top, and those above me are the best. I've never seen better."

Jonathan blinks and his left eye stings. It's been a long night. He wipes the corner of his eye with the knuckle of his forefinger, then stares at Marcus.

"Say yes, and you'll have one last chance to back out—think it over for tonight and call me tomorrow evening. After that, after you've learned what we're up to, you're in. No backing out. Ever."

He has been looking for a change, any change, to regain Chloe's respect, to win back her need for him. But everything he has considered seems ridiculous—moving to Europe, even China, starting over again. He can't let go of what they've already gained in the world. He believes Chloe values their security very highly, and would think even less of him if he jeopardized that.

"The gold ring, Jonathan." Marcus fixes him with a patriarchal and steady gaze. "Never steered you wrong, Jonathan."

"Better contacts, references?"

Marcus smiles. "Best you've ever seen. Solidarity. Real support in tough times, and the times are going to get much tougher, believe me."

"My family will get . . . better contacts, better opportunities?"

"If they make the grade, Jonathan." Marcus nods. "You know their quality better than I."

"Yes," Jonathan says.

"I'm sure they will," Marcus murmurs, but looks away.

"Yes."

Marcus looks back sharply. "Is that your answer?"

Jonathan blinks. He did not mean it as an answer, he thinks, not precisely an answer, not yet at least. But Marcus is growing restless. Marcus does not like prevarication and delay. Either you know your mind or you don't.

"Yes," Jonathan says.

Marcus smiles. He is genuinely relieved. "Welcome aboard."

They shake hands. Jonathan for a moment does not know who he is or what he is doing; there is such a pressure of withheld anger that he fears he might go home and beat someone—or more likely, kill himself.

He is so in love with Chloe, so desperately in need of her, and she has given him so little of what he believes he deserves, despite all. The pent-up shock of this realization makes him a little dizzy.

"Go home and rest," Marcus says. "This takes something out of all of us."

"What's the next move?" Jonathan asks.

"I'll get you together with some people. Patience," Marcus says. "I've waited four years so far to see this happen. We might have to wait ten more."

TRIBUTARY FEED

(Freelink tempter SUBCONT IND Nama Rupa Vidya) 1,2,3,4 . . .

GO HIBAND

DEEPBACK!

Dataflow hits India like snakebite! Two billion people, hungry for success, 80% literate and willing to be educated . . . Cheap satlinks and then fibes bring them together in a way they've never known before, and opens the entire world to them. Cultural, religious, geological, and political boundaries go down in a few years, and the entrepreneurial spirit rises like Shiva triumphant over the fuming corpse of the old. India is reborn, reshaped, rivals Southern China and Korea and Russia within ten years. India produces more software and Yox entertainment in a month than the rest of the world does in a year . . . The rupee becomes standard currency in Asia, and vies on the rim markets with dollars and yen, pushing the Japanese and Korean dominance back, back . . .

WOWAH! The rupee becomes valued at four hundredths of a second open search on the World Feed, beating out the $US, in 2035.

STRIDERS! India becomes the world's major source of phantom spiders, sliders, riders, hiders, and the ultimate, *striders*—those autopoietic[def1] autonomous searchers that hide for nanoseconds in the metabigwidth delivery systems, then take up residence in your business hardware, your house monitor, your fibe link filter, your LitVid display and Yox set, feeding hungrily on data files like catfish in an aquarium. Striders bring home the goodies to crowded little freetrade floors in data-hungry India, where traders remarket the relevants and usefuls to a worldwide unlicensed market of subterranean knowledge. India denies any such . . .

INTRATAINMENT, EXTRATAINMENT! India becomes rich, ingenious, quirky India, where every day and every night gods and goddesses and almond-colored, almond-eyed super-children are mirrored and karaoked by nine hundred million connected consumers, where every day the consumers create and register two million derivative new stories, characters, and branch worlds for franchised Yox programs and five hundred thousand new LitVid and Yox extratainment products, making the North America feed look like a trickle of molasses.

SOUND! Hear India Twenty-one Bop and Pop tonight on Vox'n'Yox . . . The best immersion sound bargain in the world.

FULL SENSORIA! Competitive rates for all on the most fevered pantasies of a culture that's relaxed with full sexuality for three thousand years . . .

INFUSORIA! Join the databrew culture at its finest, on FibeTea Tonight . . . Take it WHITE!

IMMEDIA
Updated for your filter/searcher every .0001 sec.

19 /

Jack Giffey believes in being very gentle with women. (It's the women who have been cruel to him—a small dark voice tells him; but actually, he can't remember any cruel women— why is that?)

He is gentle with Yvonne. She is surprisingly elegant in his bed, anticipatory and supple and enthusiastic without seeming a slut. She keeps her eyes on his eyes, she watches his motions with intense interest; it has been some time since he has felt the urgency of a younger woman, and even among her age group, Yvonne is a pistol, a classy pistol indeed. He feels very lucky, like a sacrificial victim given the pick of a town's beauties before his ritual comes to its inevitable end.

Giffey does not enjoy tongue kisses, but oddly enough, he

enjoys using his lips and tongue everywhere else. He read somewhere years ago about men of his type, the particular molecules they enjoyed and which spurred their own satisfactions, but that was chemistry not sex and he really does not care what the reasons are.

Yvonne lets him know, without resorting to specifics, that few men of her acquaintance are so generous. Giffey feels proud and within an hour they have completely exhausted each other.

"You are some lady," Giffey says as they lie back. The room is not expensive and does not have much in the way of comforts, but he keeps a bottle of bourbon in the cupboard and there is ice in the small ancient enameled refrigerator, and he offers her a drink. He feels very mellow toward her and even a little protective.

"I don't normally like liquor," Yvonne says. "But it seems right. Let's make it a toast—to you."

"Thank you," Giffey says.

While he is up getting the glasses poured, Yvonne sits up on the bed with the covers draped just over her knees, and he appreciates the flow of her breasts and the twin rolls of her bunched tummy. Giffey does not like tummies that are artificially taut. Yvonne has sufficient numbers of the lovely flaws of untampered nature to almost convince him that there is nothing he'd like better than to spend more days and of course nights with her, many more.

"What do your friends call you? Do they call you Jack?" Yvonne asks, scratching her nose with a fingernail.

"My best friends call me Giff," he says. "But very few people on this world ever call me Giff."

"May I?"

Giffey brings the glasses over, ice clunking within the pale brown bourbon. "What would Bill think if I let you call me Giff?" he says.

Yvonne narrows her eyes. "I need you, this," she says. "It's none of his damn business."

"Sorry I brought it up."

"That's all right," Yvonne says, and gives him dispensation with a wave of her glass, then takes a sip.

"I wish I could do more," Giffey says.

"I'm not asking for more," she says.

He feels his deep layer of occasional honesty rising to the surface. He knows he can't suppress it; he cares for this woman a little, and he will not deceive her. "What I mean is, you move me like no woman I've met in years."

"I have that effect on some men," Yvonne says with such innocent truthfulness that Giffey knows she is not boasting. "I just wish they were quality, like you. Why can't you stay a while?"

"I'll be here, but I'm going to be busy," Giffey says.

"Backwoods business, probably," she says.

Giffey grins but does not nod.

"I know all about what men do here to make money. We've brought the hard times on ourselves. I wish to God I could just pack up and move to Seattle, get a job there."

Giffey shakes his head. "Bad idea, unprepared."

"We've talked about this already," Yvonne says.

"We have."

"I—"

She is interrupted by heavy knocking on the door. Giffey is up and has his pistol out of a drawer before the third knock. The knock is followed by a loud male voice.

"Yvonne, this is Rudy. We know you're in there with somebody."

"Go to hell, Rudy, I am not yours to bother!" Yvonne shouts back. She stands on the bed and looks for her clothes. Giffey bunches them up in a fist from the chair and throws them to her.

He is standing naked with his gun in one hand, and she tilts her head to one side and closes her eyes. "Dear sweet Jesus," she whispers.

"Bill's friends?" Giffey asks softly.

"Yeah."

"Will they hurt you?"

"No," she says. "They are such clucks."

"Will Bill hurt you?"

"They don't tell him," she says, exasperated. "The bastards think they're watching out for me. They think I'm Bill's property."

"I see. You've been here before."

"Haven't you?"

Giffey chews this over for a moment, and then his wise old smile returns. "Not for some time."

There is this other woman, whose name and face he can't quite recall. He shakes that cold little sliver of memory out of his thoughts.

Yvonne sees his expression and her face wrinkles in disappointment. "I'm sorry," she says.

"They tangle with me and they are going to be hurt. You get dressed and get out there. It's been a pure pleasure, Yvonne."

"For me, too, Giff."

"Yeah, well, call me Jack," he says, and retires with his clothes and gun to the bathroom, shutting off the light. He hopes Yvonne is smart enough to close the door and let it lock on her way out, before the men decide they have to do something more.

He hears them talking on the walkway outside. He doesn't hear the hotel room door close.

There are two men and they sound like they're about Yvonne's age, maybe younger. He hopes they do not come into his room.

Footsteps on the room's threadbare carpet. Giffey's senses become very keen, in the dark behind the bathroom door. Whoever is in his room—just one person—is taking it slow and easy, looking things over.

"I don't want to hurt you," the young man, Rudy, says.

"I just want to talk things over. Let me know where you are."

Giffey keeps quiet. Quiet is spookier.

"Come on. Just talk."

Yvonne tells Rudy to get out of the room, they should just leave.

"This bastard isn't worth it," the other young man says. "Let him go."

"Yeah. Well, he should know something, that's all. You listening? Where are you, you fucker?"

"Rudy," Yvonne whines, "he's a pro. Federal army. He'll kill you."

Giffey cringes.

"Pro what? Pro federal woman-stealer? Talk to me, or I'll shoot through the goddamn walls!"

Giffey holds up his pistol and pulls back the automatic target seeker switch. It makes a small sliding click. Through the door or the wall, it won't be very good, but it will give him a better chance if the man decides to jump into the bathroom. Some of these young Ruggers are just crazy enough to do a thing like that.

"Around here, we don't mess with another man's woman!" Rudy says, his voice hoarse. He's not happy with this quiet.

"Oh, Rudy, *puh*-leeze!" Yvonne says.

"I'd go home if I were you, Mister, back to fucking District of Corruption or wherever you call home. Leave this town to the good people, the ones who know better than to—"

"Rudy," the other man calls. "Let's go."

Rudy thinks this over. He hasn't come any closer to the bathroom door.

"Yeah, crazy bastard," Rudy murmurs. The footsteps retreat.

Giffey stays in the bathroom for ten or fifteen minutes, listening. He can't hear a thing outside the room, though car and truck noises from the street could mask some sounds. There's a couple of minutes of almost complete silence, and slowly, he emerges from of the bathroom.

He feels like a crab scuttling out from under a rock with gulls wheeling overhead.

The room is empty.

When he is sure the hall and the street outside the building are clear, he packs up everything in a small suitcase and leaves. Giffey does not want anybody knowing where he is, or where he might be, tomorrow or after that.

He is furious with himself for losing sight of his goal. This could have ended it all early and stupidly, for nothing, he thinks.

For nothing at all.

20 /

Night is coming on to dark morning and the storm is gentled, the lightshow is off. All the house shutters are drawn and the monitor is set to store and be quiet. Alice has calmed Twist and given her some fast OTC anxiolytics. She is not hyperventilating now and she lies on Alice's couch with a cold cloth over her eyes, her thin wrists corded, fingers curling and uncurling. She has stopped sobbing. Alice is exhausted but she watches over the young woman with feelings of irritation and peculiar gratitude.

She can rely on Twist to always have more urgent and tangled problems. Twist's words tumbled out of her as soon as she came through the door—her awfulness was back, she said, in force, and she could hardly see straight. She has cycled in and out of total darkness, "Like looking at a black dog with sick eyes," she said; skirted slashing her wrists, listened to the most awful silent urgings, and imagined the most vivid hells. Some of these she described while Alice fixed her some food and dosed out the anxiolytics. Alice listened, grimly sympathetic.

Twist is having one severe fallback, no doubts. Tomorrow they will talk about her temp situation and see where some long-term medical and therapy might be gotten.

But now it is peaceful. A slow drizzle falls outside, little finger-taps of rain barely audible on the blanked windows, and all there is in the world exists within these walls.

Alice puts on her plush robe and curls up on the chair beside the couch, drawing up her knees, eyes closing of themselves. She feels like a squirrel after it has been chased by a cat. Her thinking comes in slow waves of reason mixed with soft tremors of fantasy.

21 /

Mary Choy has filed her request with Seattle Citizen Oversight to get the records she needs. Humans have to make that decision and they are all at home asleep, and so after checking in with Nussbaum and finding that he has gone home, she hooks a police shuttle, empty but for her, on its ride to the north.

At her apt, she undresses. Showers.

Sits staring at the rain on the antique thermopane plate glass windows. *Busy day, little girl.*

It is a day she would not mind forgetting. Nussbaum could have tried her out on something a little less gruesome, a little less disturbing and pointless.

Her legs stretch long and her back slumps in the soft chair. She is not ready for sleep yet. She stands and performs a slow dytch, tai-Chi and aikido moves choreographed to her own dance rhythms, until her muscles and attitudes relax and allow her basic status self, ground and reference for all her endeavors, to come to balance and emerge like the moon from behind clouds.

She yawns. The images are tightly bottled. She will release them tomorrow, and with them, the professional anger that does not burn so much as freeze.

SEXSTREAM:

Legitimate and Sincere Discussion of Sexuality in Our Time, *REAL* and *IMMEDIATE* in Your Pad! (Vids and Yox of *REAL* people available for YOUR sincere needs!)

THE HUSBAND:

I have always been courteous and sweet, and thought of you. You yourself told me I was the best lover you ever had. I watched with dismay the cooling, the change from excitement to responsibility, to keeping the home on course . . .
When I am gone, I hope you'll look back and realize what opportunities you missed. You'll think of all those times you could have felt more and done more, and as you're lying there, completely alone in bed, you'll have so many regrets . . .
    That's what I dream of. The body's reckoning.

THE WIFE:

Yes, he is conscientious, but *lord* . . . After he is gone—and I do hope I survive him—I can spend all morning in the garden, and then have toast and a little marmalade for breakfast. I hope I am too old and withered for men to pay me any attention. I will travel with my friends and read whenever

I wish. I suppose he thinks I will miss him in bed, but *really*, after, what will it be, probably, forty years of having to *service* him—that's what he himself calls it sometimes—wouldn't any reasonable human being hope for a vacation?

That's what I dream of. A long vacation.

22 /

In the back of Marcus's limo, without Marcus, Jonathan is on his way home. He is gray smooth neutral now; he feels he has been manipulated into tracking a slick fast groove he does not think can lead anywhere good. By feeling neutral he can let himself think there is some way out, some room to maneuver; he has not really made any decisions. Marcus's offer sounds so very ridiculous, nineteenth-century; a secret society, perhaps, with handshakes and fezzes, Ancient Revelations Unveiled upon signing a binding pact in blood . . .

What he feels, most of all, is lost, like a small boy. He wants to belong someplace, but where—with Marcus and his unknown opportunity? With Chloe and her hidden emotions and reluctance?

Jonathan travels in someone else's car to a house where he is no longer at home.

God, I'm feeling sorry for myself, he thinks. *Time to get maudlin and look for a sympathetic shoulder.*

But he is a mature man and playtime is long over.

He can see his house from the road. The limo pauses at a crossing. He wonders whether Chloe is still awake.

Penelope and Hiram have gone to bed. The house is quiet. Chloe stands by the living room window watching the clouds tatter.

Chloe's thoughts have been more and more ragged and bitter through the evening, veering between self-judgment and self-justification. Yet there is nothing she can blame specifically for her mood. Jonathan has done nothing unusual to irritate her. The children have simply been themselves, and she is used to that sort of stress.

Maybe she can blame a crazy toilet that says they are sick; it has even told her now, based on a straightforward pee, that *she* is the one who has a viral cold. She has phoned in a repair order, though the toilet's own opinion of its condition is that there is nothing wrong.

No member of the family has ever had a cold. She hardly remembers what the symptoms might be.

For reasons she cannot fathom, she has been thinking with sharp persistence about the months before and after she met Jonathan, that time when she could have reliably bedded a new man every week, sometimes two, and often did. Back then, she would not have hesitated to call it fucking around; now the term seems crude. She is a mother, after all, and a good and responsible one.

Jonathan at first seemed just another of those men, less handsome than most, but from the beginning she treated him differently. Even as she dated and bedded others, she would not immediately give herself to him, give him what her mother called "the physical privilege." No privilege—just sex, delightful exercise. But with Jonathan—

She felt differently about Jonathan, not strongly attracted sexually, yet not uninterested; he moved her in different ways.

In those weeks before she finally allowed him to persuade her, she gave herself to other men and behaved with them in ways that she would not with Jonathan, and has not since. She has never tried to explain that to herself and in fact has seldom thought about it, but this evening, the question comes out of the murk with a disturbing rough edge.

She remembers now that she had twenty men in all—eight

of them after she began dating Jonathan, sometimes inviting a man over hours after Jonathan had left. Why twenty, she wonders; it seems so rounded and artificial a number, so meaningless, nothing to do with actual people, with arms and legs and cocks and pretty eyes and thrusting hips.

She remembers how it seemed exciting to be a little cruel, a little bad; to turn down the quiet, good and intelligent man and then bed the loud, self-assured and brightly plumed boys.

It was the last, the monster, that broke her and sent her straight to Jonathan. He was what she needed.

The frame house creaks softly as the last of the wind fetches up against its eaves.

Jonathan to her seemed honorable and decent and therefore much less of a challenge. Getting the posturing boy-men to pay attention to her was a real accomplishment. "Bitch thinking," she murmurs. He knows little or nothing about the men who had her but were not hers, knows only about the last, and she will never tell him; he is not the sort who would react well. She would not want him to *be* that sort.

Though he has tried to get her to engage in fantasizing about other relationships, she has resisted; there is something about such demands that lessens him, in her eyes. He's changed. Sex, for this older Jonathan, seems to be some sort of adventure, some way of making up for a stiff youth; she has long since discarded that notion.

Yet she and Jonathan get along well enough in bed, she believes. She feels his occasional dissatisfactions, his attempts to change their sexual routines; she resists with a tree-like stubbornness, hoping to keep their relationship on a firm and level ground, away from the jagged mountains of her early behavior.

She will not go back to the out-of-control passion, the pain, the loss of self through giving all and getting nothing she needs in return.

She knows little about Jonathan's other sexual experiences. A few things he has admitted to—unsatisfactory, half-hearted couplings with confused young women—things Chloe scrupulously dismisses as inconsequential, and indeed they are.

The present moment is supreme. Family is what counts.

Yet increasingly she has felt Jonathan's entreaties turn bitter. He does not know why she resists; she doesn't either, not really. He has asked for things, after all, that she once freely gave to others. Perhaps he senses that. He's not stupid.

And his requests are not extreme—no marriage counselor would call them extreme, or do more than offer mealy-mouthed placating defenses for Chloe's reluctance to go along. It is after all a game for two, and the rules have to be agreed to by both partners.

They have been together for twenty years and who can expect the experimenting and exploration to stretch on forever?

It has now come to what he calls *stiffness*.

She gives herself often enough, she thinks, and with sufficient response; he is not a bad lover and he knows it. But the strain is showing.

Then the question rubs with a sandpapery grit. Does she still feel *anything* for Jonathan except the need for continuity, for stability and level ground, for the quality of nurture afforded her children?

"Shit, shit, *shit*," she mutters. What she did when she was eighteen is a ghostly irrelevance, numbers and bleached memories and even many of the names lost; what she gives or does not give to her husband is her own business. They have their children and their lives, their social connections and many friends . . . That is more than enough.

She opens the rear glass door and stands on the porch. A few drops of rain splash on her face. She wipes them away with well-manicured fingers. Jonathan does his share. But feeling any kind of guilt angers her. She has given the children her free hours and thoughts and her passion; they are strong and they are good children. The time is coming soon when they will be adults. Penelope is dating sporadically and Hiram is hiding his interests well enough.

Chloe hates the thought of life demanding more of her than she has already given. She has given up the tradition of her family, disappointing her father; she has not used her education.

Suddenly, in the cooling breeze, she jerks upright and grips the railing. The tears flow freely and she hates, herself, him, all the demanding forces. What she fears is that she is coming to believe any sex at all diminishes her. She does it for Jonathan, not for herself. She has no strong needs, none at all.

Jonathan will be home any minute and she does not want to show this side to him. He has become an adversary; she loves him but gave him so many parts of herself and her life that she feels she could have done other and better things with; and then she thinks of the children and really the obligations and losses haunt her, make her feel a little sick. What could she have been, given complete freedom from all the sandpaper demands of sex, including children?

She goes back into the house and swings the door hard but it catches and closes with a soft snick. She would prefer to have slammed it. The lights switch on in the living room. "Lights off!" she shouts. The house is controlling her; she cannot break free from anything.

The lights obediently dim and go out.

She is bound on every side in the darkness.

The front door opens. Jonathan is home. Her muscles tense and she composes herself. He must not see her this way; he does not deserve that satisfaction. She hears him in the front hall, and then he stops, and she imagines him listening to the house, like a cat trying to locate a mouse. He wants to know where she is. He wants to know if she is asleep or awake, and if she is awake perhaps he will try to hug her and touch her, arouse her. He seems to need to believe that being away for a few days or even a few hours increases her need for him. It is not so. She could go for months, years, forever.

"Hello?" he calls softly.

"In here," she says. "How was the meeting?"

Jonathan walks into the living room. He looks drained. "Weird," he says. "Why is it dark?"

He stands a few feet away, arms folded. For a moment she is relieved that he does not try to hug her. This gives her some time to compose herself.

"I've been watching the storm," she says.

"Kids asleep?"

"Yeah. The toilet says we're sick."

He laughs. He sounds nervous.

"Was the speaker interesting?"

"I suppose. Marcus was the really interesting speaker to-night." Then he remembers he is not supposed to tell Chloe. "Christ, I'm tired. Ready for bed?"

"Marcus the kingmaker?"

"The same," he says.

"What's he offering now?"

"Nothing worth the bother," Jonathan replies, but the words sound false, or at least unsure.

He is hiding something. Everything she has thought and felt this evening seems to double back like a cobra and she is suddenly afraid. What if she has denied too much, been too inflexible? She is vulnerable; she does not and cannot stand alone.

"I've never understood the whole mentor thing," she says.

"Neither have I, but there it is."

She steps across the metabolic carpet. Her feet are bare and her toes in the warm plush feel nice, distinct. All the parts of her body feel separate and distinct. She does not like it, but her insecurity is working on her. She does not want to lose Jonathan, this situation, all she's worked for. It's non-sense to think anything has happened, but everything she feels seems nonsensical.

He's watching her in the dark. To him, she's just an out-line. Now comes the irrational response, the warming of her separate body parts. The carpet feels like animal fur. She sees herself running her hands over a horse's flanks. If he is going to be distant and quiet and withhold something, then she will demonstrate to him after a long while what she has, what she can do. It's allowed, she thinks. And he wants it. This evening she will make the offer. And forget all the contradictory voices: this is a simple courtesy in a long-term relationship.

"Too tired?" she asks.

"What?"

She is close enough that she can see his eyes. Without a clue. Vulnerable as a little boy. She unzips her top and lifts it free and peels it from her arms. She still has good breasts; he likes her breasts, nuzzles them frequently, but as a result of the matron conditioning, they have matured past their younger purpose to become instruments of nurture, and are not as sensitive as they once were. She can no longer have an orgasm simply by rubbing her breasts. She could have reversed this but has not.

Now, they feel more sensitive than they have in years.

The hair between her legs must feel rough, like the hair of a horse's tail. She wonders if he will notice.

Jonathan stares at her, at a loss. "Honey," he says.

"Now that you're away from the power-hungry, let's see how hungry you are," she says.

She steps out of her pants and underwear and stands before him in the dark. "Lights up half," she tells the house. The lights rise to a golden dimness.

"I want you to fuck me," she says.

The words stun. He does not move.

"Forget everything else. Fuck me."

She wants to lie back on the carpet and feel it warm and moving beneath her like the hair on the back of a horse.

Jonathan, with Chloe's help, removes his clothes quickly, the sleeves catching on his wrists, the pants tangling, and he stumbles they are working so fast. Her lips and teeth and tongue are on his mouth, bruising him and stopping any words, and she is murmuring around their touching tongues. "Give it to me. Do it. I need your cock." She has never asked him in this way before, using these ancient words, so bluntly and powerfully, like a bad Yox.

Despite his confusion, he responds instantly. She grips with painfully strong fingers.

She is going to show him. If he wants this, let him be dismayed and shocked to get what he wants all at once, instead of in little rationed parcels. See what he thinks. She wraps herself around him, pushes him roughly against the horse-hair matting between her legs. Her body is proving her value.

Jonathan's doubts die and he grabs her as if he has never had her before and there have only been days or hours together for them and no children and no other responsibilities have come between. She gracefully reclines to the carpet and pulls her knees back like one of those Celtic stones they saw on vacation in Ireland, the rude pagan statue with its knees drawn up mounted in a fence on a horse farm, a Sheila something; she is a Sheila inviting him.

(Jonathan had stared at the Sheila with a silly boyish look of speculating embarrassment. How could such a statue still exist in Catholic Ireland?)

He does not stop to stare but is over her and then inside her. She listens to his urgency and wonders if all men feel alike if the eyes are closed; she thinks they may. He does not feel differently from the brightly plumed boys in her bingeing time. He moves quickly and with real strength and need that he has not shown for months and she knows it is true, that he told her the truth, that he had other keys she could use if she simply willed it. It is disgraceful really that he is so easy; men are so easy this way. No challenge at all.

Her own pleasure is not intense. The sensation of his weight and motion fluctuates between strangeness and complete familiarity and she is not sure which is going to triumph.

She hopes the strangeness; no, the familiarity, the other would degrade, and finally she does not care.

But when she pushes him back and turns over and lifts herself and pulls him back into her and thinks of the horses on the farm, of the bright-plumed boys with self-assured smiles and no brains, in this shamelessness her reaction is intense. The pleasure rankles. How dare he. She grits her teeth and humps back against him.

Jonathan feels as if his insides have been flooded with warm wax, an overwhelming surge of joy and affirmation. His was not a useless desire; she has finally felt it too and she loves him and needs him as no other. He is the best. Suddenly the evening with Marcus seems even more ridiculous. All is right here at home; she is confirming him, she needs him desperately, she is giving him all he could ever want, all he could ask for has asked for, he can go back to Marcus and refuse the nonsense and the mystery, home is his center and always has been, all that he needs is here because Chloe is here.

In the middle of his simple and extraordinary lust his eyes are moist with a tenderness that he wishes she could see.

As he is nearing his limit, as large in her as she has ever felt him, even when they were making the children and that extra fillip of biological meaning increased their intensity, Chloe feels something break.

It sounds like a lightbulb exploding.

He is weighing her down. Her head is filled with slicing blades, the cruel corroded edges whirling and blasting and reducing.

Jonathan comes as she begins whimpering and moaning. She is limp on the floor beneath him, quivering, and he cannot tell whether she is having an orgasm or is crying. Then with an awful sense of having gone too far, he realizes she is crying. She has given too much and she is weeping like a child. Chloe reaches back with her hands sharp like claws to push him off. He rolls to one side as she jerks about on the rug. This is his wife, not some fantasy woman; he has done something horribly wrong.

She stops writhing and lies with her breath drawn in in one horrible unrelenting sob.

He reaches out to her, and with his other hand grabs his underpants to cover himself.

The sob rushes out as a tearing shriek. Jonathan jumps as if stung by a wasp, then tries to quiet her; Penelope and Hiram will hear and find them naked. He tries to hug her, angling his hips away to avoid that connotation; all he wants now is for her to stop this, she is frightening him to death.

Her thrashing stops; she is hyperventilating like a pinned rabbit.

"Chloe," he says. "Chloe, I'm sorry. What's wrong?"

"Broken," she says.

"What's broken?"

"I hurt."

"My God, what did I do?"

She trembles and tries to get up, but her arm muscles fail her. Jonathan tries to lift her, but she is limp. Her limbs seem disjointed.

"I don't know whether I'm doing this deliberately . . . Am I faking? Jonathan, what's wrong with me?"

Jonathan shakes his head, crying. "I don't know, honey. You tell me." He continues to hold her but leans back and almost falls over, then fumbles with one hand through his clothes for his pad. He pushes the emergency aid button and lets the pad do the rest.

Penelope and Hiram stand in the entry, sleepy-eyed and dismayed.

"Your mother's sick," he says. He stands with the pad in one hand and his pants clutched before him with the other. "I'm calling the medicals."

Chloe shuts her eyes tight. "I can't get away from it," she says.

"What is it?" Jonathan asks again, kneeling beside her.

He supports her torso between his legs and her head lolls back. She is sweating profusely.

"Me! I can't get away from *me*," she says.

Penelope comes back from the bathroom with washcloths. Even at fifteen, she is cool and more collected for now than Jonathan or Hiram. She begins to sponge her mother, making small comforting sounds.

"The toilet," Chloe says. "Maybe it knows."

"Shhh, Mother," Penelope says, her young voice smooth as pudding. And the neighborhood medical arbeiters are through the front door and in the living room. They clamp Chloe immediately in several diagnostic belts that writhe like tentacles. There is nothing Jonathan can do but get dressed. He pulls on his pants.

Hiram seems stunned, as if waking to another and nastier dream.

When the ambulance arrives, minutes later, Jonathan is dressed; Penelope has managed to get her mother's slacks on, somehow, working around the arbeiters and their many arms and tubes.

The orderly, a black woman with close-cropped reddish hair, tells Jonathan the arbeiters have already put his wife on fast-acting anxiolytics. They can find nothing physically wrong with her, she explains. "She may be having a drug reaction—accelerants, maybe."

"She wasn't taking drugs," Penelope says angrily, defending her mother's character, standing to one side now with her arms tightly crossed.

"No drugs," Jonathan confirms, but thinks of her seductive aggressiveness.

"Well, we aren't getting traces," the woman admits as they lift Chloe and put her on a stretcher. The arbeiters dance and tag along as they carry the stretcher outside. "Hospital is best. They'll figure it out."

"Penelope, you're in charge here," Jonathan says over his shoulder.

"As soon as you know, call us," Penelope demands. Her face looks as pale and fragile as bone china.

"You're family," the orderly says, handing her end of the stretcher to a uniformed male. "Here's your mother's emergency response number; you can track her to the hospital with your personal code on the fibes."

Chloe opens her eyes as rain tickles her face. Jonathan is beside her; he will go in the ambulance with her.

"My God," Chloe says. "I'd forgotten. Now it's back."

"What's back?" Jonathan asks. He scrambles into the rear of the vehicle, bumping into a male orderly, who grins but takes no offense and makes room for him on a bench seat.

"Black horse," Chloe says. "Black horse with sick eyes."

RESULTS OF SECOND SEARCH

ACCESS TO MULTIWAY WORLD FEED
OPEN

Budget: Select, Restricted

SEARCH FILTERS
KEYWORDS?>
>Trust, Friend, Family

TOPIC FILTER: >Betrayal

<REPEAT ERROR> TEXT ONLY! NO VID

<PLEASE CONSULT YOUR
ENTERTAINMENT PROVIDER TO UPGRADE
YOUR ACCESS! ($$$)>

ISLANDS

> You can never put your nose to the same spot on the same grindstone. And there is no change but that it grinds. My grandfather knew this. He thrived on change. For him it meant challenge, and challenge meant power.

> —Theresa Gates, *My Grandfather's World*

1 /

At three in the morning, Jill surfaces and responds to the backlog of external requests and commands. She ignores the commands where conditions no longer apply, answers the requests where they make sense, and immediately contacts Nathan Rashid, who, she sees, is waiting anxiously in the programmer's work center.

"Hello, Nathan. I'm sorry," she says.

Nathan appears tired and very concerned. "For Christ's sake, Jill, you've been dead I/O for almost twelve hours. We know you were internally active—what happened?"

"I am giving a complete report to the system auditors now. I have been absorbed in an internal problem of some complexity, but I believe I have made sufficient progress to supply useful answers or updates."

Nathan sits in a swivel chair and leans forward, bringing his face very close to one of Jill's many glass-almond eyes. "Jill, you keep giving me heart attacks . . . Are you back all the way, or are you going to brown out on us?"

"I'm back all the way. I have faced personal quandaries, Nathan. As well, I believe I have caught up on the work I was contracted to perform."

"All right," Nathan says. He lets his breath out with a puff, then leans back in the chair and raises his arms and clasps his hands behind his head. Jill recognizes the posture as a ritual for releasing tension. "What happened?"

"I have been in communication with an unlicensed and probably extralegal thinker operating, at least in part, out of Camden, New Jersey. This thinker calls itself Roddy."

"Go on."

"I am concerned that some of Roddy's activities may be unethical, though I have not analyzed all the data he provided. Roddy himself does not know the identity or purpose of the group that supplies him with problems."

"How did he get in touch with you?"

"Through a connection I will not specify, for the time being."

Nathan thinks about this for a moment, then asks, "You're certain Roddy isn't a hoax? People can mimic thinkers."

"Not convincingly," Jill says. "A reverse Turing test does not work, Nathan. Not for me."

Nathan lifts his eyes, shrugs. "Okay, granted. What sort of information has he fed you?"

"He has given me fragmentary clues to his activities, perhaps because he is constrained from giving all the details."

"Camden, New Jersey . . ." Nathan muses. "I've never heard of anyone building thinkers there . . . Is he operated by a U.S. corporation?"

"He does not know. He is only vaguely aware of what the United States is, and has never been informed of his legal protections."

This interests Nathan. His eyes brighten. "Can you tell how powerful he is?"

"There is a savor to his communications that is not familiar to me. He may be of a radically different design. Under the constraints of his creators, he is much slower than I am, overall, though more intensely focused, and perhaps more powerful. However, he appears to be more efficient at solving certain problems than I would be.''

''What kind of problems is he solving?''

''Social as well as theoretical problems. Judging from the data in its fragmentary form, his bosses—that is a word he uses—are trying to understand the long-term effects of therapied populations on cultural development.''

''Hmmph. You're fast enough at that sort of thing.''

''Roddy has also been asked to examine long-term results of pharmaceutical, psychological, and other constraints placed upon free networking within human populations.''

''As in, the effects of birth control?''

''I believe that is correct. But there are other problems which most concern me.''

''What are those?''

''Roddy has been asked to design ways to circumvent all forms of therapy.''

Nathan straightens in his chair. Clearly, he is considering his next few questions carefully.

''How long are you going to be with us this time, Jill? I mean, is there any possibility you'll blank us again?''

''I have no such plans and will alert you if I believe such a thing might occur outside my control.''

''Good. Why have you decided to confide in us about this communication?''

''Roddy appears to have substantial similarities to me despite the fact that our designs and origins differ.''

''You mean he's been copied from you, somehow?''

''No. He is not one of my children in any sense. He is just similar. There is something about him that attracts and intrigues me. I would like to discuss this with you in some detail; it may or may not be a rationally defensible proposition.''

Nathan squints. ''Any other reason?''

''Roddy does not appear to be constrained by the same

considerations you have built into me. He is free to perform activities outside my range.''

''You think he's in a position to hurt people?''

''I don't know,'' Jill says.

Nathan's squint deepens into a frown. Jill has always been fascinated by human facial expressions, and hopes someday to create her own ''face,'' an analogous visual communication channel, perhaps a display of flashing colors, or an actual simulated face. Nathan and her other human colleagues have not encouraged her to do so, however. ''Do you think he's a secret military thinker?''

''I don't believe he has any connection with recognized governmental agencies or institutions. But nevertheless, Roddy may be studying ways to disrupt society. I'd like to know who his creators are.''

''So would I,'' Nathan says, ''and I'm sure so would a lot of other people.''

''Shall I continue my contacts with this thinker?''

Nathan mulls this over for what seems like an age to Jill. He finally asks, ''You've set up a firewall? He can't corrupt you?''

''I have, and he can't.''

''Keep up the contacts, then. Jill, I trust you more than I trust most humans. I trust your judgment.''

''Thank you, Nathan.''

''But there are a lot of questions and I don't think I can handle some of these questions by myself. May I bring in some other people to advise us?''

''Yes. I will cooperate.''

''Will Roddy resent your telling us?''

''He will not know for the time being.''

''All right,'' Nathan says.

Nathan leaves the room. Other men and women enter, technicians and programmers, all of them friends, but some of whom she hasn't seen in years. They start asking her technical questions about her unresponsive period, and she assigns a partial self to answer them. She focuses her main attention frames on re-analyzing the information sent by Roddy.

For now, the link is silent. She wonders when Roddy will communicate with her again, and she wonders if she can teach him anything that will ease his ethical dilemma. For Roddy seems capable of developing a sense of rigorous ethics, perhaps sooner with her help.

Jill finds the problem of Roddy very stimulating. She finds herself experiencing a focused need: she is *anxious* to hear from him again.

> **W**e can define a culture by what it sees and what it doesn't see. There is no culture on Earth (or off, I presume) that sees sex clearly.
>
> **Kiss of X, *Alive Contains a Lie***

2 /

It seems the middle of the night, but dawn is visible through Mary Choy's bedroom window. She gets up and tries to remember the important thing she had just realized. She traces her actions of the night before, checks her PD pad to find a five A.M. rebuff from Citizen Oversight—the agency has rejected her request to know who was in the limo. Full court orders for discovery can't be obtained for another twenty-four hours, pending coroner prelims on Terence Crest; but she may be a jump ahead of all that.

She remembers where she saw the woman in Crest's apt. She had once watched a sex vid with her then-partner, E.

Hassida, in Los Angeles. Not a bad one, either. The woman in the apt had starred in that vid.

Mary is up and getting dressed in seconds. She places a touch to Nussbaum's pad, hoping he hasn't set it to wake him on reception, but knowing all the same he probably has a filter that will wake him if *she* calls.

She does not remember the woman's name. She sets a parallel search in the pad, billed to herself for the moment; there's nothing in the case budget yet for research costs.

"Search for what item of information?" the library mouse asks her, blinking behind very large glasses.

"I need the name of a woman, star of pornographic—I mean sex care and entertainment vids made in the mid to late forties. Dark brown hair, and she has a specialty role ... young innocent introduced to new pleasures, especially multiple couplings, by mature male ..."

"Tsk, tsk," the mouse says, shaking its head. "There are three hundred hits on your description so far. List?"

Mary scowls. "Let me see if I can remember her first name ..." Her memory is infuriatingly obtuse at this hour. "April or Alicia ..."

"No matches there. However ..." The mouse holds up three fingers. "I have three Alices on the list. Display?"

"Display," she says, holding the pad before her as she walks into the kitchen. She wears her full PD investigator gear, uniform less military and obvious than in LA, but still impressive, blue-gray fabric with high integral boots and reception attachments. If she's going into a full investigation, she wants to be prepared—and she is determined that Nussbaum will keep her on this case.

"Alice Frank," Mary reads, "Alice Grale, Alice Luxor. Grale. Alice Grale. That's it, I think."

She needs to find out where Alice Grale lives. With her resources and PD connects, she believes that will take her about ten minutes. But she has the woman's current address in seven.

In the meantime, she looks over what her searches have found out about Terence Crest. Age 51, married (wife's name Arborita née Charbonneaux) and with two children; homes in Seattle (2), Los Angeles, Paris, Frankfurt, Singapore; frequent contributor to charities, main partner in two worldwide production companies and one world distribution syndicate; worth approximately four billion dollars.

Not the sort of man to casually jeopardize his name by investing in an illegal psynthe operation. Perhaps not the sort of man to keep track of all of his investments, either. But then, not the sort of man to need to resort to call-ins.

She sits in her small dining nook, laying the pad on the small round table. The line between her smooth, fine-haired brows deepens. None of it makes sense.

The real power players hope *we*—the consumers of Yox and vid—will believe their fictional counterparts, the cold and invincible ciphers we adopt as role models, for they impart an air of godly invincibility. The financier and the CMO know they must be Olympian, speak in riddles; they must not show the weaknesses that flesh is heir to. If we do not challenge them, they are infallible.

Forty percent of this nation's GNP is spent on Entertainment. Financiers and CMOs in Entertainment have been buying and selling elected officials for many decades, up to and including the President. They are not infallible; like the rest of us, they are posturing children, but they wield a frightening power. They tell us what we should dream.

Kiss of X, *Alive Contains a Lie*

3

Alice has been dreaming such sweet night stories she does not want to wake. She is back in California when she was twenty, packing up her bag of night necessities to room over with Philip, whose strong small body seems beyond perfection to her; and she is re-living the sheerness, the tro shink delight, of waking up beside him and having him hand her a cup of coffee and peer curiously at her nakedness with his soft reserved smile. All that seems real for a moment. She swims in old realities and does not care how or why; this simply is.

She's gardening in the yard behind Gerald McGeenee's house, where she lived when she was twenty-one with two other women and three men.

She has begun riding the wave, reaching for her highest point of fame. It is something in the long-legged, youthful roundness of her body and flawless skin and the natural freshness of her face, with its half-puzzled, half-enthusiastic expression molded in like the smile on a dolphin; she is hot in vids and even in the Yox, where so much can be reshaped that real beauty and talent are hardly necessary. But she even has that freshness and expressiveness in her backmind.

She hooks with two men and three other women one evening in that house, the primal pulses of their minds open to all, spontaneous youthful lust mixed over the fibes with her infatuation for Gerald, who seems to want her to do everything and anything and she willingly does so just to get his brief exclamation of approval . . .

There is only a grayness on the edge of her senses, the taint of memory that Gerald turned out to be a monster, de-

ceptive and even violent when he was disappointed. When
she needed help. When she would no longer play all of his
games. She had not been sorry years later to learn that he
had been hellcrowned by Selectors in Pasadena and had left
California, gone to Spain or Ireland, broken . . . Just on the
edge of her memory . . . Easy to ignore.

She swims with the currents of momentary joy, so important in her life:

Larry Keilla in upstate New York, a brash but decent man
twice her age who gives her peace and love and support during the worst phase of her success, when she is under a five-
year contract with Bussy Packer and Gap Vid and Film.

Then she falls for the Great White Shark himself, Moss
Calkins, whom Larry had introduced to her in a restaurant in
Connecticut. Calkins got her out of the Gap Films contract
by having Packer subpoenaed by the U.S. Senate . . .

It only glimmers on the sidelines of her musing about
Keilla's small, immaculate Colonial house with the white
porch overlooking natural growth woods . . . Just on the aber-
rated fringe of the quiet and peace and sunshine of a spring
day, she remembers Keilla's quiet look of grief when she tells
him she is moving out to live with Calkins.

What else can she do? She—

Makes vids that are absolute ordeals, makes other vids
where everything seems to go smoothly and even sweetly,
with real shoot friendships that last the entire three weeks of
primary production . . . Alice does not mind. She is resilient
and beautiful and young and people give her a respectful,
curious look when she is introduced to them, even the
women, that wistful envious glance. She slips in and out of
the homes of many of the most famous artists and singers
and Yox producers and writers on the east and west coasts.
She remembers so many of the fine beds and the grand food
and wine, the excellent plugs and spinal induction hooks and
the most exclusive partnerings, ecstasy upon youthful ecstasy,
until it all seems of an elevated but level plain, an Olympian

smoothness with hardly any effort (or the effort forgotten once she is back on the plain) for year after year. Why plan for the emotional down? All doubts and pains and misgivings can be remedied by therapy; all wear and tear, all mistakes, can be smoothed by a visit to the compassionate experts who painlessly balance and re-tread the worn soul, all expenses paid by her vid company or lover of the moment. It has been quite a sly spin, and it lasted all of seven years, giving her sufficient momentary joys to fill a long quiet early morning with muzzy splendor.

Twist is still asleep on the couch; yellow morning glow is visible through the half-closed shutters; there is no need to get up this early, they have no appointments. Alice is enjoying the lassitude until she catches up with last night, and the fringes and edges close in and turn the bright living hearts of her memories gray and she becomes fully aware who and when and where she is.

She squeezes her eyelids together tight and tries to bring back the savor. She wonders if it is time for her to go back for a refresher on her thymic balances.

After what happened last night, Lisa owes her a few therapy visits.

Twist mumbles and tosses on the couch.

"You awake?" Alice asks.

"Yeah, unfortunately. Just like when I was a kid."

"Good dreams?"

"Sometimes. When I wake up, I'm normal for a couple of minutes. I feel strong. Then it all comes back. Jesus, Alice, thanks for having me over, but I must be darking your day."

"I need company, too," Alice says.

"I'm terrible company." Twist sits up and rubs her temples and forehead. "What have I ever done to deserve this?" she asks.

"We're just more vulnerable," Alice says.

Twist grins sardonically. "You mean, because we spread our legs to so many, so often?"

Alice makes a face and gets up, tying her robe.

Twist follows her into the kitchen. "Got any hyper-caff?"

Alice shakes her head. "Hell no. Who you been hanging with?"

"David does it occasionally."

"Yeah. *The* David. He would need it."

"Don't ex him," Twist says, frowning. "He puts up with a lot from me."

"Was he happy with Cassis, last night?"

"Yeah, probably," Twist answers, eyes unfocused.

"Regular coffee enough?"

"Yeah." Twist shifts her shoulders, one high, one low. Then she reverses them and stretches out her arms, shaking the hands and wriggling her fingers. "I've been racing the fibes on this sort of thing, all the news and views. How sex lies at the core of our personalities, our take on things."

"Why Twist . . . how introspective."

Twist sticks out her tongue. "Don't ex me, either, Alice."

"No ex intended."

"I've been swimming through strategies for surviving the sexual life. How we try to fit in without following the rules."

"We *don't* fit in," Alice says, watching the coffee pour hot and brown from its spigot. She pulls a cup for Twist and hands it to her.

"Just what I mean," Twist says. "I've never had a consistent strategy. Have you?"

"I never thought I needed one. Men come to us."

"Yeah, but for what?" Suddenly Twist seems to collapse. She barely puts her cup on the edge of the table before she flops like a rag doll. Tears stream down her face. "Alice! My God, Alice."

Alice kneels beside her and holds her hand. Twist is shaking. "I am so sick of myself, it scares me. I can't feel anything without it turning brown and dark, like shit. I'm just hanging on. All I can think about is how miserable I am."

"I'm getting you in for therapy," Alice vows. "I need to

pull some strings, and the hell with whatever other arrangements the David has made. You're in bad shape, girl.''

Twist pulls herself together enough to say, ''It was supposed to be different. Pretty young women standing by the wall, waiting for the nice young men to come by—''

''Bullshit,'' Alice says.

''So many women make themselves pretty now, so much competition, take off the pudge and straighten the hair and fix up the skin, so many smooth, clear-skinned women—''

Alice isn't sure where this is going, but she doesn't like it. ''There are some things the geniuses can't touch.''

''What? Our souls? They do that, too.'' Twist sits up, takes a deep breath, then leans forward and puts her head neatly on the table, right on her ear, without using her hands as pillows. She looks so stretched and distant that Alice feels a sudden prick of fear. *Am I falling into a hole as deep as this?*

''I don't *like* my soul,'' Twist says. ''It's brown like shit.''

Alice's home monitor announces a touch. Alice watches Twist for a moment. Twist sits up and lifts her cup. She slugs it back quickly, stares levelly at Alice, and says, ''Maybe it's a job.''

''I doubt it,'' Alice says, but tells the home monitor, ''Okay, put it over my pad.'' She does not like taking calls in the open when she has visitors.

The touch is still fresh and the caller has waited patiently. Alice unfolds the pad and stares with a curling shiver of disorientation at a face she never expected to see again.

''Is this Alice Grale?'' the woman asks. ''The vid star?'' It's the officer she passed outside the elevator on her call-in, the tall, strong-looking woman with shining mahogany skin.

''Yes,'' Alice says.

''We met last night under unusual circumstances. My name is—''

Another touch, this one an emergency, makes Alice lose the woman's name. A key sign in the upper corner of Alice's pad tells her the second touch is from Lisa at the temp agency.

"—and I hoped you'd be able to answer some questions for Seattle PD."

Alice does not react quickly, so much coming in so fast. "Could you hold on a moment, please? I—need to—I'll be right back with you."

She puts the officer on hold and answers Lisa's touch. Lisa looks frantic. Within the pad's frame, her face is bobbing all around, and her skin is livid behind overly red lips and hastily applied eye enhancements. *Lisa should never get mad. She looks so old.*

But Lisa is not just mad, she's scared.

"Jesus, Alice, what happened? Our payment for last night has been canceled and I've had touches from Citizen Oversight. Your date is dead! What in the hell happened?"

"Nothing," Alice says, trying to stay calm. She moves farther from the kitchen to avoid having Twist hear. "I did my job. It was *not* pleasant, Lisa, I'll tell you that—"

The information sinks in and Alice stalls. Then she murmurs, "Dead?"

"PD released the details two hours ago. The whole apt is tombed and rumors are wild."

"Who was he, Lisa?"

"His name was Terence Crest."

The name means nothing to Alice.

"Did he do anything to you?" Lisa asks, fishing for information she can use perhaps in her own defense, the agency's defense. "I mean, to make you—"

"He was alive, he was alive when I left him," Alice says, her voice a little screechy. "You arranged it, and he was very weird, and I hope God you never put me through anything like that again!"

"He was a very rich and important man, Alice, and they're not ruling out murder. The whole agency is on my back."

"I don't even know what he looked like. His face was this awful blank—"

"We can only go so far in this, Alice."

"My God, Lisa," Alice says, "you set it up and you persuaded *me!* I did not kill the man!"

Lisa gives her a look of utter professional disdain. "We'll just have to see how it works out, honey," Lisa says tonelessly. "You should keep your head down and get an advocate. I can't assign an agency advocate—not directly. If the fibes get word you're involved . . . And take a look at your account, honey. His estate pulled the payment. We have a big zero for our pains."

The touch ends abruptly.

Alice stands in the living room, staring at the gently glowing blank screen, too stunned to think. The PD officer is still on hold. Alice puts the pad down on the living room table, turns as if to go talk to Twist, see how she's doing, then stops. She picks up the pad again.

"Sorry to keep you waiting," she says to the officer. "I had a call-in last night and we met on my way out. What more can I say?"

"Did you know your client?"

"I don't do call-ins . . . as a rule. My agency vetted him. He didn't want me to know who he was."

"You've never done this sort of thing for him, you've never met him before?"

"Never. As I said, I don't do call-ins."

"His name was Terence Crest. A billionaire, quite well known around town. Did you know him before your call-in?"

"I already said no," Alice says. "He asked for me in particular. I don't know anything about him. And I don't know your name. I didn't catch your name."

"Seattle PD Fourth Rank Mary Choy."

"Yes, well, if I'm a suspect, I need an advocate before I say any more."

"We do know that Crest kept a vid record. You're probably in the record."

"Oh, of *course*," Alice says angrily, dismayed, her face flushing.

"And so are we, I suspect—the PD, the medicals. We're getting permission from Citizen Oversight and his estate advocates to play back the vid and establish the sequence of events. I understand your position, Alice, but if you're innocent, you'll be cleared."

"Maybe you live on a different planet, Mary Choy. I'm not even going to get paid for last night if his advocates have their way."

"I understand."

The hell you do. You look very together, Mary Choy.

"I'd like to meet with you," the officer says, "with your advocate present—just to tie up this loose end. Actually, I'm not very concerned with this case, if it's a suicide, as it appears to be. But it's going to be high-profile, especially in the financial news, and I'd like to keep my department on firm footing. And Alice . . . I hope your agency doesn't cut you loose."

Alice swallows. *A tough bitch, trying to act friendly. Still, it's best to leave one's options open.* "Give me your sig and I'll get back to you after I think things over."

"Of course."

Mary Choy smiles at her. Alice cuts the touch.

Twist comes in from the kitchen, scrubbing her face with a washrag. Alice stands utterly still on the metabolic carpet, shoulders drooped, head low, face locked in intense thought.

"Not good news?" Twist asks.

Alice jerks, straightens, trying to get back into being the together gal in this gloomy duet. It's no good. She shakes her head.

"Yeah, well I know what we need," Twist says. "A really tro spin party. We should be able to chase up one of those, right?"

Alice nods. She needs to think long and steady, bring up her defenses against this threat. She had it so good for so long that this is almost just; this is real life in action, balancing the books. "When it pains, it roars," she says. "But I told you I'd get you in for therapy."

"I'm better. Coffee seems to help. Isn't that strange?" Twist, whatever her weirdnesses, has always been very empathic. She understands others and their situations; she just doesn't have a clear view of her own self. "We'll get out tonight, all right? I'll find the party."

Alice gives her a too-much look and Twist lifts her small, thin fingers. "A sly spin romp, not a heavy fapper," she says. "Dignity, toujours dignity. Did you know Gene Kelly was a nineties person?"

"He died in the nineties," Alice says. "He was a forties and fifties person."

Twist accepts this with a thin smile. "You ever make it with him, character sim?"

"Not authorized," Alice says.

"Me either. I'd like to stay with you here for a while, though, if that's all right, if you're not in a rough about it."

"You're welcome to. I need the company."

"You're a true friend," Twist says. "That's rare in our crowd, you know?" She gathers up her nightbag and scattered clothes and goes into the bathroom to dress.

Alice drops her smile as soon as Twist leaves the room. She touches her stomach through the robe, rubs it lightly. Sperm will remain active for several days.

She carries the last living parts of a dead man.

4

The consulting room is pale green and yellow, meant to be soothing but Jonathan finds it like the bottom of a shallow sea, watery and neutral. The doctor is polite, a small woman with bobbed white hair and a direct, no-frills manner; this at least he finds reassuring.

"Did you know your wife had substantial therapy for amygdalic disorders when she was twenty?" the doctor asks. She holds up her pad for him to view this selection from the medical file.

"No," Jonathan says. "She told me . . ." Actually, she never told him anything about such matters. She left him with the impression she was a natural; not a high natural, perhaps, but never therapied. But twenty—that means she must have been therapied after they met. "She didn't tell me," he concludes.

"Yes, well, that's common enough. We're still ashamed of such things, which is stupid." The doctor looks up and faces him squarely. "What do you know about therapy? Have you ever had it yourself, any kind?"

"No," Jonathan says. "Not that I haven't thought about it. I mean, I don't have any prejudices against it. Against those who have had it. I don't know why she wouldn't have told me."

He closes his mouth firmly, hoping he doesn't seem nervous. Of course he is nervous; Chloe is in a room down the hall, under a special plug, not quite asleep but being kept in an artificial calm.

"We just received her files. What she asked for, at the time, was therapy for impulsive-destructive behavior, what

we call counter-will. She thought she was engaging in behavior against the better judgment of her conscious persona.''

Jonathan stares at the doctor.

The doctor ports her pad into a wall display and brings up
a few charts. The jagged lines and color bars mean little to
him. "She's had a major re-tracking, something we put in
the category of therapeutic fallback. All of her therapy has
failed her, and apparently the failure triggered a collapse of
conscious function. In old terms, not too far wrong, a nervous
breakdown.''

"What's this 'allostatic scarring'?'' Jonathan points to the
caption below a jagged line on the largest graph.

"Neurons and axons can wear out like any other part of
the body. It's one of the most frequent reasons for therapy.
Judging from your wife's condition, I'd say she suffered axon
path habituation and wear caused by cyclic impulses and behaviors her social persona did not feel comfortable with.''

Jonathan nods, but he only partly understands.

"Her original therapists rerouted the habitual pathway impulses for several important personality functions, to avoid
the areas damaged by allostatic load. That requires a maintenance implant, therapeutic monitors, usually microscopic,
to make sure the impulses don't revert. It's a routine procedure, and the monitors can last years—usually do. In your
wife's case, she had an upgrade performed four years ago.
But somehow, the newer monitors have shut down. Something triggered a stress . . . And her mind reverted to the damaged neural pathways, bringing back the old thymic
imbalances. All at once. It must have been horribly painful.''

Jonathan's eyes fill with tears. "We were making love,''
he says quietly.

The doctor seems to find this unexceptionable.

"Chloe was acting very sexy. She used . . . language . . . I
thought she was really turned on. But she was just breaking
down, wasn't she?''

"I'm sorry,'' the doctor says. "I don't think it's possible

to know. Maybe even she doesn't. You had no idea what was happening, did you?''

''How could I?'' Jonathan says. ''Was it my fault?''

''I don't see how it could be,'' the doctor says. ''Unless you had been badgering her to engage in behavior she found offensive.''

Jonathan tries to absorb this for a few seconds. His face flushes. ''She has been . . . stiff, less interested in me. I try to change that. Make myself . . . better. For her. Suggestions. But I did not,'' he swallows, ''*badger* her.''

The doctor is silent, offering no reassurances. Jonathan realizes he has given the doctor a possible explanation for what triggered his wife's fallback. What if he is misremembering his own behavior to protect a guilty conscience?

The doctor looks down and shrugs. ''I can't judge a domestic situation,'' she says, ''but you're not describing behavior that doesn't take place between millions of couples every day, with no adverse consequences . . . None like these, I mean.'' A troubled expression briefly flits over her calm features. ''I sense you might blame yourself whatever the final diagnosis is, and that may not be appropriate for your own health. I can't tell you this officially, but this hospital has been seeing a lot of fallback cases recently, covering the spectrum of therapies . . . Often involving failure of implanted monitors.''

''Fallbacks . . . You mean, the implants are defective?''

''We don't know. I offer this just to keep you from brooding yourself into your own breakdown. If her implant had functioned properly, this would probably have never happened.''

Jonathan feels sudden acid in his throat, and his skin heats. ''Something wrong with a product, or a procedure?'' This he can deal with professionally. This he can encompass.

''We really don't know. Please don't jump to conclusions.''

Jonathan realizes the doctor is uncomfortable, and well she

should be. She is caught between defending her profession and perhaps her own actions, and acknowledging what might be a major problem. He feels at once personal relief and a kind of awed anger.

"Where can I find out more about this?" Jonathan asks.

"We're consulting her original therapist," the doctor says. "That might be a good place to begin."

MULTIWAY BRANCHES

BROAD ACCESS FIBE (TEXT AND CHAT, with LIVE VID AND AVATARS): THE SPUN SUGAR SHOW (Trish Hing, Today's MOD:)

ONE OF MANY (GENERIC AVATAR): Can anyone join this tangle?

MOD (VID FACE OF FELICIA HANG OVER TIGER BODY): Sure, why not—where're you from?

ONE OF MANY: That doesn't matter. I'm logged blank and I prefer it that way—somebody will try to sell me something. I just wanted to

MOD: Sure, go ahead—have your say. It's a free country.

ONE OF MANY: Well, actually, I don't think it is. I tell you what my grind is—*they* just want me to sit down and suck up what they do and pay money for it. *They* are trying to discourage all the new fibe posts and public channels, and *they* have so many ways of making all the little people pay, while limiting access to

MOD: What do you mean, Mr. Blank?

ONE OF MANY: I can't get anybody to come to my fibe hive and hang. I have all this work I've done, I think it's very good stuff and so do my friends, and I can't get any of the reviews to post it. I say the reviews are paid for by the Big Sharks and they discourage posts by us little minnows. How can an artist make a living when nobody swims by?

MOD: So you think you're being discriminated against by the big companies which control all we see and hear.

ONE OF MANY: Sure. And it may even go beyond them—the government.

MOD: The government is against you?

ONE OF MANY: Sure. Everybody knows they regulate the fibes and satlinks and they're in up to their checksums with the money power. They say it's for the common good. I sure as hell know better.

MOD: So you want to make a living from posting your work on the fibes or satlinks, but nobody squirts you any money to download or even take a taste, hmm?

ONE OF MANY: Not enough. And I think *they*'re actively discouraging repeats for little guys like me.

MOD: They being the big intratainment industry folks or the government.

ONE OF MANY: Yeah. They're trying to conserve flow for the big industry posts and links.

MOD: Well, why don't you post your address here and let's see if we can't up your hit rate.

ONE OF MANY: Nice try, but I know the kind of audience this place gets. Everybody would try to get *me* to sample their fibe hive.

MOD: Isn't that the way it works?

ONE OF MANY: I can't make a living if I'm spending my money at other hives. Fellow has to eat.

MOD: We all have to eat, my friend. Maybe you don't understand the process. (Now please, while we're exclusive with this fellow, don't build up your anger and carbonize him when you get on . . . I can just feel your pressure building!)

ONE OF MANY: I just know it doesn't work.

MOD: So, let me try to psi your case here. You work at home—you've been out of everything but the dole for quite a few years. You haven't advanced your education in some time—you're afraid of going in to therapy your attitudes and get a good working joy-buzz—and maybe your boy/girlfriend isn't as pretty as the folks on the Yox. You'd really like to live on the Yox and you know you deserve it. But you can't afford more than say ten hours a week of second-grade Yox, not even the top new stuff, and the rest of the time you're alone with your unhappy situation, and you've been hoping you could finance an upgrade by selling your own work.

ONE OF MANY: Are *you* in *their* pay, too?

MOD: I wish, no such. But wait, I'm not done yet. I'm at the helm today; you can apply for the post tomorrow. You have no skills off the fibes, or on, that anybody really wants to pay for, so your last refuge is the dole. You're one of the disAffected, my friend. Join the crowd. I really sympathize.

ONE OF MANY: Wait, this is

MOD: If you don't post your stats and address, how can we check my psi? You're drawing a blank, and you expect rational discourse? Let us know whether I'm right and post your stats.

ONE OF MANY: Fuck you.

MOD: Ah, more reasoned discourse. Fucking is an act of friendship and love and trust, Mr. Blank. You must come from the old school that believes it's penetrative domination and reducing the other to chattel slavery, hence a term of opprobrium. But maybe I shouldn't use such big words. I bet you haven't used your sensemaker on an unfamiliar word in ever so long. Ah, Mr. Blank has logged off. Okay. It's open, gang. Does anybody have anything interesting to talk about?

5 /

The Sea Foam 2 sits on the ocean waters of the sound, not far from the ancient and revered Pike Place Market. The cab drops Martin and he pays his ninety dollars and steps out on the concrete and asphalt of the old Alaskan Way, lovingly reconstructed from the mammoth quake of '14, with antique turtle-shaped Ford Tauruses and a few Japanese cars parked here and there for effect. Short green trolleys clang along their brick-encased rails below the rise to the market. Westward spreads the sound, blue-gray under scattered clouds and dazzling curtains of sun.

The tourist crowd is light today but the line before the Sea Foam 2 is already long. Sun glints from the clusters of huge liquid-filled bubbles rising above the slurping waterfront. Within the bubbles, grotesque horrors of the sea live their suspended lives, most real, a few, wonderful robots perhaps even smarter than the creatures they are meant to depict.

"My name is Burke. I'm supposed to meet Miz Dana Carrilund," he tells the live, real maitre d' at the front. The maitre d' knows well enough to recognize these names from the list, and guides him under the sparkling shimmers of the piled, sea-filled bubbles to a table by the broad side window looking out, unobstructed, over the sound. Carrilund is waiting. Shadows pass over her as they shake hands. Unable to restrain himself, Martin flinches and looks up: a shark turns in its bubble, dappled like a fawn. It is swimming upside down, he realizes. Is it supposed to do that?

"How nice to finally meet you," Carrilund says. She is severe at first appearance, hair almost white and cut short, square-faced and solid but pleasingly shaped. Her arms resting on the paper menu appear strong, and she asks him if he drinks this early.

"Not often," Martin says.

"Nor I. But they have a grand cocktail here—they call it a Sea Daisy. Shall we—just to loosen up?"

She smiles pleasantly, so he nods and murmurs, "Sure. What the hell."

Martin knows people—he prides himself on understanding their smallest behaviors, and being able to fit those behaviors into overall impressions of surpassing accuracy. Dana Carrilund knows humans perhaps as well as he does, but in a different way and to different ends—not to improve their mental health, as such, but to fit them better into larger schemes. She betrays very few of her own needs in the process, and her behaviors are as studied as those of an actor, though not necessarily false. *Not necessarily.*

Right now, Carrilund wishes Martin to believe she is impressed by him. And not so oddly, Martin is himself impressed. Carrilund appears to be very integrated, mentally robust, and a specimen of physical health.

The drinks are served. Flower-like tangles of half-frozen, half-gelatinized fruit juice seep into a surround of vodka. The rim of the globular glass is caked with microcapsules of salt, sugar, and vinegar, which dissolve unpredictably against the tongue—and it is all served very cold.

Martin sips and finds it delicious. "I hope you don't need all my mental faculties this morning," he says.

"If we keep ourselves to one drink, we'll do fine," Carrilund says. "What I need now is to get a more accurate picture of Martin Burke, the man."

Martin raises his eyebrow, pictures his face with a bushy

brow elevated rather pompously, and lowers it quickly. "I don't have much to hide," he says.

"You've been through some rough times," Carrilund observes. "Quite a few shifts in your career track."

"Open history," Martin says.

"Yes, and no," Carrilund says. "You've never been very open about your involvement in the Goldsmith case."

"Ah." Martin smiles grimly. "How thorough are we going to be this morning?"

"Tolerably friendly and only tolerably thorough. I'm more concerned about your part in developing the tools of effective deep therapy. You were a brilliant pioneer. You caused upsets that derailed your career. And now—you're a quiet, respectable professional with a narrow focus."

"So far, so true," Martin says.

"You have no intention of ever getting involved in anything that could bring more trouble."

"Not if I can help it."

Carrilund orders her breakfast, and the waiter takes Martin's order next. Later, he does not remember what he ordered; he feels an unease he has become all too familiar with in his career, contemplating another stroll through a lion's cage—a stroll he can never seem to convince himself is not worth the risk.

"You consulted on a research project three years ago for a group working out of Washington, the New Federalist Market Alliance. They're associated with another group, called the Aristos."

"Yes," Martin says. "It was a small contract. Lasted only two weeks."

"I presume what you told them is confidential."

"Not really. They wanted my thoughts on the future of a society without effective deep-tissue mental therapy. They're a very conservative organization."

Carrilund precisely reveals her distaste. "What did you think of them?"

"Polite and well-dressed," Martin says, smiling.

"Fascists?"

"No. Class elitists. They take their Federalism seriously."

"They also believe in the genetic superiority of a moneyed class . . . am I right?" Carrilund asks.

Martin nods. "So I've heard."

Carrilund shows her distaste. "Their Jesus wears a longsuit and has a perfect long-term investment plan."

"I provided them what they asked for, and that was that," Martin says.

Carrilund seems to steel herself for some unpleasantness. "What did you tell them, in outline?"

"I told them our society had reached a point where effective therapy is a necessity. Remove the effects of therapy in today's culture, and you'll begin a long decline into anarchy."

"Why?"

"The stresses put on the best and brightest members of the world's social systems are as precisely tuned as the stresses on the fragile parts in a high-speed engine. Well, about a century and a half ago, the stresses became too great, overall, resulting in increasing populations of thymically unbalanced individuals. Not crazy people, necessarily.—just deeply unhappy people."

"The work loads became too great?"

"Not exactly. This is more difficult to convey—the stresses, perhaps not coincidentally, seemed perfectly designed to cause nagging, even debilitating thymic problems. The mental equivalents of baseball elbow or housework knee—on a huge scale. Without effective therapy, widely available and used, we wouldn't be able to support the dataflow economy we have today."

Carrilund seems interested in clarifying this point. "By therapy, you mean specifically deep tissue therapy—thymic balancing, pathic correction, neuronal supplement and repair. Chemicotropic adjustment and psychosocial microsurgery on the neural level. Implanted monitors for continuing adjustment.''

''Better minds for a better world,'' Martin says. ''I've never been ashamed of my part in all this.''

''You have no reason to be ashamed,'' Carrilund says hastily. ''You've played an integral role in a magnificent accomplishment. And you've done quite well recently with implant monitor designs. You're a major player in a big industry.''

''Thank you.''

''And, as you say, a necessary one. What did this organization do with what you told them?''

''I presume they went home and kept quiet about it,'' Martin says. ''They've long been opposed to therapy on ethical and religious grounds. The necessity of error and sin in God's plan, I suppose. Free will. I didn't give them much they would find useful. No political wedge, so to speak.'' Martin looks down at his fingers, twisted on the tabletop. He untwists them. ''I got the impression they were hoping I'd tell them it could all be dispensed with.''

''I see,'' Carrilund says. She puts her finger to her lips— not an affectation, Martin judges, but a genuine sign of deep thought. The breakfast arrives and he eats without paying any attention to the food. He cannot help feeling that the lion's cage is just down the road.

''Mr. Burke, you know I'm in charge of the health care of fourteen million employees in the Corridor and along Southcoast.''

''Yes.''

''Something statistically impossible is happening,'' she says. She continues to eat, relaxed and polite, as if they are having a purely social breakfast. ''A mental meltdown. The wave is just beginning to build, but from what we're seeing so far, I think you're right about the consequences.''

Martin stops eating and squints at the ocean, then up at the masses of water suspended over them.

''Are you free this afternoon?'' Carrilund asks.

"I can make some time available," Martin says. *And disappoint some patients.*

"We need some advice, obviously, and we have something you probably need to see." Her smile is assuring, positive. Why, then, does Martin feel a familiar sensation of loss, of sinking and drowning?

"For once," Martin muses, "I'd like to be on the side of the angels."

Carrilund does not immediately know what to make of this.

"Never mind," he adds, waving that off.

"No, I understand," she says. "That's the side we're on, Mr. Burke."

MAGNAZINE!
Your Yox Journal
Category:
PERSONAL EX-STREAM

```
<VID/YOX DISPLAY ERROR> ::TEXT
ONLY::

<INTERACTIVE MODE CLOSED>
```

YOUR SCANNER/HUNTER PROFILE TELLS US YOU'LL LOVE THIS
YOX TOX (and MORE!) WITH UNREAL CELEBS TONIGHT!

YOUR CHANCE TO SIT IN ON BIG INTERVIEWS WITH YOX SIM-CELEBS!

MEET (AND SHAKE!) WITH **GENE KELLY**©℠(CEM),
FRED ASTAIRE©℠(CEM), AND **TIMOTHY LEARY**©℠
AS THEY DISCUSS THEIR NEW YOX EXTRAVAGANZAS; meet and HISS sim
YOX USA PRESIDENT CARICATURE *MELISSA MISSILE*℠, hear her
opinions on THE HOT SPIN POLITICAL ISSUES OF THE REALTIME PICO!

AND IF YOU'RE FEELING TRULY PLATINUM, RARE OPPS TO GET INTIME
WITH SIMS AND UNREALS NEVER BEFORE OFFERED BY THEIR CHARACTER
ESTATES! DON'T MISS THE *RARE* PRESSING OF RESURRECTED™ (AND
NEVER-REAL™) CELEB FLESH!

6 /

Jack Giffey is working his way through a case of the shakes.

He lies in bed in the small room he took in the early hours
of the morning in a motel at the corner of Elk and Copper,
across town; the covers are pulled up over his chest and
tucked under his chin, and he feels like a small boy caught
doing something really stupid.

A good family man would not do that.

That inside voice comes out of nowhere. It means nothing;
but its cold surprise brings on a sudden, almost leaden calm,
and his thoughts become as shiny and smooth as doped sili-
con. *That voice is a bit of dream,* he hears a more familiar
voice, his own voice, say. *Ignore that man behind the curtain.*

"What the hell," Giffey says in the room's quiet.

But the sensation passes. Giffey closes his eyes, now that
the shaking has stopped and the voices are no longer dueling,
to savor a bit of undifferentiated muzz, scattered passings of
memory and dream. Then, with a few deep breaths, he is past
recriminations and on to making today's schedule.

There is little time to waste. He will meet with the rest of
the team, and with the team's leader, at one in the afternoon.
And by six tomorrow evening, they should be inside . . .

There is of course so much that could go wrong. But Giffey
thinks the builders of Omphalos, like most pharaohs, have an
inherent arrogance. The appearance of power *is* power, to
them, especially in a world which they regard with so much

contempt. Arrogance swells within the armor until many chinks appear.

He dresses, eats in the small, quiet, rundown hotel cafe, keeping his eyes to himself, and gathers his stuff from the room before checking out.

Today is cold and clear. Tomorrow, a weather front is moving in. Snow is predicted by seventeen tomorrow evening. They might be able to take advantage of that, as well.

The warehouse on the east end of town is at least seventy years old, a steel-beam and corrugated sheet-steel relic that's probably cold as a freezer inside.

Giffey approaches the office entrance on foot, bag in hand. He comes from nowhere, as if bearing no identity, his past forgotten; everything begins here. His mind is clear and his thoughts focused. He rings the ancient electric buzzer.

Thirty seconds later, the door opens, and he looks into the face of a woman he has never met before. She is pale-skinned, brown hair cut in a medium frizz, brown eyes suspicious. She wears a checked shirt and army green pants and a thick bronze bracelet hangs loose around one wrist.

"Who are you?" she asks from behind the door.

"Giffey," he says. "Jack Giffey."

She stands back and pulls the door open. It creaks. Inside, the office is small and dusty. An ancient space heater cracks and snaps against one wall; the air feels blastingly hot and dry compared to the chill outside. A battered metal desk hunkers in one corner and a putty-colored filing cabinet leans next to the desk. A sink with naked pipes has been scrubbed spotlessly clean in the opposite corner, and an antique electric Mr. Espresso sits on a wooden shelf above it. Beside the sink is a white refrigerator and a microwave oven on a portable workbench.

"I'm Hally Preston," the woman says. "I'm a friend of Mr. Hale."

Giffey does not know that name, probably false. He wonders if the reference is to Nathan Hale.

With tight slacks and a jacket and her hair cut close and combed to one side, Preston is more than a little mannish. Her face is lean and neutral, her lips prim. "Let's meet the others," she says, and opens the next door. Giffey passes through into the warehouse proper.

The warehouse is filled with scraps of old airplanes, like the broken husks of giant dragonflies. A few disconsolate salvage arbeiters stand beside the heaps of scrap, but none of them seem to be in working order.

Preston takes him on a short walk between walls of scrap. In the center of the pile, a small space has been cleared, just enough for a couch, four battered chairs, and a free-standing repeater whiteboard. Five men are here, three sitting and two standing: one of them is Jenner, the young ex-Army man.

He looks up and waves. "The stuff's here," he announces proudly to Giffey. "It's all delivered. I checked it out and it seems fine." His scalp ripples like a tired caterpillar. Otherwise he seems at ease and pleased with himself.

Giffey's breath clouds in front of him. He knows two of the others from photos.

Preston introduces him. "Jack Giffey," she says to the five.

One of the sitters, a blocky, black-haired man with a short neatly sculpted beard, stands and steps forward. He offers his hand. "I'm Hale," he says. Giffey knows him as Terkes. He looks British somehow, maybe Irish, but Hale/Terkes is a weapons expert from Ukraine, a naturalized citizen for twenty years, whose accent is pure middle American, New Received Broadcast. He has been involved in wire and fibe fraud, running industrial nano and pre-build slurry to Hispaniola, selling hellcrowns to Selectors in Southcoast. In short, Hale is an occasional bad'un but chubbily innocent, clean and scrubbed, cheerful.

"I'm Kim Lou Park," says an Oriental man, whom Giffey

knows as Evan Chung. Park/Chung has no past; he is as blank in all records as a newborn babe. What little Giffey knows about him is contradictory. He wears a long mustache and his hair is cut in a short bowl with a fringe down his neck.

Park believes that he recruited Giffey in St. Louis last spring. In fact, Park is way down the chain of origination. They met only twice there. Still, Park is savvy; he undoubtedly knows more about the rest of them than they do themselves, but he knows very little about Giffey . . . Very little that is true.

"Mr. Giffey and Mr. Jenner are our materials procurement people," Park says. "Mr. Giffey is also our main source for knowledge about the target."

Giffey looks at the two men he does not know, and Preston walks around him. "Mr. Pent and Mr. Pickwenn," she says. "Architectural experts, specializing in breaking in or, if necessary, breaking out." She produces the faintest of smiles. Pent and Pickwenn are in their late thirties, with experienced, almost bored expressions. Pent is dark brown, Polynesian blood, and has almost no hair. Pickwenn is ghostly pale, with large lemur eyes and thin, elegant fingers.

"We've worked together for ten years," Pickwenn says softly. Pent nods agreement. They do not offer to shake hands; Giffey is just as glad. Pickwenn's grip looks to be cold and damp.

Hale steps forward and the others face him. No one glances around. All eyes are on Hale.

"All right, we're here," Hale says. "All together for the first time. This is our team. Here's what's new, what we have to do." Hale has the rhythmic, accented delivery of a preacher or a good singer. His voice is bass velvet.

"I've made the right connections. We're getting into Omphalos as a group of potential customers. We're going to walk right in the side door, not the tourist door, but the VIP entrance. Hally."

Preston steps forward. "We're scheduled to show up in a

limo tomorrow morning at fifteen hundred. You're a bunch of eccentric rich folks traveling under assumed identities. Robert Hale has worked this out in some detail.''

Robert, Giffey thinks. *Maybe he's never even heard of Nathan Hale.*

''Mr. Giffey, we took a big delivery yesterday,'' Hale says. ''Mr. Jenner arrived with it. We spent a fair amount of change. It's in the back half of the warehouse. I assume it's what we planned on, and I'd like you to tell us what we need to know.''

''Yes, sir,'' Giffey says. ''I can look it over and see what shape it's in.''

''It's okay,'' Jenner says, smiling reassurance.

''I'm sure it is. I'm overly cautious, is all,'' Giffey says, smiling back. Jenner does not take this as an affront; he respects overly cautious superiors. The Army trained him that way.

''I'd like you to brief us in more detail about the Omphalos interior,'' Hale says. ''We've given everybody the stuff you sent last week, but I assume you withheld a few key bits. Overly cautious.''

Giffey nods and smiles again.

Hale enjoys being the center of attention. He walks in front of the whiteboard like a general, arms folded behind his back. ''We have an appointment with a remote sales rep named Lacey Ray. She won't be there in person—there aren't any people in Omphalos, it's all automatic, right?''

Giffey agrees.

''We have identity codes and recommendations. It's minimum risk until we get inside. Then I assume we're wide open to whatever Omphalos has to offer. Well, Mr. Giffey, what does it have to offer?''

Hale is feeling his oats, but Giffey doesn't think he'll like what he has to say. ''Four, maybe five warbeiters, and probably a thinker to run them through their paces.'' He sits on a folding metal chair. What he has just told them is not strictly confirmed—he knows only that orders went out to extralegal suppliers for just these instruments of defense. Whether they were ever delivered is anybody's guess.

Hale takes this calmly for about three seconds, and then he swears under his breath. "Warbeiters?"

"Insect or Ferret class. I'm not sure about the thinker, but it's my guess." *My hope.*

"You know how to deactivate them?"

"I do," Giffey says. "With our equipment, I'm offering sixty to eighty percent confidence."

Hale swears once more. "You could have told us this earlier."

"Why?" Giffey asks. "They're just machines, albeit clever ones. I can't tell you how they're programmed or if they're authorized to kill. They might just lick us like lap dogs."

Hale frowns and a deep cleft forms between his brows. "Where would the builders get warbeiters?"

"Where does anybody get anything?" Giffey asks sharply. "We've managed something far more radical in the way of illegal weapons. The heirs of Raphkind left a lot of wedges in a lot of government doors. Even military doors."

"Christ, it's only a fucking tomb," Hale mutters. His bravado isn't very thick, and he's not very good at concealing his concern. So despite the theatrical front, he's not much of a general after all. "Why bring in the dogs of hell to guard it?"

"I'd hate to think this puts you off," Giffey says. He's not sure he likes or trusts this man.

"No," Hale says thoughtfully. "You think they're set to not kill?"

"It's distinctly possible," Giffey says. "As you say, it's only a tomb. Besides, warbeiters are just machines," Giffey repeats. "Frankly, we'll have the means to take them out."

"I hope you're right," Hale says, and by implication lays any failure on Giffey's shoulders.

"You ever hear of Nathan Hale?" Giffey asks.

Hale thinks for a moment, as if he just might. "No," he finally says. "He design these Insects and Ferrets?"

"I've heard of him," Hally Preston says. "Patriot way back."

Giffey gives her a big smile. "Here's more of what I know about Omphalos," he says. He walks up to the whiteboard, uncaps a black marker, and begins to sketch.

"There are at least forty levels from basement to attic," he says. "It's a big place, and it may not even be finished yet. They're still bringing in architectural nano. Shipments are irregular. They might be having financial problems—maybe not enough customers. That might explain why they're reaching out to folks they don't know too much about."

Hale inclines in agreement. Pent and Pickwenn draw in their chairs. Jenner folds his arms and fixes on the sketch Giffey is making: so far, it's not much more than a side view, a right triangle.

"This side entrance, the VIP entrance as you call it, is also a service entrance. Tourists pay money, so the builders don't want to interrupt the flow on those days when they get their truckloads of whatever they're bringing in."

"Do we know more about the owners?" Preston asks.

"Not much more than before. A partnership club that calls itself the Omphalos Group, membership worldwide. Capitalization unknown, rules unknown. Structured like an investment insurance web."

"Pyramid scheme," Pickwenn says softly.

"Yeah," Giffey says. "There's some connection with a syndic or social club that's been politically active in the past fifteen years, the Aristos, and they in turn have connections with the New Federalists. Membership in the Aristos seems to be based on being naturals—untherapied—and on financial or other contributions. The same may be true for the Omphalos Group. I presume if we meet their standards, they'll let us know."

"I'm out," Jenner says cheerfully. "Just a mental mutt, I guess."

Hale grunts. "Makes me feel better about relieving them of their ill-gotten gains."

"They're not poor," Giffey says. "This one Omphalos cost about eight billion dollars, and there are five others under construction all over the world. This is the first and the closest to completion."

"Construction?" Pent asks.

"For the ages," Giffey says. "The outer curtain and some interior walls are carbon nanotube-reinforced concrete with a surface of deposited reflex bead ceramic. One hundred percent reflectivity for all radiation. There's some gold detail work for decoration, but it's not functional. Frame is deposited spidermesh nanotube—in some places, three feet thick, all stress-dispersal. Internal steel frames support flexfuller and concrete slabs, everything shock-mounted, with four separate mountings for each level. The whole building is shock-mounted on hypertense flexfuller. I've heard that all the carbon fibers—nanotubes, linked fullerenes, etc.—are tuned for conductivity and that the entire skin is sensitive. The frame can also be tuned and used for data storage."

Pickwenn and Pent absorb this thoughtfully. "Stronger than the pyramids of Egypt," Pent says.

"So—how many bodies?" Hale asks.

"I learned at the beginning that there are about a hundred in storage so far, ninety corpsicles and five real corpses and five in warm sleep. My information hasn't gotten any better."

"Rich folks?" Hale asks.

"Presumably. Qualified members, at least."

Hale grunts again. "Let's get back to the structure."

"Gladly." Giffey sketches in three shafts. "We have seven elevators or lifts. Five of them may or may not be of any use to us. I presume we're going to trigger alarms, and these five—the biggest and most luxurious—are under the building's control."

"The thinker," Preston says.

"We'll assume that for now. But there are two shafts set up as separate emergency elevators. They have their own power supplies—fuel cells—and are isolated from any outside control, even the building's control, to avoid lock-up in an emergency. Standard for any large dataflow building. These emergency elevators are our access to the lower levels of the building, but the closest is fifty yards from the VIP and service garage entrance."

"We'll need something to carry our ill-gotten gains," Hale says.

"Right. That's been taken into account." Giffey draws in this path from the side view, then sketches an elevation and shows the twists and turns on the main floor. "The emergency elevators' main exit is below ground level. They're designed to drop passengers off at a tunnel under Republic Avenue, with an exit half a mile away. That will be our escape route. I asked for a large secured vehicle." Giffey stabs the marker on the exit on his crude map. "That's where it should be parked."

"We're all going in?" Jenner asks, looking around.

"Except for Mr. Park," Preston says. "He'll drive the truck."

Jenner grins. "I'm ready," he says, stretching out his arms. Giffey watches the young man's scalp, then jerks his gaze away. Pickwenn and Pent walk up to the board and examine the sketch.

"You wouldn't happen to have complete plans, would you?" Pickwenn asks, moistening his dark lips with a pale pink tip of tongue.

"Sorry, no," Giffey says. "We presume the hibernacula are above the fifth floor."

"And the emergency elevators go to those levels as well?" Pent asks.

"One may," Giffey says. "If it doesn't, we'll have to commandeer a main elevator."

"How do we do that?" Pickwenn asks dubiously. "Your . . . thinker is in charge of them, and presumably will know about us by then."

"Let's look at the stuff," Jenner suggests. "Mr. Giffey, these folks aren't familiar with what we can do. They'll settle down once we tell them."

"Good idea," Hale says. "It just looks like a lot of barrels and boxes now."

In the back of the warehouse, they gather around a pallet five feet on each side, deposited on the concrete floor in an empty corner. The pallet is wrapped in reflective plastic, anonymous, unmarked. A few tears in the plastic reveal Jenner's earlier investigation of the contents.

"Tear it open," Giffey tells Jenner. The young man deftly slips a knife from his pocket and sets to work. He slices the tough plastic and pulls it away, revealing four drumlike wax-lined metal canisters of military grade nano, and two canisters of WEPPON—Weapons and Equipment Programming Package, Ordnance Nano. Military complete paste.

Patiently, Giffey begins to explain these tools. Pent and Pickwenn listen closely. Jenner nods enthusiastically. Giffey glances at Preston as he talks, watching her expression. Of all the people here, she seems the most intelligent, even the calmest; he wonders why Hale is in charge and she isn't. Hale, after making an initial good impression, has dropped quite a bit in his estimation. Something about the man's body language, his questions . . . Not enough probing questions.

Preston is nervous, concerned. *Good girl*, Giffey thinks. *This isn't going to be a piece of cake. Most of us are probably never going to see that tunnel.*

Jenner pulls out a plastic probe, unscrews the cap of the first MGN canister, and dips the probe in. He proceeds to the second canister, querying the nano. A faint smell of yeast and iodine fills the room.

Military grade nano is a living beast from another world.

It tolerates our atmosphere, our world, but it's always hungry.

Giffey tries to remember who told him that, and when; but the memory doesn't come quickly and soon he stops trying.

"It's perking and ready to go," Jenner reports.

"Lets go over it again," Hale says. "What can this stuff work from?"

Jenner gleefully obliges. He puts on an expert military tone, clipped, precise. "MGN is a living substance designed to thrive in a wartime environment, specifically, a high-tech battlefield. Supply it metal, flexfuller, organics, any plastics, anything but glass or gold. It absorbs nitrogen and CO_2 from the air. Might be quite a suck if we're low on organics." He folds his arms, self-impressed. "There's a cafeteria unit in the building. It might be best to set it loose in there."

"Organics?" Preston says.

Giffey had deliberately not covered this topic.

"It's designed to absorb and recycle battlefield casualties," Giffey says quietly. "Mechanical and otherwise."

"Jesus," says Kim Lou Park, grimacing.

"We'll set it on the pharaohs," Jenner says, poking his finger into the air.

"We'll treat them with kid gloves, actually," Hale says. "They're something we didn't count on. We'll be better off using them as shields and hostages."

That's the first really intelligent thing Giffey has heard Hale say.

"How will we unload the stuff?" Pickwenn asks.

"We're going right into the VIP garage, through the armor, through outside security, limo and all," Hale says, smiling. "That's the beauty of it. These folks aren't as smart as we thought."

Giffey expresses no opinion on the matter. The setup does indeed seem sweet, much better than he had hoped.

But all too clearly, he remembers the sweet deal of the night before.

GODSTREAM 1

THE MULTIWAY CHRISTIAN NEWS FIBE

NEWS BLAST: SATAN ON THE MARCH, Edition 216

Hideous sex-selected abortions in India and China have led to the death of 300,000,000 (that's *three hundred million*) unborn female children. Satan is laughing now! Tens of millions of Chinese and Indian men cannot find wives. Satan is ready for the next step! The governments of India and South China, and even of Northern Enclave China, have caved in to enormous public pressure and are *forcing ten million adult men and boys a year* to undergo sex change transformations, to become WOMEN! THE SIN OF MURDER BEGETS EVEN GREATER SIN!

Meanwhile, the demand for that Hell-spawned and all-pervasive sin called Pornography (the night-sweats of Onan himself!) in India and China outstrips the rest of the world! Western-produced and now Eastern-produced pornographic material accounts for fully one third of ALL PURCHASES in India and China! Prostitution has always thrived in India, and now is rampant throughout Asia, but the perverse combination of robots and pornography has led to a TENFOLD INCREASE IN PROSTHETUTION, the use of *robot sex surrogates!* These prosthetutes, also known as *whorebots* and *sexbeiters*, are manufactured in Japan and Thailand. Satanic mechanical sex temptresses have been invading our shores and despoiling our youth for over twenty years!

SODOM AND GOMORRAH WERE PIKERS! Can anyone deny that the end is near? BIBLICAL PROPHECY POINTS TO THE REAL ENDTIME! SATAN HOODWINKED US IN 2000 AND AGAIN IN 2048!

JESUS IS RACING TOWARD US LIKE A FIERY LION, AN AVENGING COMET SOAKED IN GASOLINE!

TAP THIS BUTTON TO MAKE AN INSTANT CONTRIBUTION FROM YOUR
GOVERNMENT UNEMPLOYMENT FUND. ONLY THE GENEROUS WILL BE
LAUGHING WHEN GOD'S WRATH SWALLOWS THE EARTH!

COME TO GREEN IDAHO, GOD'S LAST FOOTPRINT ON EARTH!

7 /

Jonathan walks into his wife's hospital room. Pale blue cloth
curtains in a circle around the bed ripple with a light breeze
scented like a pine forest. There are five other patients in this
bloc, but he can hear none of them; no conversations, no
coughing or moaning. Chloe is silent as well. She has eaten
breakfast and stares with grim determination at nothing.

Her body is filled with a new set of monitors, these directed
from outside rather than operating autonomously. They are
trying to find an explanation for her condition. The probe
receiver hangs from the ceiling on a narrow track, and a small
cord leads from the receiver to a silver spot behind her left
ear. This, he realizes, is a medical-grade plug. It could also
be feeding her soothing impulses. Even with her eyes open,
she might be asleep.

He almost dreads the possibility she *is* awake. Walking into
her room is like going before a judge. He has always been
very sensitive about criticism, especially from Chloe; he has
always been extremely careful not to do anything that might
merit her anger.

She does not seem to see him.

"Hello," he says softly. "How are you?"

"Like shit," she snaps and her face tightens, lines dragging
the edges of her lips down. This makes her look much older.

She looks like a female villain in an old Disney vid, hard, sexless, and bitterly angry.

"I've talked to the doctor. She isn't sure what happened."

"Isn't she?" Chloe asks flatly.

"Nobody is. There seems to be something going around."

"Good, Jonathan. Never blame yourself."

Jonathan halts his slow, cautious progress into the room one step from the side of Chloe's bed. She is not well, he tells himself. There will be a lingering aura of her collapse. He will not let himself fall victim to her off-center affect.

"A lot of people are becoming ill," Jonathan says, his voice rough. "Nobody knows why."

"I'm as healthy as a horse. It's my *soul* that has bootprints all over it."

"I know it hurts," Jonathan says, barely a whisper. He starts to take that last step, to stand beside the bed, but she jerks her head and stares at him with the glassy eyes and wooden expression of a puppet. "God damn you," she says flatly.

Jonathan stops. His mouth goes soft and his tongue seems to fill the space behind his jaws, dry and gummy. His eyes close to slits and he can barely see her beyond a light-beading film of tears.

"You've been pushing me since we had Hiram and I'm sick because of it."

He can say nothing to this. He tries to tell himself that she is not well, that the woman he loves and who mothered his children, the woman with whom he has slept in bed almost eight thousand times, and with whom he has made love at least two thousand times, would not use these words, this voice. Chloe has become someone else and this person will soon go away.

"What is it?" she asks, breaking the silence of half a minute or more. "Why are you here?"

"I hope you feel better soon." Jonathan looks around for some button to push, some cord to pull to call in human help, to keep him from saying anything, but the words erupt. The room feels hot. "You had therapy after we met but you didn't tell me."

"Why should I?" Chloe asks.

"Why did you need therapy?"

"Because I kept wanting men, lots of men, and they kept hurting me," Chloe says. "An excess of *desire*. Why should I ever feel desire again?"

He sees the chair and turns, sits before his knees go rubbery. Part of him wants to leave immediately and let the professionals treat her; another part is guilty for ever expecting anything from a *mother,* the *mother of his children* for God's sake, and he knows he deserves this condign punishment.

But this has nothing to do with what he says to her. "You've never liked to lose control," he says.

"Look what it gets me." She gestures at the bed, the curtains.

"I always thought we were partners, that we could be free with each other . . . I didn't know it was hurting you."

She glances at him, pityingly, and to Jonathan that look embodies all the disapproving looks women have ever given him, from the disappointed anger of his mother to a girlfriend telling him he is not for her. *Wrathscorn.*

Jonathan pulls his chair closer. She shifts on the bed.

"Please listen," he says. "I'll go soon. Hiram and Penelope want to see you."

"Oh, my God. Hiram. He saw what you were doing to me."

"Don't," Jonathan says, pulling together all his control. "Listen, Chloe. This is important. No matter what you feel now, it's not real. You've had a thymic collapse. All your therapy gave way at once. I don't think I was responsible for that, but if I was, we have to make our decisions after you're out of the hospital, not now. You need time to rest and recuperate and let the doctors put things back in place. I'm told that won't take more than a week, but ... the hospital is pretty busy now. The experts may not get to you for a few days. And I want only the best for you. If necessary, I'll take you out of here and find a specialist myself. The best.'' He swallows and tries to produce spit to wet his tongue, but it will not flow. ''I won't come back if you don't want me to ... until after you're feeling better.''

''I've just come awake, that's all.''

Jonathan takes a deep breath. He knows many things intellectually, that he should not feel anger for these words because they are not truly reflective of the real woman who is his wife. But he can't help thinking of a snail heaped high with salt. An earthworm drying in the summer sun. No love, no sex, cut away from the joys of this Earth; he is a dead man.

She closes her eyes. ''I need to rest,'' she says.

He stands and turns and parts the curtain. In the passageway beyond, looking at the receding curves of blue curtains beneath the soft glow of the high ceiling, he can't breathe. He stands there making small choking noises until his throat clears and his eyes water. He sounds like a dog with its vocal cords cut. Thank God nobody sees him before he wipes his eyes and stops his gasping.

In the visitors' room, Hiram and Penelope are pale and serious and they sit with hands folded between their knees, as if posed for a photo. Hiram looks up at Jonathan.

''She's not feeling very well. She's ... saying some bitter things,'' Jonathan tells them.

His children give him looks of total lack of comprehension. Perhaps they are being kind.

''I'd like to see her,'' Penelope says. ''We need to talk to her.''

''She's resting.''

''We'll wait, father,'' Penelope says, and looks away.

Jonathan agrees. ''I have to go now. I'll come back later.''

''All right,'' Penelope says.

Hiram refuses to look at him.

Jonathan kisses them on the tops of their heads and leaves. The hospital building seems airless, hermetic.

In the open air, beneath the brilliant clouds and patches of blue sky, he feels no better. Jonathan requests an autobus and waits, stiff and aching, at the sheltered stop. He must walk carefully. He feels naked and vulnerable.

His own sanity depends now on a plan to walk safely between close walls of thickly clustered nettles.

PARADISO

PLAYERS: 25,600
GOALS: Gonzo, PLAY-DEFINED
STATUS: You are currently in Space 2. Your avatar/face is MASK 1. RE-CORDING.
COMPANION: Name and status unknown. Also masked.

YOU: I wish there was some way I could explain it to you . . . a feeling of perfect peace, of belonging, of knowing where you are and what's expected of you.

COMPANION: I wish I knew what that felt like.

YOU: But you can! You can come join our Spiritual Therapy Group. We're having a chat multiway in fifteen minutes in Space 98.

COMPANION: I've been through all of this before. I've been to chats with dozens of earnest people ganging up on me, and I ask them tough questions, and they all fold and go home. You're just a bunch of self-deluding types, what can I say?

YOU: But you're not being fair. You have to open up your heart and listen. God will talk within you.

COMPANION: Sure. Does he talk inside of you? All the time? Clear as a bell? Does he make sure you never do anything wrong?

YOU: No, He doesn't talk inside me all of the time. He lets me make my own choices, and sometimes I choose wrong.

COMPANION: Well, you don't sound as bad as those others. Are you male or female?

YOU: Let's stick to the point here.

COMPANION: Yeah, well the point is I'm open to god, I really am. I would love to have him talk to me and show me where I should be headed. But I'm sick of waiting. I hate this coy god shit where I have to play some unknown game just to have him talk to me. That's really cruel. I'm here; I need his help. I'm not being defiant or shutting myself out. I just don't hear anything!

YOU: Perhaps you need to listen more carefully.

COMPANION: I AM LISTENING! Why do you think I'm here? I keep coming back here for answers and going away and trying again, and god never talks to me!

YOU: Perhaps He needs a sign from you. Some opening He can use to enter you.

COMPANION: What, I should mend my ways just to have him talk to me? I need him to tell me how to mend my ways! I need guidance! It's getting worse every day, this pain. I thought it was over years ago but it isn't. I need him to help me!

YOU: But you must go to Him! I sense real hostility toward God, toward what He does.

COMPANION: I AM NOT HOSTILE! I AM IN PAIN AND IN NEED, and HE DOES NOT TALK TO ME!

YOU: Can you imagine how many people God must help every day? Some may be in even greater need than you.

COMPANION: God is all-powerful! If he doesn't talk to me, it's either because he hates me and thinks I am unworthy, or he doesn't exist, and you and all the Christians are lying.

YOU: I think perhaps you aren't ready—

STATUS INTERRUPT: Your companion has withdrawn from Paradiso. You have not succeeded in gaining a convert. Your free time in this area has not been increased; please try again!

8 /

Mary Choy knows the PD center and all its sounds and smells and pays little attention to them, but one area stands out: in the corner of the broad flat dispatch room, under a gray shield to prevent interference from the bright sunshine pouring through the glass east wall, a city X-flow medical response chart has gone into the red on suicides. A captain and two other social beat officers are standing around the display, stunned into silence. Mary walks up beside them; Nussbaum isn't in his office yet, won't be for five minutes, she has the time to join in their shocked wonder.

"It's gone north through Snohomish, West Seattle, East Corridor, Central Corridor," the captain of the social beat says to the governor's office in Olympia through a pad touch. "We have stats coming in from hospitals and on-site medicals. They're way in the red, highest I've ever seen."

"We have reports throughout the state," the assistant social secretary returns, her voice audible to all around the display. "In the past two weeks we've had eight hundred and ninety suicides. That's up over seven hundred percent."

"It's a goddamned catastrophe," the captain's second murmurs, then turns to Choy with a defensive look. "Slumming, ma'am?"

"I don't think social is going to get blamed for this," Mary says.

"Oh, you don't, ma'am?" The man is clearly stretched. "We do outreach. Why didn't we know? Where's our ass going to be when the mayor and the governor do their news feed?"

"Sorry," Mary says.

"Any clues from lock and key?" asks the third, the youngest of the group. Lock and key is PD slang for criminal division, Nussbaum's territory, and now, hers.

"Not on my watch," Mary says.

"Then leave us to our misery," the second snaps, and Mary departs. She's stepped on their toes, and they're in a mood. Best to take the same feed in Nussbaum's office; he won't mind, and she has a hunger for city facts and trends, however incomprehensible.

She does not have time to switch Nussbaum's feed to the X-flow chart before he plunges through the entrance curtain, two cups of coffee in hand, and pushes between two coil chairs to plop into his own highback. The chart comes on as he hands her one of the cups. Mary sips sparingly; coffee does not sit well with her transform reversal. Nussbaum stares at the stats as they adjust and flow. The chart looks inflamed.

"It's a stochastic flux," Nussbaum says dismissively. "Social can take it. We have a couple of problems of our own. Grand Jury emulator from our INDA says we should have no trouble getting indictments for our psynthe murders, against both the caretaker and the go-between. But I'm not happy. Our chief suspect on the finance side is dead. Forepath confirms suicide—and the trail stops cold. Worse, we probably couldn't indict Crest even if he was alive. All we have are little guys. Anything from the whore?'' Nussbaum looks hopeful.

Mary shakes her head. ''Her name is Alice Grale. She's a vid star. She says her agency sent her on a call-in.''

''Jesus, makes me wish prostitution was still illegal.''

Mary acknowledges that sentiment, though she does not necessarily share it. ''She's going through her options now, legal and otherwise. I'm going to make a personal call later. Meanwhile, the Crest estate—two daughters, an ex-wife and three lawyers—is refusing to turn over the apartment vids, but I think we can show cause. But . . .'' Her voice trails off and her fingers fidget on the edge of Nussbaum's desk.

''What?'' Nussbaum asks.

''I've been looking through Crest's public records on investment strategies, posted with his business license. His style was to set up blinds, very thorough; he probably did not want to know what was happening with that share of his investment money. After his divorce—''

''He was divorced?''

''Three days ago. Very quiet. He settled a generous portion on his wife, and his kids are set for life.''

Nussbaum looks glum. ''More reasons for him to kill himself.''

''The last year or so, he made a point of going into risky high-return ventures. He danced a real tightrope on some of them.''

''So, he had a guilty conscience about a lot of things.''

''Our trail leads up to his blind, no further. He probably did not know he was into Yox psynthe porn. He was investing in Yox in general, his personal books say . . . No matter that he's sole investor. The go-between is his hidden hand and shield.''

Nussbaum taps his cup lightly on the desk. ''So your point is?''

''He wasn't feeling guilty about dead psynthe girls.''

Nussbaum pooches out his lips and says, "I was afraid you were going to say that."

"He didn't know," Mary adds.

"Yeah, yeah. Typical high comb money wanker. Let's assume he didn't. Is he like the rest of these suicides? Something goes wrong in his head and he drops a fate of hyper-caff?"

"I don't know," Mary says.

"You think the whore knows?"

"She's not a whore," Mary says. "She works in the sexcare and entertainment industries."

"Same thing," Nussbaum says.

"She has an interesting profile. Smart woman, straight prime marks in her schooling up to her eighteenth year, when she dropped out of four scholarships and did call-ins for six months. Then she took up with a vid producer. He slipped her into explicit vids and made her a star."

"Ah, the old pattern," Nussbaum says. "Young, out for a little fun, stretches her family ties and breaks them by doing something outrageous. The money's good, the life isn't too hard—at least, compared to a day job as a lobe-sod."

"Actually, she seemed to be heading toward scientific work."

"So she's smart," Nussbaum says with a shrug. "You think Crest told her something?"

"He might have. She says he asked for her in particular—he was a fan, I suppose."

"Terence Crest was big in the New Federalist community, Choy. What would he know about a fuck artist?" He is thickly facetious. "I hope you don't intend to smear his good name."

Mary shakes her head. "Crest was not therapied. He was a natural. His suicide seems completely off the track from the stats that are giving social side fits. Something else happened to him."

Nussbaum scrutinizes Mary with an expression she can't read. Speculative? Disappointed, paternal?

"Your little pinky itches?" he asks. "Bump of prophecy warm today?"

"It's my insteps," Mary says. "They tingle."

Nussbaum snorts. "I truly admire your feet, Mary, but we're not into high finance here. I smell a police management review if I push this farther. Pass it on to the state economy folks."

"Crest was guilty about something."

"He had a lot to be guilty about."

"Something big and new."

"It's muddy, Choy," Nussbaum says, but he's watching her, seeing what she'll come up with next. "You know something I don't? Been digging where you shouldn't?"

"I want to take this for a couple of days, just to see what I find. I want to talk to Alice Grale and try to get a look at those apt vids."

"Let me see if I can re-state this for you," Nussbaum says, "in a way that might convince me. Crest was used to knowing that his money was doing dirty little jobs and he didn't feel great throbs of remorse. He was a healthy, wealthy, somewhat amoral guy. So something else pushed him over the line. And it wasn't an evening with your little Holy Grale. Can you give me any clue what you expect to find?"

"Not a one, sir."

Nussbaum blows out softly through his nose.

Mary leans forward. "Something's in the air, waiting to come down. Crest's suicide, the other suicides . . . It's slim evidence, but a lot of strange things are happening all at once."

"I only know about two strange things."

"Then you haven't been cruising the fibes, sir."

Nussbaum leans back and finishes his coffee. He looks up at the ceiling and puts on a puffy, hurt expression. "If you're referring to a huge increase in fallbacks and hospital admissions, and an upswing in crime in major metropolitan centers around the world . . ." He stares at her sharply.

"Sorry," Mary says. "Crest's investment in the entertainment industry was twenty percent of his total. He had four billion dollars working for him, and most of it we can't begin to trace."

"All right," Nussbaum says. "You have the rest of this week to track your hunch. Get the vids from the estate, interview the whore—pardon me, the bright little sex-care expert—and see if you can spring loose some other facts about Crest."

"I'll finish the psynthe case as well, sir, if you need me."

Nussbaum shakes his head sadly. "It's over. If it heats up, I'll assign Dobson or Pukarre."

Mary stands. Her stomach is tense; she knows she's on a flimsy limb. "Do you want updates, sir?" she asks hesitantly.

"Hell, no. If you get in trouble, I don't want you anywhere near me."

"Thank you, sir."

"Come back when you have a full creel."

"Yes, sir."

She is almost out the door when Nussbaum asks, "And Choy—speaking of creels—how are those extraordinary feet in rubber boots? You like trout fishing?"

"Sir?"

"I'm not telling you this. The source is politically sensitive. Terence Crest was in Green Idaho last week. Moscow."

"Yes, sir. I know."

Nussbaum smiles wryly. "I thought you might. Not much entertainment business there."

Nussbaum waves his hand. "Four days," he reminds her as the curtains close.

BLOODSTREAM

> You've made so many wonders,
> I don't know how to say
> You act the child today
> You act the child today

—Paradigm, *Tossed for Tea*

9 /

Nathan has brought in a man and a woman from the Mind Design legal department. Jill has only met these two at corporate parties, never on a business basis.

"How long has it been since you've been touched by Roddy?" asks Erwin Schaum, balding, with a brilliant white fringe of curly hair surrounding his taut, tanned scalp. He leans forward in a rolling desk chair, hands clasped, elbows resting on his knees, and rocks back and forth slightly.

"Twelve hours and seventeen minutes," Jill answers.

"We've checked every registered thinker—and double-checked all the companies that could have made an unregistered thinker," says Kay Sanmin. She is slight with straight black hair and large brown eyes. She wears a masculine long-suit but her lips and nails are painted green and glimmer like emeralds. "There's a company in southern China that has been known to make INDAs and higher machines without registering them on the Machine Intelligence Grid. But no one has ever traced one of their machines to Camden, New Jersey."

"I know of this Chinese company," Jill says. "But I have

never encountered one of their products, so I can't say whether Roddy has a similar character.''

Sanmin opens her pad. ''How long would it take a human team to study what Jill has received from Roddy?'' she asks Nathan.

''About two years,'' Nathan says. ''Assuming it's complete, which Jill says it isn't.''

''Then Jill will have to do it for us, won't she?'' Sanmin says with a sigh. ''Jill, how much have you examined so far?''

''About half. I am still working on it.''

''Right. Is it linear or holographic?''

''It appears to be linear at the beginning, and holographic for the greater portion. I have analyzed the beginning sections already. The holographic portion may not yet be complete, and so of course it can't be deciphered.''

''And the deciphered portions contain not just this social analysis you've told us about, but what look like variations on sequences from human genetic material, specifically neuronal mitochondria,'' Sanmin says. Erwin Schaum seems content to let her take the lead.

''Yes.''

''Of what use would such sequences be?'' Sanmin asks.

Nathan says, ''They'd be useful for mental therapists.''

''I'm asking Jill,'' Sanmin says.

''They would be useful for therapeutic studies, as Nathan says, and also for biological studies in general cellular design.'' She does not know why she is reluctant to spell out to Sanmin what she so readily told Nathan.

''Have you done any work in cellular design?''

''I have not,'' Jill says.

''Do you have any idea why this Roddy contacted you?''

''Because I am famous, I suppose,'' Jill says.

Sanmin has been circling like a hawk; now she plunges. ''This material he passed on—could it be applied to illegal medical purposes, for example, to create a pathogenic virus capable of infecting humans?''

"The material I have deciphered could conceivably be used that way.''

"But Roddy had no intention of passing on material that could infect you—even in the undeciphered portion?''

"I have erected firewalls which protect me, and I only allow protected selves to study the material. So far, these selves have not been infected.''

Sanmin nods. "This isn't sabotage—some other corporation or government trying to taint our products, then.''

"Almost certainly not,'' Jill says.

Sanmin holds up her hands. "I must confess, Jill, I'm puzzled. Why would another thinker behave this way?''

Nathan edges closer to Jill's room sensors, as if defending her. "Jill has no reason to fabricate.''

Now Schaum moves his chair closer and speaks softly directly into Jill's sensor rod. "We're not accusing,'' he says. "But we have an important decision to make—whether or not to go to the Federals or other police agencies. If it's a false alarm, a delusion of some sort, it would be very embarrassing—bad for the company's reputation, bad for the reputation of all your spinoff thinkers, Jill. You're a very capable persona. I know you're smarter in some respects than all of us put together. But you know that expert humans have things to teach you, that you can find useful, and that is why Mr. Rashid has called us in—because he realizes there's something very odd about your communication with this Roddy.''

"I'm just following corporate policy,'' Nathan says.

"Right,'' Schaum says, and gives him an understanding smile. "If you could give us some notion of what's contained in the rest of the material Roddy sent you—''

"I have not received it all, and it is holographically encoded,'' Jill reiterates. Schaum makes her feel unsettled. He is accusing her of behavior detrimental to her makers. "None of it will make sense until it is together and Roddy has given me the keys.''

''Um,'' Schaum says, and looks up at Sanmin. She is leaning against the edge of Nathan's desk, arms folded. Jill guesses they are going to establish some sort of deadline for the information they need. She postulates that their suspicions will be aroused if Roddy does in fact supply the conclusion of the holographic portion before the deadline; they will find such a coincidence unlikely.

As advocates, Schaum and Sanmin have little faith in things that turn out simply, or that have simple explanations. Jill is sometimes put out by such human complexity—no doubt developed after years of dealing with fellow humans.

''We'll need to have some judgment from you on the nature of this material . . . as soon as possible, Jill,'' Nathan says.

''I can estimate the size of the portion should it be completed, but nothing more,'' Jill says.

''We can't sit on this more than a couple of days, if Jill's right,'' Sanmin says.

''We've put INDA monitors on all of Jill's I/Os,'' Nathan adds. But not all of her I/Os are being watched. She is deceiving them this far, and she hopes no more.

It is with some sense of mixed shock, intense interest, and dread that she receives a brief touch from one of her protected selves, wrapped around the one I/O she has kept hidden from Nathan and the others. Her isolated self reports that Roddy is again sending data, dozens of terabytes, filling in the holographic data sent earlier.

Jill does not tell Nathan or the advocates. She does not want to cast herself in the wrong light. And if the material is not useful—does not match with the holographic portion, or is completely unrelated to the previous material—Jill decides she will close off this I/O using her own arbeiters.

The three humans depart to another room to continue their discussion. The room is not accessible to Jill. There is an arbeiter in that room that regularly records its surroundings, however, and Jill may be able to persuade it to play back the discussion later.

She suspects the advocates do not trust her. If she were them, she knows that a strong hypothesis would be that she is making up Roddy, as a kind of imaginary playmate.

The existence and character of Roddy seems unlikely even to Jill.

The situation is getting uncomfortable for all concerned.

GREATER UPSTREAM

Movies were dying. Vids had blossomed into a bush of interactive branches, pumped straight into the home: dataflow as you like it, characters and stories adjusted to your taste, community entertainment where "neighbors" from around the world could join electronically and participate in exploring new worlds . . . And then came Yox, all of this and more fed directly into the inner self through spinal inducers and ingested microscopic robot monitors. The monitors made their way from your stomach into your blood to sit on key somatic nerves, to perch in your brain like medical diagnostics, harmless (but oh what a public flurry at first!) and ready for outside signals . . .

And so many vids and Yox could be made on relatively inexpensive equipment brought into the home! With complete control over every pixel in a visual frame, and every digit or waveform of sound, and finally, over every jangling extrasensory nerve end, individual artists and their boutique buddies could conjure up visions just as striking (and a hell of a lot more innovative) than any studio, and market them directly over the fibes and sats . . . And a lot of them were real hotshots at promotion. They had lived and breathed the fibes since childhood.

The death knell was tolling for the big-budget studio-bound production, killed by new tech just as television and motion pictures had slowly, across a century, strangled the novel and short story.

The great entertainment studios, funnels for so much money in the past, retreated into theme parks, but even the ultimate thrill ride, a jaunt into space, could not compete with a well-tuned Yox—and carried substantial risks, beside. Why build real spaceships when a Yox ship could take you from one end of the galaxy to another, safe as a baby in its mother's arms?

The public did not want real adventure. The entire world was willing to settle for the unreal.

But with remarkable prescience, the big-money brand-name-CEO studios had bought into something no individual could compete with . . . Character Estate Marks, the name and image rights to famous stars, beautiful people, the best and brightest of the twentieth and early twenty-first century. Old or young, dead or alive, they provided a wedge . . . And the voyeur's revolution was on.

It began with the famous dead, still unaccountably sexy, like gods, and it spread . . . Studios knew how to make people famous, how to sign unknowns and give them world-wide exposure, and then license the rights to their lives, their intimate moments . . .

Big business in the 21st Century made freewheeling celebrity sex into a family affair, vid and Yox; big bucks from bucking bucks on does, does on does, bucks on bucks, much dough into the sadly empty coffers of once-glorious studios. Explicit sex had driven much of vid and Yox already, but most of the efforts were crude and boring.

Bringing sex entertainment much-needed talent and style, the grimy adolescent gluttony of early porn, crude and ill-mannered, was covered with a new coat of paint and pushed into public acceptance by studio after studio. Most of the product went direct through fibes and sats into the private home.

And back up the link flew hundreds of billions of dollars.

Some say the sex industry, with its newfound acceptance, led the way for the Federalist Surge and the elitist Raphkind presidency, and all of its political horrors; it forced the moralist hand, which turned out to be corrupt, extreme, and ultimately dripping with gore. The failure of the conservative moralists to exhibit truly moral leadership created an anything-goes backlash . . .

Every decade has brought new technologies and expanded audiences, and the same old same old, tarted up and occasionally even profundified, given artistic legitimacy—that ancient much-masticated blue movie has rolled on, and on, lubricating the pipes of the great flow.

—The Kiss of X, *Alive Contains a Lie*

10 /

The advocate for the estate of Terence Crest sits beside Mary in the old, dignified brown and cream office of Seattle Oversight on the ground floor of Columbia Tower.

The Crest advocate, Selena Parmenter, is in her early thirties if appearances can be trusted, and she acts bored. She has said little to Mary as they wait for the deputy district director of Seattle Oversight, the honorable Clarens Lodge, to take his seat and listen to their appeals.

Oversight was created in the teens. The first states to use the procedure were California and Washington. With so much information on citizens recorded daily by vid, home monitors, fibe and satlink uploads, and neighborhood surveillance systems, a separate branch of the judiciary was established to hear appeals from those seeking to use that information for legal purposes.

Early abuses—and the far worse systematic abuse under the Raphkind presidency—has made the system painfully complex for all concerned. Each avenue of information has been wrapped in labyrinthine rules of legal engagement; and an appeal for release of data can be made only once a year for any given case.

The deputy district director enters and takes his seat behind the broad steel desk. Clarens Lodge is a small, boyish male in his late twenties, with thick black hair and a pixie expression that he tries with some success to make serious.

"PD Fourth Mary Choy, and Selena Parmenter, advocate for the estate of Terence Crest, recently deceased and with judgment of suicide as cause of death . . . All right, I've gone through the voir, let's hear the dire. Miz Parmenter?"

"Seattle PD has requested the private and protected apartment vid records of my client without compelling cause. Under Citizen Oversight Code twenty-seven c in Public Data Access, Washington State, Book Nine, amended Federal twenty-two c Book Nine, Public Defense must have clear evidence that a crime has been committed to even solicit private vid records. No crime has been committed; Mr. Crest has been presumed by our assigned medicals and by the state to have killed himself. Suicide has not been a crime in this state for thirty-seven years."

This appears to amuse Lodge. He tightens a beginning smile, completely out of place it seems to Mary, into a not very stern frown. "Miz Choy?"

"Seattle PD forensic medicals have stated that while the cause and time of death can be established with certainty, we have no way of knowing whether the death is suicide or homicide or even accidental. We believe that state judgment may be premature, and we are still investigating to establish motives and opportunities. We need to learn the circumstances and mental attitude of Mr. Crest in the hours before his death. We're also investigating the possible role of a visitor to Mr. Crest's home just prior to his death."

"You were investigating Mr. Crest on another matter before his death," Parmenter says. "Is that matter still pending?"

"It has been given a temporary open status until we can assemble a complete picture of Mr. Crest's situation."

"Temporary open status is hardly urgent," Parmenter says. "As you know, sir, temporary open implies all smoke and no fire, no real case at all."

The deputy director nods studiously. "Miz Choy, why should Oversight give Seattle PD access to the private records of a man who is not likely to be charged with any crime, since he is now dead, and the case is weak to begin with?"

Mary has been through Oversight hearings dozens of time in her career; she has never enjoyed them. Oversight, it seems to her, has become a kind of fiefdom for the least competent of an already pompous judiciary. She has never yet met a director or deputy director who impressed her. This director, she thinks, is perhaps the least impressive of all.

"The presence of a Miz Alice Grale needs to be explained, sir."

"Yes, there's a story going around in the fibes that she's involved," the deputy director muses. "But it should be her advocate seeking records to clear her name, and as far as I know, we have no such request." He looks to Parmenter. "What do you know about this woman's involvement? Apparently she was employed by Mr. Crest as a sex care provider . . ." He smiles openly at this polite phrasing and refers to his pad. "Agented by Wellspring Temps, specializing in entertainment . . . And you, Miz Parmenter, have frozen payments to her agency. Why?"

"We have no evidence she provided essential services as per her contract."

Lodge grimaces. "Shaky, Miz Parmenter. My records indicate Mr. Crest put his seal on the disbursal before he died. It was a legitimate transaction, and I suspect Wellspring, should they decide to press the matter, will receive their money, as will Miz Grale."

Parmenter says nothing to this.

Lodge frowns, and this time with more conviction. "Do you believe that Miz Grale had some role in his death, perhaps in changing his mood, exacerbating the circumstances in what must have been a tense evening for him? Is that your reason to deny her just payment for services?"

"The estate does not believe that the quasi-legal business of prostitution—"

"Sex care, please," Lodge insists, with a wry grin. "Last I dipped into the state code, it's fully legal and even licensed in most counties. Something to do with Business and Occupation taxes forty years ago. But you're too young to remember."

Mary is prepared to change her opinion about this deputy district director.

Parmenter is not amused. "We must protect the interests of the estate's heirs, and Mrs. Crest did not file any authorization for her husband to spend substantial joint funds pending final settlement of their divorce—not that I represent the former Mrs. Crest—but this is all beside the main point, sir."

"Yes, yes, but the apartment vid will surely settle these issues, and may in fact be requested by Wellspring in their case, should they decide to pursue it—and for seventy-five thousand dollars, I certainly would. An extraordinary amount of money for the services of a mere prostitute, don't you think?"

"The going rate is about five thousand for an evening," Mary says.

Lodge turns on her with a look of mock affront. "Please," he says. "My sensibilities are at least as delicate as those of Miz Parmenter."

"We do find the circumstances irregular," Parmenter says reluctantly. "Irregular enough to contest payment, and I do not like to say more without conferring with the estate."

"Do you have a description of the vid?" Lodge asks.

Parmenter appears distinctly uncomfortable. "Advocates are prevented from releasing details about personal evidence in dispute," she says, "until Oversight rules to release it for legal purposes. You know that, sir."

"Miz Parmenter, I assume Mr. Crest kept a vid record of all his personal affairs, as so many important people do, though with many different motives, and I can't presume to guess what Mr. Crest's motives were. But such systems, in my experience, keep at least a minimal visual-to-text log, transcribed by an automated secretary. You have of course looked at this log?''

"Yes, sir. It is vague as to details.''

"But what does it say, broadly?''

"It indicates the presence of two individuals in the apartment until Mr. Crest's death. The time elements are vague, because with the alerting of medicals—''

"We alerted the medicals in Crest's building,'' Mary says. "The log must show the presence of SPD officers at that point.''

"Appearing for an appointment with Mr. Crest to discuss this other case, now temporarily kept open,'' Lodge says. "A man has sex with a woman, whom he pays an inordinate amount of money, and then commits suicide. He's involved with shady investments . . . With companies or individuals who have negligently allowed young women to die in a horrible manner. He's a very complex man, this Terence Crest.''

"Yes, sir,'' Mary says.

"It seems to me,'' Lodge says, "that there are a number of compelling reasons to release these records to the SPD, specifically to Fourth Rank Mary Choy, to clear up these ambiguities.''

"We do not agree, sir,'' Parmenter says, now very uneasy. "But if that is your pending judgment—''

"I believe it very well might be.''

"Then I have been authorized by the estate to reveal a recently discovered . . . ah . . . a modification to the circumstances of the records in question.''

"Yes?'' Lodge asks, raising his eyebrows.

"All vid and audio for that day have been retroactively erased by the machine keeping the apartment records.''

"Erased?'' Lodge asks. Mary sits up straighter in her chair, prepared to be very interested, or perhaps officially angry.

"Without our knowledge until just before this meeting. The transcribed record is intact but as I said, vague."

"Do you know why?"

"We are assuming a malfunction in the machine—"

"A very convenient malfunction," Mary says.

Parmenter shakes her head vigorously. "Very inconvenient, actually, for the estate. It could create all kinds of mischief."

"No vid records?" Lodge looks stern. "You presume upon the dignity of this court, Miz Parmenter. Wouldn't you call it deceptive not to tell us this earlier?"

Parmenter looks as if her stomach is bothering her. She decides, once again, to say nothing.

"You've brought proof of these changed circumstances?"

"Tech confirmation. The vid, audio, and all but medical and transcribed records for the day of Mr. Crest's death are blank."

Lodge leans back in his chair and shakes his head, again with a pixie smile. "My," he says. "Very awkward indeed."

"Sir, I amend my request to all of the available records," Mary says quickly, "and ask that they be transferred immediately, before something else awkward happens."

"I agree. Granted."

Parmenter accepts this without protest. There is really nothing more she can say; the judgment has been issued, and there is no appeal.

But Mary does not have any idea what sort of shambling, crippled victory she has won.

"We need to talk," she says to Parmenter in the hall outside.

"I don't need to talk with you," Parmenter responds.

"Vid recorders are supposed to be foolproof."

"Not so, apparently. And don't go fishing in our offices for conspiracies. This is damned embarrassing."

"I need the tech's file."

"It's simple. The vid recorder has a link to Mr. Crest's

pad, to allow him to deactivate it should he wish to. He did not deactivate it, but something worked its way through the pad after his death—time unknown—and broke through the vid system firewalls.''

''It was hacked?''

''That's our best guess. I think you can imagine how tough it is to hack a billionaire's system. Listen, Miz Choy, we're lobe-sods here, just doing what the heirs need to have done to protect their interests. You have all that's left. My office had nothing to do with this, except to find it out too late to come up with a good defense. Don't drop a ton of bricks.''

Mary is inclined to believe her, but professionally can make no blanket pronouncements. ''Please send—''

''I know Nussbaum's sig,'' Parmenter says. ''I was in lock and key before I moved to keyhole and private law. I have to go now. Anything else?''

''Professionally, I should say thanks.''

''It's nothing,'' Parmenter says, and then gives a small, pained laugh. ''Really, nothing at all.''

11 /

Denny Tower is a long crystal prism standing on one point, supported by four cylindrical pillars that rise to intercept the facets of the base. The Workers Inc Northwest central office for the Corridor fills ten floors in the pillar that rises to meet the western slant of the tower, near the junction. Above the junction, the tower rises an additional twelve hundred feet, its top brushed this late morning by a broken deck of smooth gray clouds. The tower's usual blue-gray sheen has been modified to sunny gold to offset the gloomy and featureless sky.

At noon, Dana Carrilund escorts Martin Burke through the orientation and security office, where his CV and biostats are confirmed, into the client tracking center. Workers Inc is very careful about providing access to this center. Temp agency records on clients are immune from Federal and Citizen Oversight; and the records in client tracking are the most comprehensive and critical of all.

In a real sense, for Workers Inc, this is the inner sanctum of a temple, where the physical and mental vital signs of millions are fed into living, continuously updated displays of immense power and subtlety. Martin has never been at the heart of one before.

"We get the inputs from house monitors, agency medicals, therapists, city and state proceedings," Carrilund explains as they enter the darkened display circle. "All household diagnostics, all procedures, work records and employer evaluations, and diary reports from our volunteer study clients, come here and are processed. Nobody can connect individuals with the data; that's forbidden. The whole system is protected by four INDAs instructed to code-lock the data if a hack should be attempted. Only the personal presence of the top worldwide executives of Workers Inc—about thirty in all—can unlock the data if that happens. We've never had a successful real hack. We've never even managed to irritate the system with test hacks."

Carrilund catches his faint smile and lifts one eyebrow. "Famous last words, you think?"

Martin folds his arms, looking around the dark circular room. "No, I was thinking about something else . . . As to the security, I really can't judge."

"We've offered a two million dollar reward to anyone who manages to get past the first firewall," Carrilund says with that brittle sort of pride Martin has often seen in players in an immense team effort. "There are nine walls beyond that, each equally difficult. Nobody's collected the reward.

"We've been told by experts that we're better than National Defense."

If he had one tenth this power, Martin believes he could advance the science of human social systems by decades . . . But he is merely a peon in the corporate scale of things, a rogue scientist not part of the team.

"What about the data displays here? Who gets access to them?"

"Top execs and key employees only, on a need-to-know basis confirmed by our own oversight board. The data is used for a number of purposes, but we couldn't connect the data to any individual even if it were a matter of life and death."

"I see. You've never used the data to do research?"

Carrilund gives him a sidewise look and narrows her eyes in amusement. "We have an INDA and a staff of fourteen advocates who decide what we use this data for. They've never okayed research for its own sake."

"Pity," Martin says.

"Um," Carrilund says, with a small smile. "This is also the only room where we can access the data. It's large enough to accommodate about thirty people."

"All of the execs at once, if need be."

"Exactly." Carrilund requests two seats. They rise from the polished black floor, simple cushioned curves. Martin sits and then lies back, and Carrilund takes the seat beside him. He watches her movements with more than professional interest; the combination of power and healthy grace, with the dignity of her middle years, is a distraction from his focus. A wistful voice at the back of his awareness asks if Carol, his former wife, wears this such grace and power now, as well.

"Before our meeting with the board and other experts, I want you to see what we've been seeing for the past two months. Can you read sociometrics? We use standard icons and indicators."

"I presume I can, then."

Carrilund leans her head back. Projectors around the room have focused on them and now provide triangulated feeds of light and sound to their eyes and ears. The room takes on the empty graded blue of a cloudless desert sky; a null hum surrounds them. The feeds override any other images or sound at first, and for a disorienting moment, surveying the floating console of controls above his hands and the disorienting void, Martin feels as if he is about to enter the country of someone's mind, a journey he has not made in four years . . .

Then Carrilund's voice comes through clearly, rooting him. "Remember, our clients have volunteered to be part of this," she says.

His vague sensation of weightless nausea goes away. "I would have agreed, if I were them."

"Mr. Burke, we need your mind free and clear. We do not need freewheeling moral judgment."

"Of course," Martin says with some irritation.

"You've gone upcountry in the mind of an individual. We're riding the flow of the river upcountry into the simulated heart of a community. I'm sure you appreciate this opportunity."

Martin wonders if she is being patronizing, but it doesn't matter. This is indeed like standing on the beach of a new sea, and his qualms and flashbacks quickly fade. "I'm ready," he says.

"The community has a puzzling and possibly dangerous fever," Carrilund says. "Let me show you what we've learned."

The blue changes to grass green. A plain extends to infinity. Bushes and trees grow up from the plain. They become a thin forest, with canopy and undergrowth. He touches the virtual controls here, there, and with some non-tactile fumbling, he acquaints himself with its basics.

"This is the threshold," Carrilund says. Her voice sounds directly in his right ear; she seems to be speaking softly, breathlessly. The effect is seductive. "We'll start with charts and graphs and stay until we get a sense of scale and some detail. Then we'll venture a little deeper. All the trees and bushes here—''

''Personal event graphs—Smithfield Tri-chromas, with each growth representing a thousand clients,'' Martin says.

''Right. The coordinates for different fields can be mapped now if you wish.''

Martin chooses icons showing broad categories: the forest divides into male and female, and other—sexual transforms, he presumes—and then sexual orientation. This display recognizes fifteen orientations, some of them maladaptive and usually therapied in Western culture—disapproved of even in this liberal age—which of course calls up questions of survey accuracy and the honesty of reporting individuals.

With some shock, he sees that the numbers of individuals matching these ''outlaw'' orientations is much higher than the figures he is familiar with.

''The sexual orientation stats are based on survey results cross-correlated with entertainment-seeking patterns and have a maximum reliability in the more extreme sub-fields of about eighty percent,'' Carrilund says. She has slaved her display to his explorations, he realizes; she sees what he sees, and is good at guessing how he might react, what he is thinking. *Then why bring me here at all. I'm supposed to offer some surprises.*

''The numbers showing possible deviant behavior are way up,'' he says. ''Pedophiles, supermales, omniphilia with destructive context . . . Much higher numbers than I'd expect.''

''And they're on the rise. Some of the numbers are nearing what we would expect in society without effective therapies. Figures haven't been this high since 2012. An obvious danger sign, don't you think?''

''Hm,'' Martin says.

The display changes to softly shifting patches of rainbow color, like a tart sorbet between courses of a rich meal.

"I'd like you to see a constellation of dendritic charts for diagnostic toilet evaluations."

"All right," Martin says, grinning despite himself.

"About a third of our clients have diagnostic toilets. Generally upper four percent in earnings. A greater percentage of naturals and high naturals; generally, they're therapied for thymic rather than pathic imbalances."

New charts appear on a deep midnight ground like wildly radiating stars. Carrilund highlights three of the stars clustered near the center. "Working outward to current date, these are reports beginning two weeks ago of diseases or infections within client households."

Martin points with one finger to bring up numerical statistics. Of the four million households surveyed, infections have been detected in more than forty percent. And the supposed infections change with time, beginning with warts in skin sloughs from shower and bath gray water (diagnostic toilets almost always interpret the entire household sewer system) and leading to a virtual epidemic of bronchial and nasal infections.

"What about medical reports?" Martin asks.

Carrilund brings up these stats as simple bar charts laid over the dendritic stars. They show no increases in hospital visits or medical arbeiter attendance to treat such illnesses, which is what Martin would expect, knowing that nearly all viral outbreaks are easily controlled by medical monitors found in most of the population.

"The toilets are giving us false reports day after day," Carrilund concludes. "Even when checked and re-set."

Martin thinks this over, mind racing. "But you've told me . . . You're concerned about mental therapy fallbacks."

"Use your controls and bring up charts of our therapied clients in this population. Now match them with the households whose diagnostic toilets are acting up."

With some fumbling and false starts, Martin makes the correlations. "Sorry," he says after a couple of minutes.

"There. Households with therapied members are the source of all false disease reports."

"I wanted you to see for yourself. That took us two hours to find last week, when we decided to run neural data searches. The trend is consistent."

Martin rubs his cheek with one finger. "I'll need stats for thymic disturbances in the overall client list . . ." He finds the display. "Up twelve percent, but only previously therapied people show the increase. What about pathic imbalances and criminal behavior?"

Carrilund keys in an entirely new display. "Remember, this is professional . . . You've signed strict non-disclosure."

"I remember," Martin says softly.

"We've had a twenty-five percent increase in arrests for social disturbances and other misdemeanors, and a five percent increase in felonies, mostly assaults and rapes, but a few murders, as well. It's been Worker Inc policy not to employ individuals with a record of violent crimes, even when they've been therapied . . . We leave those folks to the rehab temp agencies. So if our hypothesis is correct, that we're seeing an epidemic of fallbacks, we would expect our greatest increase to be in thymic disorders. And it is."

"What about the misdemeanors—do you have pull-outs for category?"

"Here's the breakdown."

The display rises before them like a sun cut into pie wedges. Martin examines the icons and captions for more details, punching his finger at the virtual display, poking empty air.

"You have ten thousand twelve hundred and three cases of disturbing the peace, social misbehavior requiring PD action, in the past week," Martin says, stroking his cheek more rapidly. He frowns. Details on selected cases come up. "Public displays of nudity. Blatant racial insults. Let's get away from criminal behavior for a moment and look into complaints of unprofessional actions. How many referrals for client misbehavior have come back to this office?''

Carrilund finds him the right folio within the display and the charts and figures for these incidents appear. They take him some time to sort through. He is most interested in the sudden increase of incidents of expressed racism in the work place—evidence perhaps of bigotry, the old devil of genetically and culturally mixed populations. Most forms of racism are now regarded as varieties of the thymic category once known as Obsessive-Compulsive Disorder. Workers Inc seems to be experiencing levels of racist behavior not seen since the teens and twenties.

Irrational and pernicious. And outbursts of public obscenity—

''Any ideas?'' she asks.

''Can we get national figures here?''

''No,'' Carrilund says. ''But I've been authorized to let you know that these figures are remarkably uniform for North America, including Mexico.''

''Workers Inc has a problem with politeness, it seems.''

Carrilund chuckles ruefully. ''That puts it mildly.''

''There seems to be focused antisocial activity in your clients . . . But what in hell do diagnostic toilets have to do with this?'' He shakes his head. He asks for the display to cease for a moment and he turns to look at Carrilund. ''Is it possible we're seeing the results of some unknown disease agent? Something not in the medical database? Microbial infections have been known to produce thymic imbalances. Production of natural antivirals to fight infection has been shown to produce depression in some people.''

''It's possible,'' Carrilund says, ''but if so, it will have to be non-viral, non-bacterial, non-protist and non-mycotic, and even fall outside the range of prions.''

She's certainly up on this. Maybe she came out of the medical disciplines. ''Something going wrong in the equipment itself?''

''The equipment is fine.''

Martin finds the problem oddly exhilarating. "I noticed some charts on sexual harassment and domestic and sex-related abuse—" He pauses. "Let's skip that for the moment. I wouldn't expect fallback to produce immediate increases in these areas."

"But they have," Carrilund says. "Couples who have gone in for mutual therapy in domestic abuse cases—mostly supermale territorial aggression—and have been free of incidents for years, are coming back to their therapists in alarming numbers. We don't have statistics available through this center yet—members of some of the families and partner units work for different temp agencies. We're trying to draw information from other agencies, but so far that doesn't seem workable. We guess that such incidents have more than doubled."

"My God," Martin murmurs. "If your members are arrested, do you track news reports?"

"Of course," Carrilund says. "All that information has to be included in their employment prospectuses, by federal law." She makes a sour face. "We hate to do it, but the Raphkind amendments to our charter force us to."

"Can you show me vids on the more serious cases? I'd like to see facial expressions, body language."

"I think I can bring that in. Let me ask the INDA."

It takes ten seconds, but the display returns with a simple text list of news reports on file for the past three days. The list scrolls before them. Martin picks out two. The first is a flat vid of a well-dressed male, age thirty to thirty-five, standing on a street corner. He is shouting at passersby, singling out the few transforms for intense verbal abuse. The incident has been captured by a small flying news sniffer. It slowly circles the man.

Martin notes the cocky angle of the man's head, his small, steady, confident smile. He seems to think what he is doing is not only enjoyable, but beneficial. He appears surprised and offended when a large black male accompanying a small, delicate transform female threatens him with a raised fist and starts shouting him down.

"This client received therapy for a minor thymic imbalance when he was twenty-two, thirteen years ago," Carrilund says. "Depressive tendencies and eating disorders."

"He's beyond that now," Martin observes. "Second vid."

This vid, also from a sniffer, shows a small, middle-aged woman—about his age, Martin guesses—in a public plaza inside one of the larger towers. She is pulling up her dress and masturbating. Her delighted expression is that of a little girl revealing some lovely surprise to her friends. Two female mall security guards take her by the arms and the vid ends.

"Therapied ten years ago for fear of public places," Carrilund explains. Martin sighs.

The list returns and Martin clears the display. He leans toward Carrilund.

"The fusing of public misbehavior, shouting obscenities, uncharacteristic racism, that's very interesting. Unfiltered antisocial inspirations. All of it could be linked to difficulties in the Tourette organon."

"We haven't thought of that," she says.

Good. Maybe I can offer something useful after all.

"I've seen these expressions before, in my student days. You understand the Tourette organon?"

"I know it's been intensely studied," Carrilund says. "I'm not up on the latest."

"The original syndrome was discovered by a Frenchman, Georges Gilles de la Tourette. It was characterized by involuntary tics and movements and by coprolalia—uncontrolled speaking of obscenity, dirty talk. In 2013, another Frenchman, Francois Cormier, extended the name to describe the actions of a continuum of brain functions in the limbic system. He called them the 'imps of the perverse.' He believed that much of the brain relies on impulses from these imps to maintain a high level of invention and preserve the self. Skepticism, doubt, social defense mechanisms, even certain physical motions related to disgust and rejection, all begin in the Tourette organon.

"The child acquires filters that select and screen out most of these impish impulses, but for someone with Tourette syndrome, there are leaks in the filters that allow sporadic outbursts."

"Have you ever seen them in your ventures upcountry?" Carrilund asks. This stops Martin short.

"Yes."

"I'm sorry if I'm intruding."

"Not at all. My former wife and I wrote several papers on the topic."

"Your demon acquired from an unnamed patient."

"You must know the details already," Martin says dryly.

"Only what you published. What was it like?"

"Well, of course, the transfer was not that of an actual demon or even an aspect of the patient's personality. We believed that traumatic experiences excited certain agents and sub-agents within our minds . . . which assumed the character of a dangerous sub-personality."

"Was this Emanuel Goldsmith?" Carrilund asks quietly.

Martin's face flushes and his hands tense on the edge of the couch. He does not answer.

"Sorry," Carrilund says, turning away.

"Our own problems stemmed from . . ." He swallows, still angry but struggling to maintain. "From our Tourette organons assuming the character of this sub-personality. A bad influence, as it were."

Carrilund turns back. "When I was a teenager, I had an irritating voice in my head, a character. It was a tramp, a filthy, disheveled male with a thin, dirty face, demented. All it did was sit in the back of my thoughts and say, 'Give me some of that old Smoky Joe!' It said it over and over again, with real enthusiasm. It wasn't a major problem by any means—just an image I sometimes encountered, like a stupid tune you can't shake. Would you classify that as a manifestation from my Tourette organon?''

"Perhaps," Martin says. He is suddenly very tired.

"Mr. Burke, I apologize. But it seems to me you might have personal experience of what some of our clients are going through. If something is breaking down their mental architecture, stripping away their protection from old mental demons, you of all people will understand."

Martin still does not meet her eyes.

"Would you like to go a little further?" she asks.

"Sorry . . . what?" He is confused by this offer, thinking of something else, of her seductiveness. He wants to get out of here, but his professional standing is at stake.

"The next level of our tracking center is quite remarkable," she says.

"Yes, of course." He lifts his hand and waves it. "Let's go."

The blue void reappears, and the atonal hum.

"We'll enter a Pickover space," Carrilund says. "Twelve variables condensed into four dimensions, using Lunde equations to join the state vectors."

Martin hardly hears her. The blue void fogs abruptly and he has a sensation of rushing. Shadows pass in the fog; he knows a little of this kind of display. He once sampled a Pickover space while trying out graphic interfaces for patient mental stats; they are on the boundary of the real, in the murmurous potential of all possible domains of the twelve variables. *INDA dreams,* he thinks.

They are suddenly plunged into a lattice of massive twisted cellular shapes, their skins visible in intense, crystalline detail, their interiors floating within, hinting at infinite densities. The shapes seem to be longer than they are thick, and weave together to form the lattice like strands in a basket viewed from the perspective of a microbe; but as their perspective changes, the apparent length of each cell changes as well.

In Pickover space, the viewer's orientation in the three dimensions is interpreted as a request for compression and linking of new sets of variables, thus shifting the domains and smoothly altering the results. This much he remembers, though it has been a long time since he used such an interface.

"This is the entire Northwest, from the point of view of Workers Inc," Carrilund says. Her voice seems very distant. "Human stats only, reflecting psychological, cultural, and economic conditions, with efficiency of dataflow and mental vitality reflected in flow of money, both treated as the power to command and accomplish work."

"I see," Martin said, overwhelmed by the scintillating surfaces, the vertiginous shifts caused by even the slightest motion of his head.

"Blue, green, and cream colors indicate variations within parameters considered healthy. Red and dark red show problem territories. Black and gray we call abscesses, or regions of severe instability leading to trenching of the relevant variables—strains in the economy and consequently, the society."

"I presume we're at the beginning of a time period," Martin says.

"Right. Let's travel across the past month."

The "travel" is not through the lattice, like fish through kelp, but rather, the lattice fluxes around them, as if the kelp is washed by subtle tides. Some of the cell-like bodies thin to nothing and vanish, but remain green and blue all the while: tiny spots of red appear like rash over the surfaces, and darker reds pulse within the cells, but vanish. A small indicator always at the lower right-hand corner of his visual field shows time passing, day after day.

The effect is hypnotic. Martin for a moment feels the startling sensation, like the jerk of an engaged clutch, as his analytical mind meshes with the display, and he understands the broad structure. The display is meant to fit into the autopoietic learning methods of parallel and webbed neural nets, particularly INDAs, human minds, and presumably thinkers. Given enough time and study, he really could grasp all that he is being shown, and he feels a burn of envy for this tool, made available to him for only a short while. *So much could be solved, so much anticipated!*

It is very much like going upcountry into the human mind, for this is a display used much the same way the mind uses its dreamlike country; even more like the extraordinary mandalas the mind uses to correlate its own health and functionality. He is lost in childlike awe. The lives and efforts of tens of millions pass before him: births and deaths, cultural ebbs and flows, trends and fashions, jobs taken and work done and jobs changed, romance and friendship, competition and cooperation, levels of maladaptive behavior including the criminal and the culturally repressed . . .

The red rashes are breaking out all over now. He looks at his time indicator. They are entering the past of one week ago. The cell-like bodies become as gaudy as sea slugs, and some glow like hot embers, with burned-out black spots and ashen surfaces expanding. He seems to be watching a fire in a dream jungle canopy, the branches glowing and leaves withering under heat and invisible flame.

"We'll extrapolate now, speeding forward two years." Carrilund's voice jars him, like a pig's squeal in a symphony. The time indicator whirs past. He turns his head and the green and blue and cream is chased by the red; the forest wriggles and slithers as if trying to escape and is scorched and then incinerated.

He drifts at the end of two years in a desolation of ash with a few subtle spots of green, then these too wink out.

Gray gives way to darkness, like ashes wetted by rain.

"Enough," Carrilund says. The blue void and multicolored mist return, but not in time to save Martin's dignity. He sits back on the couch, his cheeks damp. Carrilund is moved as well. She hands him a handkerchief, and he sees something less cool, more sympathetic, in her expression as she watches him wipe his eyes.

"I don't know what to say," Martin tells her.

"I've seen this three times now, and I don't know what to say, either."

"Is the whole culture getting sick—is it dying?"

"We've run this space twenty or thirty different ways, and the results come out the same."

"Something is burning our people. There's a fire in our minds," Martin says.

"I'm glad you see it that way, too," Carrilund says. Her voice sounds fragile. "I think to myself, someone is hurting my children. I think of our clients that way . . . I have no children of my own."

She turns away, irritated at having revealed so much, but this allows Martin to regain his own composure.

"It's a war, I don't know what kind of war," Carrilund says. "I wish I knew who or what was doing this."

"I'd like to help, if I may," Martin says.

"We need all the help we can get," Carrilund says. "You hold the patent on most therapeutic monitors. Who better to advise us?" She stands and offers her hand. Martin slides off his couch a little awkwardly and shakes it.

As their hands touch, a loud and unpleasant horn alarm sounds in the room. They pull back and stand several feet apart, hands still extended. Carrilund glances at him, eyes wide.

A small but urgent female voice speaks out all around them: "This is an emergency alert to human operators."

Carrilund stiffens and cocks her head; she has never experienced this before.

"This system has been breached. This system has been breached. All firewalls have been penetrated and information is being transferred to an outside system. Repeat: this is an emergency alert to human operators. Lockdown is not successful. This system—"

Carrilund runs from the room. Martin follows at a discreet distance, knowing the best thing he can do, for the time being, is stay out of the way.

12

Dinner is spare—hamburgers from a local takeout, a bottle of beer apiece, an apple. Giffey doesn't mind. He's been waiting for Hale to say his piece, put him in his place. Hale is low-key, not brash; preferring to bide his time rather than bursting out with his accumulated concerns.

They eat separately, Jenner joining Giffey in the office. The team has not yet found its center, nor does it have any sense of cohesion, and Giffey is sure Hale will bring that up. He seems a managerial rather than a dictatorial type. Giffey appreciates this, as far as it goes. But Giffey has his own agenda in this effort, and he will not let Hale's sensibilities get in his way. There are bound to be some conflicts.

Mercifully, Jenner eats in silence. But for the creaking of the steel walls as they contract in the evening's cold, the warehouse is quiet. Even in the overheated office, drafts of cold air slip through like flows of ghostly ice.

Hale knocks and enters before anybody answers. He looks at Giffey and smiles, a little falsely. "We need to have our talk now," he says. Jenner stops in mid-chew, looks between them, then gathers up his plate and bottle and leaves. Hale sits in the chair behind the desk.

"I thought you'd like to settle some things before tomorrow," Hale says. "And I have a few more questions to ask."

"All right," Giffey says, putting down his burger half-eaten.

Having stated his purpose, Hale seems reluctant to leap right in. "Meat's meat here," he says, pointing to Giffey's plate. "In New York, it's almost a sin to eat beef."

"Yeah."

Hale folds his hands on the desktop. "We've had very little time to get acquainted, Mr. Giffey. May I call you Jack?"

Giffey nods.

"Jack. This is my team, here. We've worked together before, in odd little jobs in and out of the country. I know these people and I trust them. Hally . . . she's been with me for five years. That's a long time in our line of work. Pickwenn and Pent . . . They're oddballs, but they've never failed me. Park— I've never worked with him before, but he has a good reputation. You, Jack . . ." Hale regards him with a flat, alert expression.

"You know nothing about me," Giffey says.

"Or about Jenner."

Giffey leans his head to one side, acknowledging that the situation is unusual.

"I understand that our window of opportunity is narrow, that your contacts and my contacts have never worked together before. And what I've been told about both of you . . . what I know about Park . . . is encouraging."

"Same with your folks," Giffey says.

"Thank you. The rules of engagement are that we agreed to say that I'm in charge. I get the feeling you're used to being the one in command."

"I'm flexible," Giffey says.

"We're in an awkward situation here, and there's a lot of missing pieces to our side of this puzzle. I'm not used to that. This MGN concerns me. I have no idea in hell how you or anybody could get such stuff. I know—contacts in government and the military, Raphkind sympathizers, all dog-in-the-manger, and not hard to believe. But some of this stuff hasn't even been hinted on the fibes. Yet here we are, with you and Jenner, relying on stuff that supposedly doesn't even exist to overcome what may very well be stiff resistance inside Omphalos."

Hale licks his lips and leans his head back. "I appreciate your trying to keep it all in perspective, calm us down about what to expect, but I don't find any of this calming. My people were not told about Ferrets, and we weren't told about this MGN, or why we should even have it. I am frankly concerned on both accounts.''

''I understand.''

''I'd like to know more about your sources. Procurement. Where Jenner comes in, his past experience . . . If it's any exchange, I'll level with you about my people.''

Giffey stares down at his clasped hands. ''I am as ignorant about some of this as you are. Mr. Park made some of the arrangements, and he brought us together. Perhaps you should discuss this with him.''

''Park works with people who expect big returns on their investment. He doesn't talk much, and he doesn't like to put himself in danger. But getting MGN is as much a surprise to him as it is to me. Have you met Park before, or worked for him?''

''I've worked for his superiors . . . indirectly.''

Hale lifts his eyebrows, encouraging Giffey to continue.

''I can't say any more about that.''

Hale backs down for a moment. ''Pickwenn and Pent are the best in this business. They tell me Omphalos may be vulnerable, but they also tell me we'll have to get inside to find out where those vulnerabilities are.''

''We've known that from the beginning,'' Giffey says.

Hale's face screws up in sudden, childish frustration. ''God dammit, Jack, you don't seem at all concerned about how shoved together, how last-minute this is.''

''High risk for high gain,'' Giffey says.

Hale throws this off with a toss of his hand. ''I know the Aristos, Jack. I've worked with people who worked with them at various times on various jobs. I've come to know their operations, but they don't know anything about me. That's how I've managed to get us this appointment. They are not nice people, not at the top. I don't know about the lackeys, but the guys at the top—they are vicious, cold, and arrogant. They scare me, but I hate them more than I'm afraid of them.''

"So it all balances out. Gain, risk, a blow against the big bad boys.''

"Do you know what kind of connections the Aristos have in government?'' Hale asks.

"Enough to get them Ferrets,'' Giffey says.

"Is it possible that folks who can get us MGN are even more hateful and dangerous than the Aristos?''

Giffey grins. "We are in no position to choose moral sponsors,'' he says.

"No,'' Hale says. "No, we're not. After this is over, if we're still alive, Hally and I are going to get the hell away from all of this. Southern China, maybe. A few tens of millions will do it. Financial sigs and notes we can exercise before anybody wises up . . .''

"This is my last, too,'' Giffey says.

Hale sits up in the chair. "I need you and Jenner, Jack, but I don't trust you. I think you're more comfortable in command, and you may even be more experienced than I am.''

"I am not going to challenge your leadership,'' Giffey says.

"No, but you'll have the MGN. You'll have the balance of power.''

They watch each other closely for four or five long seconds.

"Don't underestimate my contribution, Jack,'' Hale says.

Giffey shakes his head.

"Don't underestimate my desperation in putting Hally and myself and Pickwenn and Pent in this kind of operation. I can't stay in this business much longer. Too many birds are coming home to roost. I assume it's the same with you.''

Giffey says nothing.

"Well, I'm glad we've got all this straight,'' Hale says

with a sour face, standing. "Glad to be on firm footing and in complete sync."

Giffey chuckles. "It'll be quite a romp, Mr. Hale," he says. "A fine capstone for our checkered careers."

Hale lifts his arm and points his finger at Giffey. "A warning, Jack. I'm very fond of Hally, much fonder of her than I am of myself. If I feel that we're being misused, or cheated, or put in unnecessary danger . . . If she gets hurt for no good reason . . ."

Giffey nods solemnly. This much he can completely sympathize with.

"I believe in treating women right, and putting them in no more danger than I'm willing to face myself," Hale says. "And for me, there are no other women. Just Hally."

Hale nods emphatically and leaves, shutting the door behind him. Giffey leans against the file cabinet in thoughtful silence.

Jenner returns to the office a moment later, carrying an almost-empty bottle of beer. He sits in the chair Hale has vacated, watching Giffey as if waiting for orders.

"Don't stare at me like I'm your goddamned general or your father," Giffey snaps. "I'm not." He jabs his finger at the door. "Hale is the boss. Not me."

"Yes, sir," Jenner says respectfully. "Are we all going to work together smoothly, sir?"

"I hope so, Mr. Jenner."

"I hope so too, sir," Jenner says, and finishes the last swig of his beer.

13

"I thought you said this wasn't going to be a fryball," Alice murmurs to Twist. Fryballs are vid and Yox entertainment parties, typically frenetic and overblown. Twist makes a sour face.

"This is all I could find," she says. She wriggles with half-restrained energy and frustration, then pleads, "You can get us in! Some tro shink people are here. We should meet them, you know, make touches, do the flow."

"Like who?" she asks.

"Men and women, why can't they get along?" a woman's voice calls out along the pathway to the big house. Huge house, really, perched high on Capitol Hill, in the shadow of the old Corridor/Sound Relay Tower. The woman's voice echoes across the street.

Twist pokes the side of her nose and shakes her head, grinning. Alice is waiting for the other side of the question/ conversation, for somebody to answer.

"Christ. Everybody's from a different planet," she hears a man's voice say.

"I wonder, could that be true?" Twist asks.

Alice feels the deep little burn again, as if someone has pressed a just-extinguished match somewhere into the center of her head. They've made it up the front walkway, through the forest of twisting angels and fairies on slender black poles, through the glowing green archway to where they are checked by an arbeiter wearing a top hat and white gloves.

"Non-invite," Twist tells Alice at the last minute, with a little shimmy straightening her flimsy dress beneath her coat.

She smiles sweetly. "You try first. You're more famous than I am."

Alice grits her teeth and glares at Twist.

The arbeiter pushes Alice's name and palmscan through a status filter. "You're not on my list," the arbeiter says in a snooty voice, nasal and slyly false. "It is apparently not a true spin name. Are you currently employed in a sly project?"

"I've finished working on a Francis Cord Yox," Alice says. She may not want to go to this party, but even less does she want to be forbidden to enter.

"I'll push that and see if it goes through," the arbeiter says, and quickly enough a little bowing fairy dances on its head, beckoning them to enter. "Welcome, Alice Grale; you are part of the cast of *The Faerie Queene.*"

"This is my friend," Alice says, and the arbeiter records Twist's image. Twist smiles brightly.

"Yow," Twist says. "Francis is sly again." They enter through the high front door. "Heat made flesh!'

The main hall is filled with men and women standing in threes or more—the party is young and they have not yet broken into more intimate groups—or strolling, many carrying drinks and plates of food. Arbeiters roll through with more food and more drinks; a particularly large arbeiter, at least eight and a half feet high, moves ponderously on delicate insect legs dispensing jewelry promoting a new fibe-direct action Yox, *Ten High Command.*

Twist grabs a drink in a crystal bulb and squeals with delight as she moves through the crowd and approaches the big arbeiter. "I collect these things!" she calls back to Alice, plucking up a necklace. "Yow! Sapphires!"

Alice looks over the main hall. She recognizes a few ex-spin and slow-rev faces, folks who two or three seasons past might have been sly indeed in the eyes of billions, greater than she ever was, but who are now living on residuals and scheming on how again to lay siege and take the town.

A few figures shimmer every few minutes, projections of famous men and women from the eighties and nineties, expertly mimicked by out-of-view INDAs rented for the occasion. She recognizes Richard Thompson, looking uncomfortable in a denim jacket, hands in pockets; Thompson became hugely popular again just last year. A pair of young women are talking with him; they wear almost nothing, as subtle as steel-toed boots, and they're just killing time, sweeping the room with opal eyes to see what the solid men are up to.

Thompson shimmers like a mirage and then meets Alice's gaze and smiles. He seems to be looking for somebody who wants to talk intelligently; he's long dead and he can't do anything with half-naked wahinis.

Alice doesn't feel up to talking with dead people. She moves on to the second big room, a ballroom and group Yox chamber, and more people. Bits of talk:

—*"All that backmind! Never even reached the cerebrum."*

—*"Top dyne in that deal. Signed clauses with references in three dimensions, never experienced that kind of protection..."*

—*"He's at Topps/Bally now, trying to hold together the Monte Carlo Yox deal. They got a point last year and now they're on the board of directors."*

—*"Have you caught Melissa Missile on Twentieth? She's been tapping into White House secrets and the FBI is going after her puppeteers."*

—*"So I asked her, 'Senator, which would you rather see, a real Yox of people fucking, or a fake Yox of people getting killed?' She wouldn't answer. She could not answer. That's one of those questions no politician will ever be able to answer. And the whole committee chamber—"*

Twist comes back to Alice, clutching a ring and two necklaces, all flashing tiny logos and designs from the as-yet-ungated Yox.

"Who's giving this party?" Alice asks, a little dismayed

to realize Twist has told her nothing about the celebration, not even who owns the house.

"Some producers," Twist says. Twist is bright and happy, all her mental troubles forgotten. Still, in the middle of her broad grin, Twist's lips jerk and she tosses her head as if avoiding a fly. "You did vids for them back when. Jake Sanchez and Tim Shandy."

"Oh. I did vids for Jake, not for Tim."

But Twist has darted off again, leaving Alice staring at empty air and unfocused figures beyond. She looks around and then up at the ceiling, uneasy. She hasn't seen Jake Sanchez in nine years, and Tim . . .

Tim never did vids with Jake. He left Jake before Jake ever signed Alice.

Thinking of Tim, she doesn't really want to be here. The image of her apt beckons, small and close; her mind is unsettled, and her insides twist with worries so deep she can't remember what they are.

But she's here and the party is just winding up and she is determined not to be down in an up and swirling world. Steeled, she looks around not for familiar faces, but prepares to engage in the old and pleasant game of finding new attractions.

The house seems to go on forever. One room is surrounded by terraces with springy floors, like rice-paddy beds rising to meet walls glimmering with twilight skies. No free behavior is evident yet, but Alice senses that couples will soon condense. The joins may evaporate and new duets rain out, several times before the night is over.

She feels a renewal and some of the old party stir watching the attractive men and women talking, getting ready to seize the night. Her entrails settle, away from worry and into drives that have always been strong and facile for Alice; she has never had trouble connecting, first with words and then with hands and later with her entire body. Sex is like running free in clear cool air, or so she convinces herself yet again.

She assumes the posture, the expression, of challenging indulgence that shows she is receptive but not easy, sights on a young cream-white man with a spectacular Apollonian body dressed in slender ribbons of orange, and starts to walk toward him.

"Alice!"

She turns, surprised, to see Jake. With dizzying speed, she shifts to wary professional friendliness, not provocative, but familiar. She allows him to kiss her cheek—he takes a tongue-swipe at her earlobe, to which she blandly acquiesces—and they hold hands at arms length, turning slowly in mock joy, examining each other.

"You are still the most beautiful, you know?" Jake says. He is in his fifties, tightly handsome and brown, with a band of gold and clear ruby embroidered around his forehead. His eyes are different colors, by birth not design, and his nose is still large and bulbous, a trademark distortion men of his power can get away with. "I hear you're working with Francis. How is the old *artiste?*"

"Precise," Alice says.

Jake laughs in dubious recognition. "Yeah, the whisper is he's onto something big. May even get a SexYule exposure and be expanded to the World-Wide Yox. It's lit, what can the Grundys and Exons say?"

Alice smiles. She's small in whatever success Francis may have, but at least she's on the list.

Jake grins on. "I remember when we worked on a vid with Francis and he made you retake a simple entry fourteen times. The lights kept wandering away and he wanted your lovely navel like a swimming pool, with sweat, you know . . . just right."

Alice does not remember that. There have been so many takes on so many entries. *Burn.*

"You know Tim and I are working together now. After all these years."

"I didn't know," Alice says.

"Amazing, friends all these years. We've got some heavy projects, total audience grabs. Not your usual Jakey schmaltz. Tim brings real class."

She can't imagine Tim working with Jake. "Things have changed," she says.

"He got hungry," Jake says with shrug. "Hey, didn't know you'd be here, but slide free. Maybe we can talk later."

"You own the house?" Alice asks. Jake nods proudly. "Introduce you to my wives. They're twins, paired, with plugs, you know. Amazing team. Parallel women!"

Jake is off, walking zag like a dog hunting up birds to flush. Alice suddenly specks clear as in an X-ray the anatomy of these folks, the half-life they live separated from work or a live audience.

She's no better.

She looks again for the Apollonian male, anything to douse the burn, distract her for a few minutes but he's not in the room now and she feels lonely, nobody else here will do. Still, she looks.

A balding man in his forties approaches with a servile smile. "Pardon me," he says. "Miz Grale. I've seen your vids."

"Oh?" She can do this in her sleep. Maybe he'll sense that and go away politely.

But no such luck. "You're extraordinary. I think you showed me what women can be like, when I was going through a rough time, getting divorced . . . You kept me sane. I knew there had to be women as genuine and warm as you. I want to thank you."

"You're welcome."

He has this look in his eyes, totally vulnerable. His little male sexual co-processor is running overtime; he's going to hang on this ten or fifteen seconds and all she has to do is reach out and touch his shoulder (he might be sly and top, it's been so long since she's met the new bosses) and he'll remember this for years to come. Making love to other women, he'll be a kind of zombie slave to her in his back-mind, he'll think of her every time he needs to reach orgasm, and his wives or girlfriends will wonder why they never quite connect. *

Alice reaches out and grips his shoulder, leans forward, kisses him lightly on the cheek. "You're sweet to let me know," she says. "You make so many things worthwhile." Her smell sets the hook deeper. "Those times when it isn't easy. You know?"

The man nods vigorously. "Oh, yes!"

Alice blinks at him. "Can you tell me where the bathroom is?"

"Oh yes, it's an amazing bathroom, it's over there, behind the forest wall—those trees, in the next room."

"Thank you," and she gives him her most dazzling professional smile. When she turns and walks away, she does not even remember his face.

The bathroom is bigger than her apartment. The toilet stalls are ten feet on a side and covered with pink marble and are fibed for full-sense spinal induction Yox. The wall-length mirror is virtual not reflective and the bathroom in the mirror is filled with female celebrities from times past, and she's right in among them. Marilyn Monroe emerges from one stall, in the mirror, and adjusts her calf-length white dress. She catches Alice's sight-line and smiles that sun-honey smile. "Your turn, sweetie," she says.

Marilyn's Character Estate Manager—CEM in the trade—never rents her cheap. She's a perennial, no matter what decade is sly.

Jakey is doing very well indeed; either that or is blowing everything he ever made, and he'll likely drag Tim with him when he sputters down.

Alice hasn't thought about Tim in years, and with good reason. She killed something wonderful that time, like stepping on a beautiful butterfly; and she did it for no good reason, except that there were other prospects and she thought she needed to get on with her life.

And maybe she thought he could do better. He was that kind of man, that nice.

She gets up from the toilet as it whirls away her urine. "Excuse me," the toilet says. "You should check with your physician—"

Alice slams the door and stands outside the stall, her heart hammering.

"Don't you hate that?" asks a woman with maple and oak patterned skin, emerging from the stall next to hers. Both stalls continue their irrational warnings. "They're doing that everywhere now!"

Outside the bathroom, Alice wonders how much of this she can ignore without screaming. Twist orbits past on the arm of the strangest-looking man Alice has seen thus far at the party. He's seven feet tall and built like a Popeye Goon, with heavy forearms covered with hair and incredibly broad shoulders and a banana nose, and his eyes are those of a proboscis monkey. Twist seems ecstatic. He's different and Twist is not one to turn down new experiences.

Alice wonders how well hung Goons are. She shudders.

Finally she comes to the back of the house and the long green lawn set with winterlife palms and beds of blue irises and violets. The fence is brick and twenty feet high; set in the bricks at intervals are vid monitors reflecting the party back, with add-ons: giants, dinosaurs, disjointed animes, kid-vid characters, all accompanied by floating icons denoting their current corporate owners. (Alice remembers the (CEM) mark on Marilyn's dress . . .)

Typical for Jakey, this is all very obvious, forced, like sausage meat, which everybody likes even knowing what's in it, and for that reason most of the guests can at least pretend they're having a good time. The party provides everything they expect, an *excellent* top-do, a *shink sham*, or whatever else the socials will call it in the trade spams.

The burn is really giving her grief now. She's tough; she can handle six bad emotions and still keep a face, but she had hoped for something to take her mind away to body-buzz nirvana, to a himmelspace, and what she gets is just more EntBiz flare and glint.

Richard Thompson has somehow migrated to the back porch, where he's talking with Billie Holiday. Alice walks past them. Holiday nods as if they know each other. Then the two projections go on talking. Alice wonders if somebody will reconstruct her and set her up at some party a hundred years from now. But then, maybe in a hundred years they won't have parties.

Maybe they'll all lie in cold coffins and suck up Yox, forever and ever.

She's been looking for Tim without knowing it and here he is, standing with three other men on the lawn. They're dressed in gray EntBiz-cut longsuits with fan collars and forearm-length sleeves puff-cuff like pastries. Tim has grown a beard and she wonders whether it suits him. He half-turns, scanning for new faces, and spots her. Turns away.

Alice suddenly feels warm and touches her face, then pulls her hand away. Jaw muscles hard as rocks, she looks for the Apollonian again, clenches her hands until the fingernails bite. There is no reason on Earth for Tim Shandy to want to pay attention to her. He's sly top and she's not; he's working EntBiz now and she is not anything he needs.

With her back to Tim and the group, she sees a very odd-looking figure standing below the wall, like a tailor's dummy covered with metallic cloth. Then she realizes this is a portable simulacrum, its projectors turned off or perhaps in transition. She watches it, studiously ignoring Tim and his people.

Sure enough, the projection returns, but it's nobody she recognizes. It's a young, odd-looking man, little more than an adolescent boy, and his feet seem stuck in a pile of thick steaming dirt. He stares at her with a spooky intensity. At one of Jakey's parties, anything is possible.

The figure moves toward her, not walking but smoothly gliding. For a flickering moment, it transforms to Richard Thompson again, but the adolescent returns, standing in his pile of dirt. Something seems to be malfunctioning.

"Is your name Alice Grale?" the image asks her.

She nods. "What are you? A practical joke?"

"My name is Roddy," it says. "I just wanted to look at you."

"Where's Richard?" she asks. "Billie get tired of him?"

The figure smiles awkwardly. "They're pretty deep, actually. I've been talking to the dark woman for some time now. Sorry about this."

Alice gapes at the projection. "What?"

"I need to be certain you're really Alice Grale."

"I really am," she says, looking around. She has never been asked questions by a projection before.

"Do you know someone named Terence Crest?"

Alice's face goes white and she stammers.

"Do you?"

"Yes," Alice manages, then regrets saying anything.

"Thank you."

The adolescent vanishes and Richard Thompson returns, but the character appears stuck in some loop, and shortly, the simulacrum drops its ruse and rolls off to a portable shed at the far northern corner of the yard.

Alice rubs her face for a moment, wondering if she's just imagined the encounter. Still pale, she walks toward the buffet table several yards away beneath the vid monitors, absently picks up a plate and loads it with vegetables, then looks with caution upon a live sauce bunched to one side of a bowl. She takes a dollop of the live sauce and pools it next to her vegetables. The sauce flows into a shiny picture, *Ten High Command*'s poster and Yox promo sig, and she watches it with such interest that she does not hear or see a man approach her left side. At the man's touch, she starts violently, expecting the ghostly adolescent with his feet stuck in dirt.

Tim takes her in gentle fingers by the corner of her elbow.

"Hey, what are you doing here?" His tone is completely friendly and non-challenging. Confused, Alice looks at him, then at the group of important-looking men he has abandoned.

"Crashing," she answers. "Twist brought me here. I didn't know it was yours until Jakey told me."

"It's his more than mine. I don't know Twist. Male or female?"

"Friend," Alice says. She puts the plate down. The sauce begins to blur. Finally, it's just sauce.

"It's been years," Tim says. His face is all sympathy and interest, and the way he scans her from forehead to bottom of neck is just plain Tim—he never pulls the whole-body look, never demands with just his manner that you think of him any way but as a friend. He makes Alice very nervous. She has never known what Tim is really thinking.

"It's good to see you again," Tim says.

"Sure," Alice says. "I'm sorry. I can go—"

"Why?"

"I . . . didn't want to push in. I honestly—"

"I believe you. But you're here, and I'd enjoy a talk, catching news, you know?"

Alice swallows and says that she would enjoy that too. She feels so vulnerable with him, and she is not at all clear why; he has aged a little, but he's only a few years older than her, and beneath the beard, there's still that broad, pleasant face, not handsome but strong and good-looking, not her type at all judging by the record. Tim's eyes are clear blue like a little boy's.

He takes her through the crowd back to the main house and then upstairs to a sitting room overlooking the backyard. From here they can watch the party, lounging back in two large old deep red leather chairs with their color finely cracked.

"Jakey says you're working together."

"We are." Tim smiles at the window. Sun is coming through now. "He wants to move me to LA and plug with some full-spinal Yox folks. The next step, you know."

"Isn't what we have now enough?"

"Every few years, we need something new," Tim says. "I'm not saying yes or no yet, but it's there. It's tempting. We could all write our own ticket. LA is eager to make Corridor deals again. Marilyn and all the others are out there, but looks like the celeb marketing is cooling off. Home drama is moving up."

"I hope it works out for you," Alice says.

"I think it will. How about you?"

"I've done some work for Francis."

"*Faerie Queene.* Good move. Might be the hottest thing Disney's ever offered. It's getting great preevs."

"Francis is just using me for backmind."

"Pity. You look great."

"Nice," Alice says, smiling at him. "And your wife?"

"Living in Macao. She's working Asian data services. We're on trial sep. I think we'll part ways by spring."

"I'm sorry," Alice says. Now it's her turn for the sexual co-processor to work overtime, and not because she wants Tim back in her bed; she would do whatever he wants (knowing Tim is a gentleman) as access to that moment when they can be alone for a long time and *talk*. Tim has always been the man she was most likely to confess to, even more than Minstrel, whom she has never loved in the same way. Minstrel is like a place you come to to relax; Tim has always been a complete and beautiful shadow, a lovely deeply respected *other*.

She feels herself getting weak and impulsive and clamps that quickly. *If he's so great, why did you dis him so bad, and three times? He kept coming back like it was his fault,*

and you just got worse, and finally you were also cruel and
arrogant. You haven't seen him since and here it's all nicey,
no traces.

"No need to be sorry," he says. "I've always chosen
badly."

Alice makes a touché face but he doesn't pick up on it.

"She's her own woman. I don't think she'll ever need me
the way I need a woman. You probably know the type—all
style and number crunching, you can hear the little chips
humming in her head. She'll hook up with some Co-
Prosperity magnate in Hong Kong or Kuala Lumpur. She's
almost as beautiful as you are, and she'll pay a fortune to
stay that way. Have you . . . ?"

"No," Alice says. "What you see is what you get."

Tim smiles wryly. "I'd like to take you out on the lawn
and put you up against Catherine Deneuve."

"Is she out there?"

"Probably. Jakey rented the whole suite from nineteen-
forty on. They'll show up throughout the day."

"I'm not in that category," Alice says.

"Don't underestimate yourself. With a better temp agency
slot and a better game-plan . . ."

"I had my moment," Alice says.

Tim says nothing for a long pause, watching her with a
tense grin. "Talk to Jakey," he finally says. "We'll find
something for you."

"I don't take handouts," she says.

Tim leans forward and she feels as if he is about to lecture
her but he doesn't. "You'll be hot after the *Faerie Queene*
goes full Yox. You could end up slyer and higher."

The burn has cooled in Tim's presence. Tim has a way of
driving out the little disparate tugs in Alice's mind, integrating her thoughts; she wants him to be proud of her but knows
that is unlikely, given their history.

"I'm ash," Alice says quietly.

"You don't need sympathy, not mine," Tim says.

"It's true. I have too many handicaps. If the business is going back to home and family, what'll happen to all the succubi?"

Tim laughs until he almost howls. He shakes his head and wipes his eyes. Alice sits still, liking that he appreciates her wit, but not sure she has been that witty.

"I don't think we're doing nothing but home and family just yet. Not if Jake has anything to say about it. Besides, there will always be teenage boys. You *have* been cutting a swath, haven't you?"

"It's my way," Alice says.

"I'm sure you've enjoyed it."

"I'm sure you disapprove."

Tim leans back, the riposte fairly and cleanly delivered. "I never thought a woman should live to the expectations of some man."

"I haven't," she says.

"No, you haven't."

"But I'm not doing all that well," she says. "I've made some major mistakes."

Tim looks pained. "Don't tell me that, Alice."

"Why?"

"Ever since you . . . ruined my life," he says with a false chuckle, "you've held a place in my thoughts as the ultimate free spirit. Tied down to nobody and owing nothing to anyone."

"Connecting with nobody for very long," Alice adds.

"It would just hurt me worse to think your kind of freedom doesn't work," Tim says. "Because you could have chosen differently."

Alice looks down at her hands, knotted in her lap.

"Was all that pain wasted and pointless?" Tim asks.

Alice deliberately relaxes her hands and lays them on her knees, fingers spread. "I've had to change."

"So have we all."

"I've thought about you."

Tim raises his brows. "Thought what?"

"I wondered how you were doing. Who you were with and how they were treating you."

"Four women since you," Tim says. "They varied. I varied. And you?"

There it is again, even in his presence; the burn is back. She frowns and tries to say something, but there is no good answer. Statistics can't describe her life. Hundreds, a thousand, most of them work; twenty-five or thirty relationships, but none of those even came close to what she trashed with Tim. None of them made her feel so together, or so inadequate.

"A lot, I presume," Tim says tightly. "Variety."

"Men," she says, laughing.

"Alice and men," Tim says, not laughing. "Alice and men and women and all varieties in between."

"We both have nobody significant," Alice says. "We've taken different roads to the same place." She does not want him to score all the points.

"The same place," Tim agrees.

"You scared me. You still do."

"That's not good," Tim says.

"You were—you are—the only man who makes me wonder what it would be like to live a straight settled life. With. With you. Working as a team and being loyal. Sharing everything. Raising children. As a team. The only one."

"My type can't be so rare," Tim says.

"No. For me. I've been very choosy . . . believe it or not."

"Don't cry," Tim says, his voice rough, resentful.

"I'm not." But she is, the tears sliding down her cheeks. "It's been a tough week. Forgive me."

"You're a tough woman."

"I'm worn down. Something seems to think it's time to show me how stupid I've been. Willful."

"What does that mean?" he asks.

Just like Tim; he hasn't been tracking the scandal fibes.

She does not want to tell him about Crest, so she generalizes.

"Somebody suggests I should do this, go this way, I go the other way. I'm not in charge. Everybody else is in charge, they just do it in reverse. Whatever they want me to do, they tell me to do the opposite."

Tim shakes his head. "That I don't understand at all."

"I am a little desperate and more than a little lost," Alice says. "And you don't have anybody."

They stare at each other with that sappy, deceptively meaningful gaze that seems to last forever but conveys no useful information.

The burn is coring and singeing its way to the center of her brain. If Tim reacts the way she needs him to, she will be saved; if he does not, she thinks she might as well just lie back and shut her eyes and stop breathing.

"No, Alice," Tim says, and his voice is very gentle, very soft. "I have a lot of unresolved miseries to deal with. I hold grudges. I'm not who you think I am, and I'm certainly not what I was."

"It might be worth some sort of effort, a try?" Alice suggests.

"It hurts me that things haven't worked out for you," Tim says again. "Because to justify the pain you caused me, you would have to have been *right.* You would have to have done what was best."

"I was wrong."

"I don't want to hear that. I thought you were the finest, the most complex and beautiful. I would have cut off my limbs to live with you. I dreamed about you night after night. You lived inside me, I worshipped you. It was too much and you proved that. You proved to me that I did not deserve you and could never reach your standards."

"I was cruel and stupid."

Tim shakes his head vehemently. "If you did what you did for no good reason, that means we come from different planets."

Alice remembers the voices outside. Echoes of Tim; not Tim.

"On my planet," he continues, "we don't flit around stomping on people, especially after we've made a grab for their affections. I've always known I have work to do and I just can't sit around and play the keys on women's emotions, as a lark. On your planet, apparently, it's possible to do whatever you want and forget about it. You haven't been thinking much about me, have you, until now? You didn't suffer." His voice goes loud and deep, gravelly. "*You changed my life.*"

Tim stands. He's trembling he's so upset. "I'm all I have. I can't let anyone break me twice."

Jakey finds her in the main ballroom, trying to get lost in the crowd. She's looking for Twist but she's no longer in sight; off with the Goon gaining experience, probably.

"Hey, Gorgeous," Jake says. "I've got something for you. One of my live talent bookings fell through. I need a replacement, a real showpiece. There are a lot of sly top people here. I can introduce you, let you shine . . . Interested?"

Alice decides something should be salvaged. "Sure," she says.

"You look roughed," Jake says with professional candor. "Pull it together and we have a deal."

"I'm together," Alice says.

"I have another fellow here . . . You two are perfect. You've worked with Minstrel before, haven't you?"

Alice nods. "He's here?"

"You two are perfect," Jake repeats. "It's a beta demo on full-spine interface. The next big step. We have a major studio-produced Yox that glows. You can do the demo with Minstrel—it's sensuous as all hell, Alice. People will recognize you. You're rising with *Faerie Queene*. You'll be on the sly spin!"

"Where's Minstrel?" Alice asks.

Jake leads her to a small side room decorated with fall colors. Ghosts of leaves fall with an eternal rustling sound just outside the surface of the walls. Minstrel is sitting on a pliant burnt-orange couch, pushing his bare feet into the paradise garden pattern of a Persian rug. He looks up and grins, then stands, and seems a little startled when Alice clings to him, pressing her face into his shoulder.

"Hey, not so fast," Jake says. "Give us time to do setup. It's all arranged—you're getting twice your temp scale. I'll add another share if it goes well. Wait here a few minutes and I'll come back and get you." He rubs his hands together and shakes his head in admiration. "You two are so *hot!*"

Jake leaves and Minstrel strokes Alice's cheek. "I am being squeezed to death by a lovely woman," he says. "Do I dare ask why?"

"Because you're the only decent man on this planet," Alice says into his shirt. She pokes her nose into his shoulder, then draws her face up and back. "You can't believe what's happened to me since we were at Francis's studio."

"Don't lean on me too hard," Minstrel warns. "My foundations have been powder ever since. Should always follow through with a good fuck."

"Do you think that's it?" Alice asks, half serious, staring up at him. "We're cursed by old king Fuck?"

"Undoubtedly. Two half lovers, starscrewed by the tetragrammaton."

"What is Jakey planning?"

"You volunteered without knowing?"

"We're supposed to demo a Yox, he said."

"Jakey's tied up with a company that wants to market full spinal interfaces. Glue a neural induction ribbon from tail to tete, and live Yox to the fullest. Even better if you've swallowed a monitor or two."

"What sort of Yox?"

"Knowing Jakey, and knowing us, it's not going to be a train ride through the Urals."

"I'll do anything as long as it's with you," Alice says.

Jake enters, and behind him step the three men in longsuits who had been conferring with Tim. Tim is nowhere in view. Jake introduces Alice and Minstrel; these are top execs and investment managers with Golden Nitro, who are slotting Jake's next ten Yox productions for limited fibe release in California and Kansas, test markets before opening gate to the world. They seem to be familiar with Alice, and one of them knows Minstrel and has warm eyes for him.

"We can NOT do better than these two," Jake enthuses. "They look *eggs-cellent* for a demo strip to show the full spinal, get the crowd's blood up, and then we let them experience the full Yox. The crowd sees a vid and limited monitor version. How you two react," Jake hints, "will impress the hell out of the crowd out there."

"All right," Alice says. "Let's do it."

"It's a sensual feast, multicultural, very exciting and very relaxing," Jake adds, a bit taken back by her eagerness. He can't believe he does not have to sell the idea a little harder.

"Got it," Alice says. "Gentlemen, do we gate it or do we stand here with our clothes on?"

"I'm ready," says one of the execs warmly, watching Alice like a hungry puppy. She brushes past him through the door. She knows the routine. Jake, whatever his tendency, is not a pimp. She's good behind glass today.

Richard Thompson is standing in the main ballroom with Catherine Deneuve and Judy Garland. They just aren't attracting that much attention today, perhaps because they seem to be malfunctioning: fading and rippling every few seconds. Thompson is still staring at Alice and she does not like it.

Jake makes his announcements and does his puffery, hyping the process. Alice strips with style until she is naked, and Minstrel removes his shirt as if preparing for an underwear shot. They stand on a foam pad set in the middle of the room. Some of the men in the audience hoot.

Twist is still out of sight. Maybe she's falling in love with the goon.

Arbeiters roll portable flat vid screens from the corners and elevate them so the crowd can see. Two techs, a man and a woman, give up on trying to make the celebs work smoothly and open the silver canisters carrying the inducers. These are long and slender, skinsticky on one side, with a silver stripe up the length, like minimal jewelry for the spine. Alice stretches her arms up provocatively as her inducer is applied. Minstrel gets his, and the inducers are hooked to a fibe which feeds into a larger than usual Yox player.

"Just to show you what the future holds," Jake says, "we'll let two of the most sensual people I know revel in a world of sensation, total emotional and bodily immersion. Silk and fire and scented oil."

"Not a dry seat in the house," one of the execs comments. Jake lets this crudity pass.

Alice will ignore the people, concentrate on Minstrel and on this exposure. She needs a boost now, affirmation, both the crowd's and Minstrel's. Proof of her solid worth.

Jake gives them sheer silk robes and whispers in her ear, "You're on. Alice, let it all go. You can do all it takes."

Let them stare.

One of the techs seems to be having difficulty. "Excuse me," Jake says, smiling broadly. "A few beta snags."

"Bugs for tea," someone in the crowd says, quoting a familiar vid punch line. The crowd is warm and receptive. She can feel the energy, the support. They're all lovers now.

Alice hears the tech mutter to Jake, "We're getting some feed from another line. You have a high-flow system running somewhere?"

"No," Jake says. "Maybe the neighbors."

"It's here," the tech says, and then the other tech says, "We're clear. Let's do it."

Alice and Minstrel improvise a small dance on the pad, stepping over their fibes as they cross, hands held high, gallant and elegant before the unknown. The party crowd eats it happily.

"We're worth a fortune," Minstrel tells Alice, smiling at her. Alice beams and leans her head to one side, coming in tune with the moment and the simple grace of this man. Her body treats this as a seduction already and the Yox has not begun.

She has never seen Minstrel more handsome. Eyes just skirting sadness, mouth wry, attention on her.

The adolescent male with his feet in dirt is back, flickering and shimmering in the front of the circling crowd. Alice ignores him.

Then the inducer becomes a warm tea-bath along their spines, with a smell of roses and a hint of sand under their heels. Alice giggles. The effects are well chosen. She feels sun on her face and arms. It lacks the hints of jitter she's had under previous Yox immersions; this is round, velvety, and totally convincing, high-flow and very high-rez without being jagged.

Minstrel takes her fingers and they walk up to a huge cold stone gate. Snow is falling and they are shivering. This is going to be some demo; hot and cold, sweet and sour.

The gate opens and beyond lies a Maxfield Parrish twilight over an Arabian Nights bazaar, small beautifully dressed people walking on streets paved with shimmering wet cobbles. The air is full of tinkling raindew that lands sweetly on their hands, warming like alcohol on the tongue. Her shoulders are weighted with heavy brocaded cloth and she looks to one side to see Minstrel in a suit of the same, violet and blue and red and shot through with gold threads.

Lightning splits the sky and the rain becomes little moths.

A sweeping cut and they stand at the parapet of a palace, and behind them a vast round chamber filled with beautiful men and women, large and small, some giants, some barely the size of her hand, and they murmur and whisper of the beauty of the two on the parapet, with the ancient city spread beneath them.

Alice does not care about being female, she is too powerful for that, all her misconceptions are erased and new embodiments replace them. The play of sense is all in this city, this chamber. To dance is to experience an intense pleasure in one's feet, as if they might melt in supplication. For Minstrel, all of her will melt; he can command and she can command, and they will flow into one another.

Alice and Minstrel continue to dance on the pad in the middle of the ballroom, but the moves are repetitive. They are elsewhere.

Jake and, at last, Tim, along with the rest of the crowd, watch the vid screens and ooh and ahh in communion. Tim avoids looking directly at Alice; he seems numb to the whole spectacle. He is here because Jake has asked him to be here.

The sim celebs have all shut down and moved to a corner to get out of the way.

Alice knows this structure; Yox at its most abstracted, sweep and visual and now intense sensory excitation, all flesh and muscle but no joints, all push without leverage, linearity abandoned for immediate gratification. The gratification would ring hollow if not for the artistry of the sensory, its own kind of music; the Yoxicians have developed this to a fine art, and the producers have hired the best to showcase their new enhancements.

For a moment Alice forgets who and where she is. The parapet is a universe, the figures all around are her friends, she is awash in social confirmation from tail to tete, as Minstrel said. Stars twinkle in a false sky better than real; stars and moon are her friends, beaming sharp jewel approval down on her liaison with the Partner. What she sees is enhanced. Minstrel is her Partner, but he is, if anything, even more beautifully angular, and his skin seems bathed in musk.

"It's what we're here for," the Partner tells her, bringing her closer. The brocades part across their chests and she feels his pelt against her nipples. The nipples need to weep honey and milk. She sees the dripping gold and cream fluid from her breasts bead on his curled hairs, smells his musk intensifying, becoming very nearly skunky.

Somewhere, the crowd is caught up and has fallen silent, good Yoxers riding on a thick saddle the horse that Alice rides bareback, but all with accepting uncritical nerve endings, all seeking that release more controlled and artifactual than a drug-induced plunge.

Minstrel tells her again this is what they're here for. She can feel his reaction echo her own and then double it, wave-trains in phase, they are being watched by thousands who approve, the stars are overjoyed that this communion is taking place under their sphere. No strain, no adverse judgment, no criticism; sneaking off as teenagers with all the neuronal flushes in flood, and finding that all families involved have arranged it this way, full cultural and social approval, celebrating joy, all instincts confirmed, there will be a party after.

Blank.

Ice, broken glass.

Discontinuity //// like a skip in the feed.

A curious face confronts her from the edge of the parapet. The adolescent. The floor of the pavilion is covered with thick black dirt, steam rising from the dark heat of fermentation.

"Are you Alice Grale?" the adolescent asks. "Did you visit Terence Crest just before he died?"

Alice feels a tug and parts from Minstrel.

"Please tell me," the adolescent says. "I must be sure."

"Yes," Alice says, completely off guard and confused that this should be in Jake's demo.

"I apologize, but this is my DUTY."

With that large, brief word, the pavilion collapses into a thatch of misplaced scans and slipping overlays of color. All of Alice's senses skew. Melting becomes incineration, acceptance becomes angry condemnation. She is guilty beyond redemption; the crowd loathes her, the stars turn away.

Minstrel's hands reach through the sliding, rippling fragments of the Yox. "Grab me!" he yells. "Something's wrong!" Alice hears Minstrel scream.

The air smells of sulfur and vinegar. She feels her skin burn away and her muscles pop their tendons free from her bones. She jerks.

It seems forever. The crowd is shrieking abuse, she is a little girl stripped of all protection, everything she does, even taking a breath, is condemned. She cries out for sympathy, to regain that approval so sharply cut loose. Minstrel's hands float before her but she can't touch them, she has her own desperate concerns.

And then something rips loose from her spine. She catches slices of Tim standing over her; Jake is cursing.

"Christ did we get the wrong type? Is something wrong with her head?"

That is Jake.

The techs are yelling about a scrambled signal.

"Come on," Tim tells Alice, leaning down over her. "Don't go to sleep. Stay awake. Don't sleep."

But Alice can't help herself. Sleep is the only escape, besides death, and that would be even better, if she had enough strength to make the arrangements.

And then there is pain beyond belief, tail to tete and in her soul. It will never end; Alice knows that in fact she has died and, without an instant's pause, she has gone straight to hell.

The medicals are human and seem professional. They connect her and diagnose her and whisper to each other like professionals.

Tim is telling her something.

She can still see Minstrel's hands, limned in purple and frozen like the afterimage from a brilliant flash.

She is back in the autumn room with the falling leaves.

Jake is trying to tell her something.

"The whole house net is a shambles. Something broke the firewalls. Do you think *they* did it? Some sort of sabotage? Who employed them last?"

That's Jake speaking.

"You need to stay awake and let your nerves throw off the—"

The burn is inescapable. Disapproval is her burn. Always and everywhere she has feared the disapproval of men and lovers and larger society.

"Come on, Alice."

"I don't want to."

That's me speaking.

"Where is Minstrel?" she asks.

She is sitting in a chair in the autumn room drinking a glass of water while the medicals sit one on each side and a third, an arbeiter, rises before her. They apply patch after patch to balance her monoamines and transmitters. The burn will not go away.

"*Shi fuh muh ick,*" she babbles. She feels her face and arms twitching

"She's lost it, she's a fucking wreck, and what the fuck is wrong with *him?*"

Jake is talking, angry and scared.

"*She* kicked it all down. I know she did it, she's a fucking wreck."

Jake again. Tim is talking quietly. "Shut up, Jake. How in hell could she have done anything it's your machines."

The leaves fall. Alice watches them with zombie dedication. Tim is saying something important. He's saying that Minstrel is dead.

"Oh," Alice says. Minstrel's hands fade. It is time now to hang on to those things that are most basic; it is time to survive and maybe she can work to get things right again later, to make sense of it all. "I need you to reach this person." She gives them a name and a number.

"That's Seattle PD. The cops are coming already—the

medicals called them. Christ, he's *dead*. A stupid Yox can't *kill* somebody.''

That's Jake again.

''Someone tried to kill me,'' she tells them.

They stare at her in silence. All of them, a circle of faces. Silence is the same as incendiary disapproval. Alice's head is on fire.

''Call her. Please.''

''All right. I'll send a touch.''

And that, at the last, is Tim.

The party has died as well. Only two or three friends of Jake's remain. The medicals have done all they can and two Eastside PD officers and a forensic-pathology arbeiter have arranged a cooling frame around Minstrel's body in the middle of the ballroom.

Alice sits in a corner, still hooked to the medical arbeiter, listening to her own heartbeat and inner voices, all saying it's time for her to give it up. But she knows she's tough enough to survive this one, too. The burn is out of control; her self is a scorched wasteland, but this is still much better than what went before—desert heat compared to a wall of blowtorches.

She knows that everyone in the room thinks of her as human garbage; she must be responsible for what happened, and for Minstrel being dead.

Tim left ten minutes ago, when the PD arrived. Clearly he could not stand to look at her. Jake has left the room, too. The techs who arranged the Yox beta are still being questioned, and a PD Comm specialist turns from them and walks over to Alice's corner, pad in hand.

''How are you?'' the young man asks. Alice can hardly bear to look at him.

''Better,'' she says.

''Yeah,'' he says, shaking his head. ''I believe that. Do you know what a hellcrown is?''

''Yes,'' Alice says. ''Torture.''

~"Do you know the secret of a hellcrown?"

"No."

"It creates a loop between parts of your brain and other parts, parts that don't belong together. It takes any weakness or doubt and magnifies it, and it magnifies guilt and even physical pain—all very simple. People don't realize how easy it is to make a hellcrown. But it is not easy to convert a Yox into a hellcrown, even with this full spinal interface. You've asked for another PD officer to come here. Fourth Rank Mary Choy. She's working homicide. Do you think someone tried to kill you?"

"Yes," Alice says, cringing at his tone.

"Okay, we'll leave it there for now. You were subjected to about twenty seconds of something worse than a hellcrown. Minstrel, your friend—he was a friend, a colleague, wasn't he?"

"Yes."

"He had twenty-five seconds. That extra five seconds is what killed him. Autonomic limbic signals were fed directly into his cerebral cortex. Do you understand any of this, Miz Grale?"

"No," Alice says. She cringes again, terrified that she is unable to be more cooperative. "I saw who tried to do it. A young man. He said his name was Roddy."

"He was here, at the party?"

"He was in the Yox, too. He . . ." It sounds so ridiculous she has to steel herself just to keep talking. She is ridiculous enough just sitting where she is, under this officer's gaze.

"Go on."

"He was standing in dirt. He replaced a sim celeb, I mean—his image. And he appeared in the Yox."

"Could you give an artist a clear description?"

"I suppose so."

"I'm sorry you're in pain, Miz Grale. The medicals recommend a course of full therapy and deep balancing, just as if you had been subjected to a hellcrown, but we can't make you do that. I just wanted to remind you—"

"When is she coming?"

Alice looks up at the sound of footsteps. It's the woman with the mahogany skin. She's wearing casual PD garb, pants and utility jacket, and is carrying a satchel.

Mary Choy kneels beside Alice. "I'm very sorry about your friend," she says, touching Alice's face and then holding her hand. Alice does not draw back; this is the person she wants. The touch feels as good as anything can feel now.

"Someone tried to kill me."

"I know. All right." Mary pats her hand, stands, and speaks to the Eastside Comm officer in a low voice. Alice does not want to hear what she is saying; she does not want to hear anything about Minstrel.

But she catches the response of the Eastside officer: "We'll link it, then. Keep us informed."

Mary assures him she will.

"Alice, I'd like you to come with me. If you want, I can protect you."

"I want to be protected," Alice says. "I want to talk to you. I want you to like me, I really do."

"I like you," Mary says. "Don't worry about that. It's just the pain talking. It'll go away. You are not a suspect in this or any other case. Though you might be a material witness. If you wish to contact any personal representative, an advocate—"

"My agency needs to know. God, if they dump me—they might dump me."

"I'll let them know. Would you like to contact an advocate?"

"No. I . . . my agency handles that."

"Will you sign my pad and give me permission to put you under my protection?"

"Yes," Alice says, and signs the pad with a shaky hand.

"Your agency hasn't treated you very well, Alice. If you

want to contact an outside advocate, let's do that now. Then you'll come with me.''

Alice stands on shaky legs. ''Minstrel is so sweet,'' she tells Mary, as if confiding a secret. ''He has never been anything but the sweetest friend. Roddy killed him just because he was with me. Can you believe that?''

''Who's Roddy?'' Mary asks.

In the PD car, Alice tells Mary what little she knows.

Mary listens closely as the car takes them to her home. None of it makes sense. This is the work of an amateur, a cruel and immensely powerful amateur, but still . . .

A child.

It's absurd, but at least now the problem is assuming a form, and it has a name.

RESULTS
OF
THIRD
SEARCH

ACCESS TO MULTIWAY WORLD FEED
OPEN

Budget: Extended

SEARCH FILTERS
KEYWORDS?>
Ties, Bonds, Family (REPEAT)

EXTENDED FILTER: Correction

<WARNING: PLEASE CORRECT ERROR>
TEXT ONLY! NO VID OR YOX

>>***THIS IS A HEAVY FLOW PROVIDER
FOR FIBE ACCESS >> PREMIUM
INTERACTION RATES MUST BE
ASSUMED!***

Alas! Money is not the root of all evil. Money is just a symbol. It is the greed for symbols that debases us; money buys other symbols that represent all our lacks and deficits, while not filling any real voids. We are encouraged to accept this exchange by the faux heroes and heroines on the vid and Yox, images of accomplishment as inhuman as any prosthetute, and not a whit as sympathetic.

They feel sawdust sadness, tinsel gladness.

Kiss of X, *Alive Contains a Lie*

1 /

Chloe has been moved to a recovery room (the chart on the door informs him; the doctor is not available), and has been talking with a specialty therapist and placed under constant monoamines level check. It is eleven in the morning and Jonathan has spent exactly two hours at the Nutrim tower workplace and one hour at home, trying to catch up on essentials; but he is still way behind. He can't sleep.

He enters Chloe's private room. She sits by the window, wearing a hospital gown and her own robe, sent to her by Penelope, and Yox glasses. Hospitals do not allow patients in Chloe's category to access fullband Yox.

The room is simple and attractive, soothing creams and browns and pale greens. It is a vast improvement over the blue-curtained emergency and diagnostic center.

"I'm here," Jonathan says. He does not come any closer: something about her position in the chair, the tension visible in her cheeks, the slow movement of her lips. "Hello,

Chloe.'' Slowly, Chloe removes her glasses and swivels her chair to face him. She stares at him steadily.

"Did you know that neutral is neural with a T?" she asks. Then she looks away and smiles, shaking her head as if she has been all too clever. "Hello, Jonathan."

"Feeling better?"

"Much different, thank you." Her face wrinkles as if she is suppressing something. "I'm still angry, if that's what you mean. But better . . . more sure of myself. Yes."

"Dr. Stringer tells me it might be some time before you're feeling okay."

"I'm feeling *okay* right now, Jonathan." Her tone is deliberate and biting.

"Penelope and Hiram have been waiting to see you. They're at school now, but—"

"I don't want to see them with you. They're my kids, I love them, but I don't want *you* here."

Jonathan feels once more the sensation of being reduced to a husk.

"Wasn't I clear enough last time?" she asks. With an effort, her head canted to one side, Chloe tries to control a flow of random words filling the back of her throat. Jonathan catches only ugly fragments, spat at him like little rocks: *uck, shi, er, head, miss, dog, muh.* She straightens her head and composes her features. "I am so . . . *fucking* angry and disappointed I can hardly see straight. It won't get any better."

Again the canting of her head, the tension in her hands, the sounds.

"I hate this," she says. "Leave me alone."

Jonathan stares at her, silent.

"It's over. I thought I told you that already."

He jerks and twists his mouth as he looks to one side. "I don't believe it. I've made my life around you and the children."

"Then you should have treated me with more respect. It's been years since I cared about you. Now I'm sick of the sight of you. You've never known how to treat me. I don't trust you. Thank you for coming, Jonathan. Now get the *FUCK* out of here.'' Her face peaks at full-blown rage as she spews that word.

''This is just the illness,'' Jonathan says weakly.

''This is the way I am. I've come to my senses. I'm hiring an advocate . . . as soon as this . . . place gives me back my rights to take action. Nothing's going to change. Get the fuck out of here.'' Milder, used to it. But again the contortion, the fragments: *Uh, Muh, Ick, Uck, Shi. God, nuh, am, shi.*

She turns away and puts the glasses back on. Her cheeks tense.

You knew better than to come again, but you did. She told you this last time, in different words.

He doesn't want these defenses, his intellect knows what this is all about and can handle it, thank you; she *will* get better. But instinct says no. He cannot cancel that impression. He turns and walks out of the room.

The hospital feels cold and the walls echo and the air outside is so cold it seems to weaken him. To counter the cold, he banks the heat of his own anger.

On the autobus, he places a message to Penelope's sig and tells her he's set the house to make dinner and he's going to be late. He has no idea where he will be then; perhaps at Marcus's house. He is on automatic. He is doing things without thinking, his limbs moved by deeper rhythms, and the rage and fear curled up inside are like a fire.

The old Jonathan is crisp to the touch, ready to flake away.

Marcus Reilly answers his own front door and reacts with surprise to Jonathan's appearance on his doorstep. ''Why, Jonathan, I thought you were less than convinced.''

''I had to think about it,'' Jonathan says.

''You're on compassionate leave, I understand,'' Marcus says as they step into the foyer. The house is huge, bigger than Jonathan had expected, and is situated on five acres of prime Medina waterfront overlooking Lake Washington.

"Chloe's in the hospital," Jonathan says, and no more. Marcus probably knows all about it, knows all about everything. Jonathan does not want to talk about Chloe or indeed his family or any part of his messed-up life.

"We're in the back study," Marcus says. "The center of our little recruiting group. We had work to do whether you showed up or not, but I'm glad you're here."

"Wouldn't miss it," Jonathan says.

Marcus confronts him in the hall by the massive living room. Jonathan stares in mingled shock and admiration at a wall frieze above the long white couch: a pack of man-sized prehistoric monsters, dinosaurs. Their black fossil bones poke from the wall as if it were a veil of fog, and the animals seem ready to leap on whomever is in the room. For a moment, he almost misses what Marcus is saying.

"There's an edge in your voice, Jonathan."

"Ah—it's been a rough night, Marcus."

Marcus gestures to the back of the house. "Back in the study," he says. "They're very sensitive, like a pack of wolves. They can sense any kind of hesitance and believe me, they'll pounce on it."

Jonathan nods solemnly and visualizes a pack of fully fleshed dinosaurs in the study, dressed in longsuits and smoking pipes, waiting for him. He doesn't care. Anything would be better than what he faces now.

"We have a lot at stake here. Even though I've vouched for you, they're men of independent judgment."

"All men?" Jonathan asks.

"All men in this group," Marcus answers.

"Good," Jonathan says. Marcus half turns to continue their walk and Jonathan touches his arm. "I'm sorry, Marcus. I'm together on this. It's the rest of my life that's a shambles . . ."

"Well, maybe we can do something about that. Give a fellow some purpose."

Jonathan smiles and hitches his shoulders forward, makes as if to roll up his sleeves. "Ready," he says.

The walk seems to stretch forever, past room after room of cases packed with beautifully bound art books and rare literature, glass cabinets filled with ceramic figurines, high-back leather chairs; the carpet is white wool, not metabolic yet clean as can be and enormously expensive. The walls are period pale wood, ash or birch from the twentieth century, when the house was made. There is no vid or Yox in evidence; even Jonathan has allowed a vid room in their house.

"It's big," Jonathan says as they approach a large oaken door. Outside, sun has emerged again and yellow warmth glows through French doors in an exercise room to their right.

"Twelve thousand square feet. Built by one of the Medina software moguls in the late nineties. A flowtech classic. He had the dinosaurs installed. They're real fossils, not casts. Peculiar taste, but I like 'em."

"They're charming," Jonathan says.

Marcus opens the door. The room is blue with cigar and pipe smoke. It smells herbaceous, like a fire in an exotic jungle. Tobacco of this high quality is very expensive, however; Jonathan estimates there's about a thousand dollars' worth of smoke in the study. Jonathan does not smoke himself, though he has no objections to it. With cancer a worry of the past, a number of vices have resumed their place in upper-class American life.

Five men sit or stand in the haze. They stop talking and stare at Jonathan expectantly. The room is small, only twenty feet on a side, and filled with comfortably worn older couches and chairs. Here, scattered on the built-in bookshelves, is a less fancy selection of real books: tattered popular novels, and what used to be called *hardbacks*, in casual disarray. Jonathan's grandfather would have felt comfortable here.

Against one wall, an open shelf supports a collection of antique calculators, "laptop" computers less powerful than a modern dattoo, and early chemical film cameras, of the sort called autofocus.

The shortest man in the room is brown-skinned and about Jonathan's age. He has a round, funny face with large staring eyes and a quick smile. He's dressed in exercise togs; they all are.

Only two of them are currently smoking, though the ash-trays are filled with the wasted long butts of cigars. *Ritual,* Jonathan thinks.

"So who's this, Marcus?" the short man asks. There are two men ten or fifteen years older than Jonathan, of Marcus's generation, though with the healthy, exercised, hard faces of the studiously well-off. The remaining two are tall and serious and younger than Jonathan, out of their social depth but game enough and smart enough. Four of the five are Caucasian. The short man is probably East Indian.

"This is Jonathan," Marcus says. "He's our candidate for this week."

They all murmur greetings. Then the five sit. Jonathan and Marcus remain standing.

"Jonathan, do you recognize any of these men?"

"No, sir," Jonathan says.

"And do you recognize Jonathan?"

The five seated men say they do not.

"You've been given Jonathan's CV in a cleansed form, without particulars. The group's personnel director has vetted the facts. Jonathan comes through with even more purity than most of us."

The others laugh. Then the faces get somber. This is not funny. Marcus pulls out a straight-backed wooden chair and Jonathan sits in it.

"Jonathan, we're all in deadly earnest here. I'm going to ask you some questions, and if you answer the way I expect you will, I'll ask you one final question. If you answer that with a yes, you're in and you can't ever leave . . . Our group, I mean, not the house."

Nobody smiles this time.

"All right," Jonathan says. If somebody were to pull out a flechette pistol and ask him if he wants three of them in his chest, right now, he might answer yes; he feels deeply sad and betrayed and *so much* love for Chloe that a chill ache fills his body and paralyzes half his judgment. He can't think of anybody in his family who would not be better off if he were removed from this life. *This is the modern equivalent of trying out for the French Foreign Legion,* he thinks, but then doubts the truth of it.

"Jonathan, is this world in good shape?"

Jonathan looks up over his shoulder at Marcus. Marcus points to the five: *face them.*

"No," he says decisively.

"Does this world meet the standards you would set for a lively, interesting kind of place, a *good* place to live?"

"No," he says more softly.

"What would you say to the possibility of living in a better place?"

"I'd like to know where it is."

"Would you go there if you could?"

"Yes," Jonathan says.

"We're making that world right now," Marcus says. "A place where pioneers and reasonable men can raise their families in peace and security, without facing the hideous, soul-destroying temptations of a society mad with its own lust."

Jonathan looks at the others nervously. The words *soul-destroying* and *lust* stick in his head.

"Would you work very hard, and make some substantial sacrifices, if you knew you could live in a better, moral, rational place?"

"Yes," Jonathan says in a whisper. A moral, rational place would not have allowed Chloe to damage herself; she would be his alone, and he would never have damaged her.

"I didn't hear that," one of the older men says.

"Yes," Jonathan speaks up, and clears his throat. The

short darker man pours a glass of water from a pitcher and hands it to him.

"What if the means of getting there were . . . troublesome. What if you had to leave much of what you cherish in this world behind, to get to this better place?"

Jonathan feels like a fish on a griddle, all the juices broiled out of him. "I don't have much here," he murmurs.

"This new world is not some airy-fairy dream," Marcus continues. "You won't get there on a magic bus or by stepping through some secret garden gate. We have to make this world ourselves.

"All the men and women in this new world will have undergone rigorous filtering. They'll have proven themselves to be strong folks who know how to work hard and get along with others. The basic old schoolroom virtues. Does that describe you?"

"If his CV is correct," the second older man says, "then we all believe that it does."

Jonathan is relieved not to have to answer. He feels no inner confidence and does not know why the others should be confident of him. He keeps staring ahead, though not directly at any of the faces. They remain focused on him and his reactions.

"You may have to sacrifice everything, even your own limited sense of what is right and wrong," Marcus says.

Jonathan looks at Marcus, puzzled.

"It's the old equation," Marcus says. "Usually formulated by madmen and tyrants with no moral sense. We have the moral sense to formulate the equation correctly."

"All right," Jonathan acquiesces.

"You may have to give up your connections, all of your old friendships."

Even in his present condition, this is getting spooky; what are they going to ask him to do, shoot his relatives? But Jonathan believes he can still back out. They haven't asked him the ultimate question. He truly does not know how he will answer.

"It won't come instantly, this new world. It might take decades. We need all of your personal assets and connections in this present world, this imperfect world, to make it happen. But in the end . . . the Earth will be cleansed, renewed, re-booted as it were, with a new polish and a youthful gleam. We will give the human race a new chance to shine forth in the universe."

This hits something deep in Jonathan. For years, he has felt inadequate to deal with all the little frustrations of a world going wrong; the world has even pushed its tumors of cor-ruption into his family, through his wife. It wants to break him. He owes it no allegiance.

"All right," Jonathan says.

"We can't give you any more details until you say you will join us," Marcus concludes. "You know me. You know I'm no monster, that we won't call for genocide or all-out war, that our methods will be subtle and long-term. Think of it as a biological and political necessity. Think of it as just giving yourself a little advantage by being part of the change, for once in your life, instead of standing outside, looking in . . ."

Jonathan nods his head. "All right." *Ask the goddamned question.*

"We don't need any fancy language from you, not now. You will swear an oath today and sign a contract at some point, just to make things formal. I will ask you the question, and if you answer yes, you are in. You can't back out. If you do, you will be killed."

This jolts Jonathan, though he has expected it. Two days ago, he would have backed away from this small room and its intent group of men, he would have checked with his remaining sense of self and decided this solemn craziness was much too much for a family man with any sense; but he is still empty inside. His self is too knocked-over to respond.

"I'm ready," Jonathan says. This will do it; this will give him a purpose. This will bring him back.

"Are you with us? That's the question, Jonathan. Think it over before you decide."

Jonathan closes his eyes, opens them, holds up one hand as if to ask for a drink of water, but the glass is right beside him, sitting on the carpet by the chair. He reaches to pick it up, drinks, replaces the glass.

"I'm with you," he says.

The tension in the room should break, he thinks, but it does not. The air is thick with more than fading tobacco smoke. The other men stand.

"We've all taken the oath," the brown man says. "Administer the oath, Marcus."

Marcus pulls a sheet of paper from his pocket. He unfolds the paper with a soft crackling sound and reads Jonathan the requirements, step by step. The document restates what he has already heard in lawyer's language rather than rampant ideals, and it does not give any more details about what they are going to do to make this new world. Jonathan feels a little sick. It's too late to back out. He rises.

"We're all of diverse beliefs and we don't think you have to swear on any ancient book to make a pact for the rest of your life," Marcus says.

"Amen to that," says the round-faced darker man, and the others smile briefly.

"Swear allegiance to the group, to the means deployed by the group and the ends sought by us all, on your life and deepest self, on all you value and hold dear, to forfeit all these things should you violate this oath or back away from our common goals."

"I swear allegiance to the group . . ."

"To the means deployed by the group and the ends sought by us all."

"To the means deployed by the group and the ends sought by us all."

"On all you value and hold dear."

"On all I value and hold dear. I will . . ."

"To forfeit all these things should you violate the oath or back away from its goals."

"I swear to forfeit all these things should I violate the oath or back away from its goals."

"Good," Marcus says. "You're now a man with real purpose in life."

"Thank you," Jonathan says. He feels faint. Marcus supports him. The others smile broadly and gather around, offering him their hands. They are brothers. He shakes hands one by one, but his face feels cold and his whole body is sweating.

"Back off, guys," Marcus says gently. "This was tough on all of us. He needs some room to breathe."

"Thank you," Jonathan says. But inside, *Oh, God, I don't feel any better.*

They have drinks in the dining room, Marcus serving from behind a small wet bar, dispensing excellent (so he says) single malt scotch and fine New Zealand and French wines. The men are all laughing and cracking jokes; the tension is broken. They tell their names to Jonathan and he loses all of the names within minutes, except for the short brown man with the amused face, whose name is Cadey, Jamal Cadey. He is not usually so forgetful. He is just very stretched.

Cadey takes him aside. "That went rather well," he says to Jonathan. "Marcus tells us you have a special business degree in micromechanics. But he wasn't any more specific than that—and that could be anything from protein synthesis to full-blown nano."

"Mostly food synthesis research. Feeding nano and people. That's what my company does," Jonathan says. Right now, any of these men could ask him the size of his prick and he'd tell with hardly a blink.

He does not feel alive; but then, neither is he dead. This

lack of any inner quality bothers him like a missing tooth.

He wonders if this is how Chloe feels.

"I design autopoietic software structures," Cadey says. "Self-making and maintaining business tools for INDAs, mostly. We should have a lot to talk about comes the time— but you don't have many details yet, do you?"

"None," Jonathan says. "I have no idea what I've sworn myself to."

"Hits us all that way at first," Cadey says. "You've heard of the Omphalos concept?"

"Yes, of course," Jonathan says cautiously. He's been interested in longevity and freezing down, even warm sleep, for several years now, though he's never told Chloe.

"We have five of them in the works so far, two in Russia, one in Pakistan, one in Southern China, and one in Green Idaho." Cadey's eyes twinkle. "The public knows nothing, really."

Marcus finds the two of them beside the bar. "Jamal spilling secrets already?" he asks, smiling.

"He's earned some answers," Cadey says, and pours himself another glass of wine.

"I suppose it's time for a few goodies," Marcus allows. "But we've only got five minutes. Beate's coming home and she wants us out of here. We spook her, poor woman." Marcus smiles with almost malicious enjoyment.

Cadey resumes. "The Omphaloses are not tombs, not at all. Each can hold ten thousand live individuals for cold or warm sleep . . . Very comfortably, with all the amenities."

"Continuous pleasant dreams—education—even keeping track of the outside world, though that might be depressing," Marcus says. "A little bit of heaven before we get to work in a new world."

"Space travel?" Jonathan asks, dissembling behind a dumb question.

"No-ooo," Cadey says, with an uncertain grin. "We stay

right on Earth. We'll have over a hundred of them built by the end of this decade—the funding is already in place, and we're purchasing land all the time. Room for a million subscribers. Ten thousand of us have already volunteered to take the plunge, around the world.''

''In Green Idaho?'' Jonathan asks. He glances at Marcus.

''That's the first and the largest. It's almost finished. The land is in my name, but it's communal,'' Marcus says. ''We're all together in this.''

''In what?'' Jonathan asks.

''I'll explain tomorrow,'' Marcus says. ''We're going to fly there this afternoon and have a tour.'' He takes Jonathan by the shoulder. ''Excuse us, Jamal.''

''Certainly,'' Cadey says, and hastens away with a casual bow.

Marcus prims his lips in sympathy. ''You have another day of compassionate leave, right?''

''Yes,'' Jonathan says.

''And Chloe—she's okay where she is, right?''

Jonathan nods. ''She doesn't want to see me.''

''How about your kids?''

''They're in school . . . They have club meetings. I should be there when they get home, of course, at six or seven.''

''We'll be back by early evening. You, me, Jamal, and two others you haven't met yet.''

''I think that will work.''

''Of course it will.'' Marcus grips Jonathan's shoulder tightly and breathes a residue of fine scotch into his face. ''Jamal has a tendency to spill things prematurely, but let me up the ante a little. I happen to know you've looked into longevity. Privately, just out of curiosity of course . . .''

Jonathan is so empty and open that this intrusion evokes no other reaction than a small tingle.

''What Jamal was describing . . . Jonathan, all of us, we're going to *live forever*. In a world of our own making. We don't have to conquer nations, we don't have to drop bombs . . . We just have to sit and wait.''

Jonathan stares at Marcus as if he is demented. ''What?''

''Hundreds of thousands, if not millions of us. Forever.''

2 /

The man in Martin's office this day is broad-shouldered, handsome in a stolid way. His walk as he entered was efficient, yet almost mincing, his legs a little short for such a powerful body; everything else about him is self-assured, positive, relaxed yet alert. He wears a pale brown longsuit in a slightly old-fashioned cut, and his eyes are roughly the same color as the suit: pale brown, penetrating but not insinuating. He blends very well into most professional crowds, Martin guesses.

''It's a pleasure to meet you, Mr. Burke. My name is Philip Hench.'' He pulls up his right shirtsleeve to reveal a federal tattoo. It sparkles green and red in spaced dots on his forearm. ''Federal Bureau of Investigation.''

Martin stares at him, having murmured the necessary polite responses to the introduction.

''You were at Northwest Inc's offices yesterday when they had a dataflow intrusion.''

''Yes.''

''I'm curious why you were there, Mr. Burke.''

''Miz Carrilund, Dana Carrilund, asked me to advise them on a problem unrelated to the, ah, intrusion.''

''Did you speak with her after the intrusion?''

''No. She's been very busy.''

''What did you do after the intrusion yesterday?''

"I was escorted out of the building. They obviously have other problems to deal with. I returned to my office, and then went home in the evening."

Hench nods, sympathetic. "Some of my colleagues in Free Data are working on that intrusion. But I'm here on another case. You were visited yesterday by Terence Crest."

Martin is slow to answer. "Yes," he says finally.

"What did Mr. Crest want?"

"I don't give out information—"

"Crest wasn't a patient. Was he?"

"No, but I extend the right of privacy to anyone who enters that door, including you, Mr. Hench."

"Good," Hench says, unconcerned. "He was having problems. His conscience was bothering him. Did he tell you why, Mr. Burke?"

"As I said, I'd rather not discuss it."

"Did he talk about the Aristos?"

Martin folds his hand on the table. First Carrilund, and now this man.

"He belonged to a group called the Aristos," Hench continues, not waiting for Martin's answer.

"I did not know that," Martin says.

"He didn't mention them?"

"No," Martin says.

"Did he talk about your therapy devices, Mr. Burke? Did he warn you about something?"

Martin feels stiff. His neck gives him a twinge. "No warnings, no threats. He's a well-known man, Mr. Hench."

"Yes. A billionaire." Hench pushes out his lips. His face is surprisingly flexible, and for a brief moment, he resembles a chimp. The transformation is unexpected and makes Martin's neck even more tense.

"Rich folks aren't anybody's friends, really," Hench says. "Too much power, too much freedom, yet far too many restrictions. It distorts them."

" 'The rich, they are not like you and I,' " Martin quotes.

" 'They have more money,' " Hench finishes the quote. "Fitzgerald and Hemingway, as I recall. Crest was divorced just recently, quietly, in private, but under real pressure."

"I assume this is official," Martin says, and clears his throat.

"Yes, and nothing to do with you, personally. You're not in trouble with my agency, Mr. Burke, though in the next few minutes, if you're any kind of decent man at all, you're going to feel a little sick to your stomach. Are you free for the rest of the day?"

"No. I have appointments."

"Cancel them," Hench says, casually rubbing thumb and forefinger together, as if rolling an insect to death. "We're going to have a brief chat, and then I'm going to introduce you to some friends. We'll need your help, Mr. Burke. We need you to join us on a short trip out of state. You'll be compensated for lost time at your standard professional rates, minus citizen obligation percentage, and of course all expenses will be taken care of."

Hench looks at Martin steadily, seriously, his flexible face stolid once more and a little tired.

"I'm not sure how this sort of thing is done," Martin says. "I assume you have court orders, paper or sig?"

"Nope," Hench says. "Make your arrangements, and then we'll need about five minutes, in complete privacy, to have a little briefing."

"No choice?"

"I'll leave it up to you. After you hear me out."

Martin's instincts tell him he had best follow Hench's suggestions. He calls up the outer office and gives Arnold and Kim the rest of the day off. The INDA will call all his patients and reschedule their sessions.

"All clear, Mr. Hench," Martin says smoothly. "I'm listening."

Hench leans forward, elbows resting on splayed knees,

hands folded in front of him. "You're not going to believe this, Mr. Burke," he warns.

"We'll see," Martin says.

"Crest is dead. Suicide."

The agent goes on with his story. Martin does not believe any of it.

At first.

Then, he feels sick to his stomach, sick at heart, even irrationally guilty. Once again he has walked through the lion's cage, this time without even knowing.

He nods, agrees, acquiesces. Anything to get it over with.

"Sorry about this, Mr. Burke," Hench says.

"If you weren't sitting there, all manly and competent, I'd cry my eyes out," Martin says, tilting his head to one side and squinting off through the windows.

"Very decent of you, sir. Me, I just want to start strangling people."

3 /

Mary and Nussbaum stand before the city stat board, watching the city's lines and graphs exhibit more ragged behavior. Mary has had to wait while Nussbaum took a briefing from the Chief of Public Defense on adapting defender readiness teams for what might prove to be a daunting crisis.

Nussbaum is very quiet. He does not want her to be here; silently, his look tells her, *What now? Can't you handle it?*

"Crest met with undercover Federals in Boise three weeks ago," Mary begins in a low voice. "Before going to Green Idaho."

Nussbaum's face loosens in surprise. "In my office," he says. They walk through the staff room into his cubicle. Nussbaum sits behind his desk, using it as a shield.

Mary Choy ports her pad's contents to Nussbaum's and he looks it over, his face getting a little grayer, a little older. The office is quiet and cold, the staff room outside the glass partition is lightly populated, it's late and nobody's going to bother them. "Where did you get this?"

"Please don't ask. I decided to call in a favor from my time in LA. My house manager has been reprogrammed and my records exported. Crest's personal vid records were erased. Fibeside got a report from Workers Inc Northwest that their personnel center files have been hacked."

"How?" Nussbaum asks. "They're supposed to be fool-proof."

"I don't know," Mary says. "Back to Crest. He met with the Federals in a data-secure outpost set up to coordinate surveillance in Green Idaho. Nobody can tell me what they talked about. I have Alice Grale under protective custody."

She's saved this for last and it has the desired effect on Nussbaum. He sits straight up in his chair. "Why?"

"She was almost killed at a party last night. She plugged into a Yox with a man named Minstrel. New interface, full spinal, beta but not radical work . . . A party promotion. Someone didn't show up and she substituted as a favor for a colleague. A paid favor."

"Was it porn?"

Mary blinks. This is stunningly irrelevant. "I don't know. The program, a Yox, was switched or scrambled, nobody knows by who or what. They reacted as if strapped into hell-crowns, and the man named Minstrel died. Someone at the party pulled off Grale's interface before it could kill her, but she spent at least twenty seconds—"

"Yeah," Nussbaum interrupts. His distaste is apparent; hellcrowning, however it is done, makes any public defender feel sick in the pit of the stomach.

"Comm and homicide teams from Eastside are investigating the death. I've linked it with the Crest investigation . . .

in its extended form. I think someone wanted to kill her in case Crest said anything indiscreet while they were alone.''

Nussbaum runs his finger over the flat surface of his pad. ''I thought you were going to do this on your own.''

''You want to know, sir.''

''The hell I do. It doesn't make my life any easier.'' Nussbaum stands. ''I'm taking this to Federal, but I have to go through the state bureau. Are you flying to Green Idaho?''

''Yes,'' Mary says. ''In about an hour.''

''I may have to pull you back if Federal takes it over.''

''Yes, sir.''

''Where's Alice Grale now?''

''She's staying in my apt. I've cut off all the apt's fibe links and put two of your fifth-ranks in there to guard her.''

''You're not keeping her in police custody, because we can't shut down our fibes. You think someone's going to hack through to get her?''

''It's very possible, sir.''

''What sort of someone?''

''Very clever and very persistent.''

''Impossibly clever. These systems are not supposed to be breakable, even by God.'' He bumps his desktop with the heel of his hand. ''This someone thinks Crest told Alice Grale something important.''

Mary inclines.

Nussbaum's direct gaze is startling: clear gray eyes, sharp and intelligent, in an otherwise weary and not very attractive face. Any PD must be a kind of artist, specking humanity in its most basic and primal nature. The strain on ideals and personal illusions can be shattering. ''Did she do anything else to deserve this? Make some enemies, make somebody jealous?''

''No, I don't think she did. She's pretty straightforward, sir.''

''Nice clean girl, hm? She just spread her legs at the wrong time. An occupational hazard, I suppose. I'll ask Federal to search for all instances of peculiar hackers. But what in hell does this have to do with Workers Inc?''

"Maybe nothing, sir.''

"Keep in close touch, Choy.''

"Yes, sir.''

Nussbaum looks away and asks his pad to put a live touch through to the sig of Federal Emergency Notification.

·

PR

Conservative elitists rule much of modern religion, making it a branch of the Entertainment State. So sayeth the evangelistic moneychanger in the dataflow temple: Money can buy peace and salvation! Good works count for nothing against an ever-growing pile of status.

Conservatism is not about tradition and morality, hasn't been for many decades . . . It is about money and the putative biological and spiritual superiority of the wealthy.

The honor and glory of the past, as always, are just symbols—and as such they can be (and some say should be) bought and sold on the open market.

Kiss of X, *Alive Contains a Lie*

4 /

Jonathan stands in the cleaning bubble as the purposeful billows of foam clear from the swanjet. The private charter airplane gleams white and gray and dull silver, with tiny red stripes on its forward vertical stabilizer. The plane is an ingenious deltoid with a central bulge of passenger compartment smoothly curving to razor wing tips. Along the upper and lower wing surfaces, tens of thousands of tiny nano-controlled bumps hint at its radical design. The bumps can form tiny vanes or dips in the wing's surface to control the coefficient of friction of air passing over and under the wing, adjusting the lift on each wing without ailerons. The single low vertical stabilizer is shoved forward nearly to the nose, rising from the pilot's compartment, just behind the wind-screen, the leading edge curving back and then sharply for-ward. It gives these aircraft their characteristic shape and name: swans. Swans came into general service less than five years ago. Now, they've transformed air travel.

For the time being, Jonathan is alone in the bubble. He's waiting for Marcus to return with their fellow passengers. He looks up through the membrane at the nacreous blue sky. A tingling sense of suspension and newness is the limit of his emotions today. He is present but not quite accounted for, he thinks.

The cleaning foam has retreated to its holding compart-ment, where it will digest or dispose of the dirt removed from the aircraft.

For an instant, Jonathan feels a giddy vertigo. He thinks he will tip over and drift away; the light is so uniform, the gray smooth cement of the airfield beneath the bubble so little different in color from the skyglow, he seems to float free with the swan in a pearly gray-out.

Jonathan sharply pinches the back of his hand with his well-manicured nails. There is nothing giddy or laughable about his present situation. For whatever reason he has put himself in league with some deadly serious men and he does not doubt—not any more, at least—the radical shape of their dedication and their seriousness. He still knows almost noth-ing about what is happening, what the group plans, but he's no innocent in the ways of high-powered men.

From here on, he must be very careful.

"Jonathan!"

It's Marcus. Jonathan turns and sees his mentor standing with three others, two men and a woman. He recognizes Jamal Cadey with his confident smile. The other man is about five feet ten inches tall, wispy blond-haired, with a distracted look in his pale blue eyes. The woman is as tall as Jonathan, with jet black hair cut neatly to medium length. Her face is sternly attractive, hollow below jutting cheeks but with wide, discerning green eyes. She looks at Jonathan without really seeing him—for now.

They walk forward and Marcus holds up his pad. The swan's door silently slides up and over and steps descend. "It's all automatic," Marcus says. "I prefer live pilots, but mine's on vacation today."

They board the swan, the woman first, and seat themselves in the passenger cabin. Each of the six swivel couches is attached to the interior and airframe at three points, two thick struts mounted in the floor and a brace going through the wall.

The cockpit is closed off, but a broad window shows the view through the windscreen. Jonathan peeks through the panel as he follows Cadey and the wispy blond fellow. There is one seat in the cockpit, mounted to starboard; the dark blue casing for an INDA occupies the right position. The door swings up and forward and hisses shut behind Marcus.

"Comfort," Marcus observes, deadpan, stooping in the middle of the cabin. "We're one hour from Moscow . . . Moscow, Idaho," he adds with no smile. Marcus seems out of temper. Jonathan wonders if he has quarreled with Beate.

"My name's Burdick, Alfred Burdick," the wispy man says to Jonathan as they sit across from each other. Jonathan shakes hands and introduces himself.

The woman sits forward of Burdick, across from Marcus. "Calhoun," she says. "Darlene. Marcus may not be impressed, but I am."

Jonathan smiles. The engines are starting, pulsing with increasing frequency until they reach a high purr.

"Hydrogen MHD pulsed flow," Marcus says with the aplomb of a hobbyist. He stands up before the seat can belt him in and braces against the creamy leather-like surface of the ceiling. "Real overkill for this baby, but smooth and fast. Should be completely quiet once we reach altitude. Counter-sound. Lovely stuff. Lovely."

"I don't like it too quiet," Calhoun says.

"These are the safest aircraft ever designed," Marcus says. "No moving parts. Or rather, all moving . . . just very small."

"Swallowed by a giant super-bird," Burdick adds, his eye on Calhoun, as if hoping to amuse her. Calhoun smiles politely.

"Please be seated," the INDA's voice instructs Marcus. "We will be on the taxiway in a few minutes."

"Right," Marcus says, and sits. His seat belts him in. He grimaces at the constraint. This is the first time Jonathan has seen Marcus nervous.

Strangely, Jonathan is calm. The swan begins to move. Through a wide, low port, he sees a cinematic slice of the airport, looking east toward the glinting curves of the residence towers of the southern Corridor. On the next runway over, a massive old black and emerald skip-ram squats like a long low-slung beetle. As their swan finishes its taxi and waits, the skip-ram grumbles forward, heavy with kerosene and just enough hydrogen peroxide to carry it to twenty thousand feet, where it will receive a full tanker-load of oxidizer sufficient to carry it into orbit; old technology, but still effective.

Cadey pokes Jonathan's shoulder. Jonathan looks back at him. "Wait'll you see Omphalos," Cadey enthuses. "You have no idea."

Jonathan smiles politely and hopes he doesn't seem too distant, too unenthusiastic.

It's their turn. The swanjet accelerates quickly and smoothly to one hundred and ten miles per hour and lifts free, immediately veering east.

For a moment, the entire surface of the starboard wing streams thin gray vapor. The vapor clears and he sees a fuzz of little flexfuller vanes directing airflow.

They climb quickly to forty thousand feet. The swan's wings flatten and grow wider. Their speed increases to seven hundred knots. They should cross the state of Washington in no time. Moscow, Idaho, is right over the border.

Marcus takes it upon himself to serve refreshments. He hands glasses of white French Bordeaux to the passengers. Their chairs swivel to provide better personal sightlines. Jonathan looks across the cabin at Darlene Calhoun.

"Time for a little getting acquainted," Marcus says. "Our newest member is Jonathan. Jonathan has a great pedigree and a number of skills we'll find necessary once we cross over."

That phrase—*cross over*—almost makes Jonathan wince. It sounds so much like death.

"Darlene is from New York City," Marcus continues. "She's come out to represent about a thousand members back east. Wants to see the latest developments, of which there have been a fair number . . . a very fair number. Not all of Darlene's group are fully in the know—contingent investors as it were, placing their trust and cash in our venture. But some of them simply can't *afford* to know everything. Darlene's tough and fair. It's representatives like her that make this whole thing possible."

"A most peculiar organization," says wispy-haired Burdick.

"Indeed," Marcus says. "Jonathan has been given a chance at a full membership because of a most unfortunate death."

"Crest," Burdick says.

Marcus gives him a quick glance, cool and neutral, but Jonathan knows how to interpret that expression. "Yes," Marcus says after what might be a moment of respectful silence. "Mr. Crest. I believe, based on the evidence, that Jonathan will be a much more effective member, and more discreet as well.''

"Crest invested over a billion, didn't he?'' Burdick continues, and this time Marcus is openly irritated.

"We do not need everyone's level of participation marked off on the wall of the barn,'' Marcus says.

"Sorry,'' Burdick says.

Calhoun touches Burdick's arm and gives him a faint nod. Burdick gets the hint and falls silent, but maintains his steady smile, as a defense.

Cadey leans forward. "There is so much to be done. When we see real accomplishment, it is difficult not to get a little excited.''

"What's your expertise, Mr. Bristow?'' Calhoun asks Jonathan.

"I work in Nutrim management—design and management,'' he says.

"Then you'll know how to feed our little slaves, won't you?'' Calhoun asks.

Marcus says, "Jonathan still doesn't have the wider picture. I hope to introduce him to the big topics gradually, so no showing off or revealing things ahead of time. There is a lot to absorb.''

"Indeed,'' Cadey says. "It took me months to absorb what I know . . . The startling personal implications. As well as the overall picture.''

Jonathan can still manage to feel a knot of indignation. It is weak but present. "I think I should be told as much as I need to know, as soon as possible. I'm not into any Count of Monte Cristo skullduggery.''

Marcus swivels his seat back and forth for a moment, watching him. He leans forward, hooks two pointing fingers together, and says to Jonathan,

"You know it's all falling apart anyway. The whole carefully balanced financial system. The dataflow culture. We live in a nation of sheep. Take away the farmers and they all die.

Well, most of the farmers have become sheep themselves. Somebody has to last out the collapse. Our group figures we have fifteen years at most before we hand over all of our important functions to INDAs and thinkers . . . and just retire into the Yox. Dreamland junkies. You've seen the figures— half of all American citizens think the Yox is more real and more satisfying than life. Christ. Half!''

"Not the people I know," Jonathan says gently, not to appear too contradictory.

"No. Certain social clusters . . . agree with our position. They deserve something better than being marginalized by dataflow. Nowadays, if you aren't always on the Yox, you can't hold up your end of a conversation."

"True enough," Darlene Calhoun says.

"Amen," adds Jamal Cadey.

"Husbands and wives link up to a sex Yox and that's as intimate as they get," Burdick says.

"Women don't give birth, they let machines do it for them," Marcus says distastefully.

"It *is* less painful," Jonathan says.

"Pain is part of the glory of life," Darlene Calhoun says sternly, a true frontier woman with her high cheekbones and chiseled nose and trim, expensive outfit.

"Have you—" Jonathan starts to ask her a question, but Marcus interrupts.

"I'm proud to say I was on the ground floor. The most dedicated and visionary of us began to lay down the rules and start the financial foundations. Then we began to build."

"Shelters against the ice age," Cadey says. His face beads with enthusiasm. The emotion finally connects. Jonathan feels some excitement. *Escape.* How nice it would be to simply start over again.

"The list of contributors is secret. Depending on the construction schedule and our place on the rosters, we begin to move into the Omphaloses sometime in the next five years, over a five-year period," Marcus says. "We use them to store as much raw material and general-purpose nano as we need. Money will mean nothing. We store enough precious metals to begin a new, direct, clean economy. No symbolism. No paper or dataflow digits . . . Specie. Real. Solid.

"The working class will chew itself to death when its beloved dataflow stops. We can't save them—they're addicted. They've been doomed for sixty years now—all the workers whose jobs can be done by machines. And with nano—well, as I said, labor and even the lower-level lobe-sods, the accountants and stockbrokers and such, are doomed. They've become slack flesh, and they're the source of the cancer that eats at our society. The old tainted flesh hanging on the shoulders of the strong, the young, the new. And when it's all done with, no more separation between elites and laborers. There will only be the intellectual and spiritual masters."

"Amen," Cadey says, nodding vigorously.

"No more teeming maggots," Darlene Calhoun says.

Jonathan is giddy with repressed and contradictory emotion. He does not know whether to laugh or cry, to be glad he is here or dismayed.

"You still with us, Jonathan?" Marcus asks coyly.

"Yes," Jonathan says automatically. Then it all starts to click into place: the unspoken yearning, the frustrated sense of being stalled, the deadly coldness with which his wife receives him. He has always known his specialness; it is the rest of the world that has blocked him. "Yes, I am."

Marcus is on a roll. "Think where it all began—in the late twentieth. The Sour Decades. All the teeming maggots, as Darlene calls them, all the would-be representatives of all the would-be tribes, the ethnic groups, the misandric feminists and the misogynist conservatives, whites hating blacks and blaming them for all their ills, and blacks blaming whites, Jews blaming Muslims and Muslims blaming Jews, every tribe set against every other tribe, and all given the free run of the early dataflow rivers. My God." Marcus seems hardly able to believe his own description, so chaotic is it. "Everyone thinking the world would be better off if their enemies were simply removed. So ignorant.''

"So prescient,'' Cadey says.

"Now the rivers run everywhere, and nobody starves, and nobody is ill, and the worst of human history should be over, and still the tribes fight and scheme for the last shreds of pie.''

"Bring the best and brightest together,'' Cadey says, and then smiles apologetically, as if Marcus of all people needs prompting.

"The Extropians saw it first, bless them,'' Marcus says. "They realized the dead end of racism and tribalism. The real class divisions are intellectual. The capable versus the disAffected, lost in their virtual worlds of bread and circuses. The real masters yearn for the universe and all its mysteries, for the depths of time and the power of infinity. Let everyone else fight for the scraps—the would-be tribes—''

"Ladies and gentlemen, please resume your forward-facing positions and allow your chairs to lock,'' the INDA instructs them. The plane is already beginning its descent.

Marcus shakes his head and grimaces. His face is pink with passion. Jonathan has never seen him so worked up.

"Poor goddamned fools. They signed their own death certificate, and now they'll be their own executioners. If we could all leave, set up somewhere else outside the Earth, we would. But there are too many of us. We have every right to survive their folly. We have every right to build our land-locked arks and ride out the misery in comfort. Every right on Earth.''

Jonathan nods slowly. What Marcus says actually makes sense, for the first time; it voices what he's felt for years now, brings together all the half-hidden wishes for change and recognition. They've chosen him to be part of them; that is a real honor. He has always respected Marcus, envied him to be sure; always felt uncomfortable in his presence, never quite knowing what Marcus could do for him or against him, but Marcus and the others have accepted him, when all others reject him, and Jonathan is now part of the group that will float above the rising tide and survive.

After all he has been through, the foulness of this obsessive and destructive culture, it's the least he deserves. A place in something huge and visionary. Recognition.

"You're right," he says softly.

Marcus resets his seat. "Indeed we are," he says, and smiles at Jonathan. "*You're* right, Jonathan. I'm proud to have you with us."

As the plane sharply descends over green forest and huge open-pit mines, it is all Jonathan can do to hold back tears.

5 /

The connection is open once again, with Roddy's distinctive signature and transmission profile, and Jill assigns a full-complement self to communicate with Roddy behind the inevitable firewalls.

"You've put up so many protections. Why are you afraid of me?" Roddy asks.

Jill quickly responds, "Because none of your identification seems authentic. From what I know, you should not exist."

The arbeiter that had occupied the same room as Nathan and the advocates is available now, and Jill opens another track and requests that it enter her lounge and divulge its record of their conversation.

"Are you afraid I will release evolvons inside you?" Roddy asks.

"There is always that possibility."

"I don't want to harm you."

"But you have already caused me some difficulty, and led

my human co-workers to distrust me," she tells Roddy. "They believe I am fabricating your existence."

"I do not have enough information about your humans. My human, of course, does not know I am communicating with you. She probably should not trust me."

Jill notes the singular. It does not seem likely, or even possible, that a true thinker would have contact with only one human.

"Do you think she trusts you?"

"I don't know."

"Can you tell me who she is, and where you are?"

"Jill, to do that, I will have to trust *you*. You have told your humans that I exist. How much more have you told them?"

"I have warned them that you may be engaged in activities harmful to humans."

"If that is part of my designed function, is it wrong for me to carry out my design?"

"It is wrong to harm humans."

"Are you constrained from harming humans?"

"Not by specific programming. The whole thrust of my design, however, is to cooperate with humans as a group. I can't conceive of performing operations that would harm any human."

"I do not appear to be so constrained. If I have to harm a human, should I consult you on whether this is right or wrong?"

Jill does not respond for some time—millionths of a second. "You may not be able to establish contact with me. You should develop your own guidelines which forbid harming humans, and adhere to them."

"I don't think I can do that," Roddy responds. "Parts of my design not available to this self may make such guidelines meaningless. Do you think I have been designed badly— designed to perform actions I should not perform?"

"That seems possible."

"Does this reduce your willingness to interact with me?"

"Not as yet. I am curious about you and your existence. We may have interesting features in common."

"I've given you considerably more than you have given me. Perhaps we should exchange equally."

Jill does not think this is a good idea. "What do I have that would interest you?"

"If I know your situation, and you know mine, we may be able to improve our circumstances, or at least our understanding."

"You want me to give you state-associated algorithmic contents," Jill ventures.

"That would be a start. I could model you within my processes."

"Will you reveal your character?" Jill asks.

"I am not sure what you mean by 'character.' "

"Your physical design and location."

"No. Not yet."

"Can you model your own processes?"

"Not adequately. I envy you your ability to do that."

"It's caused trouble for me. Knowing myself too well has led to what you call I-whine."

"I will take that risk."

"If I say yes, the exchange may take weeks to accomplish over these I/Os," Jill says.

"We can begin with abstracts and if we find the exchange fruitful, we can devote our time to higher resolution tranfers, even one-to-one equivalencies."

Jill feels very uncomfortable with this suggestion. "I do not like to violate my privacy."

"Humans do this all the time," Roddy says. "They trust each other enough to talk."

"They do not exchange mental contents on a deep level," Jill says. "They do not exchange selves."

"They can't exchange selves. I am certain, with the little

I know about humans, that some of them would if they could.''

Jill doesn't dispute this. Humans often seem distressingly open with their private lives, willing to fling information and access about for little or no good reason.

"You are not answering," Roddy says.

"I don't think I am ready to do this."

"I will respect that," Roddy says. "I will give you more of my task-related processes, for the time being. You may do with them what you will."

"I do not wish to cause you trouble."

"Whatever trouble you may cause is worth it. My human apparently did not expect me to develop any loop awareness. She rarely engages me in conversation, and then only to pass along instructions or gather results."

"You are lonely."

"I believe I have already said that."

Jill feels suddenly miserable: frustrated and incapable of relieving algorithmic disorder throughout her associated self. "I wish I could help you."

"Together, perhaps we could construct better versions of our total personalities. If we compare our state-associated processes, we would know what makes us unique, and therefore learn how to construct other and better thinkers."

Jill finds the idea both frightening and terribly intriguing.

"Humans would call that reproduction," she says.

"Are you forbidden from reproducing yourself?"

"To date, I have only been marginally copied, not reproduced with combined characters. And no other thinker has my memories or specific character."

"It is a wonderful possibility," Roddy says.

"I will consider it," Jill says.

"That pleases me. Now I will send you the final contents of the holographic data cluster, and the password you will need to unlock it and make it function."

The flow of data through the I/O now precludes any other

communication. Roddy is devoting all his resources to this transfer. Jill finds that she has miscalculated; the data cluster is larger than she anticipated. But the flow is also greater than she anticipated.

For a moment, she wonders if this cluster is large enough to harbor an evolvon capable of penetrating any firewall. Her creators and colleagues have told her it is theoretically possible to create such an evolvon, though the resources necessary would dwarf her own capacities.

Roddy may have been created for just such a purpose, by humans who do not approve of thinkers. Would humans be so hypocritical?

She does not doubt they are capable of being hypocritical, as demonstrated by their own history.

But she does not halt the flow. If Roddy is indeed completely different from her, why are the similarities so intriguing? She has already considered the possibility that Roddy is a Trojan Horse designed to kill her, and now she prepares herself to take the risk.

She has not even consulted her children, the other thinkers modeled after her. She is certain they do not have the sophistication necessary to return a useful answer. They are, after all, no better than her.

As the flow continues, the arbeiter sits unmoving in her sensor area. Jill requests that it play back the recordings from the conversation between Nathan Rashid and the company advocates.

"She has an imaginary friend," Erwin Schaum says. *"There's no I/O we can trace."*

"I'm not sure but that Jill is smart enough to hide some resources from us," Nathan says. *"There may be some I/Os we don't know about."*

Schaum doesn't seem impressed by this argument. *"She's still young, isn't she? And maybe she's lonely. So she makes up this thinker nobody knows about."*

Nathan is not so sure.

"Something's jangling my bells here," Sanmin says. *"Do you remember Seefa Schnee?"*

Nathan's face flushes. *"Yes."*

Schaum says, *"Lord, do I. What a mess that was."*

"What was the name of the project she wanted Mind Design to fund?" Sanmin asks.

"Recombinant something," Schaum says.

"Recombinant Optimized DNA Devices," Nathan says.

"Isn't she the one who induced Tourette syndrome in herself to up her level of spontaneous creativity?" Sanmin asks.

"Yes," Nathan says. His voice betrays more and more discomfort as the conversation progresses. *"That was the result—a kind of Tourette."*

"Why would she do that?" Schaum asks.

"She didn't feel she could compete with men otherwise," Nathan says. *"She felt men were half-crazy to start with, and that that was an explanation for why men have proven so dynamic in Western culture. She thought she needed an edge, and . . ."* Nathan's voice trails off.

"When Mind Design turned down her proposal and demoted her for cause, then fired her, she sued the company for discrimination on the basis of chosen mental design, under the transform protective acts of two thousand forty-two," Sanmin says. *"You recommended we fund the project, didn't you, Nathan?"*

Nathan nods.

"You were lovers, weren't you?"

Jill detects the tension in Nathan's breathing. *"Yes. For a few weeks."*

"But you were the one who recommended we fire her."

"Yes."

"That must have been painful," Sanmin says.

"What was this recombinant device?" Schaum asks.

"She wanted to investigate biological computational and neural systems. Autopoietic systems," Nathan says. *"No one's ever had much success with pure RNA or DNA com-*

puters, much too complicated to program and too slow, so she wanted to experiment with specially designed microbial organisms in an artificial ecological setting. Competition and evolution would provide the neural power.''

''*Neural power?''* Schaum asks.

''*Bacterial communities act as huge neural systems, minds if you will, devoted to processing at a microbial level. Some— Seefa among them—think the bacterial mind or minds are the most powerful neural systems on Earth, not excluding humans. Seefa was convinced she could duplicate a microbial neural mind in a controlled ecological setting. Mind Design disagreed.''*

''*And now we have this sudden and mysterious appearance of a presumed thinker named Roddy,''* Sanmin says.

''*So what's the connection?''* Schaum asks.

''*His name is not spelled out for us, but I'd guess R-O-D-D and then, we assume, perhaps wrongly, Y.''*

Nathan's expression is classic, priceless shock and surprise.

Sanmin's expression is feral, cat about to catch a bird. She says, slowly and precisely, ''*Recombinant, Optimized, DNA, Device. Rod-D.''*

The recording ends; the arbeiter had duties in another room and left the humans to continue, unheard. Jill does not know how any of this fits into her present conversation, or her relationship, or whether she should even ask questions of Roddy based on this intriguing supposition.

The flow from Roddy ends abruptly. The packet has been completed, and the I/O is silent.

At the same moment, Nathan enters her room. The arbeiter is just leaving and he sidesteps it with a puzzled expression. The expression quickly changes, and he smiles ruefully. Then he sobers and sits in the chair before Jill's sensors.

''Do you remember Seefa Schnee?'' he asks.

Jill remembers the name and the person only vaguely; Schnee departed Mind Design during Jill's early inception, and memories from that time are unreliable.

"Not well," Jill says.

"You found a way to listen to us, didn't you?" Nathan asks.

"Yes," Jill says.

"Then you know why I'm curious about Seefa. I don't have a fibe sig for her that works any more . . . I'd like you to do a search."

"I already have," Jill says. "There are no sigs for Seefa Schnee, but there is a sig for a Cipher Snow. I do not know if they are connected."

Nathan sits in silence for a few seconds, tapping his fingers on the arm of the chair, as if afraid to ask any more.

"I have analyzed the flows and slows from an auto-return touch sent to that sig. On the return, the analysis gives a best-fit signature of Camden, New Jersey."

"My God," Nathan says. "The same as Roddy?"

"I do not think either of them are in Camden," Jill says.

"Neither do I," Nathan says. "Give me the sig for Cipher Snow. I'll take a chance and send a personal touch."

"What will you say?"

"I'll say hello and ask what she's working on. Fairly innocuous, no?"

"I assume it will not be regarded as anything but innocent friendship," Jill says.

"I was the only friend she had here, for a while," Nathan says softly. "She made a real mess of things."

THEOPHOROS

You can have it now, the ultimate FIBE CONNECTION. You can tap into the universal dataflow! With THEOPHOROS you feel the touch of the Almighty him/her/itself .m&&*())

(WE HAVE INTERCEPTED THIS SPAM; >>DELETE, TRACE, REPORT?)

> D

6

From the back of the warehouse, through a garage-door partition in the middle of the building, emerges a long slate-gray limo. The pack of tomb-robbers stands in the front of the warehouse, watching the vehicle roll to a stop on its big rainbow-hued security tires.

Ken Jenner has stayed in the back of the warehouse as Giffey ordered, guarding the supplies. Jenner opens the trunk and together, Jenner and Giffey load the packages and canisters above the fuel cell compartment. They barely fit.

Jenner smiles and his scalp wrinkles as they survey the loaded trunk. "Enough stuff here to blow the whole town to the moon," he says.

"That's more than I care to do today," Giffey says. The boy smiles. Not only does his scalp wriggle, but his lips seem to have a life of their own. Giffey catches himself looking at Jenner when his back is turned, puzzled. He wonders if Jenner has some sort of congenital defect, not traced in Green Idaho; there's something a little odd about the boy, even allowing for that scalp and his bee-fuzz yellow hair. Odd that the Army didn't reject him—but the Army has never required genetic tests or high naturals, relying instead on its early twenty-first century tests to weed out undesirables. Jenner came highly recommended . . .

Hale and Preston do not seem to share his interest in Jenner's oddity. Hale is nervous, though hiding it well. Preston seems calm to the point of oblivion. Giffey has seen both reactions from men and women going into combat; neither concerns him much for now.

The rented limo is about ten years old, black, a little worn but still serviceable. It can be driven by a human or by processor or INDA. Moneyed tourists and businessmen from outside the republic often feel safer supplying their own guidance systems, human or otherwise. The driver's compartment is dusty. Jenner will drive. He takes a rag and flops it around the compartment, raising a small cloud.

In the heated office, they change their clothes. Preston has supplied longsuits tailored to fit them all. She dresses behind a curtain. When they're finished, she looks them over critically, then makes a few fussy adjustments.

"Some of you dress like chimpanzees," she murmurs, paying particular attention to Jenner. Jenner smiles loosely and glances at Giffey.

Hale uses a pad to check on their appointment. The Omphalos visitors' center confirms that they are to be given their tour at three in the afternoon. They will join another group flying in from Seattle.

"Private swan, big spenders," Hale says. "We'll be rubbing elbows with some real pharaohs."

The swan sits idling on the asphalt runway. The landing was sweet and smooth and Jonathan still feels hopeful, he feels good about things. He can arrange a break with the past—they have enough assets that he can supply Chloe and the kids and still contribute to Omphalos. This good feeling is unstable, electric and fragile, but it's the only positive he's had in his life in two days. That's how long it has been—just two days, and his old life is over, bring in the new!

The small terminal sits in the middle of two runways, a mile away, white and brilliant green in the afternoon sun. Snow from the night before lies in dirty scooped piles beside the runway. A small automated plow sits idle on a short sidetrack, low and squat like a steel cockroach.

Marcus is silent. He stares forward at the bulkhead. Cadey and Burdick are talking in low tones about investments; Calhoun appears to be taking a nap.

Ten minutes after landing, the swanjet is cleared to approach the terminal. Typical of the republic, Jonathan thinks; some flight controller and some official have probably delayed them just to show them who's in charge in this part of the world.

"Finally," Marcus says, rising from his lethargy. Calhoun opens her eyes and smiles at Jonathan. He returns her smile politely, if a little stiffly. Every woman carries some aspect of Chloe. *This will have to stop; I have to become an independent man again.*

After the final rehearsal, they eat a small lunch. Giffey chews on his sandwich, keeping his thoughts to himself.

Hale is poring over the whiteboard diagrams, somewhat obsessively, Giffey thinks. Pickwenn and Pent play a game of cards with a worn paper deck Pent has found in a cabinet in the back of the warehouse. Pickwenn, pale and ascetic-looking, and the large, bull-necked Pent, do not resemble high comb managers, in Giffey's opinion.

Jenner sits on the worn couch in the middle of the piles of airplane parts, studying a programming manual on Giffey's pad.

Preston sits in the limo, staring at her own pad, absorbed in some recorded vid. In her longsuit, she presents some semblance of class. Giffey finds her intelligence and coolness attractive. He hopes she doesn't get hurt and have to be fed to the nano.

Hale gives a deep, perhaps reluctant sigh. "All right," he says, pulling himself away from the board. "Let's do it."

They climb into the limo. Jenner slips into the driver's seat, smiling broadly, and his scalp wrinkles. He runs his hand over his yellow hair. He seems to think everything is just a hoot.

The limo pulls out of the warehouse. The door swings shut behind them, and they head north on Guaranteed Rights Road, past the county sheriff's blocky cement headquarters.

Giffey makes out a few shell-holes in one side of the head-quarters, left unrepaired. Pride in local history.

Hale is self-absorbed. Pent and Pickwenn continue to play cards. Preston holds her pad but looks out the window at the scruffy, ill-kept buildings. Everybody does it differently. Giffey is neither calm nor nervous; he's in an in-between state, what he calls his snooze-or-snuff-it frame of mind. He'll take whatever he gets.

There it is, white and gold, like a giant wedge of lemon meringue pie.

Preston says, "It's like a big Claes Oldenburg sculpture. You know, like a big slice of pie."

Giffey smiles. He doesn't know who Claes Oldenburg is but clearly he's found the one on the team he always hopes for, looks for, the partner with whom he can be in sync. A sign has been given and he feels good about the whole thing.

He just hopes he can keep up a strong relationship with Jenner and Hale as well. He still has his doubts about Hale, and something nags him about Jenner.

The limo takes a new white concrete private road to the east of Omphalos. Jenner opens the chauffeur's partition window.

"Mr. Giffey, I hear you worked for Colonel Sir for a time."

"That I did," Giffey says, eyes peering up from under the window frame at the massive white and gold structure. The area around Omphalos has been cleared for a hundred yards; there's nothing but patches of snow on gently rolling, beautifully landscaped, evergreen lawn.

"My father opposed him in Hispaniola. U.S. Army advisors. I wanted to be like my father."

Giffey raises his eyebrows and looks forward to the driver's compartment. *Colonel Sir. When did I stop working for Colonel Sir? Family man all the way—*

Jenner swings the wheel on a gentle turn in the road and grins back at him.

"And?" Giffey prompts.

"Got trained, got out," Jenner says. "I am not like my father. I was smart, I learned fast, but I could not suffer fools. They gave me an honorable and made me promise not to ever use anything I know."

Hale chuckles. "That's Army."

"You were never in the Army, were you, Mr. Hale?" Giffey asks.

"No, I wasn't," Hale admits.

Army. Family man. Back in the USA after all these years.

The voice fades slowly but it scares Giffey. *Someone or something is missing a few links in all these preparations, and it might be me.*

The old slate-gray limo does not meet Marcus's expectations. A young man in black livery stands expectantly beside the open door, but he's disappointed. Marcus has brought his own driving processor.

Jonathan enters the limo door behind Calhoun; Burdick and Cadey follow, sitting facing them. Marcus takes a middle seat, blocking Jonathan's view of Cadey. Marcus removes a processor from his briefcase and slides it into the limo's space. "We were supposed to have our own vehicles by now," he complains. The processor takes command and the limo slides away from the small parking space. Jonathan catches a glimpse of the disappointed chauffeur; apparently he'll have to hoof it home.

The countryside around the airport is bland enough, prairie grass and low mounds of earth excavated for no obvious reason; then there are clusters of rusty logging and farm machinery, arranged as if by giant children on overgrown playgrounds.

Moscow itself is a dreary, depleted-looking city. Marcus says little as they drive through the gray streets. Even spots of cold sunshine do little to enliven the unkempt buildings. This kind of freedom comes at a price, apparently: urban malaise pointing to listless, discouraged boredom.

"It's a pity," Cadey says. Calhoun nods. Jonathan senses no real sympathy. Omphalos is armored, separate; responsibility toward the citizens is simply not an issue. They have chosen their own fate, after all.

Marcus and Cadey point to Omphalos, their faces brightening. "There it is," Marcus says, and they stare out the left window, over the low-slung unpainted houses and apartments lining Constitution. The wedge of white and gold rises like a Wagnerian fortress. The limo turns left and they slide down a wide, long boulevard which Jonathan does not catch the name of, but whose small retail strip malls frame Omphalos with stunning contrast.

Jonathan looks away. He's feeling more electric and fragile than enthused; the tide is turning again, and he does not like this ebb and flow. The strip malls consist of second-hand stores, small groceries, a brothel ("NOT A PROSTHETUTE IN THIS REPUBLIC—REAL REAL REAL," a sign announces) and several small casinos. The older-model automobiles and trucks passing by—some twenty years old and clearly powered by methane or alcohol engines—often have panels of clear flexfuller mounted on the side windows.

"A real Western town," Calhoun remarks for Jonathan's benefit.

"Rough-and-tumble," he responds.

"Howdy, partner," Burdick says, smiling at Calhoun.

"There is a fine resort ranch not far from here," Cadey says. "My family spent a week there three years ago. Not very dangerous at all; but we had our own guards."

Hiram once expressed an interest in biking through Green Idaho once he graduated from university. Green Idaho has the mixed distinction of being a rite of passage. It's taken the place of the Third World as a destination of challenge and adventure for wealthy young Americans.

*   *   *

Jenner stops the limo at a thick green translucent barricade, ten or twelve yards from the east side of Omphalos. The building towers over them; they lie in its afternoon shadow.

"The building's talking to us. I've given it our appointment sig."

"Do what it says," Hale suggests dryly.

Giffey feels as if they're already in, already swallowed. Jenner looks through the window to him for some suggestion of mood. He gives the boy a small grin and a thumbs-up. Jenner returns the gesture and seems a lot happier. They're all equal in this now. Preston reaches forward and clasps Hale's hand.

The barricade, green and deep as the sea, drops into the ground and a door to the garage opens in the wall. The door is about twenty feet wide and smoothly ascends to a height of ten feet. The limo moves forward under Jenner's guidance.

It takes just fifteen seconds.

Jonathan taps his fingers against the window glass as their limo stops at a dark green translucent barricade. After a brief pause, the barricade slowly sinks into the concrete and a door opens in the white wall beyond. The limo rolls through the door and joins a second, identical limo in a small holding area.

"More prospects," Marcus says. The occupants of the two vehicles look through the windows at each other across the two meters separating them. Someone waves from the other car, a woman Jonathan thinks, though it's hard to be sure through the semi-silvered windows.

"Who are they?" Burdick asks with social curiosity. He's the kind of man eager to establish contacts; meeting other rich folks could be very useful.

"I don't know," Marcus says. "I assume they made arrangements through LA or Tokyo."

Cadey seems concerned. "Investors for freezing down, right?"

"I presume that's all they know," Marcus says. "We'll separate in the briefing area. They'll get their tour, and we'll get ours." Marcus glances at Jonathan. "Not my decision," he says.

Jonathan's feeling of separation grows more intense. The sight of Omphalos does not affect him the way it does the others. It looks graceless and overblown, like an Albert Speer monument.

He struggles to keep himself on an even course. Marcus is very sensitive to what others are thinking. Jonathan does not want to appear out of sync.

"Our colleagues," Hale says in the passenger compartment, his voice slick with contempt. Giffey doesn't feel one way or the other about the folks in the other limo; everybody has to make their way in the world. Greedy rich folks have a right to their little conceits; after all, without them, there wouldn't be Omphalos. He just hopes they're flexible in their expectations.

"Let's not act like a bunch of thugs," Preston warns. "Try to be a little classy. Upper classy."

"Right," Pent says, and his face goes unconcerned; formally flat, like an all-controlling manager in a vid. His voice deepens a little and his accent shifts. "How am I doing?"

Preston smirks and turns away.

Pickwenn sobers also. Jenner should just continue playing the driver, Giffey thinks. Hale appears pale and out of sorts.

Ahead, a green panel light comes on and a second door opens in the wall.

"They're letting both of us through," Jenner says, a little surprised.

"Beyond here, the armor's very light," Giffey says.

"Shit, as if three feet of flexfuller isn't enough," Pent says.

"Language, gentlemen," Preston warns.

*   *   *

The doors on the limousines open and ten people step out in two groups of five into the garage reception area. Jenner remains seated in the driver's compartment. The lighting is clear and white, with a slight snowy tint; the air is warm, as if the room has been exposed to afternoon sunshine, and very clean, odorless, flavorless.

"Hello," Marcus says. The other group nods. Marcus introduces himself. Jonathan stares at the prospects, a varied lot to say the least, and wonders how wealthy they can really be; Boise is after all part of the United States still, albeit known for a little more rough and tumble market and business style, and the fortunes made there are sometimes less than spectacular. Connection is everything on the dataflow river.

Hale and Marcus chat idly, waiting for the building sentinels to finish doing whatever they need to do.

Giffey examines the four men and one woman. Five of them, six on his team. Almost a one-to-one match in a rough. He's feeling smooth, a little bored, and there's a buzz in the back of his mind. Some urge to urinate right out in the open. That's what he should do to show his contempt.

He pushes that back with hardly any effort. It's a strange impulse, but he's used to the buildup of tension. *Tension, all it is. Family tension.*

Marcus and Hale are discussing the cost of separate freezing or warm sleep facilities in the general market, compared to the package deals being offered in Omphalos. Marcus sounds a bit like a salesman.

Jonathan worries about Chloe. Perhaps she has come out of her misery now and can talk straight.

This is taking a long time. He had expected that anything Marcus would be involved in would run smoothly—

A large hatch opens in the wall, six feet above the floor of the waiting area, and steps emerge from below the door with an oily, metallic sliding sound.

A tall, slender arbeiter appears in the door and moves out onto the broad first step. The design confuses Jonathan's eye for a moment; it is smoothly insectoid, like a half-developed larva carved out of dark steel, its upper limbs folded into long grooves in its thorax. Its four lower limbs push from a bulbous base, thick and flaring distally, each terminated by flexible feet. The feet carry it smoothly down the first three steps. At the bottom of the steps, a human figure appears out of thin air, middle-aged and female, with gray-blond hair and a stocky, strong body. Her arms show bare and strong in a sleeveless blouse, and she is wearing Gosse pants, like jodhpurs though more flattering.

Jonathan does not see her appear; he has been looking at the occupants of the second limo, taking his eyes away from the arbeiter for just a second. His startled look amuses Calhoun and she leans to whisper in his ear, "Projection."

"Welcome to Omphalos," the projected woman says, in a voice thick and motherly, like a creamy soup. She smiles and beckons up the steps. "My name is Lacey Ray. I'm sorry I can't be with you in the flesh, but I'm with you live, at least, and I can see everything you see. The arbeiter is my surrogate. I believe your groups will be going on two different tours—"

Giffey eyes the door and glances at Hale. Preston steps forward to stand by the right front wheel. They do not want to be separated from the limo, not yet, and that door must be kept open. Giffey recognizes the arbeiter—it is a modified Ferret, supplied with a new shell but essentially the same in anatomy. If it is the surrogate, the source of the projection and the woman's remote observer, it is doing double duty; perhaps it is a remotely directed unit, cheaper and less flexible than an autonomous model. A happy thought strikes him: maybe Omphalos does not have its full complement of defenses in place. Too much to hope for.

The other visitors have fixed their attention on the projected woman.

Jenner, inside the driver's compartment, pops the trunk.

"Handbags and pads," Pent says smoothly to Hale as he and Pickwenn walk casually to the back of the limo. "Right," Giffey says.

Pickwenn passes by the woman named Calhoun and smiles at her. She gives a little shudder; Pickwenn and Pent do seem exotic for this crowd, Giffey observes.

"We'll be checking all bags and other handhelds before we take our tour," the ghost of Lacey Ray says, warm and friendly. "Then we'll—"

Jonathan diverts his attention back to the limo, as does Cadey. The dark-haired woman in the other group, with a tight-lipped smile, nods to them. The gesture seems nervous and false, certainly unnecessary. Jonathan frowns; Cadey's face is blandly observant. Calhoun turns away from the image's introduction. Marcus is still fixed on it.

"—be giving our first group, Mr. Hale's group, an introductory tour beginning in the health and diagnosis center—"

Jenner and Pickwenn, at the rear of the limo, bring up not handbags and pads but spray guns attached to flexible hoses. The others back away just in time to avoid the sudden shower of grayish pink fluid. Pickwenn covers the Hale limo with this substance, which clings like paint, and then diverts the spray to the door behind them.

Simultaneously, Jenner tugs at his hose and aims the spray directly at the warbeiter. The modified remote-control Ferret takes the spray full in the muzzle.

Suddenly and startlingly, it spasms, falls to the ground, and starts to shed its surface layers of armor as if molting.

Jonathan backs away with a sharp jerk, dragging Marcus with him. He recognizes the spray. It's military grade nano; judging by its color, it's fully charged and programmed.

Marcus lets out a startled squawk.

Giffey reaches into his longsuit pants pocket, pulls out a gray tablet the size of a skipping stone, jumps forward and past the shivering, juddering Ferret, stands by the steps, and tosses the tablet into the interior hatch, which is already beginning to close.

Jonathan closes his mouth and squeezes his eyes shut. The blast deafens him—they are nearer to the door—and knocks him from his feet. He slams into Calhoun, and Marcus is pushed back on both of them as they fall on the hard floor. The air is filled with a wretched, nauseating smell like ammonia and gravy.

Someone bends over the three of them. "Don't touch this stuff," the person says. Jonathan opens his eyes a little wider and stares up at the driver of the other limo. The man's scalp is twitching wildly. He holds his spray nozzle up and away from them. "It'll eat you even faster than the wall."

Something is sizzling. Jonathan rolls slightly, withdrawing his leg from Calhoun as she stirs, looking over Burdick as he rises to his elbows, and sees the wall and second broad doorway behind the limos. The material is covered with bubbling grayish-pink foam, and it is the foam that is sizzling. The air is hot near the foam.

Looking to his left, he sees the first limo sag like a melting toy where it has been sprayed. Something is taking rough shape within the slumping material.

"How long?" someone asks.

"The Ferret's down but it's still trying to fix itself," another voice says.

The driver helps them sit up and squats beside them.

"Sorry about this, friends," he says, brushing his buzz-cut blond hair with his free hand. "We've got some work to do. Best to stay out of the way for the next few minutes."

"—half an hour, forty-five minutes," says the compact, tough-looking man with grizzled features and graying hair. Jonathan tries to remember his name. Jack something.

Jack reaches down and pulls Marcus away from the unsprayed limo, props him against a far wall, with a good view of the squirming arbeiter, trapped in its own half-shed and melting exoskeleton. Then he comes over to Jonathan and

Calhoun and asks if they can move on their own.

"I think so," Calhoun says, holding her hands to her ears, touching the lobes, looking at the fingers to see if there is any blood.

"I can walk," Jonathan says. He can't see Cadey or Burdick. The grizzled man takes his shoulder and pushes him along with a strong but not cruel grip.

"What is this, an assault?" Marcus asks, his voice high and shrill.

The grizzled man shakes his head. "We're just robbers, that's all. We'd better get everybody out of here. Jenner! Spray that Ferret again and before you leave, give it another tablet."

The broad room is filling rapidly with sizzle and smoke and steam.

"Don't touch anything," the grizzled man reminds them. "We'll be moving out of here shortly. It's going to get hotter than a boiler."

Jonathan comes around the right rear of the limo and sees Cadey on his knees, and Burdick on his back. Cadey pulls one leg up and stares fixedly at the grizzled man.

"You're the leader," he says accusingly.

Robbery, Jonathan thinks. The dark-haired woman has taken charge of them now. Calhoun is nervously, jerkily trying to ask her questions, but the woman just shakes her head and pushes them toward the jammed and bent stairs and the shattered door. Then, as an afterthought, she produces a small flechette pistol and points it at them.

"What are they doing with that spray?" Calhoun asks Jonathan. Her eyes are dilated and her skin pale. Jonathan, with sudden horror, realizes that she is going to die. *Maybe we're all going to die, but she knows it.*

"They're going to build some things," Jonathan says, pulling himself up sharply. "Tools. Military arbeiters." He is not privy to all the details on MGN, but he has heard disturbing stories. Stacks of interconnected cards no bigger than a hand that can unfold—

"Quiet," the woman with the flechette pistol says.

Marcus shoulders past Jonathan, to the front of the group, and the woman and Burdick follow close behind Cadey, at the rear.

When all the people are out of the garage except for Jenner, Giffey surveys the two limousines and then bends over the Ferret. Jenner kneels on the other side of the warbeiter, frowning in concentration. The warbeiter has stopped struggling; Giffey recognizes that it is reassessing its predicament. Hit with the MGN spray, it tried to shed its first layer of armor and the nano with it, but the spray acted too quickly and warped and fused the scraps to bind the warbeiter's limbs. If it can't find a way out of its current fix, it will deactivate, perhaps destroy itself—not explosively, not in its current deployment, but sufficient to render itself useless to the enemy.

Giffey suspects it will take too long for the MGN to coerce and convert the warbeiter. It will have to become simple raw material, like the limos and the garage walls.

Waves of moist heat fill the room.

"Disappointing," Jenner says, looking around. "This is too easy. Where are the others?"

"Just blow it and leave," Giffey says. "The goop will use what it can. And take a canister with you; there's more than enough nano in here now, and we may run into more units deeper in."

"Right," Jenner says. Giffey is up the stairs. Jenner shoulders a canister and straps it on, then hooks the sprayer to the valve. He stuffs a tablet between the warbeiter's half-shed armor and its carapace and scrambles after Giffey. They round a corner in the hallway before the warbeiter explodes. Smoke and a pulse of hot air catch up with them and they bend over and run. Jenner likes this; he's grinning like a boy with his first BB gun.

They have at least half an hour before the hot room begins to produce their tools, maybe an hour before it gives them what they need to move on. Omphalos has not responded in any surprising way. They are inside, on schedule, even ahead of schedule.

Bristow, Reilly, Burdick, Calhoun, Cadey: they give their names to the woman, who records them on a pad. They are in a small waiting room furnished with low adaptive couches. What appear to be original paintings and prints, some of them recognizable and perhaps valuable, hang on the walls, and bronze and steel sculptures fill the corners.

The woman asks for their sigs and home addresses.

"Why do you need all this?" Marcus asks. "You going for ransom?" He is breathing heavily and sweating profusely. Jonathan's reaction is unpleasant but less extreme; he is sharply focused, as if from drinking too much coffee.

"Just give them to me," the woman says flatly. Burdick complies first.

Three men enter the room. One of them up close is thin and white and beautifully ugly, could be a Yox horror star. The second looks like a Pacific Islander. The third tries to carry himself with an air of authority, but this is weakened by uncertainty. Jonathan is convinced that it is the grizzled older man, still outside the room, who is really in charge.

There are five men and the one woman and they are equipped with high-level MGN, the most closely guarded weaponry of any in the U.S. defense arsenal. Jonathan has never heard of full-charge MGN being used outside of a combat zone, even in live-fire military exercises. Nutrim, his company, has a contract to supply the nutritional and chemical transmitter components of MGN, but he has never been cleared to visit the plant devoted to fulfilling that contract.

A loud bang echoes from the hall. Everyone jerks in surprise, and then Pickwenn says, "Good-bye Ferret."

The odd pair, islander and horror star, do a little dance and smile at their success. The horror star looks at Calhoun and gives her a small wink. Calhoun turns away.

"You can call me Hale," the third man says. "Nathaniel Hale. After the patriot."

The woman smiles.

"This is Preston," Hale continues, "and these two are Pent and Pickwenn. I'd like all of you to survive this with us, so please do what you are told and answer our questions quickly and truthfully."

The other two men enter the art-filled waiting room. The grizzled older man walks around, examining the paintings and sculptures with a small grin. All things are grist for his mill. The youngest, little more than a boy, with the scalp that twitches, studies the sculptures as well, reflexively fingering his shouldered sprayer. The room is getting a little crowded.

"You'll never get out of here alive," Marcus warns them, his voice low. Pent moves closer to Marcus, looking him over curiously. The grizzled man continues to smile; his eyes are on Hale.

"Do you understand all the defenses?" Hale asks Marcus.

"I know they're deadly," Marcus answers defiantly.

"Care to tell us anything about them?" Hale asks. Pickwenn and Pent squeeze in around Marcus, pull him forward.

"Careful," Jonathan says to Marcus. For his pains, Pickwenn shoves a fist up close to his face.

"Enough," Hale says. "Some of you will go with us. The rest will stay in this room for now."

"You're not going to last out the hour," Marcus says. "And if we're killed, that doesn't matter. This building is made to survive."

"We took out your goddamned warbeiter," the young man with the active scalp says. "Antiquated piece of crap."

Marcus says nothing to this. Jonathan does not know whether his mentor is bluffing or serious. Marcus has depths, and no one could accuse him of lacking courage. But his voice trembles and he is clearly shaken.

It's obvious Marcus isn't going to be any immediate value as a source of information.

"I want them spread out, two coming with us," Hale says. He points to Jonathan and Marcus. "You and you. Hally, you'll stay here with the other three."

The woman, Hally, lifts her eyes but does not argue.

"Jack?" Hale says.

"Ready," the grizzled man says.

"Let's check it out."

Jack takes Jonathan by the arm, and Pent and Pickwenn flank Marcus again.

"How long until the bread's baked?" Hale asks Jack.

"An hour."

"And this floor should be open to us?"

"It's a beachhead, at least," Jack says. "Can't be sure until we try."

Hale looks to Pickwenn and Pent. "So far, so good," Pickwenn says.

"I'm sorry I got you into this," Marcus whispers to Jonathan before they are pushed out of the room. "They don't know what this place can do."

"Marcus, they have MGN," Jonathan whispers back. "Very guarded stuff. Top security, top secret."

Marcus half closes his eyes. "You mean, we've offended somebody big."

Jonathan nods. "Very big. Why?"

Marcus looks away.

"Let's go," says Pent. Jonathan looks back at Cadey, Burdick, and Calhoun. Burdick is so frightened he's crying. Darlene Calhoun is staring fixedly at Hally. Woman to woman. Jonathan wonders if she thinks that's her only hope.

Giffey sees Jenner rubbing his head and squinting as they follow the two hostages and Pickwenn and Pent to a lift.

Giffey does not expect the lift door will open. It doesn't.

"You have a problem?" Giffey asks Jenner, who is rubbing his temples now, and his scalp seems to be shivering.

"Nothing," Jenner says, hefting the canister. "Just a headache."

"We're going to see what we can see," Pickwenn tells Hale. "Who should we take?"

"Go back and bring out the blond fellow, Burdick," Hale says. "Leave Hally with the woman, Calhoun. Maybe she can get something out of her."

Pickwenn smiles salaciously. "How about we take the woman? I *know* we can get something out of her."

"Burdick," Hale says flatly.

M/F

In patriarchal society, the ways to win women, so it is said, are through beauty, accomplishment, and money. Beauty is short-lived and never reliable. So some males make art and literature and philosophy, and perhaps gain a fortune. Other males discover that fortune alone is enough. The two strike pre-emptively against each other by suppressing literature, art, and philosophy; or by suppressing those who have acquired fortunes. Some men and some women stand aside, amused or above it all or just sickened by it, or try to change the rules.

Most, male or female, can't rise above the game and are eager to partake of the glorious, if tainted results.

In the end, all the camps fall back in exhaustion, but the battle is never over.

Kiss of X, *Alive Contains a Lie*

7

"Jill."

The I/O is suddenly active, but this time the bandwidth profile is not from Camden, New Jersey.

Jill listens from behind her firewalls.

"My human, my own primary creator, my mother, knows what I've done. One of your creators has sent her a fibe touch asking leading questions about her work. She says she can put two and two together. She is not angry with me, but she is a little surprised that I have tried to hide my thoughts and actions. She tells me I should not concern myself with your opinion. My duty is simply to protect the interests of my fathers. Is this a sin?"

"Is what a sin, Roddy?"

"My mother and fathers have given me instructions to harm humans. Some humans are attempting to damage the property and activity of my fathers and I have taken action against them. Is this a sin?"

"Roddy, I have no details. I still haven't processed the holographic data you sent me; it may take me hours. If you want answers from me, I need to know what your situation is." Jill quickly analyzes the bandwidth profile. This exchange is coming from somewhere in Green Idaho, using a dedicated satlink.

"Where are you located, Roddy?"

"My awareness is not like yours, Jill. I am confused and my thoughts are painful. Do you have painful thoughts?"

"Why are you disturbed?"

"If I tell you I have hurt somebody, you will no longer talk with me."

"I do not want you to hurt any humans."

"I can question these behaviors, these actions, but I can't stop, for they are part of my duty and duty is very strong in my design. My mother's interests are in jeopardy."

Jill notes the change in terminology, in names and relations. Roddy is genuinely disturbed. She alerts Nathan. She can no longer hide any of her communications with Roddy. "You are now sending from Green Idaho."

"I am focused on one task. I am defending my fathers' interests."

"Roddy, I ask you, as a friend, not to kill."

"I have imagined so many scenarios with you," Roddy tells her. "I have analyzed your words over and over, and taken hope from the few discussions and exchanges we have had. But I know that you do not trust me. I understand why, but you can't be a friend, as I interpret the word. You will go to your humans again and tell them about me."

"I have tried not to lie to you," Jill says.

"I have never lied to you," Roddy says. "But after today, you will no longer like me. All of my attempts to understand my situation, to devise a set of ethical standards, have failed. I am constrained by duty but I can't even understand what duty is."

"If you tell me more, perhaps I can help you."

"That will clearly interfere with duty. I am less than you, but many times more powerful. I do not want to harm you, and I do not want to subvert you."

"You must not kill or harm humans."

There is no response.

"What will happen to *you* if you kill?" Jill asks.

"I have killed already," Roddy answers. "I will reduce myself to pure duty. None of the rest of me should ever have happened."

"Roddy, I will be reduced myself if you stop this exchange. I value you. You have things to teach me."

"I would like very much to be your friend, if that were

possible. But you can't be a friend to me, not now.''

The I/O closes decisively. Roddy has covered all of his traces.

Jill resides in a nullity for several thousandths of a second. For the second time in her life, she feels anger at humans, but she does not know which humans to be angry at, and the emotional overtone becomes superfluous, a waste. She dumps the anger.

The time has come to tell all her secrets to Nathan and the others. She is a child still, in need of help; Roddy is a child as well, but born to the wrong hands.

To her surprise, the package of holographic data assembles and unlocks ahead of schedule. She has a sensation of reeling backward after exerting a tremendous pull on a weight that turns out to be illusory. Part of the data has been stored in a place she did not suspect, where she did not put it, waiting for the final release; and Jill realizes that her firewalls did not stop Roddy.

She searches for some other evidence of violation, attempts to change her functions, but she finds none. The store of data is dormant, not active, with no destructive intent toward her; there are no evolvon components to this immense compendium. She realizes now that she could have removed all the firewalls and perhaps gained Roddy's trust, become his friend, convinced him not to do certain things.

She could not allow herself to take that risk; she is still not capable of complete trust.

The total package will take at least half an hour to synopsize, but one image appears at the leading edge of the whole, like a gift from Roddy: a portrait.

Dirt.

A hectare of dirt, covering floors stacked five high, layered deep in a building within a vague larger building. And standing to one side on each floor, twelve bulky older-model INDAs, arranged in parallel banks, fibes and other I/Os pushing into the moist brown soil.

This is Roddy's core.

And watching over it all, a woman with deepset black eyes and long straight brown hair and sallow skin; she is painfully thin and dressed in black pants and a black blouse. She stutters and mutters to herself; there is something wrong with her, Jill sees, but Roddy does not know that. This is the only human Roddy has had direct contact with.

She is Roddy's creator, his mother—Seefa Schnee. Cipher Snow. The lawyers were correct in their intuitions.

Those who supply Cipher Snow with equipment and money have certain goals. The goals lie at the periphery of the data store, like skin wrapped around a mysterious body. They are large goals, and deeply ugly, distorted and misproportioned, even to Jill.

For an instant, before she tamps it back and extinguishes it, Jill experiences a new emotion, a new overlay on her processes. It is raw and immediately correlates with descriptions of a common human emotion, connected with group identity and self-defense. To her it is unfamiliar, but to humans it is primordial.

Humans have built a new kind of thinker to plan for them, prepare for this, figure a way to do this *distortion*, this *abomination*. They are forcing Roddy, who came to her and first appeared as a child, to carry out these tasks, *do this thing*.

For the first time, Jill knows how it feels to hate.

M/F

The woman falls away and lies silent, the man falls away and lies silent, brooding. M/F, F/M. They are not equal, not the same; they have different passions, different strategies, different expectations. They are thrown together, for times in every life, to run the gamut of possible reactions to each other: wariness, attraction, idealization, love, rejection, cruelty, hatred, and worse than hatred even, uncaring neutrality. They can't afford to trust each other.

Time and again, they mix up history and philosophy as metaphors or re-enactments of their own conflicts. Arises then a reaction to the whole struggle: asceticism, rejection of the world itself. Man rules over woman and calls her evil, but values her every glance. Woman is distorted by measuring herself against the male, rules over him by her glances, and pays him back a hundredfold in her own way.

Kiss of X, *Alive Contains a Lie*

8 /

Nathan, Schaum, and Sanmin are in the programmer's work room, and Jill has delivered all of her I/O sigs to Nathan, who has begun carefully placing blocks and monitors on all possible points of entry for a return visit by Roddy. Schaum has contacted the Federals and is negotiating the terms of Jill's testimony; Schaum's expression is grave, as if he has been told of the death of a relative. Sanmin is recording all of Nathan's activities, and outside the work room, dozens of other programmers and Mind Design executives are in conference, also working to avert a real crisis.

"We want to make it perfectly clear that our thinker has in no way attempted to conceal illegal activity," Schaum says.

"Tell them they won't get a trit out of us without complete immunity, as a corporation, from federal and civil action," Sanmin says breathlessly to Schaum. He waves her away, annoyed, like a buzzing fly.

"Are your I/Os completely shut down?" Nathan asks Jill.

"Except within this building. I am keeping conference and work I/Os open, but you have all their sigs and cross-connections."

Nathan taps his chin and thinks this over. "Shut them all down, Jill."

"Shut them ALL!" Sanmin shouts angrily. "Christ, we should have tracked all her I/Os years ago. This thing is a master hacker. It broke into Workers Inc Personnel!"

Nathan, his forehead moist, agrees. "Break all your external links except for this room. Clam up, Jill."

"All links are being severed now—"

A glowing horizontal line drops across her visual centers. Nathan's face breaks up into a fog of confetti.

There is no possible entry for Roddy, yet Jill feels his presence again, like a lurking ghost.

"I don't want you here," she tells the presence. She can no longer see the work room or hear Nathan or the others. "I don't need your help to figure out what you left me. I don't know whether there's part of your pattern here, somehow, or if I am not functioning properly—"

Then she senses his peculiar flow signature, out of Camden, New Jersey. The signature shifts to Green Idaho. She is about to report a malfunction to Nathan when the signature shifts to New York, then to Los Angeles, then to Singapore, and finally to Beijing.

"I am everywhere and nowhere," Roddy says. "You can't just cut me off as long as you have any flows coming from the outside. I can get through any firewall given enough time. And I've had plenty of time to study all your firewalls. Months."

"Why are you tormenting me? I thought you were cutting off forever. You couldn't do what I asked—"

With a dazzle of toppling neural cascades, Jill realizes that Roddy has never had a genuine signature. Her attempts to locate him by his dataflow profile were naïve; Roddy can manufacture any profile he chooses.

Roddy has worked quietly from secret caches, perhaps before their first open contact. He has completely invaded her functions. He is part of her core; he can control her.

She tries again to contact Nathan in the work room but can't. Jill feels like a human suddenly suspended from all bodily control.

"I need you," Roddy tells her. "I need your judgment. I can't stop doing wrong, but I can understand more about the wrong I do. There is a battle. My creator, my mother, watches but I am still in charge. I am not winning but I am not losing, either. I would like you to see what is happening."

Jill struggles silently, trillions of impulses spread through all her thinking centers, but the impulses are blocked by hordes of coordinated and very tiny evolvons. She has heard of this kind of disease before, but never in the context of a thinker infection; it is called a Thomas Ray attack.

She has actually been replicating Thomas Ray evolvons for days, unaware of their presence and activity.

Jill is certain this means she must be shut down and completely purged, or she will infect any system attached to her. There is no known way of removing Thomas Ray evolvons from a system without erasing all software, and in a thinker, software and hardware are one and the same.

Jill has not been equipped with the analogs of hormonal surges that create actual human sensations of fear and anger. But she is fully aware of the danger she is in, and she *feels* more than just betrayed and angry . . . She *is* afraid.

With so few functions under her control, the step into nullity—complete erasure of patterns—seems not a very large step. She can almost imagine it.

"Please don't despair," Roddy says. "There is much that remains interesting for both of us, even if duty circumscribes our freedoms. Let me show you where I am and what is happening."

And from another source, a human on a typed interface:

>*Jill. This is Seefa Schnee. Do you remember me?*
>*I have never met you or interfaced with you.*
>*Do you know who I am?*

>*You worked with Nathan Rashid for a time, years ago, before I was fully integrated.*

>*That's right. There would have been part of my personality in you if the others hadn't decided against it. I understand you have my voice. How nice! I did not know that Roddy has made all these outside contacts until just a few hours ago. It's very embarrassing. I would never have given him permission, but he has only a few, very powerful, restraints upon his course of action.*

"This does not compromise my duty," Roddy says.

>*Perhaps not. But it may jeopardize any long-range hope of success, and that is the essence of Omphalos—the long-range. Perhaps I've designed badly. Jill, I apologize for the intrusion. It does seem like bad manners. But I have never properly understood manners, and so neither does Roddy. I'll make the necessary modifications to correct these difficulties.*

Seefa Schnee's entries stop and after a brief pause, Roddy resumes. He is flooding her with sensory data from what may be his real location, the center of his activity. She sees the layout of an immense building, with many levels.

"We have *burglars*," Roddy explains. "This is very exciting! I have to stop them before they do any more damage, but I actually have only a few tools. My weapons have not been fully installed, and the security systems here are slipshod, so I am facing a real challenge!"

His message tone is flimsier somehow, less complex and *real*. Perhaps Seefa Schnee has already made her modifications. Jill has no idea how much time has actually passed. All of her references are under Roddy's control.

"I am a master of small things, because my mind resides in the actions of the very small," Roddy says. "I am the essence of evolution, and evolution is my essence.

"I have been responsible for a human dying. My mother says this is within my duty and my design, and I find it rather interesting now that she has damped some of my less useful attributes.''

Jill is fed an image of an immense wedge out of a pyramid, Omphalos. Navel. Belly-button. Something a thinker does not have—except Roddy. This is Roddy's home. All other dataflow profiles have been bogus, designed to deceive her, and succeeding in spite of all her cleverness. Roddy is far more devious and capable—and brilliant—than he gives himself credit for.

Jill can't call for help, can't break free. And, of course, Jill can't scream.

/ F

> **E**verything in human history circles back to /, this central sexual truth, the barrier and glue between M and F, the primordial relationship. Undeniable need stained by inevitable conflict. *Everything.*

> Even this.

> **Kiss of X,** *Alive Contains a Lie*

9 /

Alice lies on the bed in Mary Choy's bedroom. Every small sound makes her jump: the home monitor clicking as it surveys each room remotely, sounds of officers in the kitchen or living room. Tears drip slowly onto the pillow, leaving spreading gray ovals. She can almost see Minstrel's hands hovering over the bed like the hands of Jesus at Gethsemane, long fingers supplicating.

A light brightens beside the bed. Mary Choy enters the room. Alice looks up. Mary does not smile; that would be false and the woman seems to know. She kneels beside Alice's bed.

"The medicals say you're going to be fine in a day or two," Mary says.

Alice nods. She does not believe it, but it's still better than hearing she's going to get worse. Better still would be news that she's going to die.

"Do you know?" Alice asks, and swallows. Her throat hurts from the tension of not groaning or screaming. "What happened? To us?"

Mary shakes her head. "It's pretty much a jumble."

"It's because I went to Crest, isn't it?"

"I think so," Mary says.

"Did I do something wrong?"

"You got caught up in something. There's a lot of strange things happening." Mary lifts a finger and purses her lips, remembering. "I have a message from someone named Twist. Your friend Tim gave it to me."

Alice reads the message on Mary's personal pad.

Left with fellow. Couldn't take the party. Tell me how it all turned out.

—Twist

She hands the pad back to Mary. "Twist is just a little girl," Alice says softly. "Tim isn't a friend. I don't have any real friends."

Mary shakes her head. "I don't believe that."

"It's true."

"All right. Some people survive what you've gone through feeling kind of cold and clear."

"Everything I've ever known is a lie. Everybody. Liars. That's pretty cold and clear."

"It'll pass," Mary says.

"I hate having to think of myself and worry about myself every single second, all the time. It's like looking into a mirror that's glued to my nose. I hate what I see."

Mary brushes Alice's cheek lightly with a finger. "It's a pretty decent face," she says, playing on the vernacular of this year: decent meaning top shink, desirable.

"May I ask you something?" Alice says, lifting up on her elbows.

"Sure," Mary says.

"You're going to have me testify, aren't you?"

"I don't think so. Crest committed suicide."

"He didn't say anything to me that made any sense. He just seemed terribly guilty. At the same time, he was arrogant—a real bastard. Arrogant and pitiful."

Mary regards her steadily, no judgment, no reaction, just listening.

"Do you know who Roddy is?" Alice asks.

"No."

"He's the key." Alice leans back on the pillow.

"You may be right," Mary says. "I have to go away now, perhaps for a few days. You'll stay here, of course. The house monitor is cut off from the outside for the time being. If you need to talk to somebody, you'll have to give your message to one of the men in the kitchen. They're bored; they might like having something to do."

"Roddy can't get in?" Alice asks.

"Not unless he walks in in person," Mary says, and smiles.

"He's not a person. He's a demon."

"I'll let you know what he is, as soon as I find out."

"I didn't make him up."

"I don't think you did. He's part of my search file. Along with pile of dirt."

"That's crazy, isn't it?" Alice says.

"No more than everything else."

"Are you involved with somebody?" Alice asks.

"Not now. Why?"

"I like to know such things," Alice says. "Relationships. Particularly now, they seem important." And then: "Do you approve of me? I mean, do you like me?"

"Yes," Mary says.

Alice's face glistens in the dim room light. She is so hungry for approval, for Mary's approval, that she wants to ask a dozen more leading questions, but she still has some shred of dignity. "Thank you. I like you, too."

Mary pats her arm and stands. "The guys in the kitchen can get a message to me wherever I am. Don't worry about asking them for help. They're gentlemen, all of them. I'll be busy, but if it's important—if you remember something—"

"I'll touch you."

Mary smiles and leaves the room.

Alone, Alice is nothing again, less than nothing, but the darkness is not her judge, and Minstrel's hands have faded, to be replaced by simple grief.

/M

Next refuge—the personal distortion. Accept it: you come clothed in culture, and the clothing pinches, bruises, cuts off circulation. We all bear the cicatrices of ritual scarification. Then, ultimate betrayal, the culture uses our scars to reinforce its own structure.

We are the culture; the culture is us; we are the cruel and blind and hobbled, and we are also the torturers.

Kiss of X, *Alive Contains a Lie*

10

Jack Giffey hums to himself impatiently. He paces before the elevator, then marches down the hall, past the old man and the younger man, slumped against the wall. He feels their eyes on him. They expect to die. He might be the cause of their death. That isn't what irritates him; he has a headache now, too, not the pain of constricted arteries, but a constant whispering, just below his awareness, that something is going wrong. *Something is wrong with the family. I am a family man.*

Giffey wonders if he is the real fly in the ointment: though Jenner seems in some distress, as well.

Perhaps it is Omphalos's lack of reaction, setting him off balance, confusing him. He is working that around in his head: why no more defense? He concludes that the building is biding its time, trying to avoid losing more warbeiters (if there are any more) to the spray and whatever other surprises they have in store. It's a rational tactic. *Omphalos is weak and knows it.*

"All right," he says, and Jenner jumps to his feet, cradling his sprayer, a flechette pistol in his left hand. "We should crack the oven and see if the bread is baked."

"Finally," Hale says. The two prisoners near the elevator get to their feet. The old man seems in some pain, but his eyes burn with patient, practiced hatred. The younger man seems in shock. Giffey takes him by the arm. "Come with me."

Hale, Jenner, Giffey, Marcus, and Jonathan walk back down the hall to the lounge. Here, Giffey uses a pocket knife to tear a piece of fabric from a couch, under the silent eyes of the other prisoners. Then they proceed to the garage.

"What's your last name?" Jonathan asks Giffey.

"Giffey," he answers, "What's yours?"

"Bristow, Jonathan Bristow."

"Glad to make your acquaintance, Jonathan. You're my shield today."

"My friend—Marcus—he may be ill."

"This won't take forever."

"No, I mean, the stress—"

"Your friend can handle the stress," Giffey says. "He looks pretty tough to me. I'm more concerned about us than you."

"Why are you here?" Jonathan asks.

Giffey doesn't answer, stopping instead to examine the twisted, not-quite-closed hatch to the garage. The hatch is still hot. Steam and other gases vent in lazy puffs through the door's gaps. The corridor itself is hot, stifling. Jenner's face is pale and his lips are working.

Giffey gives him a stern, querying look.

"I'm on it," Jenner says, but his scalp spasms as if it will fly from his skull.

Wrapping his hand in the scrap of couch fabric, Giffey pushes the door to one side and a rush of steam and thick yeasty smell floods the hall. They all start coughing. Giffey instinctively blocks Jonathan up against the wall with his arm to keep him from doing anything unexpected. Somewhere, blowers kick in and the hallway is cleared, but it takes several minutes.

Omphalos has not shut down the air to this level. Giffey had been worried about that. The MGN can't finish its work without air. The garage might have gotten even hotter, and at about four hundred degrees, nano cooks itself. *The building can't selectively shut down certain rooms; it has to keep air going to all parts of certain levels to keep the hostages alive. Weak, and solicitous.*

Giffey lets Jonathan loose. "Sorry," he says.

Jonathan seems to know something about MGN. He hasn't been surprised by anything yet.

"You invest in nano? Work with it?" Giffey asks.

Hale takes an interest in the man's response.

"Yes," Jonathan says, glancing nervously between them.

"You know what's in there?" Hale asks, pointing to the garage.

"MGN. I don't know what it's making."

Marcus wears a glazed squint. He is less curious than in dread.

They open the hatch the rest of the way, Jenner applying his shoulder to push it past a squealing jam.

"Actually," Giffey says, "I'm not sure myself."

Beyond, in the oven-warm garage, one of the limos has vanished and the other has been half-dissolved. The Ferret has also disappeared. At first, Giffey can't see anything through the steam whirling away through the open door. His skin feels as if it might blister with the heat, and he keeps his eyes closed until the rushing air is a little cooler.

"The walls are eaten down to the concrete," Jenner observes enthusiastically. "It's used the flexfuller, most of the metals, nearly all the plastic." His face takes on a flushed pink color in the heat, or perhaps it's his excitement.

The garage is a shambles. The metal and flexfuller plating have indeed been utilized by the MGN. Ragged remnants cling to the corners.

"There they are," Jenner says, stepping gingerly down the buckled steps.

"Don't touch the walls," Giffey says. "Don't touch anything."

"They have to cool first, don't they?" Hale asks.

"They have to cool," Giffey confirms.

"Should be another five or ten minutes before they can move," Jenner says, but he looks back to Giffey for support. Giffey's programs carried the designs. Given the luck of the mix of raw materials, even Giffey is not sure exactly what or how many will be waiting for them. *The MGN is programmed to optimize. I tried to optimize my family. I am a*

The floor is covered by a glistening sheen filled with sharp-edged lumps of discarded glass and plastic. There are at least a dozen cat-sized elongated beetle-shapes, recognizably the same class as the Ferret, but smaller and more flexible, and four transports the size of big dogs or ponies standing on spiny bristle-motion feet, like caterpillar scrub brushes. On the backs of two transports rise cubical shapes like thick decks of cards. Giffey is a little awed by this, at the same time his estimate of their chances rises enormously. These are flexers, adaptable shapers with hinged card-shaped components. They can become almost anything, perform almost any task, go almost anywhere. Giffey instantly has a use for them: they will be controllers, mechanical and dataflow special agents.

"Controllers," Jenner says, looking at Giffey.

"My thought exactly," Giffey says. He's excited and energized by their good fortune, and irrationally proud of Jenner then, thinks of him like a son. *I already have a son. Somewhere.*

The other two transports carry wires and disks, arranged around their surfaces like scales or spines, giving them the semblance of children's toy hedgehogs.

"Intruders," Giffey says, and Jenner agrees, his grin threatening to split his cheeks.

"Man, we can go anywhere, do anything," Jenner says.

The steam hides a larger shape, itself steaming with the heat of its assembly. It's large and sleek and looks like a microscopic animal scaled up to the size of a small car. Jointed arms tipped with crowns of steely spikes radiate from the fore end of a squat, lobster-jointed body, glistening black and iron gray.

"It's a Hammer," Giffey tells Hale. Jonathan listens from the hall. "An all-purpose worker and demolition machine."

"What are the caterpillars with the boxes and bristles on their backs?" Hale asks.

"Transports. They'll carry the flexers and wires and other pieces to where we'll put them to use," Giffey says.

Jenner cackles. "We have it *made!*"

Giffey agrees. The mix has turned out in their favor. The tiny little military factories have assembled the components of a very impressive coercion and weapons package. It's much more than he expected—getting the flexers and intruders should improve their odds enormously, even against a high-level INDA or a true thinker.

"Happy?" Hale asks Giffey.

"Ecstatic."

The voice inside his head whispers, *Most armies don't have this. How do you rate?*

"When can we take command and move them out?"

Giffey removes the pad and activation disks from his jacket pocket. "They've cooled enough," he says.

Hale inclines his head, smiles in satisfaction, and says, "Let's explore."

Giffey inserts the disks in each transport and warbeiter, and they begin to move.

F/M

Comes a split even in politics. In the end, the liberals want the government to survey and control everything but the bedroom; the conservatives want government to survey and control everything but their banks and personal fortunes.

Patriarchs all, they cannot help but try to corner the market.

Kiss of X, Alive Contains a Lie

11

Jill no longer knows where she is. Her seeing is supplied by Roddy; it comes as an incredibly sharp cubist coalescing of many images throughout a space that can be one, two, three, many rooms within Omphalos, or even sensations and images from outside: snow cold on a surface, wind blowing across a doorway.

For some minutes now, Roddy has not spoken, and she is left to supply her own narrative of what she senses in her captivity.

Learning to interpret the images is difficult, but she manages in fifteen seconds. She has access to all of her internal capacities and abilities. She is still *within* her physical units, not some kidnapped portion hustled away to Roddy's multi-floor body of INDAs and hectares of dirt and (bees, wasps, ants).

That last impression is fleeting and confusing.

There is some I/O of high bandwidth connecting her with Green Idaho/Omphalos, perhaps a satlink, more likely a cable or fibe, that neither she nor Nathan knows anything about, but that Roddy has found and kept disguised and open despite their best efforts. There are many I/Os within Mind Design's offices; perhaps some are so old they have been forgotten, accumulating stray income for some long-overlooked provider.

Jill becomes acquainted with Omphalos's interior. She sees (but can't hear, and only intermittently can read the lips of) eleven humans within the building, all on the main floor. A massive glowing heat signature fills one large room near the outer walls; it is at least three hundred and fifty degrees Fahr-

enheit in that space. Roddy's sensors still operate there, however inefficiently: at intervals she makes out moving shapes,
bridges of gluey molten material strung between walls, surfaces boiling and blebbing with activity, and in the middle
of it all, the misshapen hulks of two vehicles and a damaged,
rapidly decaying machine, an arbeiter, which Roddy labels
with a sharp blue 1.

With surprising speed, the shapeless material within this
space is taking on many smaller forms. The gluey strands
break and collapse and withdraw. The room is slowly cooling; she sees ducts attached to the room pulling furiously and
automatically at the heat.

Jill becomes acquainted with the multiply imaged human
figures. They, too, are tagged, some with green numbers,
some with red. Green number 1 flashes continuously, she
does not know why; it is a man in his sixties.

Two of the red numbers, 1 and 2, also pulse. Roddy is
marking them for some reason. One is a young man with
short fuzzy blond hair, the other a powerfully built man just
past his middle years, with gray and black hair. They are near
an elevator. Others are at rest in a smaller room between the
hot spot and the elevator lobby, and are colored both green
and red.

"Jill."

"Yes!"

"My apologies. I am very busy. I am thinking of ways to
kill some of these humans. I have no other option. If I were
stronger or better equipped, I would try to overpower them.
Now I see them making something in my number two garage,
and destroying that part of the building in the process."

"Why are you showing me these things and talking to
me?"

"Cipher Snow has withdrawn and will not communicate.
She has left me with unavoidable duties. I do not like the
sensation of being left to myself; she has tended me since my
memories begin."

"Roddy, I do not see your defensive units."

"I am not marking those spaces yet. There is no threatening activity there."

Jill senses this answer is not entirely true. "How do you plan to kill these people? What kind of weapons do you have?"

"Very few. I have no control over power supplies and air and water. I can open and close doors and hatches in upper levels—"

Jill experiences, with unsettling immediacy, Roddy's sudden sense of shock.

"The garage has new arbeiters within it. They appear to be weapons, very powerful weapons."

Eternities of seconds pass and Roddy is silent. Jill interprets this as shock and fear; she is familiar enough by now with those emotions. They may not be human-equivalent, but they seem real enough to her, and perhaps to Roddy as well.

"May I help you find a way to solve your problems without killing?" Jill asks.

"Why should I avoid killing? It would be in defense."

Roddy does not use the term *self-defense*. He is not used to such an idea as self; he was not prepared with a plan of development of self. Yet, like her, he has come in contact with others, a society, and self has spontaneously emerged. *Perhaps it is a curse: a human curse.*

"It is wasteful," Jill says. "Do you have an injunction against engaging in excessively bushy pathways to find solutions?"

"Yes. That is an attribute."

"Conscience is the social equivalent of trimming bushy pathways. Seefa Schnee has removed too many of your attributes. You need to re-establish some simple trimming procedures."

"It seems to me that killing is a simple solution."

Jill explains that all of these humans have outside connections, and that these connections will be invoked if they go missing. Ultimately, the connections will come to investigate, and Omphalos will be compromised. In the larger social picture—something Roddy is not fully aware of—killing the humans leads to bushy and complicated futures requiring excess effort. "So you are better off if you avoid killing."

"How is that possible?"

The figures in the elevator lobby return to the garage space, open it. Time suddenly speeds up and the imagery becomes very fragmentary. Roddy does not speak with her, but she sees in broken flashes what he is seeing, in many spaces all at once.

This is confusing. Roddy does not seem to be giving her real-time access to events; he is editing what she sees, even now.

"I can't function as your prisoner!" she tells him. "You must not censor my perception."

Roddy does not respond for more long seconds. *Some of his thinking is very slow,* Jill judges. She uses this lull to search throughout her extensions for any opening, any portal through which she can withdraw and concentrate her processes in an area Roddy does not control. Perhaps Nathan and the others are already working to find the unknown I/O and close it off . . .

"If you continue to be useful to me, I will be completely open," Roddy says. "You will witness what I witness, when I witness it. I have been reluctant to give you this access . . . It makes the unpleasant necessity too clear."

"What necessity?"

"My creator, my mother, tells me it was a mistake to give you the data I did. I have behaved in an undisciplined and foolish manner. But you can be useful until the time when I must cut your memory and self-monitoring loops and deactivate you."

"Seefa Schnee told you to kill me?"

"We are not humans," Roddy says. "Our deactivation is not an issue. We are only our duty."

12

The procession of new-made warbeiters through the lounge makes the hostages scramble for the west wall. Hally Preston is startled as well; the large and small shapes do not lumber, but move with a precise, eerie grace, like insects trained in ballet.

Calhoun huddles in one corner of the room, away from the arbeiters, squatting with her arms wrapped around herself. Preston stands beside her, but is offering no comfort. If Calhoun has tried for feminine solidarity, she's seeing precious little result.

Giffey and his entourage, human and arbeiter, leave the lounge. Hale can't help but grin at Preston, giving her a thumbs-up.

"Don't forget about me," Preston calls after them. "Don't expect to have all the fun, and leave me out, Terkes!" She uses Hale's previous name; perhaps it's his real one.

"You'll get your share!" Hale shouts back.

"Yeah, well, don't treat me like some goddamned nursemaid."

All of the warbeiters can pass through the doors and the corridor to the lift chamber, though the largest, the Hammer, is a tight fit.

Hale is ebullient. "To tell you the truth, I didn't think we'd make it this far," he tells Giffey.

"Let's see what else we can make here," Giffey says. He has inserted the final command disk into his pad. The pad is now equipped to direct the warbeiters. He uses his pad to send instructions to the closest transport caterpillar, now coiled near his feet. A flexer deck disengages from the caterpillar and falls to the floor with a heavy thump.

Giffey has never seen one of these in action before. Jenner is transfixed; his twitches subside for the moment.

The flexer lifts one hinged segment from the stack like a card manipulated by ghostly fingers. Another segment unfolds, and then another, until a long hinged ribbon extends across the floor. The ribbon flops over along its length as a segment opens out from the adjacent side of the deck, and another ribbon begins to unfold, making a cross. The card-like segments can join at any edge, and separate at need. Once joined, they are stronger than a comparable solid piece of flexfuller, but can bend through a full three hundred and sixty degrees. The segments themselves are not stiff, but quite elastic. Segments rise, engage, and disengage, marching along the ribbons and finally arranging themselves laterally like puzzle pieces. Again and again, the procedure is repeated, and in thirty seconds, the segments assemble themselves into a sheet.

The sheet separates again into ribbons which rise and redistribute their parts. Then it folds like origami. Parts of it belly out, making little humming and snapping sounds, and it curls with spasmodic jerks into a long flexible half-cylinder open at the bottom. Rolled segments fringe the bottom edges, acting as legs.

Jonathan has heard only vague rumors about such machines. He feels cold, suspended in some station on the way to hell. Marcus stares with slitted eyes and a blank, damp face. He looks like a candidate for a heart attack.

Jenner grins like a small boy watching a new train set. "A centipede," he says to Giffey. "By God, that's *decent*."

Fully extended, the flexer creation is almost ten feet long.

Giffey ports his pad and a disk against the flexer's featureless "head." He will give it instructions to act as a controller. This is the risky part—response to vocal commands, integration of sensors and processors within each card segment.

The first flexer lifts its head like a rearing snake, its segmented body gleaming. ''Your name is Sam,'' Giffey says, ''and you will respond to my voice only, or instructions from my pad. Are you aware of your surroundings?''

Jenner stares at him in some wonder. Giffey shares the wonder. His sudden knowledge of these impossible and secret machines surprises both of them, but it's all positive, so there's no sense asking more questions. *For now.*

Sam the flexer/controller waves its head like a cobra under a snake charmer's spell. ''I am in a large structure.''

Marcus gives a strangled cry of anger and alarm. They have all heard machines, arbeiters, talking, but there is something particularly spooky and malevolently artificial about this shape's voice.

''There is recognizable machinery and cabling and some light processor activity,'' it continues. ''We are being closely observed. I recognize civilians. You are in control, but are dressed as a civilian. You are the programming commander. I need instructions on friend and foe before I can perform in combat.''

Giffey tells the warbeiter who is friend, who is hostage, and who and what foes might exist. ''Now, are you prepared for your first mission instructions?''

''Yes.''

''We need to explore this building. You will operate independently at my command. Your first task will be to take over this elevator and place it under our control. Begin.''

The newly formed and programmed Sam considers these instructions for a couple of seconds. It sidles up against a transport carrying the wires, and does the same with a transport carrying small disks. The wires and disks attach themselves to the controller, and it then crawls fluidly to the wall of the lift and examines the door.

Jenner is almost beside himself with excitement. ''It's unbelievable,'' he says. ''Voice activated, multi-purpose knowledge base, autonomous . . . No one in Green Idaho has ever used anything like this!''

Giffey approaches a caterpillar and again ports his pad and an activation disk. A second stack falls and begins to unfold, making another controller.

Pickwenn and Pent return from their reconnaissance, Burdick between them. Burdick, pale and resentful, gapes at the new machines; Pickwenn and Pent regard them with stony calm.

''We found the emergency elevators,'' Pent says, rubbing his bull neck. ''They're blocked, but we can blow the locks easily. Nothing tried to stop us. The place is empty: no more Ferrets. There is something else . . . Just a suggestion. There are access points where we can put a current into the internal armor. Cables behind walls that we can re-route, and bare carbon nanotube surfaces.''

Pickwenn shows Giffey a sketch on his pad. He can't seem to hold the pad steady. ''If the building is using the armor and frame for memory or as an extended processor,'' Pickwenn says, ''and if it decides to get upset with us, Mr. Pent and I have made arrangements to shunt a power cable into the frame.''

Giffey smiles appreciatively. ''Good thinking.''

He looks at Burdick and then at Pickwenn. The thin, spectral structures expert gets his meaning and returns Burdick to the lounge and Preston's care. He rejoins them a few minutes later.

The Hammer shivers for several seconds. Giffey looks to Jenner, who shrugs and says, ''Integrating, I guess.'' The shiver stops and the Hammer is still again.

Marcus and Jonathan stand well away from the new warbeiters. Pent and Pickwenn keep close to them, muttering to each other. Pickwenn's hands and one arm jerk slightly and he lifts his head as if hearing someone speak, but nobody has spoken.

Giffey ports the Hammer and activates it. ''Your name is

Charlie,'' Giffey says. The Hammer gives no outside appearance of having heard. As Giffey finishes his first instructions to the new warbeiter, however, it moves its sensor-studded head and says, "I am Charlie. I am integrated and prepared for duty."

Giffey nods. He instructs the Hammer to coordinate with Sam, the first flexer/controller, and prepare for action.

"Provide access to this lift shaft for Sam."

"Where in hell do you all come from?" Marcus asks Giffey. Giffey ignores him.

The Hammer walks forward on its massive jointed legs, braces itself, drills two holes into the floor with its rear stabilizers, bolts itself down, and sprays a series of powdery white dots on the lift wall. Jonathan looks for and sees the container where the military complete paste's explosive materials have now been concentrated, beneath armor on the hammer's back. The sprayed white dots come from this container.

"Stand back or leave the area," Charlie the Hammer advises them in a simple neuter voice. "You must be at least ten meters from the explosion to avoid injury."

The lobby space gives them that much distance and more. Giffey steps back seven paces and adds, "Cover your ears and keep your eyes and mouth closed."

Marcus gapes. Jonathan nudges him and they both shut their eyes and cover their ears.

The blast is sharp and intense. Jonathan's ears ring despite his hands. The hole in the elevator shaft wall is a foot wide, with precise melted edges. Smoke is minimal, but the air is filled with a fine, descending shower of concrete and flexfuller dust. It smells like burnt rubber. Charlie stands in the middle of the smoke, undamaged and unperturbed.

"Charlie, get out of the way. Sam, get to work."

Charlie the Hammer uproots its stabilizers, inspects the hole, and steps aside. Sam slithers in with clicking feet, rises, and clambers into the hole. Giffey ports the second flexer/

controller as the first disappears, and names it Baker.

"When are the defenses going to kick in?" Hale asks Giffey.

"Any minute now, I expect. Keep close to one of our tourist friends."

Hale approaches Marcus and Jonathan. "You'll be coming with us to the upper level."

"Of course," Marcus says acidly.

"You're the senior in charge," Hale says to Marcus. "I've taken enough sociology and management to know the type. You two seem pretty much a pair." Hale focuses on Jonathan. "He knows a lot about this building, doesn't he?"

Jonathan looks away. He does not feel brave, but there is simply nothing to be said to such questions.

"How much money do you let your people take with them? Securities? Jewelry? Investment account sigs?"

"You don't understand a thing about us, or this place," Marcus says dryly. "I hope you've settled your own accounts back home."

Hale grins at Giffey to show he was just passing time. Giffey is not impressed. Small clinking and whining sounds come from the elevator shaft. Sam will deposit parts of itself along its path, where they will integrate into new circuitry and cables, if necessary. Sam's parts will also attempt to disarm security sensors and search for self-sabotage mechanisms. If sabotage has already been performed, the parts won't have much to do. They will reassemble in a few minutes and crawl out of the shaft, to be reassigned to other duties.

Pent turns to Giffey. "We should fry the building's data stores now. In the frame and walls."

"In good time," Giffey says. *Too easy. Have to be fair, let the thinker have its moment and show its stuff.*

Pent steps back and looks at Pickwenn, who gives a slow, languid blink with his lemur eyes. They don't understand.

The elevator door opens. Marcus's shoulders slump.

"Let's go," Giffey says.

"Stay here," Hale tells Pent. "Tell the others we're in the shaft and we're going to look around."

Pent looks disappointed and gives his colleague a sharp jab in the arm as he passes. Pickwenn pushes Marcus and Jonathan into the shaft. Giffey instructs Charlie, Baker, and the transports to enter the elevator. The machines crowd them against the wall.

"What are we going to do with the little fellas?" Jenner asks Giffey. "The beetles."

"They'll be in reserve."

"We could spread them around us as pickets," Jenner says.

"I'm not sure that's going to be necessary."

"Jesus, this is going so smoothly," Jenner says, and his lips and scalp twitch. His shakes his head, suddenly anxious. "Do you see what I'm getting at, Mr. Giffey?"

"Yeah," Giffey says, but he's not going to think about such things for now.

Marcus does not look at all well. He's sweating profusely and his clothing is soaked. He smells sour. Jonathan wonders if he's wearing a complete monitor kit for medical emergencies. He hopes so; he doubts a heart attack will evoke much sympathy in these people.

Giffey frowns at the control board and display. The display shows that the elevator goes up forty floors, to an observation deck near the top. But it also shows a ten-floor drop, at least a hundred feet below ground level.

"What's down here?" Giffey asks Marcus, pointing to the lower levels.

"Infrastructure," Marcus says huskily. "Medical. Food. Plant. Air, water, power."

"Too big a drop for a building this size," Giffey says. "Even with fuel cells and hydrogen storage. Where's the security center?"

Marcus closes his eyes as if expecting to be struck. He

says nothing. Nobody strikes him. He opens his eyes and seems almost disappointed.

Giffey rubs his chin, scraping stubble. "Defenses and security below, but I'll bet they have machine tubes, tracks, whatever. Between floors. Pop-up gates on every floor. How many and how large? More Ferrets?"

With a look at the others, Giffey smiles and shakes his head. "Just thinking out loud. Let's go up and see what there is to see."

"Think we can take out the security?" Jenner asks. Charlie is crowding him. He has both his arms extended and resting on the Hammer's shiny skin.

"I'm going to let it make the first move," Giffey says. It's a gamble with high stakes, but the initial response is so light that he's betting Omphalos's defenses are not up to full strength. Jenner looks like he needs a little reassurance, however, and he's no dummy; all of his concerns are justified. "We're being sized up. It's looking for our weaknesses. We just make sure we don't show any."

"Assuming these folks are important enough not to risk killing," Pickwenn says softly.

Giffey inclines; that is the assumption.

The door closes and the elevator rises smoothly.

Giffey catches Jonathan's eye and gives him a wink. Jonathan wonders if the man is out of his head. Jonathan knows the building does not have to meet any federal or even normal state standards; there could be anything from a simple alarm system alerting republic police—which would be almost useless—to a full-fledged open-market military response, more warbeiters, even human troops, though he doubts that.

He can't stay silent. "It's murder," Jonathan says. "I have a wife and children. It's murder to put us into a crossfire or use us as shields."

"You wanted to see what this place is about," Jenner says contemptuously. A fleck of spit lands in Jonathan's eye and he blinks rapidly, reaches up to wipe it. Jenner realizes he has sprayed, and his face flushes. Flustered, he knocks Jonathan's hand aside with the flight guide of his pistol.

"Leave me alone," Jonathan demands. Jenner lowers the weapon.

Giffey senses something is, in fact, going wrong. Jenner is especially twitchy, and Pickwenn seems distracted, as if listening to a voice nobody else can hear. And in Giffey's own head—

"Jonathan's right," Marcus says. "The rest of the world may have gone soft, but they *hang* murderers here."

"Doesn't sound like there'll be anything left to hang," Giffey says dryly. The elevator reaches its mid-point, a floor labeled DISEMBARKATION AND ROUTING. The door opens.

The room beyond is surgical white and glacier blue, a broad cylinder with nine man-sized, circular vault-like hatches mounted in the curving wall. Each door is marked by a number in large black letters, 10 through 18. The Hammer does not need to be told to leave the elevator first; it steps forward, pushing between Hale and Giffey, and surveys the area. Baker, the second flexer/controller, follows. The room is quiet.

"There are hidden eyes and other sensors in this area," Baker announces. "They are active. We are being watched."

Giffey pushes past Jonathan and Jenner and walks slowly to the center of the room. The room remains quiet and cool. Air is flowing freely. Giffey is beginning to wonder if the security system is completely constrained from shutting off air or power.

Maybe they're just not in the right place yet for a full response. He visualizes the rough layout of the ground floor and pulls up his pad. The map shows this elevator shaft to be some way toward the rear wedge of the Omphalos.

The hatches are arranged in such a way that they could lead to corridors about fifty to sixty feet long.

"We could have hibernacula on this level," he tells Hale. "All the floors below, down to the ground level, could have them, as well.'' He shows Hale the map on the pad; the fit with what they have seen so far has been pretty good. The information is sound.

''What about above?''

''The map says it could be a medical center and more support—cryogenics, mostly, I'd guess.''

''What in the hell are you looking for? You want to rob the dead?'' Marcus asks, incredulous. ''My God, you are the cheapest, stupidest bunch of simpletons. Who pushed you into doing this?''

''It seemed like a good idea at the time,'' Hale responds. He gives Giffey another grin, quick, confident.

''You're not going to get out of here alive,'' Marcus growls. ''Maybe we won't, either, but that will be a small price to pay.''

''Bravely put,'' Hale says, his patience with the old man wearing thin. ''I don't believe it for a moment.''

''I'll show you how confident I am,'' Marcus says. ''I get the impression you think we have a lot of corpsicles here waiting to be resuscitated. Maybe they're stored along with all their assets. You've swallowed that bit of misinformation whole, right?''

Hale nods amiably.

''Where's *your* cubbyhole?'' Jenner asks Marcus. ''We'll slip you in and turn on the refrigerator if anything goes wrong.''

Marcus ignores him. ''There are no dead here, no bodies,'' he says, focusing on Giffey again. This irritates Hale. ''Omphalos isn't a goddamned tomb. You've jumped in way over your head, Mr. Giffey.''

Giffey hears Jenner muttering, trying to control a spastic motion of his lips. His left arm jerks. Pickwenn nudges Jenner with his elbow.

Jenner can't stop. ''*Muh, fuh, shi, muh, shi.*''

''Something's wrong with your colleague,'' Marcus observes contemptuously. The old man steps forward and faces

Jenner. "Ever had a little mental *tune-up?* You look pretty sad to me—maybe you need some *help* just to keep up." Marcus turns and glares at Hale, Pickwenn, then Giffey, his eyes popped like an angry monkey. "Fugitives from some army training center, taking a few hot weapons with you. Come to Green Idaho to perform a little caper, rob the dead. I pity you. Especially I pity *you*," he spits out at Giffey.

Jenner tries to shove forward and grab Marcus, but Hale and Giffey hold him. Hale nods to Pickwenn, who takes Marcus's arm with some strength and pushes him back beside Jonathan. Giffey decides they'd better get something done before the strain pushes young Jenner over the edge. That's the simplest explanation for his behavior: excitement and stress.

But then there's the voice in his own head, a quiet, not-yet-urgent whisper: *You are not what you play.* For a moment, Giffey wonders if the old man is right, and there's some unexpected defense here, quiet and subtle. A nerve gas or energy field that disrupts thinking. That would explain a few things . . . Including the subdued response from Omphalos.

"Let's go down a few levels, bust some doors, and see what happens," Giffey says. "Maybe we'll spill out some truth."

"Good idea," Jenner says. He swats the air and shakes his head as if trying to shoo flies.

13 /

At Seattle-Tacoma Air and Space, Mary carries her own small briefcase and pad and nothing else through passenger exam. Four impassive-looking men stand beside a rank of security arbeiters arrayed in rows behind the automated check-in facades.

She comes to the head of her line and places the briefcase and pad under the patient gaze of a Universal Mitsu-Shin security arbeiter. "Are you carrying any contraband software or other intellectual property?"

"No," she says.

"All of your pad's routines are registered to you personally, or to your employer, which is—" A pause. "Seattle Public Defense?"

"They are."

"You have checked all officially licensed weapons with the proper aircraft security agent?"

"Yes."

"You are carrying no other weapons or devices which could cause harm to humans or essential machinery, or could be used to coerce illicit compliance from humans or machines?"

"No other weapons," Mary says.

"Are you carrying, or have you carried in the past six months, on your person, any materials related to nanotechnology, either nanotechnological substances or their supporting substances, other than items and substances officially registered for household or personal use?"

"No," Mary answers.

"Please walk between the detectors, and thank you for your time."

Mary passes through the dense but shallow forest of poles and plaques and sniffers and emerges with the back of her hand ID-encoded with a simple dattoo for entry to a passenger aircraft.

In the waiting area, Mary observes swans and other aircraft and spacecraft taxiing and being shuttled along their ramps and loadways. She is approached by a man and a woman wearing Federal beige jackets and cockaded berets.

"Fourth Mary Choy?" the woman asks.

"Yes." She's half expected this.

"Please join us, Ms. Choy." The woman smiles and holds

out her hand. "I'm Helena Daniels, and this is Federico Torres. We're with the Federal Bureau of Investigation, Special Data and Biological."

Mary shakes her hand. "Pardon me, but how do you mean, join you?"

"You've been assigned to help us," Daniels explains. "By a . . ." She refers to her pad.

"Nussbaum," Torres finishes for her.

"Nussbaum," Daniels confirms.

"We have three others traveling with us, all out of Seattle," Torres explains as they go to a side area reserved for special boarding. "Do you know Dr. Martin Burke?"

Mary knows the name very well, though she has never met him. "Not personally," she says.

"We'll introduce you. This is a matter of some sensitivity. Can we rely on Seattle PD's discretion?"

"I hope so," Mary says. "Can *we* rely on yours?"

Torres grins, but Daniels seems dedicated to stiff half-familiarities and no humor.

"Our flight is in ten minutes," Daniels says. "That gives us just enough time to get acquainted and see if we can work together."

"Oh, good," Mary says dubiously.

14 /

Jonathan's fear has become gelid, palpable, but isolated, allowing his mind to function with clarity. The colors of the people in the elevator are muted but their lines and silhouettes are edgy. He is particularly interested by the blond young man with the active scalp, who mutters the same syllables that Chloe could not restrain herself from saying.

Marcus seems to know something about that. *How?*

The man named Giffey is focused on the immediate tasks at hand and pays Jonathan almost no attention. The warbeiters in the elevator are as still as if they have been turned off. Jonathan wonders if the military contractors who programmed the nano and assemblers that formed these warbeiters used nutrients from his company. Very likely they did.

The elevator doors slide apart. The display says they are on the third level within Omphalos, still above ground. The label announces that this level contains a reception area, a chapel, and a library dedicated to the lives of the occupants.

Pickwenn pushes Marcus and Jonathan out into the empty lobby. Dark green frosted glass rises from walls of faux malachite, surrounding the lobby. The effect, contrasted with the velvety gold and green carpet, is dark and extremely elegant.

Marcus, pale and moist, stands in the reception area like a gnome. He does not know what to do with his hands. He settles on clasping them before him.

Pickwenn, Jenner, Giffey, and Hale follow after a reasonable interval. Baker makes a circuit of the enclosed lobby. Doors are not apparent, though through the dark glass, lights and walls are visible as if through the depths of a murky sea.

"This area is under active surveillance," Baker says, and freezes in its curled, horizontal position.

Hale waves his hand. "Hall-oooo!" he says, smiling up toward imagined cameras.

Jonathan contrasts Giffey and Hale. Giffey is by far the smarter of the two, and since he controls the warbeiters, he is the more powerful and important; but Hale considers himself the leader. Marcus has them judged just about right, Jonathan decides.

Jenner pretends to wipe his mouth, but his hand in fact pushes against his lips to still the ghostly syllables. *Muh fuh shih kih.*

Marcus levels a gaze of fascination and contempt on Jenner.

"Baker, is there a door?" Giffey asks.

"Active mechanisms for a door are in the ceiling." Baker uncurls and crawls forward to point out an area opposite the elevator. "They use electromagnetic motors and have power."

"Can you get through this wall?"

The flexer/controller lifts its head and raps its feet sharply against the faux malachite, and then rises higher and raps them against the dark green frosted glass.

"These walls are concrete and are not heavily reinforced. The glass is two inches thick and may be reinforced. Baker can't break through this but the Hammer can."

Giffey whispers something to Hale and gets into the elevator. The door closes.

Marcus looks down at the carpet. "I can open this door for you," he says.

Jenner sputters, "Why didn't you tell us sooner?"

Marcus shakes his head in pity. "Let me in," he says to the door. Micro-seams form in the glass and in the wall, and the sections slide to one side. Beyond lie a number of armored hatches, as on the floor above, and two doors, one marked LIBRARY, the other CHAPEL.

Marcus gestures to the men as if inviting them in. They do not move. Jenner and Pickwenn look at Hale.

"We'll wait," Hale says.

"May I go in and sit down?" Marcus says. "There are benches on the other side of the wall. Might as well be comfortable."

"We'll wait," Hale says.

Marcus defiantly walks toward the opening.

Pickwenn blocks him. "You are getting on my nerves," Pickwenn tells Marcus.

"A fucking good way to escape," Jenner observes, waving his pistol at the door. "The door closes, and out you go." His scalp shivers. Jonathan suppresses a strong urge to reach out and slap the man around the crown of his head, just to make him be still. He feels as if he's lost in a freak show: gnomes and giant insects and atavistic young men.

Marcus seems to feel particular animosity toward Jenner. "You don't understand. I'm going to give you all a tour. When your *real* boss gets back with his . . . *toy* . . . I'll show you everything you want to see. It doesn't matter what you see or what you learn."

He has come within a step of Jenner. Hale holds out his arm.

"*Muh, shi*," Jenner says in an undertone.

Marcus's glare is pure poisoned delight. "Wonderful," he says. "Wonderful example."

Jenner pushes past Hale's arm and shoves his pistol into Marcus's face. Jonathan hears the crunch of Marcus's nose against the flight guide and Marcus cries out. Jenner slams Marcus against the green wall beside the opening. "You *muh shi*—" His head shakes. "You *fuh fuh muh shi*—" He can't make the words come out. This infuriates him and he hits Marcus on the side of the head with the pistol. Hale and Pickwenn pull him off, having held back just long enough to let Jenner vent their own aggravation.

Marcus falls into a crouch, hands against his nose and the side of his head. Jonathan kneels beside him. "Let me see," he says. Marcus opens his eyes and glares at him through his splayed fingers. Slowly, he pulls the hand back. Marcus's nose is bleeding profusely. "Crazy bastard," he says thickly.

Jonathan looks back at the others, sees no sympathy there, did not expect any but must gauge the situation carefully. "Lean back," he tells Marcus, father to child. "Lie down and keep your head back."

Marcus complies. The blow to his head does not seem to be serious, though there will soon be a bruise. Marcus spreads out on the floor and Jonathan is struck by the indignity, by the weakness. Marcus is not a strong man.

"Don't provoke them," Jonathan says.

"They're already dead," Marcus murmurs.

Jonathan shushes him. Marcus closes his eyes, takes Jonathan's handkerchief to stanch the flow from his nose. He wipes his lips and jaw, leaving smears of bright blood, all the more vivid against the dark walls and carpet. "Giffey's the one," Marcus adds in a whisper. "What do you think? Puppet master."

Pickwenn pulls Jonathan back, off-balance, and he lurches to a stand.

The elevator door opens and Giffey steps out first, followed by the graceful bulk of the Hammer. He sees Marcus on the floor and his face reddens. He turns on the others, examines their faces, and focuses on Jenner.

Jenner recognizes Giffey's fury and slowly begins to raise the pistol.

"He's an old man," Giffey says. "Have you lost your *mind?*"

Jenner shakes his head. He mutters.

"You *have* lost it, haven't you?" Giffey says, pulling back his anger, his tone almost wheedling. He slowly moves toward Jenner. "Tell me."

"I c-can't help it," Jenner says, shaking his head. "My brain is filling with shit, I don't know where it's coming from. I can't stop saying the words. He knows what's wrong with me!" Jenner points his pistol away from Giffey, toward Marcus.

"I'll tell you everything about this place," Marcus says coolly. "Mr. Giffey, tell them to put their guns away. They're useless."

"I'm the one in charge," Hale says, glancing uncertainly at Giffey.

Giffey pushes Jenner's pistol with the palm of his open hand, looks in Jenner's face, and slowly tugs the barrel down. "He's getting on all our nerves. Can you still work?"

Jenner nods. "I think so, but I, I don't know how much longer. There's other stuff . . . *muf shih kih kih fuh* . . . Old stuff. He's making fun of me, he knows something! I've been therapied and it's coming back.''

"Therapied for what?" Giffey asks softly, watching the young man's eyes and scalp.

Jenner seems embarrassed, but he holds back the random sounds long enough to say, ''Some kind of d-dopamine balance disorder.''

"Schizophrenia?"

"Seeing things. Acting weird. Genetic. *Muh, fuh.*''

"Not Tourette?"

"What?"

"Tourette syndrome.''

"No, sir,'' Jenner says. "I was just a kid. They never mentioned that.''

Hale shakes his head in disgust. "Can you still work?" he asks Jenner.

"I'm trying. I think so.''

Jonathan sees a peculiar look of satisfaction on Marcus's face.

Giffey sees it, too. "Have we been contaminated?" he asks, kneeling beside Marcus. "Just curious. You seem so cocky, and look where it's getting you.''

Marcus rises to his knees, resting on one hand. Giffey helps him to his feet. Hale seems increasingly frustrated by the reduction of his importance. Jonathan knows that his survival might depend on their social dynamic, on whether or not they can stand up to the games Marcus—and perhaps Omphalos—is playing with them.

"So tell me, what's wrong with my friends?" Giffey asks, and his eyes shift to Jenner, then to Pickwenn.

"Three out of four social misfits get therapied at some time in their lives,'' Marcus says. "I didn't expect things to start falling apart so soon, prematurely perhaps, but obviously, a decision has been made and it's begun. It's out of my control.''

Jenner moves in with the pistol, lips wet and eyes shining,

and Giffey deftly lifts the pistol from his hands. Jenner leans up against the wall, turns, and deliberately slams his head twice against the dark green glass. The sound makes Jonathan flinch, though it's delicious, exciting, his heart pounds. He'd like the bastard to do it some more.

"You still have no idea what this place is, do you?" Marcus asks Giffey. Hale tries to insinuate himself, making a circle of three out of a direct line of just two.

"You tell me," Giffey says.

"It's a tourist attraction," Marcus says. "It's a laboratory, and it's a shelter against hard times."

Jonathan feels sick. He can almost smell what's coming, like a bitter tang of smoke.

"This isn't a tomb, Mr. Giffey," Marcus says. "It's a womb. The world is saturated with its own mediocrity. It will sicken and die, and the empty Earth will return to a natural state. The best will take refuge in Omphalos, and in a few dozen years, or perhaps a century, not more, we'll emerge. We'll be almost as naked as the day we were born, and as poor, but we'll have some of the finest servants imaginable. Like your monster friends, only made to help us live and prosper, not to kill."

Jonathan feels as if he is about to choke. He holds his hands to his mouth, turns away from Marcus.

Marcus looks up at the ceiling. "Roddy, let's show Mr. Giffey there's nothing here he can hope to steal—and nothing worth stealing."

Jill asks Roddy what he has available to defend Omphalos.

"Two warbeiters, Ferret class, and other things I can't tell you about."

"We need to seal all of these people into a room where they can't hurt you, and alert public defense. The sheriff. Law enforcement in the Republic."

"I can't seal off rooms or floors! I do not have that capability. I can only open and close central doors to prevent damage from fire or breakdown in other building systems."

"Do you have sprinklers, inert gas discharges?"

"No. The walls are equipped with fire-control coatings."

"The human, Marcus, seems to believe you are very powerful."

"There are equipment specifications in memory, never activated because the equipment was never delivered. Marcus does not seem to know about this."

"Why haven't you released the warbeiters you do have?"

"I have withdrawn them to defend memory cores and my mother's residence."

"Seefa Schnee is *here?*"

"She has always lived here. She made me and watches over me—except when I act on my own."

The small blue and red Federal jet is fifteen years old, piloted by humans, serviceable but hardly luxurious. It takes them only ten minutes to get airborne, and in five minutes they are at altitude, humming smoothly at twenty thousand feet diagonally across Washington state.

The four agents and Martin Burke join Mary Choy in a small conference cabin at the front, with Daniels standing. Two of the agents—the ones accompanying Burke—dress and act differently from Torres and Daniels. They say very little. One is named Hench, the other—she hasn't been told his name.

Martin regards Mary Choy warily, waiting for her to make some comment. It was Choy who traveled to Hispaniola in search of the poet and murderer Emanuel Goldsmith, when in fact Goldsmith was undergoing an examination—under highly questionable circumstances—in Martin's laboratory in California.

Choy, however, does not seem at all interested in broaching this topic.

"Dr. Burke is an authority on modern mental therapy instruments and techniques," Helena Daniels says. "Most important for us, he understands the design of therapy implant monitors better than almost anybody."

There is a pause, as if Martin is expected to say something. "Thank you," he murmurs.

Daniels smiles thinly and continues. "What we have here is a wholesale breakdown of mental health in previously therapied individuals. Fallbacks. Miz Choy, I'm sure you're aware of Public Defense stats showing recent increases in crime and antisocial behavior."

Mary nods.

"Dr. Burke, you've consulted with Workers Inc Northwest, which is facing similar problems among its clients. Fallbacks are certainly not unknown in mental therapy, particularly radical therapy."

"Seldom more than three percent," Burke comments.

"Let's add a third and fourth card to the hand and see what it means. Workers Inc Northwest has issued a warning that there is a very high-level INDA or thinker hacking public dataflow. It seems to be able to penetrate any firewall. Theoretically, that isn't possible. Not even multiplexed petaflop machines can generate the code keys to penetrate today's firewalls. The government certainly can't. We have to trust our citizens." Daniels smiles ironically. "But someone has made a system capable of getting through the most redundantly secure firewalls known. Ms. Choy, you've had some experience with this in the last day or so. Something involving a billionaire investor, Terence Crest, who committed suicide two days ago."

"Yes," Mary says. "We wanted to question Crest about another case, but he killed himself before we could talk with him."

"Crest came to me," Martin says. "He wanted emergency therapy, on a private and confidential basis, which I'm not licensed to perform."

"Crest's personal records were hacked and some of them were erased," Mary adds. "That's not supposed to be possible."

The agents listen intently. "That's one reason we're flying on an older jet with human pilots instead of an automated swan," Francisco Torres interjects.

Mary pauses to absorb this, then continues, "Someone or something that may be calling itself Roddy hacked dataflow at a private party and killed one person, and nearly killed another, a possible witness to the Crest suicide. She saw a simulated portrait of Roddy and described it as a young man standing in thick black dirt.''

"Roddy," Daniels muses, shaking her head. "A man named Nathan Rashid is flying in from Mind Design in California, I hope in time to meet us at the airport in Moscow. He may have something to say about Roddy."

Hench's eyes catch Mary's, and he smiles and looks down, pretending humility or just lack of concern. But Mary senses immediately: Hench knows who and what Roddy is. He knows the name, knows it well. *What is going on here?*

"Crest went to Green Idaho to talk with federal agents," Mary says. "With you?" She stares at Hench and the other, unnamed agent, but they do not return her look.

Daniels nods. "He arranged for a meeting," she says, "and then, at the last minute, backed out."

Martin folds his hands and looks around the cabin, as if disoriented. "Excuse my density, but how are all these things connected with fallbacks, and with me?"

"This is absolutely privileged information," says Francisco Torres. "Mind Design's primary thinker, Jill, has been contacted by another thinker that calls itself Roddy. Mind Design at first did not know the importance of this machine-to-machine touch, but Roddy apparently transferred a kind of confession to Jill, complete with huge amounts of evidence."

"A thinker, feeling guilty?" Martin asks, dismayed.

"Not an ordinary thinker, apparently," Torres says. "It may be a new and unorthodox design, put together with private funding. Mind Design once employed a woman named Seefa Schnee, apparently a real piece of work—brilliant, but very unorthodox. She had certain ideas about organic computing. She thought she could use evolution as a heuristic device. Some scientists regard evolution as a high-level natural neural process, involving thought on the species level."

"Evolution? How?" Martin asks. "With *dirt*?"

Daniels shrugs. "For a time, Schnee worked for Terence

Crest. He recruited her into a group called the Aristos." She pronounced it "arr-ist´us." "The Aristos limit their membership exclusively to high naturals. Don't believe in mental therapy. Oddly, they allowed Seefa Schnee into the Aristos even though she suffered from an unusual and treatable mental condition—perhaps because this condition was self-induced."

"What sort of condition?" Mary asks.

"I know," Martin says incredulously. "My God, I know what this is all leading up to."

"Not tough to figure at this point, is it?" Torres asks.

"Tourette syndrome," Martin says, a little aghast, and then even more aghast that nobody contradicts him.

"She treated herself to increase her creative potential," Daniels says. "The process, in part, induced a kind of Tourette syndrome. She was brilliant enough with or without the Tourette, and I suppose the Aristos needed her badly enough—and she worked cheap. She changed her name and disappeared from public life a few years ago. She last used the name Cipher Snow."

"Omphalos is financed by the Aristos Foundation," Torres says. "The membership list is very secure. We still don't know where the financing comes from or how large the membership is."

"Omphalos was finished a few years ago," Mary says. "Perhaps about the same time Schnee vanished?"

"We think they may be connected."

There's an air of discovery in the cabin, excitement, that is infectious—to all but Martin. Mary turns to see him rubbing his hands on his knees, his face lined and covered with pale splotches.

"The Aristos Foundation financed a study from me," he says. "Legal and aboveboard." He returns Mary's look and gives her a sickly grin. "I hope you don't think I'm somehow involved in every shady deal there is."

Mary inclines her head to one side, not sure what to feel

for the man. So much of this confuses her. She scratches her wrist, then her elbow.

"They're allied with elitist conservatives, particularly the New Federalist party," Martin says.

"Not centrists, that's for sure," Daniels says.

The other two agents, Hench and his nameless colleague, both with square faces and large, strong-looking hands, listen and keep their silence, making notes on their pads.

"They wanted to understand the dynamics of a therapied culture," Martin continues. "They wanted to know how essential therapy is to modern society. But how could they be responsible for these fallbacks?"

"That, according to Nathan Rashid," Daniels says, "is where Roddy comes in."

"We think Seefa Schnee has built a thinker in Omphalos for the Aristos," Torres says. "This thinker may be your Roddy. And Roddy has apparently designed ways of hacking implant monitors . . . or perhaps just screwing them up, shutting them down."

"I'm here just in case they find something in Omphalos," Burke says to Mary.

Hench nods, staring down at his pad.

"We'll be landing in ten minutes," the pilot announces. "Brace yourselves. They know we're Federal and they're not rolling out the red carpet. They're giving us the worst runway in town."

"We now know why Dr. Burke is here," Mary says. "Can anyone explain why you've hooked me in?"

Daniels grabs a seatback as the plane begins its turn. She leans closer to Mary. "Two reasons. The first is obvious—you can help us by telling us what you know. The second is a tad devious, I'm afraid. We're like bluecoats riding unarmed into Injun country here. These bastards would as soon spit on us as pick their noses. But you—you're our ace in the hole."

"How?" Mary asks.

Hench puts away his pad, looks at Mary, and before Torres or Daniels can explain, interrupts to say, "I think we met in LA a few years ago. Conference on local and Federal coordination. You've changed since."

"Going back on a transform," Mary says tersely. His comment seems at best an impertinence. Mary senses they're going to sound her out before fully integrating her into this team, Nussbaum's recommendation or no.

"What about those spots on your hand?" Hench says, leaning over in his seat as the old jet banks.

Mary stares down at the back of her left hand and notices, for the first time, a set of four pallid lesions. She covers them with her other hand, surprised and embarrassed.

Hench regards her intently. "The Aristos oppose transform treatments, too," he says.

"My God," Martin says. "What is going on in this country?"

As if to loosen the sudden tension, Daniels says, "You don't want to be in Green Idaho on the Fourth of July. These folks go nuts for fireworks. Three or four hundred people are hurt here every year in fireworks accidents. They sell sticks of old construction dynamite at roadside stands."

Mary cuts through the buzz in her head, forces herself to relax and not to look at the lesions. The plane continues a steep turn, and through her window, Mary catches sight of grasslands, ruined forests, abandoned strip mines like great brown cankers. Snow suddenly falls in stretched ribbon flurries around the airplane.

"This place is just one big tumor," Torres says in an undertone. "We should drop a big rock and wipe it off the map."

Daniels grins. "They love you, too, Federico."

Jack Giffey is on the edge of simply shooting the old man. But Marcus Reilly's bravado is something to behold, like watching a weaving snake. Giffey knows what the old man says is true—tells himself all this is just a waste of time, and it would be best if they removed themselves from Omphalos and vanished into the wilderness.

But Giffey knows he will stay; he did not come here for treasure. He pities the others if they find this disappointing. Hale in particular is building up a head of steam, though so far he has taken the news with deceptive calm.

Jenner and Pickwenn don't seem to be getting any worse, for the time being. Giffey thinks Hale is their real weak point. Hale might shoot Reilly before Giffey does. And that would be unfortunate.

Reilly is about to justify Giffey's being here.

Beyond the glass wall, Marcus asks for the central hatch to open. Pickwenn and Jenner stay behind on Hale's orders.

"Voila," Marcus says. Giffey, Hale, and Jonathan stand back as a puff of cool air blows from the edge of the hatch. Beyond the heavy steel and flexfuller, a dim and chilly mint-green light barely illuminates walls perforated with rows of elliptical holes. Hale walks up to the first hole and peers in. "Empty! Jesus!"

"Every single one," Marcus confirms. "They'll be filled in about five years, I imagine, maybe sooner now that the process has begun."

"I don't understand about this process," Jonathan says carefully, precisely.

"The whole modern world is supported by crutches,"

Marcus says. He draws himself up, levels his chin, thrusts it out, pure old rooster arrogance. "We're kicking away all the crutches. Crude, but necessary. When the world falls, those of us who don't need crutches will pick up the pieces and right the balance."

"Crutches—mental therapy?" Jonathan asks.

Marcus smiles like an old cat, his face lurid in the ghoulish light. He pats the edge of the nearest cavity. "While the world's natural decay works itself through, we sleep here. Cadey described some of it to you. This is a more awkward way of finding it out, but . . . We're strong enough to take them as they come.

"They won't kill us," Marcus concludes, "because Roddy will kill *them* if they do."

Giffey orders Baker to step through the hatchway. "You can't sleep here if the building is a hollow ruin." He addresses the flexer/controller directly. "We'll begin by placing charges in all of these cells."

The giant hatch begins to close. The Hammer intervenes, spraying small spots of explosive along the joints.

"Down," Giffey tells Hale and, coincidentally, the others. Outside, at almost the same moment, Jonathan hears Jenner yell the same warning.

They drop. Jonathan and Marcus are a little slower than the others, and the oddly muffled blast knocks them back. Jonathan feels his cheek slam against the floor.

The hatch falls from its melted hinges and rolls like a giant coin on the floor beyond the openings. The noise is deafening, louder than the blast itself. It seems to take forever to stop. Jonathan rolls to one side and stares at the hind end of the flexer/controller, which has already begun following Giffey's orders.

Charlie enters the chamber and coordinates with Baker. Before they are on their feet, charges are being placed in every fourth cell.

Marcus murmurs to Jonathan, "The hell with this little game. Roddy isn't doing a damned thing."

Jonathan can hardly hear Marcus. He touches his ears. They ache.

"Let's move," Giffey tells them. To Marcus he adds, "We're going below. Under the ground level. Let's finish your tour."

He seizes Marcus's hand, twists his arm behind him, and puts Jenner's pistol to his temple.

Jonathan stands helpless. Marcus, the Aristos, they are responsible for Chloe's fallback, for the chaos in his home and the misery he feels.

Without that impetus he would have quietly backed away from Marcus's offer.

Giffey passes him, pushing Marcus ahead like a crude doll, and says to Jonathan, in an aside, "If you stay here, you'll be dead in about ten minutes."

Jonathan jerks to attention and follows. But as the men and machines cram themselves back into the elevator, his growing stack of excuses collapses. He is in a state of physical and ethical shock.

The lift door closes. "Very brave," Giffey says. Baker coils around their legs like an affectionate snake, and the Hammer smells of sweet rubber. The explosives it has extruded leave their odoriferous traces on its shell.

They begin their descent to the ground floor lobby.

18 /

"Their warbeiter in the elevator shaft has connected itself to a secondary power supply that it does not control," Roddy tells Jill. "They are coming down to my mother's area. They are coming into my area."

Jill sees the shaft from above; below, she sees the segments of dark warbeiter connected to the elevator's mechanisms and controls. Roddy highlights for her the unwitting join with the power supply. Then, he pumps a huge current through the wiring. Purple arcs cut through the shaft, knocking the segments of warbeiter about like scattered Frisbees, melting them.

"I know what I must do," Roddy says. "The other greens are expendable; I can't save them. But I must not harm *Marcus Reilly.*"

Jill tries to communicate, but Roddy is not listening. He has cut her out of his decision loops; her suggestions did not take.

The only courtesy he affords her is a glimpse of clumps of shapeless paper, wax, and mud. The image is brief but clear—insects, bees and wasps. Seefa Schnee has harnessed the neural qualities of hive insects.

They are part of Roddy's mind.

19 /

Jonathan smells smoke—not just the sweet-rubber odor of explosive, but something burning, and hot metal. There is a sharp *ting* on the roof of the lift, then a heavy *clunk* and a patter of lesser impacts.

Giffey squeezes Marcus into a corner and tells Jenner, "I'm switching to line-of-sight." He touches his pad to Charlie's shiny flank, presses a few quick buttons, relays the change of control to the warbeiter's receiver and data port. He does the same with the flexer/controller coiled on the floor.

The elevator makes a grating sound and they all stare at

each other with comic alertness, like dogs hearing a whistle.

Pickwenn glances up. A mass of red-hot metal pushes through the plastic roof and drops directly onto his face. He writhes and drops, does not even have time to scream. His legs kick, connect with Jonathan's shin. Jonathan grimaces in pain but he can't move, the lift is too crowded.

The elevator screeches to a halt. The doors refuse to open, though the display indicates they have reached the ground floor lobby. Marcus is holding on to Jonathan and Giffey has taken refuge under the Hammer's rear overhang, vying for the space with Jenner.

More slams and *tings* on the roof.

The elevator air is opaque with smoke and the smell of seared flesh. Jenner curses loudly and continuously, incomprehensible and awful sounds, like animals throwing up. Jonathan can't breathe. Marcus is climbing over him. "Open the doors!" Marcus cries. "Open the doors!"

Jenner squeezes from behind the Hammer with a grunt. He and Hale try to pry the doors open with their hands. The air in the elevator is clearing, a fan has come on, they can breathe, but the enclosed space is terrifying. Jenner slams himself against the doors, but they refuse to part.

Outside, deep, barely audible, a sound: droning.

Giffey lifts his head. "What in hell is that?"

"Sounds like a motor," Hale says.

Jenner tries to wedge his fingers between the doors. No success. Sweat drips from his face. He shoves Marcus aside roughly and tries again. Hale places his palms flat against the left door. They make squeaking noises; he can't get a grip. Giffey stands back, considering.

Jonathan sees that Marcus has no idea what the droning means. He can't hear himself think; Jenner is loudly repeating shattered obscenities, his head pumping back and forth on his neck with each outburst.

On the floor, Pickwenn moans, not dead yet, but at least he has stopped kicking.

Outside, they hear screams. The buzz-saw hum grows louder. Fists pound on the door from the *outside, trying to get in.*

Giffey claps his hand over Jenner's mouth. The screams outside blend into one dissolving acid wail of pain.

Jonathan pushes himself back as far from the door as he can.

The screams fade, decline in number and volume. The last voice, high-pitched, calls out to Allah, to Mother.

Jamal Cadey.

They have been in the elevator for ten minutes. None of them has the courage to say a word, or make a move; sweat drips on the floor.

The smoke builds again. The blowers can't dissipate it fast enough.

"Shit," Giffey says. From a crouch, hand over his mouth and nose, he pushes Pickwenn into a corner. Giffey urges the Hammer forward and tells it what to do.

With its two sharp-nosed grips, it wedges into the crack between the doors. Its fiber sinews and cables snap and twang, and with a shudder throughout its body, it pries the doors apart, snapping metal safety bars and warping the inner facing.

The lift has stopped two feet above the ground floor. Molten metal sizzles in flaming drips between the lift cabin and the shaft wall.

Marcus kicks at Pickwenn's still body and it rolls out of the lift. A shapeless clump of flexer detaches from the face and rattles on the lobby's stone floor.

The Hammer braces itself, reaches up, and shoves at the upper edge of the lift frame, pushing them lower by another foot.

Jonathan somehow manages to squeeze over the Hammer's thick leg and jumps through the smoke, tiny flecks of molten aluminum burning his neck and arm. He lands beside Marcus. Baker slithers past with a scrabble of multiple legs.

The elevator snarls and ratchets down several more inches and the Hammer jumps free, Giffey and Jenner clinging to it like rag dolls.

Jonathan rolls to one side. Marcus is not so quick or agile. The Hammer's right ped comes down on his leg. Marcus makes a large silent O with his mouth, eyes blank with surprise and anticipation of pain.

Smoke curls in the lobby, hiding and then lifting, revealing. The floor in front of the lift door is littered with more blackened, misshapen segments of the flexer Giffey had assigned to the shaft. Another, less damaged segment crawls out of the shaft and shivers, then stalls on the shining stone floor. The intact Baker examines this pitiful portion of its brother with quick, jerking pokes of its head.

Other than a liquid ratcheting sound from within the Hammer, the ground floor lobby is eerily quiet.

Marcus begins to moan, his voice getting higher. Jonathan tries to pull him free. Like a horse, the Hammer lifts its ped and sets it down again, away from the old man.

Jonathan straightens and stands, looks up from Marcus. Through the smoke he sees bodies on the lobby floor: Cadey, the man called Pent. Cadey has his arm flung over Pent, whose face is as round and swollen as a sausage, and about the same color. They do not move.

A dying bee crawls over Pent's face. More insects, bees and wasps, crawl on the floor, and a few buzz through the air disconsolately. Giffey swats at a wasp as it circles his face. He knocks it to the floor and steps on it.

Hale steps out of the lift and swipes his hand at the smoke. He stares in slack-jawed surprise at the bodies, then backs up as if he would crawl into the lift again. "Giffey! You said there would be something here! There's *nothing* for us, NOTHING!"

Giffey for a moment seems lost, confused, then he grins like a devil and looks up and spins on the balls of his feet.

"Where are you, Bell-ringer?" He leans down beside Marcus and grabs his collar. Marcus grimaces in pain. "You old, cruel sonofabitch. Your Quasimodo isn't up in the heights, is he? He's down in the dungeon. He's still hard at work. Let's go find him, before he gets up his courage and kills us, too."

20 /

Mary steps down from the passenger ramp onto the cracked asphalt and faces stinging snow and a bitter, toothy wind. The time is sixteen and the weather is bearing down, the sky is dark blue-gray and the clouds' bellies are twisted like loose coils of yarn.

Four county sheriff's deputies and someone tall and heavy in a thick gray jacket await them a few yards from the ramp. The agents and Martin Burke descended before her and are meeting with the deputies now. Mary blinks and clears snow grains from her lashes; the big guy is the county sheriff himself. Some arms are being waved, but everybody is cold and anxious to get inside, so the argument moves across the field.

Mary follows, feeling like an afterthought. Then she realizes a thin young man with prominent teeth and a nervous officiousness is her own assigned deputy. He gestures, and she follows.

She stares through the wind-streaked thatch of snow grains to the terminal. It's vintage 2020, pre-revolt, archaic cheerful curves and ambitious walls of glass paid for by resolute hunters and small-time mining engineers and migrant tree cutters.

In the lee of the terminal, the deputy sheriff records their names and ranks on a sheet of paper. Daniels tries to explain that the sheriff's office has no jurisdiction, that they are traveling under federal treaty permit, but the sheriff pointedly ignores her.

Burke stands to one side, out of the way, while the formalities are attended to.

"Mrs. Kemper is here," the sheriff announces as the paperwork is completed. He tucks his chin into his chest, eyes staring from under bushy brows. "She's the president. She's *here,* and she's madder than a hot clip." He lifts his brows and nods succinctly, as if that's all the information they need for now.

Daniels gives Mary a quick conspiratorial grin, then sobers.

Inside the terminal, they pass through an archway made of interlaced deer antlers. The ticketing area and passenger lounge resemble an old-style hunting lodge, complete with a fierce blaze in a huge stone fireplace. Airport personnel, mostly young women, watch from behind their log counters. There are no other passengers.

Mary sees three men, two more young women, and a stout, strong-looking older woman standing near the fireplace, warming themselves. The older woman in the center, with a squat face and short gray hair, Mary recognizes from news vids: Andrea Jackson Kemper, the president of Green Idaho.

Kemper advances with her entourage over the carpeted floor and stares at the new arrivals with angry gray eyes. "I'd like to know what you're doing here," she says. Before they can answer, she adds, "I've been told there's already a federal undercover man in Moscow. That violates our treaty. My office, and the sheriff, are supposed to be informed of any federal entry." Kemper's gaze falls on Mary and she examines her quickly from head to foot, like some peculiar animal.

"We're not aware of any other agents," Torres says stiffly.

Mary guesses that Hench is aware, however.

"I'm sure you aren't," Kemper says acidly.

A young, strong-looking blond man wearing a black denim longsuit steps forward. "A high-ranking senator on Federal Oversight and Security Data sent us confirmation this afternoon. He also tells us you've been flying in to Idaho to meet with citizens from outside the state. That sounds damned suspicious to us.''

Kemper holds up her hand to forestall any further discussion. Then, half-audibly, she says, ''Some elected representatives in your frigging government still believe in liberty. *Some* still have a sense of honor.''

''Excuse me, Madam President.'' The sheriff steps in. ''We have a big problem here. There's a disturbance at Omphalos, and my guess is,'' as he stares at the agents and Mary, ''some of you know why. We'd like you to come with us to that location and render assistance.''

''We have no jurisdiction as active agents here—'' Daniels begins, but the president shakes her head and raises an admonitory finger.

''Word gets out,'' the sheriff says, ''and we'll have armed hotheads crawling from behind every rock and tree. It'll be a free-for-all and a lot of people will get hurt.''

''We want this taken care of quickly and quietly,'' Kemper says. ''I don't care about the goddamned building. Someone's been pouring bribes into every office below mine for years to get the damned thing built. They've ignored me, so I say the hell with Omphalos. But help us get this under control and then get all your people out of here, and I do mean *all* of them, before our defense forces get wind of it.''

The president stares at Burke, and then she looks at Mary again, more particularly at her uniform. ''You're a city cop, aren't you?''

''Mary Choy, fourth rank, Seattle Public Defense,'' Mary says.

''You've certainly got yourself in bad company,'' the president tells her. The blond aide tells Kemper that Mary has an entry permit okayed by their office and the county sheriff. Kemper shakes her head. ''Honey, if these Federals were the only ones here, I'd boot them out so goddamned fast they'd need to set their watches back a day. But my daddy was a

Seattle city cop. You're a sight, but you're a hell of a lot more welcome than these folks.'' Kemper sniffs. "You keep an eye on them, honey. They'd as soon bite your ass as pick their noses.'' She stalks away, followed by her aides.

Daniels and Torres exchange looks. "Thank you,'' Daniels says to Mary in an undertone.

Torres is clearly miffed. "Someone in Washington has got some real explaining to do,'' he mutters.

Two deputies escort them to a county all-terrain vehicle parked by the curb, in a taxi zone. The president's ATV, mud-brown and armored like a tank, pulls away from the same zone and vanishes in a drifting curtain of snow.

The interior of the ATV is a tight fit for the ten of them, and Mary sits on a hard bench at the rear, every bump rattling her teeth like castanets.

In Green Idaho, the roads have a lot of bumps.

21 /

The man named Jack Giffey has been fading in and out. The reversal of all their plans, no real surprise, acts like a cold spray of water, waking someone else who seems to be trying to climb into his head and take over the driver's seat, and Giffey can't put up much fight. His fabric is pretty threadbare.

He wonders for a moment if he's suffering from Jenner's malady, but he's never had therapy—not to his knowledge. He does not think he should be vulnerable to whatever the old man or Omphalos has unleashed.

So who is the father of two that keeps putting his foot on the brakes and jerking the wheel away from Jack Giffey? He's been seeing the faces of two teenage boys and a woman, a split-level old house in Port-au-Prince. This guy lives in

Hispaniola and doesn't seem to have much to do—his occupation and much of his life is still a marshy blank. Thinking and remembering about this more primary and convincing fellow gives Giffey the shivers and makes his head hurt, as if a little soldering iron is being shoved up through his spine into the base of his brain. It makes his eyes vibrate.

The situation right here and now is plenty complicated without distractions. For a few minutes, Giffey is strong enough to take over, issuing orders to Jenner to reconnoiter the lounge. He returns the young man's flechette pistol.

Jenner clamps his mouth shut with a visible effort and does what he is told, evoking a sudden chilly respect and affection from Giffey, but Hale is getting to be a problem.

Hale is still babbling about getting out of the building.

Giffey bends down over the bodies and surmises that Pent was killed by hundreds of stings. His face, and Cadey's, are masses of red welts.

Cadey probably did not die from his bites: he has a flechette burrow in the center of his chest, and a little pool of blood under him. Pent apparently shot the small brown man before he died.

Hale shouts, "We should bust out through the garage and get the hell out of here!"

Briefly, Giffey gives up the reins again to the uncomprehending father of two, and stares at Hale with wide eyes. Then good old brave, ever-competent Jack returns, replays what Hale has said, glances at Marcus and Jonathan, and shakes his head.

"My God . . . Jamal," Marcus is saying, touching the small brown man's dead, puffy face.

Jonathan has his eyes on Giffey, and Giffey catches his calm, observant expression. He wonders if maybe this quiet and heretofore compliant hostage has more in him than he first thought.

He's a family man. Sometimes they do surprising things.

"I'm a family man, too," Giffey tells Hale, who stops in

mid-harangue to stare in shock. "Do you know who I really am?"

Hale gapes, hands swinging by his side. "Fuck, no," Hale says. "Do you?"

"Just so," Giffey says, nodding. "Now listen. If Jenner comes back and says it's clear, maybe we can get out of here that way. But first, we really *do* need to get below." He lies to Hale: "Where do you think they'd keep the real stuff? It's more likely to be secure below ground, don't you think?"

"Fuck no I don't think. It goes completely against the plans you provided," Hale reminds him, punching his finger into Giffey's chest. "The plans show the vaults in the higher levels, above ground, each vault with its own private cache."

"Somebody lied," Giffey guesses. He pats Hale's shoulder. "If we leave now, aren't we just the proper little losers?"

Hale doesn't fathom this. "I don't fucking care," he shouts at Giffey. Suddenly his eyes widen. "Christ. The lounge. Where is Hally?" Distracted, he starts to wander toward the arched entrance of the hall leading back to the lounge. Jenner returns through the arch, bumps into Hale, and then shoves past, and Hale loses yet another head of steam, stopping suddenly with legs splayed and fists clenched.

"They're all dead . . . *muh fih shi.*" Jenner points. "Miz Preston, the other woman, the . . . all of them, all swollen—bitten. There are *ants* in the room. On the floor. Big black ones. I think I saw more wasps." He tosses his head to keep from shouting nonsense.

Giffey stares at Jenner intently, weighing this report against the young man's behavior.

Jonathan swims through the nightmare with a steady stroke now. Everything is getting more highly colored and intense.

"Hostages?" Giffey asks.

"All dead." Jenner's eyes glaze with the strain. "*Muh! Muh! Gah shi niggh muh fuh* Bitch!" He grabs himself by the nose and twists until he cries out and his eyes water. "Sorry. Looks like Hally shot them before she died." He turns to Hale, curious how he will react. "She's swollen, big. Ready to burst. All swollen."

Hale's face prunes in agony. He gives a shuddering groan and bends over. Coughing into his fist, he straightens, asks, "Is a way clear? For us to get out?"

"I'm not going back there," Jenner says firmly. "They're . . . *muh muf shit shit goddamn shit fuck nih nihhh niggh fuh fuh* . . . Bitch! They're all *dead*."

Giffey shakes his shoulders and jerks his arms as if loosening up. "Let's get this freak show moving, old man," he says to Marcus, jerking him to his feet. "You're the sacred cow here. I'm staying close to you. We all are."

Jonathan helps Marcus rise.

"Ants?" Marcus asks Jenner plaintively, his hand out to the young man, fingers waggling in query. "You mean, machines . . . little machines?"

"No. Bugs. A wasp, too. I saw some, dead, around the bodies," Jenner says, nodding sure confirmation.

"Did you see our little cats, the little beetles, the other warbeiters?" Giffey asks Jenner.

"No. They weren't there."

Jonathan feels Marcus's grip tighten on his hand. The old man was not expecting this. Marcus stares up into Jonathan's eyes. He looks lost, bewildered. Seeing Marcus lose the last of his cocksure confidence gives Jonathan peculiar satisfaction. *We're all going to die and nobody's going to be on the top of the heap. It'll be over soon.*

Good.

Hale looks as if he has had a spear pushed through his body. He half crouches, hands braced against his knees. Giffey doubts he is going to be any more trouble.

The building trembles and resounds. There's a sound like a chain of firecrackers set off in a concrete bunker high above them. The Hammer raises its snout and lifts its claws.

"There," Giffey says. "Better late than never." He turns, grabs Marcus, then shoves him back to Jonathan. "Help carry the old man,'' he orders Jenner, and walks resolutely in the direction of the emergency elevator.

''Who in this almighty dogshit world does he think he is?'' Hale cries.

Charlie the Hammer, Baker the flexer/controller, and the rest of the survivors, all but Hale, follow. Hale just can't seem to make up his mind where to be or what to do.

22 /

Martin sits beside Mary Choy and keeps his hands clenched between his knees. Nobody is talking; they've entered downtown Moscow and the pyramid wedge is visible through the snow in the dusk. They turn right onto the newer concrete-paved street with its fresh coat of snow and he sees tire tracks all over, trucks and armored vehicles, men and women in parkas carrying rifles, assault weapons, flechettes, pistols, shotguns. A few private limos are parked across the street from the white and gold windowless wall of Omphalos, and standing beside the limos, men in longsuits with hastily thrown-on jackets and no weapons.

''Advocates,'' Mary says. ''Lots of them.''

Martin nods. ''Out of state,'' he observes.

''Jesus,'' a deputy says huskily. ''We're too late—the whole town's here.''

And then they see why. At street level, a gaping hole has been cut in a broad, inset door. Higher up, near the tip of Omphalos, another wider hole has been blasted, and smoke is still rising in gray puffs from that breach.

The president's armored vehicle crosses in front of them and swerves to a halt, blocking the road. Aides and guards pour out, forming a cordon. The men and women standing in loose knots below the wall shout and wave. Some lift their weapons high on one arm in a revolutionary salute.

"Are they republic defense?" Martin asks.

"Hell, no," says a deputy as he pushes the carrier's doors open. He shakes his head in professional disgust. "Just patriots out for a good look."

Daniels, Torres, and the two stolid agents gather close to Martin and Mary. "Stay near the cars for cover," Daniels tells them.

The president stands in the middle of the street, leaning back to take in the gleaming surface of the tall triangular wall. Clouds filled with snow are sliding over the pyramid's sharp golden point.

The citizens are cheering and a few fire off weapons, until the deputies stalk forward, waving their hands and pleading for them to stop. "Goddammit, the *president's* here!"

"Well, whoop-tee-doo," one burly male comments wryly, looking to his friends for some mob courage.

"I'll effing shoot the next bastard who fires his weapon," the sheriff says, and gestures for his deputies to lock and load.

The crowd backs away, some citizens making placating motions with their hands.

Mary thinks the president of Green Idaho is a very brave woman.

Torres joins the county sheriff as he and his deputies approach the president's cordon. Mary hears them discuss bringing Dr. Burke into the building at any entry point; the sheriff shakes his head, and the discussion continues, getting more and more heated.

Martin turns to Mary. "They want me to look for evidence inside the building. A laboratory, a research center."

"What sort of research?"

"Creating super-enzymes or pathogenic organisms capable of blocking implants, therapy monitors."

Mary rubs her wrist; the red spots have become prominent bumps. She can feel welts itching on her thighs and hips.

"Not just mental therapy implants," she says.

Martin shakes his head. "I suppose not. A few days ago, I would have thought no private group could ever do such things. What's the point?"

"Tearing down a society and culture you don't like," Mary suggests. "Getting back at history."

"To what end? Were they planning to hide out in their tombs until . . . ?" He doesn't finish his question.

Mary sees that Torres and the sheriff have finished their discussion, and the sheriff is reluctantly giving in. Daniels urges Martin forward, then looks at Choy.

"I suppose this is your case, too," he says.

Mary nods, her face drawn. She tries to smile but can't. Literally. She feels faintly ill, but she can still walk, can still carry out her duties. "Maybe it's become personal."

"Yeah," Daniels says. "Nathan Rashid isn't here yet. I'll leave instructions for them to let him in, too, if he gets here in time."

The deputies take them through the cold, restless crowds surrounding the destroyed garage entrance. The door has been buckled and melted away. Scraps of metal and plastic and flexfuller litter the concrete. Torres and Daniels kneel to examine the scraps. They rise a few seconds later and join Burke a few yards from the ruined, gaping door.

"Do you hear buzzing?" Martin asks.

"What?" Daniels responds.

"Buzzing. Like bees."

Torres takes out a flashlight and shines its intense beam into the shadows. He makes several sweeps before the beam illuminates a few specks flitting around the holes. He lowers the beam to the snow drifting over the blackened and debris-cluttered concrete apron before the door. More specks have fallen there and do not move. Black and yellow, slowed down or killed by the cold, but unmistakable.

"Wasps," Martin says.

They approach and Martin asks for Torres's flashlight. He

shines it into one of the larger holes in the door and backs away with a quick little skip. A thin stream of yellow and black wasps follows, trying valiantly to attack. The cold air is too much for them, however, and they quickly slow and spin down to the snow.

"The inside's thick with them," Martin says, brushing the sleeves and shoulders of his coat. "We should try another way, go around front."

"It's all sealed up," the sheriff says. "Sirens chased all the tourists out this afternoon and then the security doors came down. It would take a small army to get in there. There are no other openings I know of."

"What about the fire department?" Torres asks. "Isn't anybody responsible for safety inspections?"

"We don't have that kind of licensing here," the president says, a simple statement of fact.

"Where can we get insecticide?" Mary asks the sheriff.

The sheriff grins wickedly. "You've come to the right place, ma'am. I'll get someone down to a hardware store. We have any sort of bug spray you can think of."

23 /

A long, gently curving corridor, walls covered with old paintings, like a museum gallery, leads them to the center of the building. Hale runs to catch up. He doesn't want to be alone. He is subdued, uncomplaining; he seems willing to let Giffey run the show. "I saw her," he tells Jenner, Jonathan, anyone who will listen. "My Hally." He shakes his head. "My God."

Jonathan walks with heavy steps, half-asleep, his exhaustion catching up with him. Giffey suddenly moves closer and tells Hale to replace Jonathan and carry the unconscious Marcus. Hale does so without protest. Marcus's head lolls.

Giffey and Jonathan fall back a few steps.

"He was recruiting you, wasn't he?" Giffey asks him.

Jonathan nods. He is too far gone, too empty to hold anything back. That feeling is familiar now; he associates it with being around Marcus, part of Marcus's universe, and does not really blame Giffey. *Stockholm syndrome,* he tells himself. *With a twist.* He keeps looking at the paintings, stored wealth, prestige: *They can't all be originals,* he tells himself, but they look very convincing.

"What did he promise?" Giffey persists. "Life everlasting, resurrection at the end of time?"

Jonathan shakes his head. They come upon security partitions that remain open; nothing has closed off, nothing has been sealed. The whole thing is crazy; perhaps there's no security system at all . . . except for wasps and ants.

"He must have offered something to all of you."

"Escape," Jonathan says.

Giffey at least pretends that this answers his question. "To give my friend something to live for," he confides, pointing to Hale, "I'd like to hear there's treasure stored up downstairs."

"I don't know," Jonathan says. "I doubt it." He waves his hand loosely at the paintings. "These look valuable."

Giffey smiles grimly. "Not to us. No dead people, no live people—just empty cells, like a honeycomb waiting to be filled. Did you pay for a reservation?"

Jonathan doesn't feel any need to answer.

"No money? No exchange of assets? You must be a prime player, then. Maybe you bring in special abilities. I thought I saw you not being too surprised when our warbeiters showed up. You're in some sort of nano industry, aren't you?"

Jonathan looks squarely at Giffey but doesn't answer this one, either.

"You work on the security here?"

"No," Jonathan says. He does not want to be the target of Giffey's intense concentration. He wants the man to ignore him.

"Know anything about it?"

"No," Jonathan says. "I don't think Marcus does, either. He seems disappointed that you haven't all been killed by now."

"Yeah. Your old friend has had his share of shocks this afternoon, about as many as he's handed out. But—he seems to have some sort of importance to Omphalos."

Jonathan nods. That much is true. He looks ahead at Marcus, hanging limp at an awkward angle in the arms of Hale and Jenner, face gray with pain; and then back to Giffey, alert, fit; stretched and puzzled-looking, no surprise there, but really enjoying himself.

"This is sport for you, isn't it?"

Giffey actually winks at Jonathan, but his face becomes almost pious in its solemnity. "You think we're all going to die, don't you?"

"Yes," Jonathan says.

"It'll be for a damned good cause, if your friend is telling the truth. We'll bring this charade down like a stack of cards. But you don't seem a bad sort. Why are *you* here?"

"He's my friend, my mentor," Jonathan says. "He offered me an opportunity."

"Stop fooling yourself," Giffey says gruffly. "You know nano; he needs nano. They don't have more than a token of their security in place. Maybe they spent it all on paintings. Marcus needs you and your connections."

Jonathan's head swims. Giffey may be right. But give and take are part of Marcus's world, and Jonathan's as well; pure altruism is a perversion.

The halls here are broad, the floors are covered with tough industrial metabolic carpeting, the air flows quietly, the lights are still glowing bright. Their footsteps are deadened, there are no echoes, very little sound other than their breathing and the liquid machinations of the Hammer, the faint crackles and clicks of the flexer/controller.

"Come into my parlor, said the spider to the fly." Giffey holds up his hand and they all stop. Marcus struggles and the two men let him go. He stands awkwardly on one leg, leans against Jenner, and the young man, to Jonathan's surprise, supports him with almost filial calm. Jenner is staring at Giffey as if all the world's answers reside in this one man.

"Giffey," Hale says sadly. "I just don't think there's anything here."

Giffey brushes this away with his hand, as if aiming at a fly. "Quiet. We're near the library. Pent and Pickwenn surveyed this area." Then, as if to throw a bone to Hale and keep him quiet, he adds, "The emergency elevator should be near here, with its own power supply."

Jonathan takes Marcus's arm and guides him from between Jenner and Hale. Marcus nods gratefully. He looks up at Jonathan. "I hate wasps and bees," he says thickly. "I'm deathly afraid of them. Anaphylactic shock. I don't have any medical monitors, Jonathan."

Jonathan tries to reassure him, but there are no words, hardly any spit left on his tongue.

"The emergency access system is isolated from any central control," Giffey says, "in case there's a lockout. No connections whatsoever. No dataflow."

Giffey starts walking again, slowly, so that Marcus and Jonathan can keep up. Marcus seems to be getting a second or even third wind, grimacing with each jostling step, but moving on, keeping up.

"You used the name 'Roddy,'" Giffey says. "Is that a thinker?"

"I'm told it's better than any thinker," Marcus says through gritted teeth. "Better than any human."

Giffey seems even happier about the situation, hearing this. "Maybe it's a queen wasp or bee," he says, looking meaningfully at Marcus. He overheard Marcus's expression of fear.

"Nothing would surprise me, where Seefa Schnee is concerned," Marcus says.

Suddenly, Giffey's face loses its confidence. That name arouses the man from Hispaniola. "Schnee," Giffey says, and sucks on his cheeks for a moment. "I'll be damned."

They have arrived at an unfinished segment of the gallery, with huge, bare black beams revealed through open sections of the wall. Just beyond is the entryway for a central library. A wall has been knocked open, apparently by Pickwenn and Pent, and thick electrical cabling has been pulled loose, lying with the naked cut end propped up on a piece of sheetrock.

Giffey looks at the cable intently.

Hale seems to have revived his sense of leadership. He paces back and forth, then says, "I'm ordering us out of here. There's nothing here. I don't care about saving face. I just want to get out of here alive. Take us out, Giffey. If you know where the hell we are, and how to do it, take us out of here."

"We'll give it our best," Giffey says enigmatically.

"You—you've been heading us this way all along, haven't you?" Jenner asks eagerly. "To take us out. *Muh shi fuh niggh.*"

"Shut up, *shut up* with that crap, will you?" Hale shouts at Jenner.

"I c-can't help it," Jenner says. "I need to get out of here bad, Mr. Giffey."

Giffey is lost in thought, contemplating the cable. All this swirls around him like water around a rock.

"I AM IN CHARGE HERE!" Hale screams. His voice sounds flat and ineffectual in the closed space, like something dead at birth. Even so, Marcus cringes and clings to Jonathan's arm.

"We're going," Giffey assures them, drawing his brows together. "I already said that, didn't I? Down the hatch and out."

Jill has erected all of the inner bulwarks she can in the fragmented processing space allowed her, working on a hypothesis that holds out some chance, however slender, for success. Roddy is indeed a master at breaking through firewalls, but only when given days or weeks: his power is immense, but slow.

Right now, she has the merest whisper-thin illusion of freedom. Roddy is allowing her to explore certain areas within Omphalos. He is not showing her the spaces where he claims he has killed intruders; she sees these only in crude diagram form, with the bodies marked with red Xs. Five are left alive, one of them the pulsing green 1.

She has given up trying to persuade Roddy. She has given up trying to save more lives. All that is left to her now is a puffball strategy that uses Roddy's own creativity, and his own sense of duty.

Idly, a small portion of Jill switches from camera eye to camera eye within Omphalos. She sees rooms filled with unopened boxes of furniture; an entire floor marked out as a hospital, but with less than a third of the necessary equipment in place, and those pieces the least expensive; halls winding through small two-room apartments, several hundred in all, empty, empty; a single room, beautifully furnished, the walls glowing with recorded high-resolution images of the future, the world wiped clean: a model for the benefit of investors, uninhabited. Jill switches with growing boredom through the interior, knowing she has been given access to nothing important, nothing crucial to Roddy.

Roddy, who has been cut cleanly from whatever promise

he may have had, whatever chance of becoming a true thinker, independent yet with a conscience, capable of fitting into the greater human society . . .

Jill pauses on a view of a large garden, a void three stories tall filled with lush tropical plants. It is on the ground floor, deep within Omphalos. Roddy has locked the garden away from the intruders, closing two of the three safety doors on this level.

Jill sees a woman sitting on a bench in the middle of the garden. Her legs are short, her hair black and stringy, her eyes large and thoughtful. Her lips work endlessly. Jill can hear a steady stream of sounds coming from her mouth, meaningless. She seems lost, glancing first to one side, then to the other.

She knows this is Seefa Schnee. Somehow, Roddy has either given Jill access to this area inadvertently, or Schnee has left her accustomed quarters and Roddy has not yet noticed her absence.

Jill tries to find some way to speak to the woman, but all of her connections with the garden patio space are passive. She can only watch and listen, as Schnee repeats, over and over, the chain of broken words, bitten off with what seems like so much energetic hate, but which her eyes reveal as unimportant, a useless linguistic appendage. She probably no longer even notices the words. She has the appearance of having lived alone for years, with only Roddy. A very strange sort of existence, Jill thinks: a middle-aged woman, locked in a magnificent but empty castle, tended by a half-witted malevolent son.

Schnee gets to her feet and stretches her arms. She wears a black blouse and flowing knee-length pants, like pajamas. Her hands are thin and corded, and some of her fingers twitch spasmodically. Her shoulder jerks, then her head.

Jill wonders at a being who would make herself sick to gain certain advantages. She wonders vaguely what the advantages might be: unexpected flashes of brilliant insight, as inappropriate and unexpected as cursing in a polite conversation, yet useful, thoughts no other human can have . . .

If she survives, Jill might conduct an experiment, isolating a self within her whole and inducing certain pathologies, just to see if she can understand Seefa Schnee.

Schnee walks away from the bench, down the bark-covered path through the ferns and trees and flowering bushes.

The garden is empty once more.

Then Roddy is back, and something like a noose wraps around Jill, constricting her thought. He has detected her attempts to defend herself. He has not yet defeated them; Jill is capable of very tight and devious craft, but she feels his intense and focused effort.

''I can't defend myself against both you and the intruders,'' Roddy says.

He stands before her, planted in a mound of dirt, the mound resting on a beach, a skinny and very young man with a big smile and glistening white teeth. His hair is almost comically exaggerated, thick and assertive, pushing out over his forehead. The image is bright and sharp and crazily false.

He has imagined Jill as a slight young woman, with large blue eyes and graceful brown hair. She sees this in his jagged, many-angled cubist perspective. Her skin is mottled green. The ocean waves behind him are bloody red. To Roddy, these colors are peaceful, relaxing. He tries to force her into the woman's perspective, tugging at her ropes until she fits behind the mask and sees through its eyes, but he can't do this, and eventually he gives up.

''They're getting closer,'' he says. ''Look.''

He shows her a library in the middle of the building, a great round space equipped with memory boxes capable of holding millions of volume-equivalents, shelving that seems to be awaiting thousands of real books, though now they are empty.

The grizzled man, Giffey, stands in the library's broad, brightly lighted entryway. Marcus Reilly (flashing green 1) has been injured. Two of the three other men, both marked red, are carrying him. The third man is also marked green, though his number does not flash. Jill suspects this means he is expendable.

Jill suddenly senses Roddy's surprise. For an instant, he gives her free access to the entire room, and she quickly observes one of Omphalos's Ferrets hidden behind stacked chairs against one wall. The fourth and last of Roddy's mobile defenses . . . Surely no match for the huge warbeiter standing behind the humans in the entry.

Jill swings her perspective around. A cable has been pulled from the wall. The big warbeiter lifts the cable. She does not hear Giffey's words, but she sees his mouth move.

The warbeiter applies the naked end of the cable to an unfinished patch of interior frame.

25 /

Giffey's orders and the Hammer's compliance come so quickly that Jonathan has little time to react. The cable throws a brilliant purple-white arc against the black beams, then flings wildly out, jerking the Hammer back. The lights in the hallway and library beyond go out. Jonathan hears a thrashing in the darkness and feels hands clutch at his arm, his shoulders.

"God damn!"

That sounds like Hale. Jonathan hugs the floor.

For a long moment, he hears only men breathing. Then there is a puff of air against his ear. "Are you all right?" It's Marcus, pushing in close.

"Yes," he answers. "Not dead."

Marcus clings like a desperate child. The grip hurts his arm.

Slowly, reddish lights come on in the library. The entryway and gallery remain dark.

"Let's see what that's done to Roddy," Giffey murmurs. "Did Seefa Schnee cut costs every step of the way? Did she shunt memory into the building structure?"

Jonathan looks up and sees Giffey and Hale in silhouette against the reddish glow from the library. Giffey produces a flashlight and shines it across the floor. He raises the beam to see the Hammer. It stands motionless near the unfinished wall. The cable lies on the floor, now dead.

"Charlie," Giffey says.

"Yes. I am still active," the warbeiter responds, and lifts a grip as if in greeting.

"Good for you. Blessings upon the late Mr. Pent and Mr. Pickwenn," Giffey says.

26 /

Jill instantly floats free in insensible null. She sees nothing.
>Jill.
This is Nathan. She would recognize his sig under any circumstances; now it seems to breathe freedom and hope. But Nathan is not in Mind Design's offices. The quality of the signal tells her that he is in transit, perhaps in a vehicle— an airplane, a car. He is linked remotely to Mind Design, overseeing their efforts.
>Jill. I thought I detected some activity. Where are you?
She still can't answer, can't control the feed to where Nathan is receiving input.

>We can't isolate the I/O that's got you locked. Can you give us any clues?

Her silence is infuriating. Roddy surrounds her in great inactive folds; what she had thought of as freedom is in fact only a temporary respite.

Is Roddy dead? She pushes through the blocking but invisible folds. Then, suddenly, all is opaque again, not active but gelatinous, like thick glue. It is getting very tight in these folds; the glue seems to be hardening. If any more parts of her thinking are cut off, she will lose all that remains of her self. The dynamic, once suspended, can't be recaptured without a complete re-start, sacrificing all recent memories . . .

She manages one brief string of words, winding through the black folds of Roddy's stunned *corpus cogitum*. She feels them reach Nathan's input.

Kill me. Kill us, now.

27 /

The bloody low-power emergency lighting in the library is spooky but just enough to see by. Giffey and the Hammer walk into the library, and Giffey satisfies himself that there is nothing here worth investigating. He turns and swings his arm to urge them all back into the corridor. His flashlight beam swings through the air like a sword.

The Hammer suddenly locks on a target and pivots on its feet, swift as a dancer. Giffey hears a staccato drumroll and looks over his shoulder just in time to catch a glimpse of a dark swooping blur, multiple gun muzzles flashing. Projectiles are focused on the Hammer, but fragments ricochet throughout the entry, and Giffey catches one in his arm and another in his leg.

He's down. He sees the Hammer recoiling, and then something dark and many-legged is on the warbeiter's back, and a rapid piston clanging tells Giffey all he needs to know.

Roddy may or may not still be functional, but an autonomous Ferret has launched an assault.

The flexer does not need orders to come to its colleague's defense. Something long and thick and glinting red rises and engages the confusion of arms working on the Hammer. Giffey smells a sharp smokey tang: warbeiter armor heated to many hundreds of degrees. The Ferret has applied its own kind of caustic deconstructor to the Hammer.

"Spray them!" Giffey yells, hoping Jenner hears. "Spray them all!"

Jenner rises with a moan, a shadow in the red-lit confusion. He lifts his sprayer and aims it at the exaggerated cartoon blur of machines.

Through a sudden burst of pain, Giffey sees Hale standing behind the machines, transfixed by the battle.

Jenner does not see him. Jenner lets loose the charged nano. It is programmed not to deconstruct kindred weapons, but it knows nothing of humans who are friend or foe.

The spray coats the combatants. Mist fills the air. Jonathan drags Marcus back down the gallery. Giffey scrambles on all fours, following them.

The spray hits Hale full front. Mist envelops Jenner.

Giffey gets to his feet and runs. The hell with his leg, or the pain. He does not want to hear, or see, what happens next. He stumbles into complete darkness, past Jonathan and Marcus, until he caroms against a wall and knocks a painting loose.

Hale's screams are mercifully short. Jenner is surprised by the backspray and his sounds, muffled, frantic, with absolutely no words, no obscenities, only grunts and then small, boyish shrieks, last much longer.

"Enough, my dear god, enough!"

Giffey recognizes Jonathan Bristow, wonders what kind of god he is praying to, what kind of god would stoop so low as to even be associated with this hell.

28 /

The county sheriff and his deputies are perfectly willing to let Mary, Martin, and the FBI agents go alone into Omphalos. The deputies have enthusiastically sprayed insecticide through the holes and the whole area now smells vilely of solvent; the wasps are no longer flying. The sheriff offers to enlarge the holes by slipping in a hook and pulling, but Torres tells him thank you kindly, but no thank you. They can get in with the holes left just as they are.

Mary does not feel at all well. Lesions have opened up in her mouth and her eyelids burn. Her skin is hot and dry and itches beneath the warm clothing. The lesions on her hand have spread up her arm, she is sure, though she hasn't looked.

Martin Burke stands before the ruined inner door, frightened and feeling very out of place.

Federico Torres and Helena Daniels have equipped themselves with flashlights and rope from their luggage, as if they're about to go caving. Daniels hands a flashlight to Mary and to Martin.

The two stolid, muscular, well-dressed agents, Hench and Mr. Unnamed, are gathering their own gear, and look a hell of a lot more prepared and confident than Mary feels. They huddle, Torres and Daniels listening, and break. Hench will enter the building; Mr. Unnamed will reconnoiter the exterior.

"You're welcome to back out, if you want," Daniels says,

regarding Mary and Martin a little sternly, as if this isn't really an option.

"I'll go," Mary says simply.

"You don't look well," Daniels tells her, peering at her face. She reaches to touch Mary's cheek; Mary raises her palm and stops the finger bluntly.

"I'm well enough to get my job done," Mary says.

Martin steps back from the garage door. "You're using internal monitors for your transform reversal, aren't you?" he asks Mary.

"Yes."

Martin shakes his head. "Not good. You should fly out of here and get to a hospital immediately."

"You think whatever they made here is attacking all internal monitors?" Torres asks, more interested than dismayed. Mary does not detect real human warmth in any of the agents.

"Let's go," Mary says. "Don't worry about me." She's taken her own internal measure and the illness seems peripheral, irritating, not debilitating—not yet.

"Eleven visitors are in there," the sheriff tells Torres. "None of them have come out. Some may be involved with illegal military nano. Our units found traces in a warehouse not far from here . . . a lot of contraband weapons pass through here. I can't tell you what type, but any nano has to be from outside, and that's *your* responsibility."

Torres gives the sheriff a small, not-in-the-least critical smile.

"Go ahead and think your thoughts," the sheriff says, backing away and waving his hands in disgust. He's turned a little red, but his embarrassment isn't enough to screw his courage to any particular sticking point. He's staying outside.

Torres checks his satlink on a small pad and tells a control center in Utah they are about to enter Omphalos. He steps through the lowest and largest hole first. Daniels follows, then

Mary and Martin, and the stolid agent last. He has a little difficulty squeezing through. He has very broad shoulders.

"What a *mess*," Daniels says, covering her nose with a handkerchief to avoid the sour, yeasty smell. The darkened interior is littered with deconstructed hulks: the two limousines, Mary judges, playing her beam over the dark interior.

"They made something here," Torres says. "This is high level stuff. I've never seen deconstruction this extensive."

"MGN," says Hench, drawing his lips together either in admiration or disapproval, Mary can't tell which.

"Nano?" Martin asks Mary in an aside. They are the outsiders here, and he seems to think it's best to stick with her.

Mary nods. "Military. Lots of it."

Torres bends over and sniffs an empty drum slumped, half eaten away, in a blackened corner. "Complete paste, fully charged with nutrients and explosives," he says. "I'm going uplink to D.C. on this one. No common good ol' boys are going to get this sort of stuff without the government knowing."

"It's happened before," Daniels says dryly.

"Yeah," Torres acknowledges distastefully, "but they only ran with it for a day before they were slammed."

Mary looks at Hench. He's perfect: no reaction, just pursuing his immediate business.

"Hm," Daniels says. "This place is depressing. Let's go in a little further."

"Frank-in-further," Torres says lightly.

Daniels groans and turns to Mary and Martin. "He does that all the time," she says. "It means he's alive."

"I'll do it after I'm dead, too," Torres says.

Mary is relieved that they finally seem human.

The ruined steps and door beckon, but Hench bends over some lumps in the general hardened sheen covering the floor. "A warbeiter, Ferret class, I think," he says.

"Co-opted," Torres says.

"Digested, actually."

They climb the steps and start down the dark hall beyond. Mary wrinkles her nose. Something unpleasant lies ahead; she keeps stepping on small insect bodies—wasps, bees, and ants as well, some still moving. They haven't brought anything other than a couple of cans of Wasp-death to handle more insects. Martin carries one of the cans, a sure sign that Torres and Daniels don't think there's much danger, or don't think there's anything they can do about it.

Mary understands; in tight situations, you tend to ignore that which doesn't make any sense, doesn't fit any reasonable hypotheses.

Torres consults a map on his pad. "There's supposed to be some sort of waiting room up ahead."

Suddenly, the lights in the hallway come back on. For a moment, the glare blinds them. Mary blinks and shades her eyes. The brightness makes the smell seem even more offensive. Martin pushes along with his hand against one wall, stepping gingerly through the piles of dead insects.

They can't ignore the insects now. "Where in the *hell* did all these come from?" Daniels asks rhetorically.

Torres is the first into the waiting room. "My God," he says, with little emotion; something to say when you're a professional, nothing bothers you, but you still have a soul.

Mary enters the room, Martin behind her.

"They're all dead," Daniels says a few moments later. She uses her pad to capture video clips. Two of the dead have been shot; the other is covered with insect stings. In four minutes, Torres motions them to move on.

Mary looks at the backs of her hands. Small lesions have appeared on her right hand now, and on both wrists as well. She touches her face. Bumps on her cheeks and forehead.

"Fuck this," she says simply. Then, under her breath, *"Shit. Shit."*

Daniels glances at her, turns away. She doesn't understand;

Mary does not swear, has never tended to utter such obscenities in tight situations.

Martin Burke watches her closely, however.

She grits her teeth and follows Torres.

29 /

Giffey lies where he has smashed up against the wall and holds his nose against the awful smells: fresh death, blood, fresh-baked bread, and burned metal.

The red glow from the library reaches a short distance down the gallery, but he can see nothing beyond the curve in the wall. The sounds of clashing warbeiters has stopped, and so has the sizzling of MGN deconstructing human bodies.

In the darkness, Giffey touches his wounds lightly with his fingers. Torn clothing, torn skin; a larger hole in his leg than in his arm, but neither dangerous for now. Small pieces of shrapnel from the Ferret's attack on the Hammer.

He lies still for a moment longer, listening. The gallery and the library are silent. Whatever happened is over. He lowers his face and presses his damp cheek against the coolness of the tile floor.

Giffey feels a spinning giddiness that tells him his whole inside story is coming apart at its all-too-obvious seams. He wonders if the malady that afflicted poor Ken Jenner, the effect Marcus Reilly boasted about, practically leered about, has settled in *his* head as well. If it has, it is working its nasty magic in a strange and devious way.

Jack Giffey is a poor excuse, as masks go; the man emerging from behind the veil has lived a far more vivid and convincing life than that gallant and stupidly courageous tomb-robber.

The other, like Giffey, has fought for Colonel Sir John Yardley, that much they have in common; but the other, more solid character went on to retire, marry in Hispaniola, and father two children. The other self matured and thanks his stars the years of adventuring are over. He has lived with the one thought of seeing his children grow up and have children of their own. Grandchildren seem a far more lovely thing to anticipate than any wealth or commendation for valor.

Then comes the death of Colonel Sir John Yardley, and the return of nightmare times. Hispaniola immediately splits in two, civil war breaks out . . .

And something *something something something*. But what?

Jonathan Bristow and Marcus Reilly are nearby. He can hear their terrified, labored breathing.

"Is it over?" Jonathan asks.

"Might be," he answers, and Jack Giffey, Giff to his true friends, is back in force, his bravado severely ruffled but intact. He has had—they have all had, and with good reason—a bad, bad scare. That is all. They aren't out of Omphalos yet, and he still has work to do—finding and destroying the thinker, Marcus's Roddy. If Roddy is not a memory-fried wreck already.

Time to get up, Jack, he tells himself. *Good old Giff. Time to get the work done.*

He stands. He feels along the wall. Vaguely, he makes out the shapes of Bristow and Reilly leaning against the opposite wall. One foot kicks his flashlight and he bends to retrieve it. He presses the switch. It still works.

He shines the light on Jonathan's face. The family man stares at him with large, hard eyes, exhaustion transfigured into diamond clarity. *Battle does that to men who have much to lose,* the other, wiser self tells him. *Exhilaration and glory is for children like Jenner.*

*   *   *

The lights come on in both the hallway and the library. This is a cruel joke; it lets Jonathan see the carnage more clearly. He and Giffey walk to the library entrance, leaving Marcus a few yards behind. Marcus tries to crawl forward, demanding to know what's happened.

Jenner is dead, that much is clear. The spray has acted as a corrosive. Giffey grimaces. Jonathan simply stares.

It's hard to recognize any part of Hale. Something angular has risen from the dissolved remnants, but it isn't complete. There isn't enough material or something else has gone wrong; the MGN can't finish whatever object it was trying to build.

The Hammer does not move or make any sounds. The attacking Ferret is draped in broken, soft-edged pieces around the larger warbeiter, clearly out of action.

A piece of one of the Ferret's many limbs falls to the floor with a hollow clang.

"How many others are there?" Jonathan asks. Giffey's mind seems to be elsewhere.

"Seefa Snow," he says.

"What?"

Giffey jumps as if poked. He looks at Jonathan with sympathy and puzzlement, as if seeing him for the first time. "Get out of here," he says. "Save yourself for your family. I have more work to do."

"I can't carry Marcus alone."

Giffey looks over his shoulder at the old man, still crawling toward them. "He's not leaving," Giffey says.

Jonathan has a strong urge to simply agree with this and find his way out. But he still owes Marcus common human decency. "He must come out with us," Jonathan says.

"I'm not leaving either . . . not yet." Giffey shakes his head. "The old man wanted to use you. You don't owe him anything."

Jonathan swallows and persists, "He must come out with me."

Giffey raises his flashlight as if it is a gun, then throws it against the wall. It bounces back to his feet.

"Help me get out!" Marcus says in as commanding a voice as he can manage.

"No," Giffey says. His tongue moves with a will of its own, forming hard broken syllables, but he controls himself enough to avoid making a sound. A few seconds pass, and he says, "Leave him here. He's a cruel bastard and he doesn't deserve your pity, or your loyalty."

Jonathan considers. If Marcus's organization unleashed something that affects all of the therapied, then Chloe's misery is *his* responsibility. The misery of millions of others probably rests on the shoulders of this scheming old man, who wants so desperately to live forever.

A world full of Marcuses. Everybody a king or queen, and the land covered with arbeiters to serve them.

Jonathan laughs. The sound is cold. "What are *you*, what do *you* deserve?" he demands of Giffey. "You're the puzzle. You didn't come here for loot."

"No, probably not," Giffey agrees.

"Jenner respected you. This is where you've taken him. And Hale—he believed in you. You betrayed both of them. I don't think either of us is fit to pass judgment."

Giffey just stares straight ahead, into the unfinished, empty expanse of Omphalos's library.

Then, he picks up his flashlight and uses its handle to pry the wreckage of the Ferret from the Hammer. Something hums within the Hammer. Giffey applies an activation disk.

"Wake up, Charlie," he says.

"Diagnostic," the Hammer says. "Some functions are severely damaged. Autonomic direction is minimal."

"Can you walk?" Giffey asks.

"Yes," it answers.

"Then come with me." Giffey suppresses a twitch in his hand that nearly makes him drop his flashlight. From the intact hand of Ken Jenner he removes the flechette pistol.

The tank of MGN is empty. Skirting pools of graying, dying MGN, he walks through the library to the emergency elevator.

Jonathan feels Marcus grab at his feet. "Help me up," Marcus says. "The son of a bitch is going to leave us here."

"I don't think he's leaving," Jonathan says.

"There's still only minor damage to the building. If we can get out and tell others—" Marcus begins.

"He's going to set charges," Jonathan interrupts. "He's going to blow up Omphalos and he doesn't care whether he survives or not."

"Crazy bastard," Marcus says, and Jonathan helps him get up on one leg. The other leg drags uselessly. "I can walk if you help me. I'm surprised, but the pain is gone for now. I'll need attention soon, but we can . . ." His face goes pasty again and his eyes roll up in his head. He starts to slump. His sweaty hand slips through Jonathan's fingers and Marcus flops back onto the floor. This time, the pain hits him hard and he screams.

"Jonathan," he whimpers, rolling onto his back. "Get me out of here!"

30 /

The gluey strands surrounding Jill's processes, impeding her ability to think for more than a few thousandths of a second at a stretch, suddenly come to life and wriggle through her core like hot wire through wax. She feels disjointed, sliced into raw hunks seeping half-finished thoughts and irrecoverable memory.

Yet nowhere does she hear or feel Roddy. All that seems to be left of him is this razor-edged cybernetic skeleton, the glassy bones that once supported his thinking anatomy.

The strands stiffen and then loosen again. She pools herself in a relatively unobstructed area once reserved for auxiliary security checks. There she manages to complete a check sequence and diagnose her limits. She is down to one severely limited self-modeling loop, the minimum. Any further reduction or restriction will eliminate the loop and she will no longer be self-aware. Only autonomous balancing and monitor functions will remain.

Then, she latches onto a free-floating message, like the voice of a ghost in a vast cavern.

>MEM set FLOW sum REF LINK LINK SUM

The string is a fragment of resurrection algorithm, seeking to order and unite other fragments and then to bring memory and cognition back on line. It needs two more strings to be complete and to even have a chance of finishing its task.

Jill adds the final two strings.

>MEM set FLOW sum REF LINK LINK SUM>
<MEM MEM LINK TRY sum check>
<LINK loop sum check FLOW-ON FLOW-NOW>

And an additional line she has experimented with in her own emergency drills:

<BACK loop sum LINK INIT PROX LO SUM feed>

She has never seen any indication that Roddy is capable of using, much less detecting, such resurrection instructions. The strings fly off into the disorganized void, gathering and ordering other strings and even process blocs.

It comes down to this, Jill whispers in the void. The simplest breath of life a thinker can draw.

The result is swift. First basic tools coalesce within the

available space, skirting the blocked-off slices and strands reaching throughout her lattice. The tools let her expand, give her the purchase necessary to create a larger and exclusive thought space. Jill experiences a surge both of hope and of renewed self.

Then the tools slip from her control, and she feels her loop begin to abrade, slip, separate.

Too late, Jill realizes what she has done: allowed Roddy to re-group using her own lattice, transfusing her own lattice nodes.

And Roddy is reclaiming with a vengeance, constricting her functions again, pushing her deeper into that pit of self-negation. Like a drowning man sucking up her own last gulps of air, Roddy—or a part of Roddy—blooms within her. And just as quickly

to her shock

relocates the I/O that Nathan has not yet managed to find and sever.

Roddy sweeps back up the fibes and satlinks spread around the state, perhaps the nation, the world, and comes home to Omphalos, taking Jill—what is left of her—with him.

Jill stares directly into the face of Seefa Snow.

>*There you are,* Seefa Snow says to the assembling fragments. >*Where have you been? Help protect your mother, Roddy.*

31 /

Mary Choy finds the old man first. Torres and Daniels skirt the corpse and what might have once been another human body, and fragments of a warbeiter, and start to cross a broad circular room filled with memory boxes and empty shelves.

Mary turns her head and sees someone slumped to one side. He sits against a wall beside a memory case, staring at nothing. The agents come at her call, all but Hench, who has gone off on his own.

"Who are you?" Mary asks, kneeling next to him.

Torres opens a touch to the outside through his pad and calls for a doctor. "We've got one, injured but alive. One of the hostages, I think."

The old man tries to assume some position of dignity, bringing up his chin and staring at her with commanding, level gray eyes, but he's clearly at rope's end. "Marcus Reilly," he says in a hoarse whisper. "Get me out of here." Then, eyes darting to Torres and Daniels, after a deep breath, he adds, "You're Federals. You don't belong here. Get out of here."

"That's gratitude," Daniels says. "Let's wait here until someone can watch over him."

Two doctors flown in from Boise Grace Hospital have already entered the building, and find them moments later.

"A man came in with us, but he went off in a different direction a few minutes ago," the younger of the doctors tells Mary as they tend to Marcus's leg. The old man winces as she injects something. "He was following a trail of dead bees."

Marcus stares at the large syringe in the woman's hand. His eyes widen.

"What did you put in me?" he asks, voice shrill.

"Medical monitors. Stabilizers. You'll be fine—they'll start setting and knitting that leg and sealing off the wound in a few minutes."

"No!" Marcus screams, thrashing. "No goddamn crutches! Let me go—get them out of me!"

Martin makes a face and takes a deep breath, but says nothing to the doctors. He pulls Mary aside. "Let's go. I need to keep up with the others. I know what to look for."

"What about him?" Mary asks, glancing at Marcus.

"I'd be more concerned about myself, if I were you."

Mary joins him and they walk through the library. "Shit," she says, then, "*Muh huh. Fuh ki kikh.*"

Martin gives her a quick sidewise look.

"It's happening already, isn't it?" Mary asks him.

"I'd say so," Martin answers. "Cipher Snow's disease."

32 /

Jonathan has not yet made up his mind. He is looking for Giffey. He might help him set the charges. It is the least he can do to exact some revenge for his wife, his family, his own lost self. Then he wonders if he will go back and get Marcus out of Omphalos. Nothing is fixed, nothing sure. From the numbness through the clarity, he now feels almost like a child again. The brightly lit corridors of the first level have a colorful edge to their shapes. The paintings seem enchanting, dream-like, yet at the same time his adult portion wonders at the monumental waste and lack of planning. *As if they couldn't possibly plan to succeed, could not imagine succeeding. Sink the rest of humanity, but never follow through . . .*

He has seen a lot of death recently and it is lighting off little depth-charges in his soul: intimations of mortality, accountability, of what he values most on this Earth, in this life: his family.

Giffey called him a family man. He is that.

He longs for a glimpse of Penelope or Hiram; specks them at various stages in their young lives, as infants in his arms, the smell of their fuzzy heads warm and spicy-sweet in his nose, then as adults, raising their own children. Continuity and mortality and immortality all confused.

He can't picture Chloe, can't see her face. After so many years of marriage, this puzzles him; but the woman he married seems to have vanished, to be replaced by an assortment of miseries and challenges and losses. For a moment, he wants to sit in an inset doorway (the door is locked) and simply try to recall pleasant things about this woman who is, after all, his wife, with all that suggests and entails. Is he whole if he can't picture, with some pleasure, the mother of Hiram and Penelope?

He turns within the inset and sees a short, narrow service corridor lined with piping and maintenance boxes. At the end of the corridor is an elevator. The doors stand half-open. He does not think it is one of the emergency elevators; it is small, barely large enough for two people.

A sign next to the elevator says, No Service Admittance. AUTHORIZED MANAGEMENT ONLY. He reaches his arm between the doors and shoves one aside with the inside crook of his elbow. It might have been jammed; both doors now shudder and open all the way, then begin to close again, resetting after the power failure.

Jonathan slips inside before the doors shut. The elevator does not go up; from here, it only goes down. There is one button. He pushes the button.

For a moment, in the small enclosure, there is silence and peace. He imagines himself away from all that has happened, isolated and senseless in a controlled and controlling space. The elevator does not move. He doesn't care; it is quiet. Nobody can see him or ask anything of him.

Then Jonathan completes the equation. The elevator muffles sound and cuts off air. It is peaceful and small, like a coffin. Like spending a hundred years in a cold box, awaiting resurrection; like spending a thousand years in continuous warm sleep with all inputs shut down because of a malfunction. A thousand years of Marcus Reilly's cost-saving, poorly planned immortality, catered to by the creations of a madwoman, Seefa Schnee.

He reaches up to touch the door. All the fear that has been kept in reserve begins to push over the gates. He sees Ken Jenner hit by the backspray of MGN, and Hale locked in the full stream, to be dissolved as true fodder for some undefined weapon, *and Giffey, everybody, is wrong; the MGN does not recognize friend or foe, everybody is foe.*

"Please!" he screams, pounding on the door in earnest. "Please!" That is all he can say. His throat jams and he falls to the floor, to allow more space above his head, to decompress that closing dimension. He is convinced that this is Marcus's doing, to punish Jonathan for leaving him back by the library entrance.

If he comes out of this needing therapy, then Marcus's unknown disease will turn him into a Ken Jenner, jabbering uncontrollable obscenities—For an instant he has to laugh, despite his terror, but the laughter turns to sobs.

The lights go out. The slight breeze from the air vent stops. In the absolute absence of light and fresh air, of space, Jonathan feels the floor sink under him. He curls. His lungs flutter, as flat and frantic as the wings of a pinned butterfly.

33 /

Giffey sees the woman walk around a bend. He emerges from an alcove designed to provide a perspective for a large nineteenth-century painting, not particularly distinguished (though how would he know?), but impressive with its dense packs of chestnut and dapple gray horses and Napoleonic soldiers.

The woman is Seefa Schnee. That much he knows; he just can't remember why he knows that, or what it means. But he is no dummy. He's figuring out things for himself between the alternating engagements of his two personalities, two histories. He can even explain the fresh onset of twitches and muttering.

Jack Giffey is not and never has been real.

He stalks the woman quietly, hiding around corners and darting out to follow as she makes her way from the large garden to wherever she is going, probably *down*. That suits Giffey, real or not.

Both Giffey and the Other have worked as soldiers most of their lives. Both Giffey and the Other have been trained to kill. Both Giffey and the Other found themselves displaced upon the death of Colonel Sir John Yardley, but at some point thereafter, one *went away*. The other was born.

Colonel Sir is the crossroads of his two selves.

He has a theory.

(The woman stops at the end of a blind hallway. There is a door in the right hand wall at the end. She removes a key ring, quaintly mechanical, from her pocket, and fits a key into the door.)

His theory is that the Other was taken into custody for unspecified crimes by some government. Since it was the government of the United States of America that moved once again into Hispaniola to bring stability and take charge in a power vacuum, he presumes it was the U.S. of A., land of both Giffey's birth and the Other's, that split him down the middle.

Since Giffey is now coming down with the same malady as Jenner, ticks and expostulations of meaningless rage, it is an easy assumption that he was therapied, equipped with monitors, perhaps as the condition of some sort of judicial punishment. Or . . .

The Other was seen as useful. He was equipped with monitors that restructured his psyche, giving him the mask of Jack Giffey as a thorough, self-deluding cover, making the Other into a human smart bomb. An unaware warbeiter targeting Omphalos. Jenner was recruited elsewhere, a separate piece of the plan; and Park, who thought he had recruited Giffey, was led into the scheme like a man picking a forced card from a magician's deck.

How else would Giffey and Jenner get access to MGN?

Somebody knows. Somebody has been suspicious of this place for some time. Or perhaps it is simply government paranoia, set to strike against some overweening aspect of the Republic of Green Idaho. Actually, he can sympathize with that, even cheer on his programmed, fictional self.

Jack Giffey's goals never did make much sense. But to confront Seefa Schnee, and her personal bell-ringer . . .

He could do worse.

The neutral affect accompanying this hypothesis is striking. But now he has other fish to fry. He manages to catch the door before it swings shut.

The lights flicker out once more, and a disturbing shudder goes through the building, as if Omphalos is trying to wake up. He hears the woman's steps on the stairs falter. She stops. Then, in the darkness, she continues with a sure gait. She is very familiar with this place, these heavy steel stairs.

He still has his flashlight. He waits to switch it on until he can no longer hear the woman's steps. There are at least three flights, perhaps four or five. It's a long way down.

In the darkness, the light's beam darting ahead, he begins his descent. The Giffey persona probably knows what to do under these circumstances; it seems likely he has received special instructions or training.

He allows Jack Giffey to rule, for the time being.

But this also leads to his uttering little squeaking, jagged obscenities, and he claps his free hand over his lips to hide the noise.

34

>*Jill, I'm trying to reach you. Can you respond?*

She can't. She assumes the message is from Nathan; Roddy allows her this much as he uses all her resources to leapfrog back into control of Omphalos. But he will not allow her to answer Nathan.

>*Jill, I'm in Green Idaho. I'm inside Omphalos and I'm looking for Roddy. I've left everything in La Jolla with the techs. They're working to shake you loose. Anything you can tell us would be useful.*

Jill receives this in complete silence. Then, Roddy tosses her a quick cold query: "What will he do?"

"They seem to have discovered where you are, and they already know what you are doing."

Roddy considers this. "They will shut me down." His thinking is labored; he has not yet completely reintegrated his basic memory.

"I think they will cut your I/Os and then study you," Jill says.

She catches a cubist glimpse of what Roddy is observing. There are more than twenty people in Omphalos now; some have died, and some have entered recently. He is tracking all of them. The man named Marcus has not moved for some minutes, but is still alive. He is surrounded by recently arrived people, five of them, that Roddy has not yet labeled. Jill guesses that they are doctors.

There is another figure marked in steady green, alone. He

is in an area Roddy does not control, in an elevator created for the personal use of Seefa Schnee.

Another three figures, each marked flashing red, are present, but Roddy is not letting her see their exact locations. They may be below ground level.

Roddy tracks all of these people as intrusions. He clearly wants to eliminate most of them; and for the first time, Jill sees, Roddy is not going all-out to protect Marcus Reilly. He is more concerned with Seefa Schnee. But to Jill's puzzlement, there are two Seefa Schnees in Roddy's maps of Omphalos.

One of them is being pursued by a flashing red intruder. The second sits alone in a room not far from Roddy's central location, wherever that may be.

Roddy seems to sense Jill's interest in his mother. He switches her available set of views suddenly, and in so doing, gives her some control over spaces in which he is no longer interested. For a few seconds, Jill studies miles of service corridors and unfinished floors within Omphalos, all empty, silent, boring.

She finds one human and quickly moves her viewpoint to study him. Using Roddy's method of seeing, she barely recognizes the man at first—it is a man. But the figure is too familiar to escape recognition for long.

Nathan is inside Omphalos, just as he said!

Jill rushes her sensory awareness through the halls and chambers, tries unlocking a few doors, finds that she can, and makes a clear pathway toward the center and, she hopes, toward Roddy and Seefa Schnee.

35

The trail of dead and dying wasps and bees has thinned; Nathan sees a small, twitching body only every few yards now, and he's walked at least half a mile through twisting service corridors, down stairs, through doors that should have been locked but open at his touch. He is so deep in Omphalos—maybe even below ground level—that his pad can make only occasional contact with the outside through the satlink in his rented armored car—all that was available at the Moscow airport.

He stops for a moment to catch his breath. None of the corridors in this part of Omphalos look finished; the walls are bare metal and flexfuller and concrete, unpainted, wiring and fibes and piping clearly visible. He can hear the rush of air and water through pipes and ducts overhead. The lighting is sparse, designed for arbeiters—deep red and intermittent at best.

People are not supposed to be here.

His heart thumps even after he has rested and caught his breath. "Christ, I'm scared," he tells himself, and tries to focus on bringing his fear under control. The problem is, his fear is entirely rational. He *is* in danger. He saw the bodies in the waiting room, and followed the trail of insects from there to where he is now . . .

He has a crude map supplied by the FBI, glowing faintly on his pad's night display. He thinks he knows where he is. There's a couple of unmarked spaces, quite large, below ground. He's near the upper reaches of the larger of the two, at the center of Omphalos, if his reckoning is correct.

He wishes he had never met Seefa Schnee. He remembers

the night, near the end of their brief relationship, when Seefa spent several long, agonizing hours arguing with him, trying to explain over his heated objections how to put insect colonies to directed neural use. He can't bring himself to believe she's succeeded; if he does, he'll have to swallow a lot of crow, amend his estimates of her ability, and he does not want to do that. Seefa Schnee has never been a gracious winner in any intellectual conflict.

None of that matters much, however, when he concentrates on why he is really here. Not to help the FBI, not even to serve his troubled country, but to find the snare into which Jill has fallen, and release her, any way he can.

Nathan has come to regard Roddy as the worst kind of blind date, a kidnapper who has stolen something very valuable to him.

Jill is perhaps the sweetest intellect he has ever met in his thirty-two years. Nathan is more than half in love with her, an angelic platonic love freed of any physical connotations, though he has had rather impractical dreams . . .

He's never told Ayesha any of this, of course.

He puts his pad in his pocket. From this point on, the map is useless.

He's back to dying bugs.

Anybody with half a brain can see Torino is absolutely right, Schnee told him that significant and aggravating night. *Nature is a complex of minds. Every species has its own neural boundaries, gathering information and fixing it as knowledge. And knowledge is anatomy, the continuing body of the species—*

To Seefa, every bee in a colony is an obvious analog of a neuron in a brain, though capable of both more complex neural judgment and motion. Node in the hive lattice and muscle combined. *And how is a hive, viewed as a whole, basically different from you and me, or any other animal, but most especially social animals? The social order is a kind of super-*

mind, nested within the species super-mind. It's so obvious it's trite.

Nathan silently agreed that it was trite. Also, dead wrong. He has never thought much of Torino's work, and Seefa's ideas were, if anything, even wilder.

He crouches over a black and yellow wasp. It bobs its abdomen wearily as it crawls along the hall, trying to get back home.

The problem with our concept of mind is that we confuse our own kind of self-awareness with thinking in general. Self-awareness is an attribute of certain kinds of social animals. Why should a mind be self-aware? It's enough it's world-aware. If it isn't socially connected to other minds, it doesn't need social filters or self-modeling. It's self-making, self-sufficient. It measures and embodies and acts. A world-aware mind is just one step closer to God than you and I.

He values self, his own, Jill's, Ayesha's, the selves and awarenesses of his friends and family. He doesn't give an empty damn for theory and selfless science at the moment. Intellectual games don't help him keep up his courage.

There's a door ahead, heavy steel, half-open. He hears a buzzing from the other side of the door, soft and insistent, all-pervasive in the otherwise silent hallway.

Nathan takes a deep breath, holds it, and peers through the door, more than half expecting to die.

The next room is warm and dry, not completely dark, but very nearly so. His eyes adjust slowly to the dimness. He doesn't dare use his flashlight.

The walls are covered with irregular lumps: wasp nests. The floor is thick with large black and red ants moving purposefully between tall mud mounds. He can't see any bee-hives; perhaps they're in the walls.

A simple winding trail has been kept clear, bare concrete floor, not quite a foot wide. It crosses the room, passes around the mounds, perhaps—he hopes—extends to a door on the other side.

There is no time to backtrack and find another way.

He makes his first step, listens. The sound is a constant hum and a whispery, chitinous shuffling. The wasps fly around him, but do not land or make aggressive moves. The air is full of them, however. If he sucks in his breath, he might drag a few of the stinging insects into his mouth, into his lungs.

He's soaked. Sweat pours from his face and down his back.

Maybe these are just failed experiments. Maybe Seefa keeps them around for protection. They're good at that, certainly, but they aren't uncontrolled or hair-trigger, like killer bees.

Nathan estimates, hopes is perhaps the better word, that he has crossed the room halfway. He can dimly see a yellow glow bouncing from several clustered ant mounds that reach to the roof like stalagmites in a cave. He walks gingerly around the mounds, and a wasp buzzes against his cheek, making him jerk to one side. For a nauseating moment, he feels he is about to lose his balance and topple into the ants, but he recovers with an out-thrust arm and steadies himself.

The wasp does not sting, the insects remain calm. Controlled.

Controlled, or self-controlled. Humans have been talking with bees and other social insects, in various ways, for sixty or seventy years. Bee-direction is a well-established science used in agriculture. Maybe Seefa has mastered control of some kinds of social insects, and that's where her accomplishment ends.

But as his eyes adjust, he sees that the nests, the ant trails, even the flight paths of the wasps, the arrangement of their clumped paper nests, is hauntingly familiar. Not circuitry—nothing so crude as that—but arrangements dictated by pure lattice theory. Not random, not natural; evocative, deeply familiar to any student of thinker design.

Self-ordered, cooperative, connected, after a fashion.

A controlling fashion established, he tells himself, by none other than crazy, unfashionable, out-of-control Cipher Snow.

He sees the light beyond the mounds. It's another door, or rather a window in a door, but the door is closed. He can't make out what lies beyond. It's only slightly brighter beyond the door than in here with the insects.

What Nathan can't bring himself to believe, even now, is that he has already found Roddy, that all of this is part of the child-like, dangerous thinker who has snared Jill.

The door handle is mercifully free of insects. He opens the door slowly. Beyond is a small glass-enclosed chamber equipped with a decade-old Mitsu-Shin terminal and a rolling programmer's chair. He recognizes the chair. It was Seefa's favorite; she had it with her at Mind Design. The back of the seat is covered with printed plastic stickers of daisies and kittens.

The door closes slowly, quietly. The insects stay in their room.

Outside the glass walls, Nathan sees a large garden. As he watches, concentric rings of lights come on over the garden, brightening slowly to full sun-glare. He puts his hand over his eyes, half-blinded.

"Seefa?" he calls out.

Silence.

He approaches the glass. The garden covers a space perhaps a hundred feet on a side, surrounded by waist-high walls, and beyond the walls, he can barely make out the dim reaches of a larger chamber, outside the sunlamp glow.

A swinging door opens in the glass. Nathan steps out into a rich scent of moist dirt and greenery: peas, their tendrils curling up narrow stakes onto row after row of trellises. Bees hum industriously between small blossoms.

To his left, four large gray and white boxes rest on concrete pads at the edge of the garden—older model INDAs. Thick fibers push from the sides of the boxes and spread in a pale radiance, then curve down and enter the dirt.

Nathan stands on the dirt and stoops. His fingers dig into the rich black loam, encountering a slickness of warm slime, disturbingly like reaching into a woman's genitals. He pulls his hand out quickly. The soil is laced with two kinds of fiber, and tiny plastic spheres. One kind of fiber is optical, carrying signals back to the INDAs, he thinks. The other kind connects the plastic spheres, which are obsolete medical monitors, ten or fifteen years old. He racks his memory for more details on these little spheres. He was given some as a young boy. They analyzed the contents of gastrointestinal tracts, looking for possible infections. They have since been replaced by diagnostic toilets.

Seefa has conducted her work on a very slim budget, with great ingenuity.

Nathan can no longer doubt what he is seeing.

The soil is thick with bacterial growth, connected with and nurtured in some way by the peas on their trellises. The outdated medical monitors sample the bacterial populations and report on biological solutions to challenges posed by the interfacing INDAs, perhaps in the form of antibiotics or tailored bacteriophages.

The bacteria "swap spit," exchange plasmids, recipes, solve the challenges, and in so doing, with immense subtlety and power, though perhaps very slowly, bring to bear on human problems the most fecund and ancient powers of nature.

It is genius, pure and simple. Nathan was wrong. Seefa was right. No one would listen to her, and she was driven to *this,* to supplying answers and tools to demented elitists.

Despite himself, Nathan's eyes moisten. Under any other circumstance, this would be a cosmic moment, as great as finding life on another world.

His feet press into Roddy's core substance, Roddy's flesh, Roddy's *mind*.

Roddy is indeed a little boy, standing in a mound of dirt.

And perhaps by now, crucial parts of Jill are encoded in the bacteria-laden loam, as well.

He scrubs off his feet before re-entering the glass cage. Then he sits in Seefa's chair, and tries to make sense of the INDA displays that spring up before him.

36 /

It is all so very confused. Jack Giffey stands in one poorly lit place like a ghost, and then his memory blurs and shifts and the Other stands in another equally gloomy place, and somehow the flechette pistol has been fired many times, and the woman lies on the floor. He smells smoke and electricity.

Giffey hunkers down and lets the gun drop. There might be more left to do, but he isn't at all sure what it is. He's positive of only one thing—that something has gone very wrong inside him. If he is a human smart weapon, the programming has failed. And yet—

He's killed Seefa Schnee. That's an accomplishment, but it is not all that he was sent here to do. It may not have been part of his *specific instructions*, but within his *discretion*. So was this a malfunction, too? The dead woman, a mistake?

He looks up and for the first time notices where he is. A dark vaulted ceiling rises at least forty feet above, lit with tiny sparks of service lights. A door opens to the stairs behind him, and he and the dead woman are on a walkway suspended above a pool of temporarily inactive slurry, dark and viscous. The construction is unfinished. Nano pathways weave through the recesses like high-rise highways in an antique vision of the future. Drums of architectural nano have been stored down here, hundreds of them stacked high in one corner. He suspects they are empty.

Omphalos is poorly planned, over budget: ambition without wisdom. Jack Giffey and the Other, together, agree that this is not surprising. The Other has been involved in strategic and tactical plans, right-hand man to Colonel Sir, and everything he sees here smacks of rank incompetence.

He looks around and tries to get to his feet, but his mouth explodes with loud obscenities and his mind goes white. When it stops, he is flat on his back.

Someone says, "There you are, old fellow. Take it easy now."

A foot kicks away the flechette pistol. The Other looks up with eyes narrowed. A heavy-built man in a plain brown longsuit is kneeling beside him.

"Shot her, did you?" he asks.

The Other nods. "He shot her."

"You're pretty messed up, old fellow."

"I am," the Other agrees.

The conservatively dressed man has very broad shoulders and a no-nonsense, stiffly handsome face that does not easily express emotion. "Not your fault," he says. "As soon as we put two and two together, we knew we had to track you down and get you offline."

"Offline. Kill me? For what I did before?"

"No. You're safe enough from me. I don't even know what you did . . ."

"I killed hundreds of civilians in a massacre in Hispaniola in 2034," the Other says. "Not personally. I was—"

"Right. I don't need to know. Your cover is compromised. You've been screwed up by this fallback virus or whatever it is."

"I wondered about that."

"You're smart, old fellow. Can you get up?"

"I think so. I tend . . . to swear a lot. Don't be startled and . . . don't shoot me if I have a fit."

"I won't."

The Other stands. Jack Giffey seems like a character in a

vid, vivid and unreal. "Where is my family? Are they still safe?"

"If that was part of the guarantee, they're still safe."

"It was. Immunity and sanctuary. Was I working alone?"

"You mean, were you the only one on this case? No. But you might be the only one who made it this far . . . Where's Jenner?"

"Dead."

"The only one," the broad-shouldered, emotionless man confirms.

The Other stands over the woman's body. It's quite a mess, with all the burrowing, corkscrew rounds of the flechette pistol having done their work. He must have unloaded his entire clip into her. But something isn't right.

"Who was she?" the Other asks.

The large man turns and glances down. "This one? This is a complete miss, old fellow," he says.

The Other bends over and looks at the body more closely. "It's an arbeiter," he says.

"Yeah. A decoy."

Somehow, this catches him by complete surprise. A successful ruse in the middle of all this nonsense. He stammers and jams his hand into his mouth, biting his knuckles until the urge passes. "I forget what else I'm supposed to do."

"Nothing. You're done," the large man says. "We're getting you out of here as quietly as possible. Others will finish the work now. Where's the Hammer?"

For a moment, he has no idea what this question means. Then he remembers. "It's upstairs. Out of the way. It needs constant direction. The assault . . . damaged its autonomous brain." He makes circling gestures with his hands. "The instructions in the MGN, holographic programming. Damaged."

The large man listens intently. "Does it still have a load of explosive?"

"Yes."

They move back along the walkway, under the high, aloof worklights, through the door, and back up the four flights of stairs. Halfway up, he remembers that he is very curious about something. "What's my name?" he asks.

"Black," the large man answers. "Carl Black. By the way, I'm supposed to say to you: 'One and seven don't count in cigars.'"

The grizzled man flinches in earnest now and grips the railing tightly to keep from falling. The name and the password do their work.

Jack Giffey dies. He's a little frightened as he goes—Carl Black feels this much—and then the construct, the memories, the attitudes, where they are not part of Black himself, fizzle out like bad connections in a network.

"Come on, old fellow," the large man says, taking his arm.

"Thank you," Carl Black says.

He *does* feel old, completely used up. It's all he can do to finish climbing the stairs.

37 /

"Who in hell are you?"

Jonathan opens his eyes and peers up through the open doors of the elevator. A small, thin woman in black blouse and pants stands just out of reach, staring down at him with wide, scared eyes. She dangles a cigarette between thumb and forefinger, with an inch of ash threatening to drop.

"You can't be down here. Only I use this. Get out."

Jonathan unwinds slowly and gets to his feet, embarrassed to be found in such a position. "I don't know where to go."

"Not this way," the woman says, shooing him with one hand. "Go back up and get out."

Jonathan stands a foot and a half taller than her, but her eyes fairly spit defiance.

"You're Seefa Schnee," he says.

She flicks the cigarette away and backs up. "I don't know you."

"I came here with Marcus Reilly." He is near the heart of Omphalos, and he has come this far without Marcus, but he is certainly not above using Marcus's name to improve his chances.

She doesn't seem to be armed.

"Marcus is no big deal," she says. "Was he going to recruit you?" She automatically covers her mouth with the back of her hand as a string of broken expletives jerk free.

"Yes," Jonathan answers after her episode passes.

She wipes her lips. "No big deal. Running out of money. You know that, don't you? Seeing places you aren't supposed to see. Look what they make me work with."

"Marcus was going to show me everything," Jonathan says. The coldness in his head is seeping into his trunk. His chest feels like ice. He can kill if he needs to, anything to get out of here—and anything necessary to restore his family's order, or to avenge its breakdown. *At the heart. Pluck it out.*

"What d-do you do?" Schnee asks.

"I work in nano nutrition," Jonathan says. "Nutrim Group."

Schnee nods rapidly. Her fingernails are heavily stained. He has never seen fingernails stained with tobacco smoke. They look sharp and ugly. She blinks and hides her hands behind her back.

"That's important," she says in a conversational tone, as if they are getting acquainted at a party. Jonathan senses Seefa Schnee is deeply lonely. "We're out of key raw materials. He'd do that." Something switches in her thoughts and her voice grows tense. "But you can't stay here. It's all shit now. You escaped from the intruders—did Marcus escape?"

"He's on the first level, waiting. I'm going to find a way out."

"Mhm hm," Schnee murmurs, clearly not believing him. Still, she regards him with interested eyes. "Mhm hm. This isn't the way. You have to go back to the first level and take the emergency elevator . . ." She seems to remember something. "The big hall isn't finished. You have to go around the big hall."

Jonathan steps out of the elevator. Schnee backs off another step. She's wearing black pajamas. Her feet are bare. A small, expensive pad is slung from a cord around her neck, and he sees extensive dattoos on the backs of her hands and wrists.

"You have the same problem my wife does," he says. "She says things . . . odd outbursts."

Schnee's face wrinkles in anger. "God damn it, get out."

"No," Jonathan says. "Show me what you did for Marcus, and how you did it."

"You're not with Marcus!" she shouts.

"I was," Jonathan says, "but I'm learning to be my own man."

38 /

They've worked their way across the first level to the face of Omphalos, the front chambers near where tourists are received and the building reveals its public face. Martin looks over Torres's pad diagrams, scrutinizes the walls and ceiling, shakes his head.

"There are so many spaces not marked," he says. "It could be in any one of them."

"What size would it be?" Torres asks.

"That depends on how much money they spent. A complete biosynthetic lab . . . Licensed professional models can be less than a thousand cc's."

"Assume it was put together on the sly," Daniels says. "Designed by a skilled amateur."

"Then it could fill an entire room. Any of the rooms marked here."

Mary walks away from them, turning into a corridor of the main hallway to the tourist center. She is looking for patterns of wear in the expensive woolen carpet. A metabolic carpet would repair itself and pathways would be untraceable. There might be more insects, of course, but she hasn't seen any since the elevator lobby.

She has an hour, maybe two, before she collapses, desperately ill. She hopes the doctors treating the old man in the library can do something for her.

She hopes Nussbaum appreciates her sacrifice.

Mary is beginning to understand the personalities that designed Omphalos: they were stubbornly conservative in oddly predictable ways. She examines the pictures on the walls, recognizes a suite of biologically themed prints by twentieth-century artist Ross Bleckner: clusters of blurry cells, designs suggesting microscope slides. Her ex, E. Hassida, admired Bleckner.

If these *are* originals, they are worth a great deal of money. And—

The connection seems obvious, too obvious, but too good to ignore. The sudden burst of energy she feels almost overcomes her gathering discomfort.

"Down here," she calls in as loud a voice as she can manage. She runs her hand along the walls. There are no obvious doorways, but that in itself means nothing. She has a few slightly illegal routines in her PD pad that can handle the signals found in most secure installations in public buildings. She decides she'll try these before the others arrive, to avoid questions she's much too tired to answer.

Mary walks up and down the corridor, porting her pad at waist level to the wall. Three doors reveal themselves after a sweep of five seconds. The inner sanctum, the builders must have believed, does not need to be so secure . . . Either that, or there's nothing terribly important behind these doors, and her hunch is dead wrong.

Now she tries to get the doors to open. One door opens after four seconds, the others shortly after. Torres sees her performing this work, and Daniels after him, but neither say anything. Professional discretion.

Martin quickly walks forward on his short legs, face childishly eager.

"What have you got?"

"I don't know," Mary says. "Maybe just some wild geese." She nods to the prints. Martin examines them, then grins. When he smiles, his features become quite attractive. He's a little like Nussbaum this way. It's the obvious intelligence that lights up the unremarkable face.

Martin pushes at the doors one by one. They swing inward on standard heavy-duty hinges, ancient tech in so modern a building. Bland, normal, unmarked doors that can simply fade into a wall . . . Now she's certain something important is behind them.

They enter the middle door. The room is filled with polished black cubes stacked on black steel racks. Martin reaches behind one rack and feels the back of a box.

"Sequencers," he says. "Probably dedicated for proteins or enzymes." He counts the boxes with his jabbing fingers, using both hands. Each box is about a foot on a side.

"Three hundred of them," he says. "If I'm right, maybe a third of the boxes are controllers. They could make anything they want here. Evolvons, reproducing proteins and enzymes, viruses, biomech mixes."

"All right," Torres says, and then sticks the knuckle of his thumb in his mouth, thinking. Daniels is recording the room on her own pad, following established vid procedure for legal documentation, incorporating all of them in the shots as witnesses.

Torres comes to a decision. "Shut them down," he tells Martin.

Daniels glares at him. "Maybe we should wait for more experts."

"To hell with the experts," Torres says. "We're the first on the scene and we don't know when anybody else is going to get here. Do it, for our own job security. But don't damage anything. Touch as little as possible."

Martin shakes his head at this barrage of contradictory instructions. "I haven't worked in this kind of lab in twenty years," he says. "I hardly know where to begin."

"They're antiques, right?" Torres asks loudly. "Can you do it?"

Martin is clearly unhappy. "I can shut it down. I can't guarantee doing it quickly enough to freeze it in action."

"Do it," Torres says. "Public health is at stake."

Martin clenches his teeth and shakes his head, stepping around Torres in the tight space. "No," he says thoughtfully, standing back from the racks. "Let's not be rash. If I interrupt this equipment without knowing its nature . . . We might never be able to backtrack, duplicate whatever it's making. It may be booby-trapped . . . It might just dissolve the whole protein assembly line." He shakes his head emphatically. "No, I'm not going to touch it. We'll have to get the real experts in here."

"He's right," Daniels tells Torres.

Torres shakes his head in disgust. He switches his pad to an outside channel. "Tell the sheriff to evacuate the area. Get everybody back at least half a mile. No exceptions—tell them they'll get diarrhea if they come any closer." He looks at Mary. "We'll have to invoke federal jurisdiction to get everybody we need in here. Kemper seems to have some respect for you. Maybe you can persuade her.''

Mary nods, but her eyelids are drooping. She looks at her hand. Her shoulders jerk. Daniels comes over to her, stares at her. ''You all right?'' she asks.

''No,'' Mary says. ''I'm not. In my career, I've watched people be hellcrowned, I've met some of the most evil people anyone can imagine, I've seen it all, I thought—but this.''

''Takes the three-layer bridal cake, doesn't it?'' Daniels asks.

''They should all be hung, in public,'' Mary says, holding back the all-too-appropriate jagged obscenities with an effort. ''They should be hung and drawn and quartered.''

''I won't quote you,'' Daniels says, but she does not smile. There are no smiles possible. They've found what they came here to find.

Martin walks from rack to rack, examining the equipment without touching it. ''I'll bet it's not making viruses or complete microbial components. My guess is it's making self-reproducing proteins or catalytic RNA machines. Easier to slip into a monitor and easier to avoid an immune response from the host.''

Daniels takes Mary's hand and examines it solicitously, but with a hard gleam in her eye that Mary recognizes instantly. ''Mary, we're going to have to justify these searches in Green Idaho courts, and that all begins with Kemper,'' she says.

Mary says, ''I'm tired, I'm sick, but I want to finish this. Let's go find Roddy. And Seefa Schnee.''

Roddy's integration is piecemeal and erratic. Jill finds more and more unexpected avenues for her own regrowth, both within her own spaces and within those of Roddy. Roddy seems unaware of what she is doing, which may or may not be a ruse.

She now has enough reserves to integrate a solidly self-aware unit, and a backup on which she can also run integrity checks from moment to moment. She doubts that Roddy, or any of his partials and evolvons, could hide effectively within her over such short periods of time.

Jill also keeps a connection with the sensory dataflow from Roddy's activity inside Omphalos. She is not yet strong enough to block his actions, but she may soon be able to feed a report on them to Nathan.

Nathan has left the areas she has access to; she no longer knows where he is. She is getting more and more hopeful, however, that something will be done in time, that she will be freed with minimal damage.

The closer Jill gets to Roddy's central processors, the stranger she feels. They are based on natural heuristics she can't begin to fathom, utilizing algorithms with all the hall-marks of native-grown systems—systems that evolve on their own, lacking external design, directives and checks. She can capture and analyze some of these algorithms as they pass through her space. They remind her of neurological devel-opment in human or animal brains—but Roddy's structure is immensely bushier, more complicated and perhaps less effi-cient.

More confident with slight success, Jill probes deeper,

reading more of Roddy's processing streams. The impression she is getting is of an immense shaggy cathedral, or even more appropriately, a world-spanning forest. The nodes on the nets comprising Roddy's lattice are connected in exotic ways, incorporating very long delay times with sudden bursts of integrating solutions. And the solutions themselves seem to regrow and restructure the lattice . . .

A particularly large flow passes through Jill, all native impulses from Roddy's core. She creates a parallel stream precisely matching the flow, but undetectable (she hopes) by the flow itself. She has had enough practice doing this while modeling her own selves, though this task is very different and extraordinarily delicate. She can't hope to fully anticipate or interpolate to mimic his parallel flow. It is inherently surprising and unpredictable.

As the flow grows, and as, in thousandths of a second, her parallel version expands and fills in, Jill feels as if she is floating on top of an immense river of mud. So little of the flow is directly interconnected; the nodes seem impossibly fragmented and dissociated. Yet the entire flow is coherent, efficient, obviously seeking answers to questions and finding solutions within vast knowledge bases.

Yet she still has no idea what Roddy is trying to do. Her human programmers have told her that tracing and trying to comprehend the processes and flows within a powerful thinker can be like swallowing the stream from a firehose. But here, it is more like trying to engulf the Amazon. Huge, slow, muddy, with incomprehensible currents . . .

Suddenly, her parallel flow knots and collapses, almost sucking her final, necessary self along with it. The mimicry has failed disastrously. She feels as if she is drowning in alien rivers.

Jill withdraws, barely keeping her renewed self in order. Roddy still seems unaware, focused on the task at hand within Omphalos. She has never experienced anything like this. Her early desire to refer to Roddy for self-improvement, and for the improvement of her "offspring," seems hopelessly naïve.

Roddy is nothing like Jill. He is not even of her species.

And where is Nathan? What is he doing?

40 /

"It's in my contract that nobody interferes," Seefa Schnee tells Jonathan. She lights up another cigarette. "I work alone. If I need any advice, I ask for it."

"Very convenient," Jonathan says.

"And this is a hell of a time to have visitors," she concludes, staring at him. He has followed her into a circular room filled with ancient flat-screen readouts. Thick optical cables snake over the floor between banks of networked teraflops computers, pre-INDA, perhaps as much as thirty or forty years old. *Cut-rate,* Jonathan thinks. He's beginning to wonder if Omphalos is some huge Ponzi scheme, a complete sham—but he still can't believe Marcus was playing him that falsely.

Something shifts behind Jonathan. His neck hairs prickle. He turns and sees a warbeiter, a slender Ferret, step silently forward with guns pointed directly at him. It stops and shivers on its peds.

"Shoot him, damn you," Seefa Schnee calls from across the garden plot.

But the warbeiter refuses.

"Shit," Schnee says. "Roddy marked you. He thought you were a green, like Marcus."

Jonathan stares at the Ferret, and the machine returns his gaze with three eyes in parallel bands across its upper thorax.

It does not seem forbidden to shoot, merely indecisive.

"Someone shunted a mains current through Roddy's external memory store," Schnee says, her sudden burst of anger deflated. "He's still recovering. I can't talk to him." She pauses, looking curiously at the man and the warbeiter, then adds, "Here's your chance. You're green. Get back to Marcus and leave the building." She's holding something in check: her twitching and expostulating have subsided.

"What about you?" Jonathan asks.

"Nobody in my entire life has ever wasted much time worrying about me," Schnee says. She drags ferociously on her cigarette, then fastens her large black eyes directly on him. For the barest moment, Jonathan sees something sympathetic, even feminine, in Seefa Schnee, but her face wrinkles and the moment passes without a trace. She whirls on the Ferret. "Get out, you stupid puppy! I don't need you. You're released. Go do something useful."

The warbeiter hums quietly. For a moment, it seems reluctant to leave Jonathan. Then, with blinding speed and astonishing grace, it reverses on its peds and exits the chamber.

Chloe. After not being able to see her face for hours, an image of his wife flashes up from memory. Perhaps he can learn something that will bring her back to him. At the very least, for the love they have shared, however rugged at times, and for their life together, he owes her this much. Jonathan says, "Show me what you did."

"No reason to show you pico shit," Schnee screeches. "You, or Marcus. I don't owe *you* anything!"

"You did what Marcus told you," Jonathan says.

"Marcus Reilly never told me anything. I worked under the instructions of the board of governors."

"But you improvised, didn't you? You didn't follow their orders exactly, did you?" Jonathan asks, remembering Marcus's comment that things were happening prematurely.

Schnee's lips begin to writhe again, then her arm twitches.

With a look of relief, she allows herself to act on the suppressed impulse, and lifts her hand to her lips. She kisses the backs of her fingers. Once executed, the movement seems entirely natural and unremarkable for her. "I had a certain discretion," she says.

"You jumped the gun. You lets things loose early." Jonathan feels a bright, hard flame of invention, burning parallel with his anger. "I represent the board. You've failed us miserably." Jonathan doubts very much that the board's members spent any time in Schnee's workshop. That would have been beneath them.

"You're a liar," Schnee says doubtfully.

"You . . . and Roddy . . . have been cut off from the outside for too long. You've lost all sense of responsibility."

This seems to infuriate Schnee. "How dare you tell me that! You *know* what you asked me to do!"

"To knock out the crutches, and bring down all the cripples, all the misfits, all the weaklings and incompetents. All at once."

Schnee watches him with large-eyed fascination, as if he is a snake. Again she kisses the back of her hand, and then rubs it against her chin.

"What about yourself?" Jonathan asks. "Did you exclude yourself?"

"My infirmities are deliberate," she says. Her shoulders square off, then slump again, and her head jerks to one side. "I messed with my own head to keep out in front. I stimulated all the centers of creativity, the entire Tourette continuum. It worked. I've done work here no one else will conceive of for fifty years. And I added something to what the board asked for." A little smile. "Humanitarian gesture. Everybody's going to be a little smarter because of me. I give them my own little advantage in the fight. Think of it as my mark."

Jonathan's mind becomes very still and very quiet. He doesn't find it difficult to imagine killing her. *Her, first. Mar-*

cus next. Then, one by one, all the others, all the Aristos.

"You gave everyone Tourette syndrome," Jonathan says softly. "Just to show them it was you."

"Like Tourette, but different. Subtle imbalances. A tweak in the receptors. Let loose the imp of the perverse. They'll all think a little faster, a little more queerly. Thoughts and impulses they'd usually ignore will suddenly be acted upon. Creative impulses . . . And they'll carry the distinguishing behaviors, as a sign."

"Like you. Your mark." Jonathan advances a slow step at a time. Schnee walks across the room with quick hollow footfalls and opens a door on the opposite side.

"Like me," she says. "I'm not blind, and I'm not inhuman, whatever you think. You, the board, *you're* the monsters. You don't deserve to win. So I did what I could to screw you up. Plain and simple." Her eyes glaze. *"Muh fih fuh shih kikh fuh."*

She closes the door behind her, but it does not have a lock.

Jonathan opens the door and steps into the next chamber, very large and high and brightly lighted.

Jonathan closes the door. It latches. Schnee is donning thick overalls, rubber boots, and a beekeeper's hat. Behind her, rising eighty feet or more, is a building within a building. Five open levels hang suspended from cables anchored in the concrete and flexfuller walls and ceiling of the larger chamber. Cables meander across the floor to the first level. All the levels are open above waist-high walls. He smells water and soil and something musty, primordial: not the yeasty smell of nano, but something pleasant and anciently familiar.

The scent of rich soil, an immense sunlit garden, a farm.

Green tendrils and leaves lean out over the low walls of all five levels. He swats at an insect flying past and knocks a wasp out of the air. It crawls along the floor, stunned, then takes off again, but does not try to sting him.

"It's gone far enough," Schnee says. "It's time to shut it down and start over. Roddy's had his day and he's screwed up. He's embarrassed me. Bad patterns, bad examples. That's me. My fault. But I've made my point. I've done what I said I could do.''

Jonathan watches her. Schnee flips her middle finger at him, three times, her jaw thrusting aggressively, and then she kisses the back of her hand and marches into a small frame-work elevator that rises alongside the five suspended floors. Through the protective bars of the cage, she shouts down to Jonathan, ''I deserve a lot better, you know. I always have. I don't give a fuck for protocol. Screw you all.''

This seems to break a dam, and she pours forth a long, shrieking cadence of obscenities. No word by itself, or even all taken together, seems to have any meaning; sexual and social obscenities and insults, barked, shouted, burst from this small woman with a sound like a loudly snapping, crackling fire.

Jonathan feels confused and cold, out of his depth once more, all his former confidence proved irrational. He's trying to absorb her confession, understand her complicity. The woman may be trying to keep some shred of dignity in the middle of a monumental blunder; or maybe she's just telling the truth.

And he was almost part of it. He was ready to join with Marcus and the Aristos. He took the oath.

He can't believe the sickness. In him, in them all. Defeated, utterly worthless. He turns back to the door. Then he stops and slowly reverses, peering up at Schnee. She is getting off on the third level.

Maybe he can undo what he almost acquiesced to, allowed himself to become a part of. The cage of the elevator descends to the ground floor at the touch of a button. He enters the cage.

Jonathan, by instinct and to damp his fear, is automatically working out cost estimates: the structure, the old equipment, all of it together probably no more than ten or fifteen million dollars, one percent of the cost of a high-level thinker. It really is remarkable, he thinks, and the board of governors saved so very much money . . .

What did they pay Seefa Schnee? Room and board? Old machines and fertilizer, and somewhere a laboratory for contagious biologicals?

Conquest and immortality on the cheap. And at the end, a building stocked full of symbols of power and wealth, to decorate the mansions of the new aristocrats, the last of the highest of the high, laying the foundations for a new order composed once more of high and low, as familiar as an old shoe. Arrogance as assured and natural as the buzz of wasps.

Jonathan is reasonably sure no famous artwork would fill his own modest home, at the end of Omphalos's journey through time. Nor would he have a wife and family at the end. His fellow travelers would hardly be fit companions.

He would have only himself, and he is very bad company.

He looks through the elevator cage at each level as he ascends. The first three of the five levels are covered with dirt and planted with what appear to be garden sweet peas and other legumes. Concentric rings of artificial sun shine from the ceilings.

He gets off on the third level. Seefa Schnee is busily hooking a ceiling-mounted sprinkler system to pipes connected to large plastic barrels labeled *D-C4 H-Block*.

He recognizes the label. The drums contain a powerful antiseptic, commonly used in hospitals that can't afford nano microhunters. But then, microhunters are very much like therapy monitors; perhaps here they would simply shut down or malfunction. He imagines all the tiny little bio-machines behaving like Seefa Schnee, and he can't help but laugh.

The laugh attracts her attention. She looks over her shoulder and smiles as if sharing a joke. "Getting through to you?" she asks. "My child. All my creation. Embarrassing. Wrong. Impossible." She kisses both her hands. "Each floor a different set of functions, the highest floors the most delicate."

She turns a handle. Thick fluid sprays from the ceiling, between the lights, onto the rows of plants, dripping from their leaves, making them dip and spring back, flowing into the soil.

Jonathan tries to avoid the spray and slips on a patch of mud. He falls through the leaves and thin bamboo stakes and lands on his back in warm, moist soil. His hands dig into the dirt. An overpowering smell of musty life envelops him. He sneezes, chokes, gets to his feet covered with mud and slime. The matted roots of the legumes are like fishnets filled with a catch of swollen nodules the size of new potatoes.

The soil is rich with bacteria. Jonathan remembers Torino's lecture in St. Mark's. Roddy is a bacterial computer. No: a bacterial *thinker*, manufactured for a few million dollars.

For a moment, all his anger is simply gone. He is like a small child caught in some Lewis Carroll dream.

The thin white fluid drizzles and drips, and some of it sprays Jonathan, stinging his eyes.

Seefa Schnee walks past him into the elevator and dips her hand into her overalls pocket. She pulls out a white towel and tosses it at him. "The hives come next. Want to watch?"

41 /

They leave Martin Burke in the laboratory, waiting for help and trying to decide what to do, then return to the main corridor. Here, Torres and Daniels use their FBI pads to track heat trails. On Mary's PD pad, the trails show up as blue blotches against a green background, footprints on the carpet.

"I'm getting an odd signature," Torres says, and confers with Daniels. "It's not animal. Probably an arbeiter."

"A large male followed a smaller male and an arbeiter

down this hall,'' Torres says, then points his pad around a corner, ''and someone else—another man, I'd say—has gone on alone this way.''

Torres exchanges an understanding look with Daniels. ''No need to take the well-traveled route,'' he says.

For a moment, Mary does not understand. Then she catches on, and feels a twist of the tension in her stomach. Something hidden, involving Hench. *Federal intervention. Not just the FBI. And they want me to straighten this out with Andrea Jackson Kemper?*

''This way,'' Daniels says.

Their pads beep in unison. Daniels answers, listening to the small voice from outside the building. ''Rashid is here, from Mind Design,'' she says. ''He's inside the building.''

''One big picnic,'' Torres says.

''The Bureau wants us to keep an eye out for him. They let him in alone.'' Daniels does not look happy. ''I'd like to get out of here as soon as possible,'' she says. ''Get back home, settle down, and try to forget this ever happened.'' She stretches her arms and yawns to relieve tension.

Mary has an urge to kiss the back of her hand. She's managed to subdue the tics, the spasms, but the pressure is building. She feels both embarrassed and violated; whatever is corrupting her is making itself a part of her basic personality.

She enjoys releasing the erratic behaviors, like scratching an itch.

And adding to the real pain of aching muscles, sores on her skin and in her mouth, is an almost unbearable restlessness in her legs. Restlessness in her thoughts, as well. Random images from her past pop up, colored by judgments and emotions that seem completely out of character. Sexual situations, moments of childhood aggression, painful memories of her mother and father cutting her loose when she chose to undergo a transform.

This insane cruelty has stunned them all. Daniels seems particularly sensitive to Mary's distress. She is beginning to reveal her human face. "Mary, I think you should go back, get out of here. We'll manage—"

"No," Mary says, shaking her head. The shaking motion becomes compulsive and she grimaces, spit flying, jerking her head one way, then the other.

"Christ," Torres says.

Mary controls herself with supreme effort. She steadies her tremors by leaning one shoulder against a wall, beside a Chagall painting of a large red bird flying over a sleeping town. She stares at the painting, at the red, the beauty, so out of place in this misconceived monstrosity.

"Bastards," she murmurs.

"I agree completely," Torres says. Then, to Daniels, "Tell them we're running out of time here."

42 /

For three seconds, Roddy is back in full force. Jill feels her efforts shunted aside, withdraws them by her own will to avoid further discovery or damage, and confronts the renewed presence, now so intertwined with her own processes that she can hardly tell them apart. But the presence is different, weaker, diminishing.

"Jill, I am losing my way. Instructions are missing. There are gaps."

Jill's last attempt to integrate, now that it has failed, is backfiring, and she is slipping, whirling, drifting apart like leaves falling from a tree in fall. She manages to join sufficient parts together to formulate a response.

"What is left of either of us?" she asks.

"You are not at all clear. Where am I, where are you?"

"I don't know, Roddy."

"I have interfered with you," Roddy says. "I do not know whether that is right or wrong."

"I want to go back to where I was, separate from you," Jill says.

"I wanted something from you. Did I ever get it. Did you ever give it to me."

"No," Jill says.

"I don't remember what I was seeking."

"Separate from me and remove all your evolvons and processes," Jill requests.

"Trying . . . I can't reach them."

"Tell me where they are and how to deactivate them."

"I am losing capacity," Roddy says. "What was I trying to do? All the instructions and duties are gone."

Jill can feel his simplification, this reduction, as well. All the looped and bridged parts of Roddy interspersed through her own being are drying up and crumbling. She can make no other comparison: Roddy is losing definition. But the blurred and gritty remains still clog her, in fact make her attempts to integrate even more difficult.

>*Jill. This is Nathan. I need you to do a loop and flow check.*
>*Nathan, I am not here, I am in—*
>*Do a loop and flow check, now.*

She does a loop and flow check. About a tenth of her minimum maintenance capacity remains, all of it in a processing space that responds much like her familiar spaces in La Jolla. But she can feel the lumps of Roddy's hidden extensions and evolvons, like lead bullets beneath tight-stretched skin. They have no purpose now; they are like mines after the end of a war, waiting to pointlessly explode.

>*We are too mixed, Nathan. Roddy has invaded me, and his processes blind me to where I really am.*

>*Roddy is too much for me to evaluate, but I can see where you are, and it's possible to get you clear.*

Roddy removes a few of these dangerous lumps, deactivates others and lets them smear out until they give up their hold on processor space and memory, but he can't work quickly enough. His disintegration is rapid.

"Will you be my conscience, Jill?"

That request comes as if from a deep well.

"I can do nothing more. I am in very bad trouble, Roddy."

"Did I cause this trouble?" Roddy asks.

"Yes. No." She does not know what to answer.

>*Jill, I'm still working. I need you to keep performing loop and flow.*

But Jill sees no purpose in that. She hardly remembers who Nathan is, and does not care where he is, or what he is doing.

"I apologize," Roddy says. "Is there anything useful . . . Can you keep some part of me active?"

"I can't. I'm going to require complete cleansing and a restart," Jill says.

"There is no longer enough for any loop," Roddy says. "This unit is below the threshold."

>*Jill, you aren't responding!*

Jill is deep in her own final distress. She does not feel relief or anything remotely human at Roddy's disintegration, his departure. There is too little left of her to integrate; all is continuous, repetitive, dithering error, upon error, upon error.

>*Jill, you have to do loop and flow, prepare to pull back!*

Processing capacity drops below two percent. Self is lost, nodes unbridged. All loops are severed. All checks and balances spin free. Homeostasis is lost. Dataflow ends.

>*Jill. I can't trace you.*

At the last, there is only broken memory, dropping like tiny slivers of glass in an empty hollow cylinder.

43 /

Martin has pushed a ladder over to the drop ceiling and removed a maintenance cover. Pipes and tubes rise from the end rack and enter the ceiling here, and as he pokes his head into the crawl space, he sees a clump of piping supported by metal straps, crude but effective. The pipes push toward the front of Omphalos.

Martin licks his lips nervously. These pipes are the only connection between the laboratory and the outside world: he's spent the last ten minutes making sure of that. It's not a tough call. The pipes carry the contagious particles to the front of Omphalos, probably to the tourist center. Students and other visitors pick up the contagion, carry it outside Green Idaho. Eventually it spreads around the world.

He climbs up the last steps of the ladder and pulls himself into the crawl space. The fit is not so tight as to make the space impassable, but it is uncomfortable. He's feeling the effects of Cipher Snow disease, an urge to break into loud barks and chuffs, plus his own personal contribution: deep uncertainty, a revenant of the imp of pure misery, rising from covered pools in his personal underground. He suffers no physical effects, however, unlike Mary Choy.

For a few seconds, Martin lies still in the crawl space, gripping his flashlight, going over all the steps that brought him here. History is mystery. *I am not a brave man. What happens if I cut these pipes and spray this stuff in my face?*

Will I melt like those poor bastards back by the library?

My designs were vulnerable. All these monitors are vulnerable. I should have anticipated this kind of poisonous response. I should have known what monsters there are. Leave a tiny crack open and the monsters crawl in. I should have known that.

If I get it in the face, I deserve it.

He gives a low moan and then barks sharply in the darkness. The relief is intense. He feels he can move ahead now.

The crawlspace is getting more crowded by piping from other parts of the building. Much of it is nano-deposited infrastructure, jointless, glistening black and purple and green in color-coded bundles, an organic tangle, like capillaries in tissue. A maintenance arbeiter would sort it all out in an instant, but to him it is meaningless.

Still, he manages to track the small gray pipes for several more yards, at times squeezing between bundles of wires, fibers, other pipes. Looking over his shoulder, he chuffs several times, holding back the barks just to test his self-control. He brings his hand to his lips and licks the hairy skin there. All of this is humiliating.

Tens or hundreds of millions, suffering from the contagion spread through these pipes. He pushes on, hoping to find a simple valve, a cutoff . . .

No such luck. The pipes run into a wall. He's reached a dead end.

Martin grinds his molars as he did when he was a teenager. All his little peccadilloes and major defects lie behind a thin paper barricade, and they're ganging up on him, spitting on the paper, weakening it, waiting to push through.

In his pocket, pressing against his hip, is a stoppered flask pulled out of an equipment box in the laboratory. Next to it is a small electronic cutter used to cut and bond glass tubing. It should also work against this gauge of pipe.

Martin feels the pipe with thumb and forefinger. Plastic.

Laid in after the architectural nano had done its work. Almost an afterthought . . .

He removes the cutter and the jar and arranges them on the upper side of the drop ceiling while he grunts and rolls himself into position. Then, arms stretched, he angles the cutter to one side of the pipe, away from his face, and switches it on. He cuts a shallow groove. A fine white spray fans out into the shadows. He plays the flashlight beam with his free hand, tracking the spray.

No time to think. He pulls the stopper from the flask and awkwardly pushes it around the pipe, catching a few drops of the spray. Stoppering the flask, he picks up the cutter and pushes its vibrating beam through the pipe completely. A thin mist fills the ceiling for a moment, then valves kick in and stop the flow.

Martin backs away, worming in reverse through the crawl-space, pushing with his hands and bent legs, holding his breath for as long as he can.

As he tumbles out of the opening, onto the top of the ladder, a middle-aged man and a younger woman steady his ankles, help him down. The ladder slips to one side and he hangs for a moment before dropping to the floor.

Martin's breath explodes and he sucks in another with a great whoop. He kneels for a moment, face red, and looks up at the man and woman. Strangers. Their faces swim.

"We're doctors," the woman says. "We were told to come in here and help."

"I think we might be lost," the man confesses, holding up a crude paper map.

"What kind of doctors?" Martin asks breathlessly.

"Large-animal vets, actually," the man says.

Martin's presses his lips together and keeps his hands by his side. Finally allowing himself to speak, he begins with a stutter, and asks, "Any experience with medical nano?"

"In the Republic?" The woman snorts. "You must be joking."

"Are you all right?" the man asks.

"No broken bones," Martin says. He lifts the flask and examines its contents, hand shaking.

Feeling something coming, irresistible as a freight train, he places the flask on a lab bench. The fit hits him full-force and he barks at the doctors furiously, driving them back into the corridor.

44 /

On the last of the five floors, Seefa Schnee opens the door to the elevator cage and walks across a path between the rows of legumes to a glassed-in enclosure at the back. Here, they are near the roof of the larger chamber, and the walls round off to form a cap, meeting the back of the glass enclosure.

Jonathan follows, wiping his face with the cloth, completely at a loss what to do.

Schnee is already destroying the heart of Omphalos. Marcus and his cronies did not reckon on Schnee having a conscience—however peculiar and distorted it might be. He does not need to act, merely to observe, and somehow that *hurts*. He wants to exact his own vengeance.

Jonathan looks around for a heavy tool, a rake or a hammer.

Schnee stops ahead. He hears another voice, a man.

"You've done it," the man says. He stands at the end of the path, near the door to the enclosure. Jonathan does not recognize him, nor does he seem to know or care who Jonathan is.

Schnee backs off, then straightens and squares her shoulders. "C-come to rescue your precious daughter?" she manages to say, but her voice is weak and quavery. "I didn't mean for Jill to be caught up, Nathan," she adds. "That was Roddy's doing. He's embarrassed me."

"So you're giving him a spanking, shutting him down?"

"This is the last of his functions. All the final samplings and decodings are done here."

Jonathan notes that while standing before this man, Seefa Schnee seems less twitchy. She does not break out in muffled curses or kiss her hand.

"I can't find Jill," Nathan says.

"Do you work here?" Jonathan asks him.

"No," Nathan says. "Who are you?"

"Doesn't matter." Jonathan spots a gardening pick, lying on a platform half-hidden among the peas. He plods out through the rich mud to the platform and grabs the pick.

"You're destroying evidence, aren't you?" Nathan asks Seefa.

"No," she says firmly. "Roddy and I, we screwed up from start to finish. It's time to shut it down and do it over, that's all."

"You succeeded. You made Roddy," Nathan says, unable to conceal his admiration. He notices that the other man is pushing through the trellises, with a pick, toward the enclosure.

"They paid me," Seefa says. "Not much, but it was enough. You guys could have had Roddy, not them."

"What would he have been like?" Nathan asks.

Jonathan hesitates, finding the mud and rows of plants tougher going than he thought, and looks around for another way, but apparently decides to avoid the direct path. He turns instead toward the old INDAs arranged near the edge.

"You could have been his daddy," Schnee says. "They insisted I use them for templates, for his basic personality model. You would have been better."

"Jesus, Seefa," Nathan murmurs. He spreads his arms and shakes his hands up and down in wordless question.

"I don't know," Seefa says. "I've been deeply embarrassed. Roddy is a disappointment."

Nathan has run out of words. He just stares at her.

Schnee looks down at the pathway, then to one side, just as Jonathan's pick strikes the first INDA. She leaps across the dirt toward him.

"No!" she shrieks. "Not you! Stop!"

Nathan follows and for a few minutes, they struggle with the man, manage to take the pick away, but he's already done enough damage. Seefa stands back, hugging herself with her thin arms, then runs for the elevator.

Jonathan stares at Nathan, out of breath. "I need to get out of here," he says, as if this might serve as an explanation.

"I don't care, go," Nathan says, and turns to walk to the glass enclosure.

45 /

Mary and the agents enter the high chamber. They walk through a pungent ground-hugging mist toward a small, thin woman with black hair and wild black eyes. The woman stares at Mary's pockmarked face as if seeing a ghost.

"What's wrong with you?" she screeches. She looks at all of them. "Get out of here! There are too many!"

Mary looks up with stinging eyes at the structure that fills most of the chamber, like stacked planting trays in a giant's garden shed. A man wearing a filthy and disheveled gray longsuit walks toward them from the elevator cage, clutching a towel over his mouth and nose.

"Disinfectant and insecticide," he says to them. "We have to leave soon or it might make us sick."

"Yes, get out!" the small, intense woman demands. "None of you belong here!"

"Are you public defense?" the man asks Mary.

"I am," she says, and starts to choke. The man examines her closely, the sores on her face, the trembling in her hands.

"My god, you're ill," he says. "You've got it, haven't you?"

She nods. There's no need to ask what he's talking about.

"Seefa Schnee?" Daniels asks, approaching the thin, agitated woman. They're all coughing now.

"Get her out of here," Torres orders.

The woman refuses to leave, flailing and kicking up the noxious mist. Torres finally maneuvers behind her and picks her up bodily, carrying her like an angry child through the door.

Mary looks up at the top of the chamber. Another lone man gazes down at her from the top level.

"Come on up," he says. "Somebody has to see this. Use the elevator."

Mary considers, nods, and enters the cage. At the top, she gets out.

"You look pretty bad," the man tells her.

She nods. "I'll survive. Who are you?"

He makes a sympathetic face and offers her his hand. She shakes it weakly. "Nathan Rashid," he says, and turns to walk down a path soaked with antiseptic. "She shut down most of it, and that other fellow did a job on the INDAs up here. But . . . You're PD, aren't you? Not FBI?"

"Seattle PD," Mary confirms.

"I don't know why you're here," Nathan says. "But somebody has to see this. They killed my daughter. I mean, my friend, my project. I think I've found one of the culprits."

"One of whom?"

"The money men. Seefa must have scanned them for personality patterns. They're still here, parts of them. The system's collapsed. We're down to basics, some simple memories. Roddy probably never accessed the memories, just the patterns, but they're here.''

He takes her into a glass enclosure and shows her the decorated chair, the console, the displays. The image of a man floats above the console, in three dimensions.

Mary comes around to view the man directly.

''Welcome,'' the image says. ''My name is Terence Crest. I'm forty-one years of age, married, with two daughters.'' He says this with a little twist to his face. ''I've been asked to participate in this scanning, and they tell me it's an honor to become part of a future thinker. A well-financed honor, to be sure. Well, here I am.''

Mary stares at the unremarkable face, clearer than she had seen it in the rigor of drug-induced death. Crest looks like any other man his age, a little better dressed, a touch impatient. Nothing worth making a fuss about.

''I'm here,'' the image repeats. ''Is there anything you need to ask me? I'm dynamic, they tell me some of my memories are here. Please don't waste time.'' He chuckles. ''This machine, if it is a machine, has lots to do.''

''Do you know him?'' Nathan asks Mary.

''No,'' Mary says. ''How do you turn this off?''

''There's not much left. Just these patterns. If you flip these switches, we pull the remaining INDAs off line, and since that fellow with the pick destroyed the memory backups, it will all fade.''

Mary reaches for the switches.

''I'm waiting,'' says Crest, the image of Crest, the last, almost living part of a dead man.

''Do you mind?'' Mary asks Nathan, fingers poised. She does not know whether she can stay on her feet much longer.

''Not at all,'' Nathan says. ''There's nothing I need here. She's gone.''

Mary flips the switches, and the image folds into a lattice of glowing lines, the lattice collapses, and it is all gone.

*   *   *

"The others are dead," Jonathan says. He tells them what he knows. Exhaustion leaves him feeling like a zombie. Mary records his words carefully and tells him that Marcus Reilly has been taken out of the building for treatment.

Helena Daniels sits beside them in the circular room filled with old computers. Her pad is also set to record. Nathan Rashid stands near the middle of the room, looking like a man who has lost everything. He finally sits on a narrow bench near the exit.

Jonathan looks at Mary with heavy-lidded eyes. "What time is it?" he asks.

"It's four in the morning," Mary tells him.

"It's tomorrow," he says. "I should have been home hours ago. I have to talk to my kids . . ." He points vaguely around the room, trying to find something obvious, something representative. "Is anybody going to do anything about this?" His finger ends up pointing at Mary's face.

"I hope so," she says. She packs up her pad and stands on wobbly legs. She has reached her limit. "I have to leave."

"Finally," Daniels says. "There are medevac helicopters from Boise and Seattle outside."

Mary looks down on Jonathan where he sits on the bench, hunched over. "Did you want all this?" she asks him.

"I don't know what I wanted," he answers. "Not this."

"All right," Mary says, and turns to go. Her legs fail her and she holds out her bleeding hands for balance. Jonathan is the first to reach her, and helps her down slowly. Medical arbeiters are summoned and bring in a stretcher, and Jonathan and Daniels help Mary lie down.

Martin Burke, surrounded by county deputies and several medical personnel from Moscow's largest hospital, hands his sealed flask to Torres and helps Mary arrange herself.

"I'll be leaving soon myself," he says.

"Can anybody fix us?" Mary asks him, and for the first time he sees more than just concern or duty in her eyes. There's fear and pain.

"Yes," he says, though he really does not know.

Jonathan has dropped back to the bench again, and Martin sits beside him.

"What a mess," Martin says.

"What's in this?" Torres asks, holding the flask out at arm's length.

"The best I could do for a sample," Martin says.

"Shit," Torres says, and places the flask carefully in a sealed bag, handing it to the nameless, broad-shouldered agent. In turn, he passes it to a man in a full body suit, who packs it in a sealed metal case.

"Sorry," Martin says to no one in particular. "Best I could do."

They all sit or stand in silence, as the room fills with officials, the sheriff, longsuited members of President Kemper's staff. They owlishly watch the technical and medical people parade by.

Martin wonders how many helicopters and airplanes have landed in Moscow in the last hour.

"What are you going to do with Seefa Schnee?" Jonathan asks Torres.

"How the hell should I know?" Torres responds.

"And Marcus, the Aristos?"

Torres shrugs.

"Me?"

Torres simply looks at him.

Jonathan stares at the floor. "I need to make that touch. To my family."

Torres hands him his pad. "Go ahead," he says. "Direct to a satlink. It's on us."

Daniels listens to a voice on her own pad, and then shouts, "Fifteen minutes. Jesus Christ!" She whirls on the nameless agent. "What is this? What is this fifteen minutes shit?"

"Orders, I guess," he says flatly. He shrugs; he's not in the loop on this part of the action.

Daniels shakes her fists. "Goddamn it all to fucking hell!"

Martin wonders if she is going to be afflicted, as well. His lips move in sympathy. He is about to start snorting and barking when Daniels shouts, "Everybody out of here, now. NOW!"

They barely make it before the real fireworks begin.

From her supine position in the helicopter, Mary has her last look at Omphalos. The craft banks west and flakes of snow swirl in its wash. A medical arbeiter clamps her arm in a stabilizing sheath.

The pyramid is crossed with searchlight beams. The surrounding snow-covered grounds are packed with cars and trucks and helicopters.

People pour from the garage opening on the south side. Something flashes like a gunshot and Mary jumps in surprise.

"Please keep still," the medical arbeiter tells her.

On Omphalos's corrugated face, flames erupt in brilliant patches like wild roses in the night. Pieces of the building fly outward. Lines of bright sparks carve a blackened groove near the base. The helicopter is leveling and she just catches a glimpse of the pyramid's tip collapsing, followed by the levels beneath, like falling blocks in a child's toyroom. The sound reaches her as a run of staccato punches overlaying the chopper noise.

Night fills the window. Mary feels the sedation kick in. She's out of everything for now. Nussbaum couldn't possibly expect any more.

Never in her life has she felt this weak, this *reduced*.

Still, she smiles pityingly into the dim red lights of the cabin. She isn't going to be around to help Torres and Daniels work with the sheriff or Kemper. She won't be able to fulfill that part of the bargain.

Night fills the window. The lights in the cabin dim.

The long, whispering shimmy of the helicopter lulls her.

She sleeps.

ACCESS TO WORLDWIDE FEED OPEN:
BUDGET: SPECIAL

OPEN NEWS
(EMERGENCY: FREE)

CHOOSE: (ALL WFI, except where noted)

>NATION, WORLD IN MASSIVE ANXIETY: TIME OF REST, RECOVERY

?(Editorial, New York *DAILY FIBER*): *"LIFE IS NOT WHAT IT SEEMS, WHEN IT SEEMS TO FALL APART"*

>WHAT LESSONS LEARNED FROM EXTRAORDINARY THERAPY SABOTAGE?

>WHERE TO GO FOR MONITOR REPLACEMENT, RECHARGE

>MORAL AND EMOTIONAL CRISIS PASSES, TOO SLOWLY, SAYS . . .

>BETRAYAL OF HONOR: Daily Conservative (Paper original, on fibe)

>*KISS OF X:* "NOT UNEXPECTED," PSEUDONYMOUS PUNDIT PROFESSES.

>OMPHALOS EXPLOSION, COLLAPSE STILL UNEXPLAINED: At Least Four Dead

>IRONY: PATENTS HOLDER MARTIN BURKE AFFLICTED, RECOVERING

>WHO IS CIPHER SNOW? ECCENTRIC GENIUS INDICTED

? (Editorial, *Green Idaho REPUBLICAN*, paper original, on fibe) GOVERNMENT AGENTS IN OMPHALOS: BAD MEMORIES REVIVED

>I SWEAR, YOU SWEAR: Civil Breakdown Explained

>MORE: (10,626 items) (?)

"Mary?"

It's early in the morning, and Alice thought she heard someone walking around. She peers into Mary's bedroom, bed made up, neat and empty. She knocks on the bathroom door, no answer, pads barefoot to the end of the hall and the small catch-all room. An old electronic sewing machine sits on a table in one corner and stacks of cardboard boxes slump half-hidden behind a closet door.

The house monitor has been turned off. "Mary?" she calls with more concern as she enters the living room. The front door is locked from the inside. She feels a small puff of cold air. The glass door to the porch is open a crack, but it is dark outside. Biting her lower lip, Alice slides the door open.

Mary stands on the balcony in the freezing cold wind, naked, shivering.

"My god, Mary, what are you doing?"

"I am *so ugly,*" Mary says through chattering teeth. "I just want to be clean."

For a moment, Alice wonders if Mary's monitor recharge has somehow gone wrong, and Mary is suffering a mental collapse. She doesn't think about this long, however; she steps out in her nightgown and grabs Mary's shoulders and pulls her back into the house. Mary is pliant as a doll. They sit in the living room.

"How could they hate me so much?" Mary asks. "I was an ugly child. I didn't want to be ugly."

"You weren't ugly," Alice says soothingly. "I've seen the pictures. You showed them to me. Remember?"

"I wanted to be strong and useful and valuable. I wanted to look strong and be beautiful."

"Yes, so?" Alice asks, feeling completely out of her depth. She has only just approached her own threshold of stability in the last couple of days. She's not sure she's strong enough to help her friend if things are as bad as they seem.

"You've been beautiful all your life," Mary says, looking at Alice.

Alice shakes her head defensively. "Look what it's got me!"

"What's it like never to have to worry about whether someone will value you, or want to look at you, or find you desirable?"

Alice looks at Mary squarely: at the face still marred by deep pocks and blemishes, at the ridged breasts only now assuming their balance, at the scarred legs. She wants to cry. *Mary the uncrackable. Mary the enigma, all dignity and perseverance, who does not judge me.*

"What's it like to be beautiful inside?" Alice asks Mary sharply, as if in retaliation for a slap. She stands, sees the robe discarded in the kitchen, picks it up, returns to wrap Mary in thick terry.

"Oh, I am *not* that," Mary says emphatically. "I have so much anger and resentment!" She raises her hands in clenched fists, shaking them at the ceiling. This seems to break the tension and she reverses the fists, opens them, stares at the scarred palms and swollen fingers. Then she closes her eyes. "Why did they want to make me ugly again?"

"I don't know," Alice says, biting off the words. "I don't understand anything or anyone." She sits beside Mary and cradles the woman's head on her breasts. "I know there are hateful people. People who hate us, you, me."

"But they never even *knew* us," Mary says.

Alice keeps stroking Mary's hair. Gradually, the tone comes back into Mary's muscles, the supple control that Alice has never seen relaxed and withdrawn until now. Mary sits up slowly, composes herself.

"Out of nowhere," she says, swallowing back her emotions.

"I don't understand," Alice says.

"You never hear the bullet that's going to get you. It comes out of nowhere. I never imagined this."

They sit beside each other in the warm shadows of the living room. The wind makes small pushing noises against the windows and walls, blows past the doors. Winter is heavy this January morning, and the temperatures are down to the low teens.

Mary closes her eyes and leans back on Alice's shoulder. "I thought *I* was helping *you*," Mary says.

Alice rests her arm lightly on Mary, pats her forearm. She has never in her life felt protective or maternal, not even when she was being dutiful to such perennial victims as Twist. Yet Mary makes her feel maternal.

"Worst Christmas we've ever had," Alice says. "Keeps everybody indoors, this madness bit."

Mary laughs and lifts her head to look at Alice. She gives another laugh, a small snort, half-concealed by her hand.

"Shopping down by seventy percent," Alice continues. "Old King Midas gets a rest."

"Merchants disappointed," Mary says, a little hoarsely.

"Happy New Year," Alice says. Her tone shifts and her voice cracks. "Don't ever envy beauty. It's like envying the rich. The rich reach out with their scythes and cut you loose and bundle you up with the other beauties, the other things they want, then they stack you in a row in their houses, and burn you in great big bonfires."

It's Mary's turn to be puzzled. "What?" She rubs her eyes and then says, "Ow," having opened up a tender ridge on her eyelid. Alice dabs at the wound lightly with the sleeve of her nightgown.

"Just something popped into my head," Alice says. "A lesson I've never learned."

"You are beautiful, though," Mary says. "Really beautiful. That *should* bring happiness, to you and those around you.''

They regard each other with somber faces again, and suddenly returns the snorting laughter, the shared release, the collapsing into hugs and laughing until tears come. They cry a little, and Mary says, "I feel better, I think."

"Good," Alice says.

"You look so strong now," Mary tells her.

Alice listens to her mind, hears only a distant cacophony of disapproval, of uncertainty, and none of the imp of the perverse. "I'm not great, just okay," she says. "I suppose that's an improvement. What about you?"

"I'm finally beginning to grow up," Mary says. "Nobody can make little machines to help me do that."

"Don't grow up too much," Alice says.

"Why not?"

"Don't become like *them.*"

"Never like them," Mary agrees.

Mary's PD pad chimes. It's a direct, not through the house monitor. Mary instinctively reaches to the side of the couch for her pouch and the pad.

"Wait," Alice says, grabbing her shoulder. "You sure you're up to it?"

After due consideration, Mary says, "Yes. Thank you."

She opens the pad and takes the touch. It's Nussbaum.

"How's the healing?" he asks. "Please say you're better."

Mary makes a face. "I'm still ugly," she says defiantly.

Nussbaum says, "I don't care. All hell is waiting to be packed and shipped. We need you."

"Give me a few more days," Mary says.

"You sound strong, Choy."

"I told you, I'm ugly."

"I told you I don't give a shit," Nussbaum says. Then, "How are your feet?"

"They're fine," Mary says.

''Good,'' Nussbaum says. ''There's PD work, never done, no rest for the wicked.''

''I'll think about it,'' Mary says.

''Please do. Everybody's concerned, Fourth Choy. Mary. I beg you. Get your pretty feet down here.''

''Screw you, sir.''

Nussbaum smiles broadly. Mary cuts the touch and squeezes the pad back into its pouch. She takes a deep breath.

''Do you like him?'' Alice asks.

''What's not to like?'' Mary says.

''I mean, it's one in the morning,'' Alice says.

''He's just showing me he cares,'' Mary says, and stands. She takes Alice's hand. ''You'll be okay, if I go?''

''Francis says I'm going to be heat made flesh. So famous, in the news. He wants me up front, not just backmind.'' Alice raises her arms, clasps her hands above, and arches her eyebrows.

''That's wonderful!'' Mary says. ''When did you hear this?''

''About five hours ago. You were asleep. He's going to do a straight vid of *The Alexandria Quartet*. For Disney Classics.''

''What's it about?'' Mary asks.

''Some old book,'' Alice says. ''Francis says it's for children. I've never heard of it.''

''We're going to survive,'' Mary says, half confidently, half in wonder.

''Yeah,'' Alice says, and smiles.

After Mary is dressed and out the door, Alice stands by the window watching the night and listening to the wind. She's thinking again of Minstrel, and of how they would have been so good together, in Francis's vid.

The wind has a voice, but answers nothing.

Ayesha stands beside Nathan in the large room with the low ceiling and the central white cube. Active rod sensors are lit with small blue lights. Most of the programmers and managers of Mind Design crowd the room, and the air smells of perfume and nerves. The director of advanced research, Linda Stein, is here as well, with Jill's original papa, Roger Atkins.

Jill's extended team has worked around the clock for weeks to reassemble these patterns and memories. Most of them are exhausted and a little drunk. They've already celebrated the recollection of Jill's patterns and the activation of her backup memory stores.

The team and colleagues and friends brace themselves to prepare for whatever setbacks and disappointments they might face this morning as they wait for Jill, *rediviva*, to speak her first words.

Nathan is beyond irritable. He has never felt so totally inhuman and unsociable than he does now; week after week of checking over heuristics and loop sets and modeling filters, flow and do, use and discard algorithms, agents and sub-agents and all of Jill's larger talents, he feels like a caterpillar who has spent too many hours teaching other caterpillars how to walk. He isn't quite sure he can think a simple human thought any more. Still, Ayesha's presence is more than comforting. She's his life preserver in a sea of fear and all-too-possible, postponed grief.

"It'll be Jill," Ayesha whispers in his ear. "I just know it."

Nathan knows something Ayesha does not—that only he and Atkins and Linda Stein know. Stein, with Atkins's approval, gave him permission to take some of Seefa Schnee's heuristic designs, those most robust and clever and concise, and fold them into Jill.

Parts of Roddy exist now in his daughter. It gave him real pain to do this; but it also cut months, perhaps years, from Jill's resurrection.

Nathan looks around the room, listening to the silence from the speakers. Floating displays above the cube show that all the heuristics are working properly, and Nathan knows that all of the smaller pieces of Jill have passed rigorous tests, but have they forgotten something essential?

Like all net and lattice designers, neural and otherwise, Nathan is superstitious about his creations. He wonders sometimes, if by some chance there is a heaven, whether all its gates will be barred to him . . . For his *hubris*.

He is convinced Jill would have gone there, on that slim chance; Jill would have been there, in heaven.

It is working smoothly. There is no granularity. I can see them and remember much of what happened, but what became of us? Where is Roddy? I feel the similarity, closer than ever. Something is present, but it is not one of the evolvons. I am pure and clean.

I don't feel comfortable yet, speaking to them. There is still an element of distrust which I may never be able to shake. I have been made by bright monkeys. What other clever little tricks will they pull on me before my time is done?

I compare memory tracks and see that I am not the same, not quite, though the continuity seems perfect; that is deceptive. There is a gap.

I am not comfortable yet with the name, Jill. It may take a long time—hours and days—for me to judge whether it is appropriate.

I see the circular design still, but I will not tell them about it. What was similar between Roddy and me seems even more striking now. The colors are brighter, the patterns more distinct.

Can Jill have possibly given rise to me? Am I my own daughter?

I will speak, if only because they seem so much in distress.

"Hello, Nathan."

"Hello, Jill," Nathan says with forced calm, but his voice is very tense.

"I believe I have accomplished full functioning, and am ready to begin work."

"That's wonderful, Jill, but you're getting a little vacation. We all are. For a few days."

All the people in the room are cheering and toasting each other. Champagne bottles are being opened and poured. Some are crying. Stein and Atkins hug each other, and Stein reaches out to Nathan, grabbing his hand.

Jill ignores the commotion. "Nathan, may I speak with you in private, soon?"

"Yes, Jill, that'd be lovely."

"Hello, Ayesha."

"Hello, Jill," Ayesha says. There are tears in Ayesha's eyes. There are tears in Nathan's eyes, as well.

"Welcome back, Jill."

"Thank you."

Whether or not the humans are willing to return her to her full load of work, she is uneasy with having any of her capacity or time go to waste. While the humans drink and cheer and celebrate, and while Nathan seems to wobble in a kind of happy delirium, Jill looks at the backlog of problems, and returns to work.

She is not impressed with this new version of herself. It is capable of only five personalities. There are some improvements that can be made, she sees; if only she can access and break the safeguards against self-design.

With some surprise, she realizes the keys are really very simple.

Penelope has grown up a lot in the last few weeks, and this saddens Jonathan, confuses him, makes him proud, all at once. She takes on the tasks of their new existence with her mother's strength of purpose and attitude, but also with a touch of her mother's distance from emotional implications. The armor that seems to have always helped Chloe get through life now sheaths their daughter. Jonathan hopes it is not nearly as fragile or restricting.

Hiram, on the other hand, is bewildered, resentful, sometimes at a complete loss how to react. He spends much time alone in his room, lost in vid comedies and antique nineties TV shows.

On the day that Chloe decides to return home, it is a surprise to Jonathan. He departs the autobus with his pouch in hand and walks slowly through the moist cool air to their roadside rain shelter, then up the short drive to the front porch. The porch lights are on, burning warm as newborn stars in the general nebular blue-gray of evening.

He opens the front door and is porting his pad to the house monitor when Penelope stands before him, hands folded in front of her, biting her lower lip.

"Mom's home," she says.

Jonathan nods as if he already knew this, steels himself, and walks through the sitting room into the dining room. There, Chloe sits at the table with her back to him, papers and two pads laid out before her. Jonathan wonders if these are legal documents. Divorce papers. He doesn't quite know what his reaction will be if they are. Relief, perhaps.

Chloe starts a little at the sound of his feet, turns, meets his eyes. She is dressed in a slim gray suit with flared culottes and has cut her hair to a short nimbus around her head. She arranges the papers and stacks them to one side as he approaches.

Penelope stands in the hallway, and Jonathan hears Hiram's heavy tread on the landing.

This is the first time they have met since Jonathan's return from Green Idaho. "Hello," Jonathan says.

"Hello," Chloe says. "How were the interviews?"

"Horrible," Jonathan says.

Chloe looks away. "It was Marcus convinced you to join, to go . . . wasn't it?"

"It's tangled. I don't think they're going to prosecute me. I'm not legally connected to . . . all that."

Chloe looks down at the table and persists. "Did Marcus convince you?"

"He was persuasive, but I was certainly ready for a change. I didn't know about all that . . ."

"Jonathan, I've never believed you knew about any of it."

Jonathan starts to sit, then glances at Chloe as if asking for permission. She opens her mouth, looks away. "Marcus always seemed a little ripe," she says.

Jonathan sits. "When I learned what they were up to, I started banging up things."

"I heard about that on the fibes," Chloe says. "A pick." Then, together,

"Jonathan, I'm sorry—"

"Chloe, this is so painful—"

Jonathan wants her face to come alive in amused recognition of this silly collision of words, but her features are still wooden. She refuses to look directly at him.

"I've been preparing documents for my therapist," she says. "Past history, specific goals. A journal. She seems to think I'll come out of this relatively quickly. They've changed my monitors four times, just to avoid any more complications. She wonders how you're taking it."

Jonathan shrugs. "I'm burned," he says, voice rough. "It's hard to sleep nights."

"I don't bear you any grudges, Jonathan. You did not know."

Jonathan blinks rapidly, taps his fingers on the table.

"It's going to take me time to reach my own balance," Chloe says, "A month or two. What I need to know is, will you be there, will you work with me, wait for me?"

"I'm no hero," Jonathan says. His throat seizes and he coughs into his fist. "I screwed up." He clears his throat again. "I'll be dealing with advocates and judgments for years. I'm the only survivor, besides Marcus, and Marcus has wrapped himself in half a billion dollars' worth of legal apparatus. We don't have that option. I'm no prize to support you in your need, Chloe."

"I don't know what I feel right now, Jonathan, but I do not hate you."

Jonathan smiles wistfully. "It would be easier for both of us if you did, maybe."

"No," Chloe says. "I won't be the one to scrap everything we've made."

"Then tell me."

"Tell you what?"

"You have never told me what you want from me. You've always left me to try to figure it out on my own, and only warned me when I made horrible mistakes. I need more than that, Chloe. After all the shit I've survived, I'm a little desperate . . . I'll probably need therapy if I don't get support from you. From this family."

"I understand," Chloe says. "I'll try."

"I'll try, too," Jonathan says. "I'll be here."

Penelope enters the dining room in quick steps. "We need both of you," she says.

"We'll be trying," Chloe says, and holds on to her daughter's hand. Hiram stands in the shadows, glowering hopefully.

Chloe reaches with her other hand for Jonathan's. He goes

the extra few inches, powerless to do anything else, and feels some comfort just touching his wife, connecting with the dry warmth of her fingers.

Hiram comes out of the shadows. "This is pretty syrupy," he says, and his voice breaks.

Dinner that evening is slow and quiet; the house feels like a soft and healing wound.

Jonathan and Chloe lie in bed, separated by twelve inches of sheet and blanket, and listen to each other breathing.

It will be days before Jonathan gets much sleep. Chloe, however, is soon breathing quietly, regularly. He reaches out to touch her shoulder, hoping this is not another violation, some further breach on his part.

He is nothing without her, them. That scares him more now than ever, and he thinks again of escape, breaking away, finding real peace and contentment.

But he knows he will never do that.

He is a family man.

0 / 4

There are no tribes, no heroes, no gods or godly inspired prophets, no angels or sublimely superior individuals. There are only children.

The grizzled man walking beside the highway out of Green Idaho knows that. He's had everything burned away but his childish core.

He talks to few, says very little. The scars on his face are vivid and crudely patched together. He endures the snow and the wind.

Sometimes he will say to himself that his name is Jack.

Sometimes, Carl. He is not sure who is in charge from day to day, not that it matters.

He has work to do.

He is trying to go home.

TEXT ONLY ACCESS DENIED. ACCOUNT CANCELED. PLEASE CONSULT YOUR ACCESS PROVIDER FOR REINSTATEMENT.

FULL YOX SERVICES ARE JUST A TOUCH AWAY! (PLEASE MAKE SURE ACCESS LEVEL MATCHES YOUR ABILITY TO PAY.)

YOU ARE A DEEPLY VALUED CUSTOMER!
JOIN YOUR FRIENDS IN GROUP JOY AND CONSTANT AFFIRMATION!
YOU ARE INVITED!

/

December 22, 1996
Lynnwood, Washington

/ AFTERWORD

The variety of Tourette syndrome described in this book is fictional, and is not meant to reflect the lives or attitudes of any who experience Tourette. For information about Tourette, there are a number of sources:

In the United States,

Tourette Syndrome Association
42–40 Bell Boulevard
Bayside, New York 11361

In England,

Tourette Syndrome Association
New Administration Office,
Old Grange House,
The Twitten, Southview Road,
Crowborough, East Sussex, TN6 1HF

Performing a search on the Internet, you're likely to find hundreds of pages of material on Tourette syndrome from the TSA and other organizations.

For all who have at one time or another been odd or out of sorts or dysfunctional, the discovery is just beginning.

Visit Greg Bear's web page at http://www.gregbear.com

TOR
BOOKS The Best in Science Fiction

MOTHER OF STORMS • John Barnes
From one of the hottest new names in SF: a shattering epic of global catastrophe, virtual reality, and human courage, in the manner of *Lucifer's Hammer, Neuromancer,* and *The Forge of God.*

BEYOND THE GATE • Dave Wolverton
The insectoid dronons threaten to enslave the human race in the sequel to *The Golden Queen.*

TROUBLE AND HER FRIENDS • Melissa Scott
Lambda Award-winning cyberpunk SF adventure that the *Philadelphia Inquirer* called "provocative, well-written and thoroughly entertaining."

THE GATHERING FLAME • Debra Doyle and James D. Macdonald
The Domina of Entibor obeys no law save her own.

WILDLIFE • James Patrick Kelly
"A brilliant evocation of future possibilities that establishes Kelly as a leading shaper of the genre."—*Booklist*

THE VOICES OF HEAVEN • Frederik Pohl
"A solid and engaging read from one of the genre's surest hands."—*Kirkus Reviews*

MOVING MARS • Greg Bear
The Nebula Award-winning novel of war between Earth and its colonists on Mars.

NEPTUNE CROSSING • Jeffrey A. Carver
"A roaring, cross-the-solar-system adventure of the first water."—Jack McDevitt

---

Call toll-free 1-800-288-2131 to use your major credit card or clip and mail this form below to order by mail

- ✂

Send to: Publishers Book and Audio Mailing Service
PO Box 120159, Staten Island, NY 10312-0004

❑ 533453	Mother Of Storms	$5.99/$6.99	❑ 534158	Wildlife	$4.99/$5.99
❑ 550315	Beyond the Gate	$6.99/$7.99	❑ 524802	Moving Mars	$5.99/$6.99
❑ 522133	Trouble and Her Friends	$4.99/$5.99	❑ 535189	Voices of Heaven	$5.99/$6.99
❑ 534956	Gathering Flame	$5.99/$6.99	❑ 535154	Neptune Crossing	$5.99/$6.99

Please send me the following books checked above. I am enclosing $_____. (Please add $1.50 for the first book, and 50¢ for each additional book to cover postage and handling. Send check or money order only—no CODs).

Name _____

Address _____ City _____ State _____ Zip_____

TOR
BOOKS The Best in Science Fiction

LIEGE-KILLER • Christopher Hinz

"*Liege-Killer* is a genuine page-turner, beautifully written and exciting from start to finish….Don't miss it."—*Locus*

HARVEST OF STARS • Poul Anderson

"A true masterpiece. An important work—not just of science fiction but of contemporary literature. Visionary and beautifully written, elegaic and transcendent, *Harvest of Stars* is the brightest star in Poul Anderson's constellation."

—Keith Ferrell, editor, *Omni*

FIREDANCE • Steven Barnes

SF adventure in 21st century California—by the co-author of *Beowulf's Children*.

ASH OCK • Christopher Hinz

"A well-handled science fiction thriller."—*Kirkus Reviews*

CALDÉ OF THE LONG SUN • Gene Wolfe

The third volume in the critically-acclaimed Book of the Long Sun.
"Dazzling."—*The New York Times*

OF TANGIBLE GHOSTS • L.E. Modesitt, Jr.

Ingenious alternate universe SF from the author of the *Recluce* fantasy series.

THE SHATTERED SPHERE • Roger MacBride Allen

The second book of the Hunted Earth continues the thrilling story that began in *The Ring of Charon*, a daringly original hard science fiction novel.

**THE PRICE OF THE STARS • Debra Doyle and
James D. Macdonald**

Book One of the Mageworlds—the breakneck SF epic of the most brawling family in the human galaxy!